This book is dedicated with love to the source of all the humor in my life . . . my husband, Robert.

With more than thirty romantic humor novels under my belt, I must confess that I don't have a comedic bone in my body.
Or at least I didn't until I met Robert, who was a professional softball player at the time (I kid you not!) He even makes me smile in these dire financial times, despite his being a stock broker. Need I say more?
Years ago, when I had a very sexy, romantic stepback cover depicting barely clad (except for a silk sheet) cover models John D'Salvo and Cindy Guyer in the sack, Robert wanted to have the artwork enlarged and framed to hang in his office.
He planned to put a plaque under it which read: "She lost her shirt in the stock market, but does she look like she cares?"
You gotta love a man with a sense of humor.

Viking In Love

Sandra Hill

AVON

An Imprint of HarperCollinsPublishers

AVON BOOKS
An Imprint of HarperCollins*Publishers*
10 East 53rd Street
New York, New York 10022-5299

Copyright © 2010 by Sandra Hill
Excerpts from *How I Met My Countess* copyright © 2010 by Elizabeth Boyle; *Viking in Love* copyright © 2010 by Sandra Hill; *The Vampire and the Virgin* copyright © 2010 by Kerrelyn Sparks; *Nine Rules to Break When Romancing a Rake* copyright © 2010 by Sarah Trabucchi.
ISBN 978-0-06-167349-8
www.avonromance.com

First Avon Books paperback printing: February 2010

Avon Trademark Reg. U.S. Pat. Off. and in Other Countries, Marca Registrada, Hecho en U.S.A.
HarperCollins® is a registered trademark of HarperCollins Publishers.

Printed in the U.S.A.

10 9 8 7 6 5 4 3 2 1

Viking In Love

CHAPTER ONE

☘

O*h Lord, from the fury of the Norsemen . . . uh,*
Norsewomen, deliver us . . .

"Is he dead yet?"

Breanne asked the question before glancing
around the earl's bedchamber at her four sisters, all
of them daughters of King Thorvald of Stoneheim
in the Norselands. As usual, each had an opinion
and did not mind speaking over the others.

"For the love of Thor! How would I know?"

"We will ne'er find husbands if we keep killing
men."

"This is the first one we have killed, you lackbrain."

"Well, how was I to know that? The rest of you
performed the task with ease."

"The rest of us? Hah! We are *all* responsible for
this . . . this happenstance."

"*Happenstance?*"

"Oh, gods! We shall all hang."

"Or be drawn and quartered."

"Or have our heads lopped off."

"I, for one, do not feel guilty. Not one bit. He was a beast."

"What is that green substance coming out of his nose?"

"Snot, you halfwit."

"Oh. Are you sure? Methinks it might be his brain oozing out."

"Yecch!"

"Brains do not ooze. Do they?"

"Something stinks. Dost think he soiled his braies?"

"For a certainty. Ooooh, look. I have ne'er seen so much blood."

"Tsk, tsk! Do you not know that head wounds always bleed profusely?"

"Then mayhap he is still alive. Someone should check to make sure."

"Uh-uh! I get a rash around dead people."

"I am not going to touch him."

"Me, neither!"

"The very thought makes me bilious."

"I would not know a dead body from a salted lutefisk."

Much nervous laughter erupted.

Momentarily silent, they all stared down at the body of Oswald, earl of Havenshire. Except for one sister, who was huddled in a chair in the far corner, whimpering as she held a possibly broken arm against her chest. Ofttimes referred to as Vana the White because of her Icelandic white-blonde hair, she had more than earned that title today with her fair, deadly white skin contrasted against a blackened eye and a cracked lip, seep-

ing blood. The finger marks about her neck, old
and new, resembled a black and blue and yellow
torque. Vana was the wife of the late Oswald . . .
late as of five minutes ago.

Breanne's back went rigid with anger. Truly, she
would gladly kill the brute all over again for what
he had done to her gentle sister. She could only
imagine what a nightmare Vana's one-year marriage had been. If only they had left the Norselands earlier to visit her in her Saxon home!

There was a light knock on the door.

Everyone stiffened with alarm.

They must needs dispose of the body, but Breanne had no idea how they could manage the feat
in a keep filled with housecarls and servants, all
loyal to the beastly nobleman. Now it was too
late.

Breanne stood and motioned for Vana to step
forth. Despite her condition, Vana would have to
answer. Limping toward her, Vana stood bravely
and faced the closed door. "Who is it?"

"Rashid."

Five sets of shoulders sagged with relief.
Rashid was the assistant to Adam the Healer, a
physician, Breanne's sister Tyra's husband. With
a snort of disgust, Tyra—who was extremely tall
for a woman and very strong, having once been
a warrior—jerked the door open, grabbed Rashid
by the arm, and yanked him inside, shutting the
door behind him.

Breanne had the good sense to lock it.

"What are you doing here? Following me?" demanded Tyra, hands on hips.

"Allah be praised, it is good to see you, too, Tyra."

Rashid spoke in heavily accented English, and he still, after all these years, wore the traditional Arab garb of hooded robe with rope belt, over Saxon tunic and braies. "Your husband asked me to follow and see what you were up to . . . I mean, to offer you protection in the event of . . ." He slapped a hand over his heart as he noticed the nobly clad body lying in a pool of blood on the stone-flagged floor. "For the love of a camel! What have you done?"

"When we arrived for a visit unannounced, we found the spineless lout beating our sister with his fists and a whip," Tyra explained. "When I broke his whip, he came at me with a knife, which I turned on him."

They all glanced at the knife, which still protruded from his belly.

Some of the sisters began to weep.

Oh, good gods! Not the tears again! Breanne stepped between Tyra and Rashid. "It wasn't just Tyra. We all played a part. I, for one, hit him over the head with a poker when Tyra's knife thrust did not immediately fell him."

"And I kicked him when he was down," Ingrith said on a sniffle, her blue eyes sparkling with fury. So hard was she shaking her head that strands of golden-blonde hair were coming loose from her long braids.

"I kicked him, too. In the head. Just to make sure he was bloody well dead." Drifa paused. "Is he dead?"

Rashid went down on one knee and put his fingertips to a certain spot on the earl's neck. "Dead as a fly on a cobra's tongue."

Rashid always had a way with words, especially proverbs, one of which he spouted now as he stood to his full height, wiping his hand on his robe with distaste. "Death is a black camel that lies down at every door. Sooner or later every man must ride the camel. Like yon earl."

"We are in big trouble, since we brought that camel. The earl is a member of the king's Witan. He has friends in high places," Breanne disclosed.

"But you had just cause," Rashid said. "They only have to look at Lady Havenshire's battered body to understand how this came about."

"That does not signify." Vana surprised everyone by speaking up, and with such vehemence. "Dost think they care? His housecarls and servants, friends and foe, all knew good and well how my lord's temper could be set off at the least thing. He blamed me for not yet breeding him a son, but any excuse would do for his fist or whip. A missing comb. A broken bowl. My monthly courses."

"Still," Rashid argued, "there are laws."

All the women shook their heads. The *wergild* for a woman was ofttimes barely higher than a cow, and less than a horse.

"Well, then, we must make haste to hide the body," Rashid said, lifting his hands with resignation.

Finally, someone is using their head for thinking and not leaking tears.

"How are we going to hide the body? And

where?" Ingrith asked, wringing her hands. And weeping.

" 'Tis impossible," Drifa said. "We are doomed." More tears.

"The difficult is done at once, but the impossible merely takes a little longer."

"Are you saying we can cover up this . . . accident?" Tyra looked imploringly at her husband's good friend.

"Do not stand in the midst of rain and ask Allah for a hat. Allah helps those who help themselves."

Her sisters looked toward Breanne.

Even though Tyra was the oldest, her sisters always expected Breanne to lead. " 'Tis agreed . . . we need a plan. Rashid, pull off one of those bed drapes so we can wrap the body. Ingrith, take some linens out of the chest and mop up the blood. Drifa, get the pitcher and bowl of water and try to remove the stain on the floor."

In the meantime, Breanne opened the door carefully to check on any guards who might be passing in the hall. There were none. It was late evening, long past dinner. Sounds of laughter could be heard coming from the great hall, where the men were no doubt downing cups of ale and tupping every maid they could get their slimy hands on, willing or not. They probably thought Lord Havenshire was up here in his bedchamber doing the same. For all they knew, Vana's sisters, come to visit, had been led to separate bedchambers on another level and would greet their sister for the first time in the morn.

"Mayhap we could put the earl's body in the chest," Ingrith suggested.

"He's too big," Vana said, her upper lip curling with distaste, no doubt having suffered for his bigness way too many times.

Ingrith had a better idea. "We can scrunch him in."

"Scrunch? A body cannot be folded like a blanket. Can it?" Drifa pursed her lips in puzzlement. "Oh! Mayhap it gets scrunchy when dead."

Breanne rolled her eyes. "Assuming we could fit the body in the chest, where could we hide it that would never be found?"

"We could burn the chest," Ingrith suggested.

Breanne shook her head. "The fire would attract too much attention. And it would smell . . . I think."

"The river?" Drifa offered.

Again Breanne shook her head. "Bodies tend to rise to the top eventually, no matter how weighted down."

"I have an idea," Vana said brightly. You had to give the girl credit for being able to smile. "Bottom of the privy."

They all chuckled.

"How appropriate! Havenshire always was a piece of . . ." Ingrith, ever the earthy one, guffawed at her own jest.

"No, you missay me, sisters," Vana said. "There is a new garderobe just now being built on the back side of the castle. The hole has been dug and loose stones are being laid down."

"Aaaah! We throw Havenshire's body in the

hole, then toss loose stones on top." Breanne had
to admit the idea had merit.

"No one will go down in that cesspit, even in
the beginning . . . um, dry state," Vana elaborated.
" 'Tis far too deep."

"So, the privy, it is." Breanne looked to the
others for agreement. "What will we say when the
earl's men ask for him or his whereabouts?"

Rashid glanced toward Tyra, stroking his mustache thoughtfully. "Tyra, you are much the size
of Oswald. Mayhap we could dress you in his
clothing."

"With the fur-lined cowled cape he favored,"
Vana added. "And using the back stairway
through the scullery."

"Somehow you must be able to saddle a horse
and ride away from the castle, with the guardsmen seeing you but not being able to identify you
as any other than their lord," Rashid said.

"Agreed," Tyra said, "but someone needs to
distract the stable hand on duty."

"I can do that," Drifa offered. Half Arab, half
Viking, Drifa was a petite, beautiful, well-formed
woman with raven hair and slanted eyes who attracted men easily.

"The sentries will not be suspicious at the earl's
leaving the castle so late. He has a mistress in
Whitby. Ofttimes he goes to visit her and stays
overnight. Or longer when he is especially lustsome." Vana did not appear the least disgusted
imparting that news, since his mistress had spared
her some of his vile attentions.

"But the day after tomorrow, his riderless horse will make its way back to Havenshire, and the first clue will be planted that he is gone. Perchance killed by villains out to rob peaceful wayfarers." Breanne thought for a moment. "It just might work, as long as we all stay here to support Vana and act suitably horrified and grief stricken. We must not panic when someone asks, 'Where is the earl?' Nothing to attract suspicion."

"How will we get the chest to the cesspit?" Drifa wanted to know.

"The two guardsmen Father sent with us are down in the great hall exchanging glares with Havenshire's men. They are up to the task, if they have not imbibed too much ale," Ingrith pointed out. "If one more Havenshire clodpole refers to Norsemen as lacking in battle skills, we will have a war on our hands."

Hmmm. That would provide a distraction. "Nay! Our men cannot be involved," Breanne asserted. "The less people who know about this deed the better."

"No matter!" Rashid said. "Ingrith, you stand guard in the scullery. Drifa, up to the ramparts where you will distract the sentries. I, along with Tyra and Breanne will carry the chest down the back stairs, through the scullery, to the outside privy." Rashid raised his eyebrows at each of them in turn.

He made it sound so easy. Breanne knew it would not be.

Still, they all nodded.

Silence permeated the room then as they contemplated the formidable, almost impossible, task ahead of them.

Why do my sisters and I always manage to land in the most ungodly trouble?

"Mayhap we should pray?" Vana suggested in a small voice.

"To which god?" Ingrith snorted.

It was a good question. Many Vikings practiced both the Christian and Norse religions, and then there was Rashid's Moslem heritage. They all bowed their heads for a moment.

"Prayer is well and good," Rashid said then. "Even so, trust in Allah, but ride a fast camel."

Camels again!

All Breanne could do was give a mental shout, which was more like a squeak: *HELP!*

And then they all said, as one, "Good-bye Earl."

CHAPTER TWO

Home, home on the range . . . uh, motte. . .
He was almost home.

After nine long months in the king's bloody service, which was supposed to have been only six sennights, Caedmon could almost see Larkspur in the distance through the morning mist. His hauberk creaked as he rose in the saddle. They were still too far away to get a clear view over the rise.

Two of his fellow knights, landless nobles who had chosen to remain in his troop, rode beside him. Behind him followed four dozen hirdsmen and various others that served a warrior's needs . . . armorers, blacksmiths, cooks, and stable hands leading ten war horses. The great destriers—worth their weight in gold, including his own Fury— were a fighting man's best friend in battle but too high-strung for regular riding. There were even several women who had attached themselves to some of his men.

"By the rood! You reek, Caedmon," Geoffrey, his best friend and chief hirdsman, said, clapping him on the shoulder.

"Well I know it. I had to nigh hold my nose when I slept yestereve." He glanced over to his right at the blond-haired, lean-limbed knight, who was too pretty by half. Women were known to swoon over his handsome looks, a bounty he took full advantage of, without apology.

"You are a bit aromatic yourself." This from Wulfgar, on Caedmon's left, who craned his neck to see Geoffrey. As fair as Geoff was, Wulf was the opposite. A giant with black hair, dark eyes, and a gruesome scar running from forehead to mustache and bearded chin, causing his upper lip to lift slightly. Still, women favored him, too.

And, truth be told, Caedmon attracted his fair share of women. He had no complaints.

"All of our garments will no doubt fall off our bodies in rot once we remove our armor," Caedmon remarked.

"I cannot remember the last time I bathed. Mayhap it was last month in Wessex. Or was it the month before in Norsemandy?" Geoff grinned at him, his white teeth stark against his stained leather helmet with nose piece and eye guard. "Methinks my *brynja* will leave half circle marks all over my body. The women will love it. Like the tattoos those Scots warriors favor."

"You are a lackwit," Wulf proclaimed.

"There are three things I will order once we arrive at Larkspur," Caedmon informed them on a long sigh. "A tun of cool mead. A warm bath. And a hot . . ."

" . . . wench," Geoff finished for him.

"Amen," he and Wulf agreed with a laugh.

Those men riding close behind them, who over-heard, laughed, too.

Caedmon shook his head with mock dismay. "Actually, I was going to say hot *fire* to warm my weary bones. Then, I would like to sleep for a sennight in a bed with clean linens and a soft pillow."

"K-A-D-mon!" Geoff exaggerated the pronunciation of his name, as he was wont to do when making jest of him. "Forget sleep. Me, I prefer mead, bath, and a good tup. A pillow is not where I intend to rest my head tonight."

Caedmon had already sent riders ahead with just such orders. Well, not about the women. He would never order women to open their thighs to a man, not even a thrall, especially having been in the company of their King Edgar and his sordid proclivities these many months.

It had been bad enough when Edgar and his closest guard had stormed a convent at Wilton Abbey, and Edgar had taken captive one of the nuns, Wulfhryth, her screams heard throughout the camp that night and many nights thereafter. No matter that Wulfhryth was of noble birth or that she later gave birth to a daughter, Eadygth. No matter that Edgar was married to Eneda, the "white duck." Edgar just went on his merry, wicked way. And Edgar had allowed those of his men so inclined to make sport with the other nuns.

The last straw had come when Edgar put a javelin through his half-brother Aethelwold's back for want of his beauteous wife. That was when Caedmon and his hirdsmen had decided to part with the royal company and head for home. If Edgar did not like it, then so be it! Thus far there had been no repercussions, but then Edgar was probably having to deal with the rage of Dunstan, Archbishop of Canterbury, who was sure to levy a huge penance on the king's overzealous cock. Then again, mayhap not. The only penance he had levied for Edgar's rape and impregnation of the nun was that he could not wear his crown for seven years. It was probably too heavy for his little head, anyway.

"Well, my castle is still standing," Caedmon said as the mist began to part and they could see Larkspur in the distance. A pretty name for an austere fortress. Calling it a castle was an overstatement, but that is what his childless uncle Richard had named Larkspur before passing it on to Caedmon on his death ten years ago.

It was a stone-and-timber garrison built in a motte-and-bailey fashion. Sitting atop a high, natural flat-topped mound, or motte, of great size and height, the castle itself was surrounded by double walls of palisades and ramparts, as was the vast bailey on the ground level with one wide gate in front, opening onto a drawbridge. A majestic wooden tower atop the keep stood watch over the land in four directions. At the bottom of the motte and still within the bailey were the exercise fields set off by neat hedgerows, castle gardens, and outbuildings: stables, blacksmith's forge, weaving, leatherwork and milk sheds, bakehouse, brewery, cow byre, pigpens, chicken coops, and sleeping quarters for his guardsmen who chose not to reside within the castle. The outer palisades were surrounded by a moat.

Beyond that were the cotters' huts and fields
of oats and barley. Inside, the bailey had enough
room for all the villagers to gather in the event
of an attack, not uncommon here in the wilds
of Northumbria, where brigands abounded and
Scotsmen came raiding from the North. Just past
the village was a peat-infused river, only twenty
paces wide, fed from the Cheviot hills runoff,
wending its way toward the North Sea, a mere
trickle of a burn, or creek, in dry, high summer
but a torrent after a storm.

Northumbria, so called lands north of the
Humber, was a land unto itself. To the southern
Brits, the mixed breeds of British, Anglian, and
Norse, with a bit of Scot thrown in, appeared wild,
uncouth, hard-drinking, and annoyingly inde-
pendent of spirit. This high country was just too
bleak . . . and dangerous, wedged in as it was by
the English kingdoms in the south, and the Scots,
Cumbrians, and Strathclyde Welsh to the north
and northwest. They saw only endless moors, like
a wilderness of sorts, and the occasional hills and
fertile dales. And remains of the ancient Roman
walls.

Caedmon, on the other hand, saw beauty in
its clean air and icy streams. The sweetness of
wildflowers and new grass being crushed by
their horses was like the finest perfume from the
eastern lands. To him, leastways. In a few short
months, vast areas would be covered with purple
heather.

For many years, Caedmon had been a landless knight, like his two close comrades, and he

knew too well how blessed he had been to inherit his uncle's estate. He would do everything in his power to keep it for himself and his heirs. Even if it meant service to his depraved king.

A tangled mess awaited him at Larkspur after his lengthy absence, but Caedmon felt peaceful here in his homeland. And lonely. But it was a good loneliness. One he cherished. He smiled to himself at that ill logic. *A cherished loneliness!* He must be going barmy.

"Leaving Henry as castellan was apparently a good decision, despite his advancing age," Geoff observed, interrupting his reverie.

Caedmon nodded. "Yea, reports are that the keep itself is in turmoil, but the troops are in good order, having suffered only a few minor attacks within the estate boundaries."

"Turmoil?" Wulf arched his brows . . . He had removed his helmet and his hair stood out in unruly spikes.

"It appears the children are running wild. Amicia is refusing to serve food in the great hall, where the dogs have made a mire of the rushes. A chambermaid was caught in bed with two men. Some of the housecarls have taken to swordplay in the solar. Father Luke has locked himself in the chapel and refuses to come out, not even to say Mass. A loose goat ate all the herbs in the kitchen garden. Other than that, everything is normal."

There was a momentary silence before one of the men behind him yelled out, "What was the name of that chamber wench?"

Both Wulf and Geoff grinned at him, and Caedmon could hear more chuckling behind him.

"Is Father Luke that half-brained fanatic who is always mumbling about fornication and the fires of hell?" Geoff asked.

"He said I was a dreadful sinner. Can you imagine?" Caedmon made a moue of innocence.

"And is he not older than Adam's rib?" Wulf added.

Caedmon had to laugh. "Yea, Father Luke has passed more than eighty winters, I would guess, and he was half brained afore he came to us. Think on it, what priest worth his salt would want to preside over the souls of such a small keep in the northern wilds, inhabited by 'sinful soldiers,' as he ofttimes calls us?"

"All your bratlings did not help any," Geoff noted.

"You have heard about the wagers, have you not?" Wulf inquired.

By his teasing tone, Caedmon decided he did not want to know.

But that did not stop Wulf.

"We are wagering on how many children you will have by now."

"Pfff! There were ten last time I counted, but God only knows how many are really mine. And, yea, I am certain there will be more by now." Caedmon had wed and buried two wives, leaving behind three legitimate children, the nine-year-old Beth and six-year-old twins Alfred and Aidan, but he had also had his fair share of unfortunately fertile mistresses and bedmates over the years. He was, after all, thirty and four. He grinned then. "Can I help it if I am a virile man?" *And dumb as dirt when it comes to keeping my cock in my breeches.*

"Methinks your virility is going to come back and bite you in the arse one of these days," Geoff said.

It already has, and that is why I gird myself with resolve. I will ne'er marry again, I vow, and I will exercise caution in the bed furs. God willing.

He could swear he heard laughter in his head. It was probably God.

"When I was in Baghdad, I heard about a method for preventing a man's seed from taking root in a woman's womb," Geoff said of a sudden.

All ears perked up at that announcement.

When he just grinned at them, Caedmon prodded, "Well, do not stop now, lackwit."

"You take a small, thick-skinned apple. Cut it in half, and pare out most of the pulp. Then you insert it into a woman's channel, far up, like a tiny cup. And that prevents a man's seed from entering her womb." Geoff preened as if he had just gifted them the secret to turning grass to gold. "It is supposed to be done with lemons, but since we have none here, I am sure apples would suffice."

There was a lengthy silence as the men digested what he had said, turning it over in their minds. One never knew when Geoff was jesting or not, although he did know a lot about the bed arts, or so he often told them.

"I would like to meet the woman who would allow you to do *that*," Caedmon finally scoffed. *Really, I would.*

Geoff smirked, as if he knew a few.

"And how in bloody hell would you get it out?" Wulf wanted to know.

Geoff fluttered his fingertips at Wulf as if that were an insignificant matter.

"The woman would be pissing apple juice for a sennight," Wulf remarked. "And dropping apple seeds hither and yon."

"We have all been in the saddle too long. Our brains are melting," Caedmon concluded. *But I wager there will be apples aplenty missing from the larder this night.*

"Little Women" they were not . . .

Breanne sat in the Havenshire ladies' solar, where she and her sister Tyra were sewing on a tapestry stretched onto a large wooden frame.

The earl rested at the bottom of the now-in-use—*Eeeewww!*—garderobe, and they waited on tenterhooks for the call to come that he had been found.

Which had not happened, of course

And would not happen, they hoped.

Still, she and her sisters declined to use that particular privy for fear the corpse would somehow come up and bite them in their bare arses.

Vana, whose face still carried the marks of her husband's beating despite wearing a wimple and head rail held in place by a silver diadem, was down in the great hall, engaging in the chatelaine's morning rituals of a great keep. Giving the steward orders for the day's work. Doling out rare spices and foodstuffs from the locked storeroom

for various meals. Raking up and spreading new
rushes sprinkled with winter savory and balm
leaves in the great hall. Laundering everything in
sight, including some oddly stained bed linens.
During all this activity, Vana sobbed to one and
all that she was worried over her "beloved" husband, who had been missing a full sennight now.

Ingrith had planted herself in the scullery
today, where she was no doubt bothering the Havenshire cook with her own, superior versions of
particular dishes. If the past was any indicator
of the future, the cook would soon explode over
Ingrith's interference and threaten to quit.

Drifa remained outside, basking in the unsea-
sonably warm weather, taking cuttings from various plants and flowers. The gods only knew what
she intended to do with them.

Rashid was in the stables extolling the virtues
of his Saracen stallion to some of the Havenshire
housecarls. His advice before leaving them after
breaking fast this morn had been: "The camel
senses when a dust storm is coming. Be prepared!"

Camels be damned! They were already as nervous as nuns in a brothel, except for Rashid, who
would probably say he was as nervous as a camel
in a harem. That was why Breanne and Tyra were
now in this ladies' chamber, sewing. *Sewing!* They
might just as well have been trying to spin gold
from dross.

Breanne's calloused hands kept snagging on the
silk threads, and she swore under her breath for
about the hundredth time since they had buried

the hated earl. Truly, she was much more at home
building things with wood than engaging in the
womanly arts. From a young age, studying a piece
of wood, she saw visions in her head of what it
could become. Same was true of buildings. Thus,
of her very capable hands had been born benches,
bedsteads, trestle tables, pretty garden fences,
even a pigsty one time, with finely carved runic
symbols along its eaves. Her father had nigh had
a falling over fit at that one. Yea, it was an odd
talent for a woman, but then all of King Thorvald's
daughters had unusual interests.

Tyra, of course, had been a warrior, forced
into that role since she was the eldest in a family
with no sons. Smiling at her older sister across
the chamber, Breanne saw the look of disgust on
Tyra's face and knew that she was just as uncomfortable in this domestic role as she was.

They both cocked their heads to the side to
study the tapestry picture as it was evolving. Then
they burst out laughing.

"Your peacock looks like a *drukkin* chicken,"
Tyra chortled.

"Hah! Your fine lady has worms on her face,"
Breanne countered.

"Those are eyelashes," Tyra said indignantly.

Breanne squinted closer. "Eyelashes down to
her mouth?"

"I will tell you this, sister," Breanne said, "if
ever I was convinced that I will ne'er marry, I have
good reason now. I hate sewing. Besides, men are
vicious trolls, like Havenshire. At best, they are
just not worth the trouble."

"You say that because you have ne'er fallen in love, but someday . . ."

"Tyra! I am five and twenty. Hundreds of men have passed through our father's keep. Dozens more I have met here in Britain. If it were going to happen, it would have by now."

"Someday . . ."

Breanne held up a halting hand. "Nay, I am realistic. Look at me, sister." She touched her head where red hair hung in one long braid down her neck, tendrils of the hated curls already escaping. "Didst know that a young squire once likened its color to old rust? 'Twas not a compliment."

Sympathy immediately flashed on Tyra's face. "Who was it? I will bash his face in with my favorite sword."

I already did, with my fist. "You cannot blame someone for speaking the truth," she said prissily. "Keep in mind, I tower over many men, even if I am not as tall as you are. And I am too slender, with no bosom to speak of. Believe you me, men do not rush to gain my favor, except when they learn of my dowry. Even then they are easily dissuaded."

"You are too hard on yourself by half. I must admit, I am surprised that you would be satisfied staying home with Father. What will you do when he passes to the Other World?"

"I have plans." Breanne smiled to herself.

"You have a secret." Tyra clapped her hands with glee. "You cannot stop now. Tell me."

"You must keep it to yourself for now, but Father told me that if I am not wed by the time I have seen thirty winters, he will give me my dowry to use as I wish. I intend to buy myself a small manor, or an overlarge cottage, near Jorvik, where I will make my fancy chairs and tables and sell them in the trading stalls of Coppergate."

Tyra's mouth dropped open. "A woman merchant! That big vein on Father's forehead will surely burst with displeasure. You would ne'er do such!"

"Yea, I would. Rare though it be, there are other ladies who have followed such a path. Like your own aunt-by-marriage, Eadyth of Ravenshire. She sells her honey and time-keeping candles in the markets." Breanne lifted her chin defiantly. "I have already commissioned Father's agent to look for a suitable place."

Just then, a horn could be heard blaring outside the keep, announcing a visitor.

"Oh, gods!" Breanne moaned. "Someone else has come looking for Lord Havenshire, I warrant. The flummery begins again."

Every day as word spread of Oswald's disappearance, more and more visitors came, expressing their concerns and offering to help search for him. Thus far, they had only been neighbors and distant relatives. With each of them, though, Vana and her sisters had put on a good act, pretending concern and grief as they nigh gagged over such words as the "great loss" or a "kind and generous man."

Not one of them had expressed outrage on Vana's behalf over the possibility of Oswald's visiting a mistress. And it had been their good for-

tune that the mistress in question was nowhere to
be found. Mayhap she had run away from Oswald
before knowing of his absence. Would that not
be the greatest irony? Whatever the case, her absence made some think there was a connection to
Oswald's absence, as if the two of them were off
somewhere engaged in adulterous acts.

"Just so it is not the king." Breanne bit her
bottom lip with concern.

Turns out, it was even worse.

The door swung open and Vana rushed in,
tears welling in her eyes. "I have terrible news.
Havenshire's chief hirdsman has requested King
Edgar's aid, and he has just received an answering missive." Vana paused, her lower lip trembling. "Archbishop Dunstan, King Edgar's closest
advisor, is on his way."

"Well, we knew the king would send someone," Breanne said, helping her sister tó sit on a
wood bench.

"But Dunstan is the worst possible emissary.
Didst know he is a raging women hater? Truly, he
believes all of man's woes can be laid at women's
feet, or rather betwixt their legs. Eve was the devil's handmaiden, thus making all females unclean.
I heard him say so."

"What has that to do with us?" Tyra asked.

"Whether they find the earl's body or not, he
will blame me. I know he will. 'Twill be my luck
if the worst thing he does is confine me in a nun-
nery."

"Could he do that?" Breanne asked Tyra.

Tyra shrugged. "Many say he is the most influential man in all Britain, more powerful even than the king himself."

"That settles it then. We must leave afore he gets here," Breanne declared.

Vana's pitifully bruised face brightened. "Where will we go? Back to Stoneheim?"

Breanne shook her head. " 'Twould be impossible to arrange passage to the Norselands so quickly."

"To Hawkshire then?" More hope rose in Vana's face.

Now Tyra shook her head. "I would love to have you all come to my home, and Adam would welcome you, too, but I fear that is the first place the king's men would look."

They were all silent, trying to decide their best choice of action.

"There is one place we could go," Tyra offered hesitantly.

"Where?" Breanne and Vana asked as one.

"A distant kinsman of Adam's lives in the far north, one day's travel by horse. Larkspur, his estate is called. Yea, we could go 'visit' Adam's cousin Caedmon, a high-ranking knight. Surely, he would not deny us hospitality."

"That might work." Breanne tapped her closed lips thoughtfully.

"And, really, it would only be a temporary imposition," Tyra added. "I will ask Adam to get the support of his Saxon family in our cause whilst we are gone. We have naught to worry about."

Breanne was not so sure about that.

What do we know about this Caedmon?

CHAPTER THREE

❧

*H*ome, not-so-sweet home . . .
Caedmon had no sooner entered the great hall of Larkspur than he was assaulted from all sides. His steward, Gerard; his castellan, Henry; and what seemed like a dozen children.

Ominously, one of the serving maids stood nearby holding a wailing newborn babe. The whelp could not possibly be his, but still the hairs stood out on the back of his neck.

Wulf and Geoff chortled with humor and went off searching for ale. Lucky men!

First, his steward, Gerard: "Cook has quit. Slipped in the offal on her way from the kitchen, and—"

"Awful what?"

"Not awful. *Offal,*" Gerard gave him a disgusted look, and translated succinctly: "Dog shit in the rushes."

"Oh." *Already the turmoil starts.*

"Amicia says she will not return 'til new rushes are put down."

"So, why not lay down new rushes?" *I feel as if I live in the land of idiots.*

"Because she also wants the dogs put outside."

"Ah!" Caedmon knew that the men liked to have the dogs about to catch the odd bone. "What else?"

"We have run out of meat. The larder is nigh empty. The cotters were late planting spring oats and barley due to the rains. There are weevils in the flour. The sheep need shearing. A half dozen cows are in heat and need to be serviced, but we have no bull at the ready. Lice have infested the chicken flock, and—"

Mayhap going off to war with Edgar is not so unappealing, after all. Caedmon raised a hand. "Leave off for now." Then he turned to Henry.

"We must needs replenish our supply of arrows and small swords. Three attacks by brigands did we sustain in your absence, and our weaponry is sorely diminished. In addition, cattle have been stolen in recent sennights. No doubt by those bloody Scots, the MacLeans. John the Bowman was killed in one of the attacks, and his widow is wanting more than a widow's share for *wergild*."

Without waiting to hear more, Caedmon exhaled with frustration, then gave his attention to the children he saw running about. Their garments and faces and hands were looking more than filthy. His widowed sister, Alys, who had been given charge of the children, had much to answer for.

"Where is Alys?" he asked no one in particular.

"Gone to Jorvik with a passing merchant. She said—" Henry stopped mid-sentence, as if he'd said too much. His aged face, framed by overlong white hair, bloomed red.

Caedmon arched his brows at Henry in a manner that said he best speak up or suffer the consequences.

Henry sighed deeply, then revealed: "She said Bowdyn . . . that is the merchant's name . . . has wicked fingers that bring out the sinner in her. And she said she has been a saint too long, that she has waited overlong for you to find her a husband. You should have heard the lewd moans and groans coming from her bedchamber." He rolled his eyes meaningfully. "Personally, I think the children got to be too much for her."

What else is new? Well, one more problem to be dealt with, Caedmon decided, but naught he could do about it at the moment. Besides, Alys was thirty, far from a girling. As for him finding her a husband, she had buried three already.

Back to Gerard, he hesitated to ask, "Any problems with the children?"

Gerard rolled his eyes, then put two fingers in his mouth and let loose with a whistle that caused Caedmon to nigh jump, the dogs to bury their heads betwixt their paws, and, amazingly, ten children to scurry forward and stand in a line, at attention, like a troop of grubby little soldiers. There were ten of them—*Ten!*—ranging in age from one to twelve, or was it thirteen? Gerard introduced each of them in turn, as if Caedmon would not know their names, which was a distinct possibility.

It was an impressive exercise . . . Gerard calling

Caedmon's children to order with a whistle. He would have to try it himself. So angelic did the wee mites look, he would not be surprised if they burst into song.

But it did not last long.

First, nine-year-old Beth launched herself at him. He caught her about her tiny waist, and she clung to him with her skinny legs wrapped halfway around his hips. He could feel her tears wetting his neck. This oldest and only child of his first wife, Elizabeth, ever was the sensitive one. Elizabeth had died way too young, after being thrown from a horse a year after their marriage. Beth kept whimpering, "Father," over and over. The sweet girling always was overly needful of affection.

One of the six-year-old twins, Alfred, or was it Aidan, clutched his thigh and held on tight, cutting off blood flow to an important region of his body. Much more and he would have no need of apples. The other twin kicked him in the shin. These were his second wife, Agnes's, contributions to his flock before succumbing to the childbed fever.

Eight-year-old Mina was an incredibly pretty, black-haired, cat-eyed girl, born of a brief liaison with an Arab *houri*, Nadiyah. Being a favorite of a *sheikr*, Nadiyah had not wanted the babe, especially with Caedmon's blue eyes, for fear of losing her hierarchy in the royal bed. It had not signified that the *sheikr* was short, stout, and of a mean spirit. Reminded him a bit of a certain Saxon king, except Edgar was blond haired and much younger.

Piers, a one-year-old tow-headed rascal, was waddling around with a thumb in his mouth. He wore only little half boots and a sagging nappy. And he reeked. Sad to say, Caedmon could not even recall who his mother was.

Just then his eyes narrowed as he noticed his twelve-year-old son Hugh skulking away. His oldest, born of a serving maid prior to his first marriage, was supposed to be in Mercia, fostering with a distant cousin, Ealdorman Aldhelm.

And there were other children. Five-year-old Angus with flaming red hair and a temper to match. *And wasn't that name a clue?* Caedmon seriously doubted that Angus was of his blood, though his mother swore that he was, before taking off for the Highlands. *Highlands? Hah! Another clue!* Likewise, two other boys and one girl, Oslac, Kendrick, and Joanna, all seven years old, born on almost the same day. They bore a striking resemblance to some former comrades-in-arms, all brothers from Wales, who had been visiting at the time. He would like to confront them about their responsibilities, but they had been conveniently absent of late.

And, God help him, there were even more children he could not name. Hell's teeth! Someday they could make up his very own army.

While he had been perusing the children, they had been jabbering away at him.

"Father, I need a horse."

I need a horn of ale.

"Father, I have a boil on my bottom."

And you expect me to do . . . what?

"Father, Aidan hit me."

"Father, I only hit Alfred because he ate my custard."

My head hurts.

"Father, I want a sword." This from five-year-old Angus.

For the love of God!

"Father, you need to change Piers's nappy."

Not if I can help it!

"Father, why do you have a frowny face?"

Because my head hurts.

"Father, how old do I have to be to tup a maid?" seven-year-old Oslac asked.

What . . . WHAT did he say?

"Oslac's cock thickened one night," Kendrick took delight in informing him.

He probably had to empty his bladder.

Oslac punched Kendrick for divulging that private fact, which caused Kendrick to punch him back. Soon they were rolling around in the dirty rushes getting dirtier than they already were.

With one last survey of the jabbering children, he remarked to Gerard, "How long since any of them have bathed?"

Gerard straightened with indignation. "M'lord!" Gerard always called him a lord, even though he was far from it. "M'lord, they are alive and none are missing any limbs."

"All appears to be in order then. And I must compliment you on that great trick . . . whistling them into order."

"I am still working on it," Gerard muttered.

Caedmon grinned.

Gerard, who had more gray hairs than when Caedmon had last seen him, did not grin back. Children would do that to a man, especially Caedmon's children. Apparently Caedmon had insulted him by adding child minding to his duties. Ah, well, he would calm his feathers later.

Kissing Beth on the cheek, he set her down.

Now, for Father Luke.

Caedmon knocked on the chapel door.

No answer.

He yelled, "Father Luke. Open up. 'Tis I, Caedmon. You can come out now."

Still no answer.

Exhaling with a whooshy breath, he kicked at the door. Once. Twice. Three times before it splintered open. The smell that hit him was putrid. And there was Father Luke, kneeling on his *prie-dieu*. Dead as a door hinge. Must have expired weeks ago, and no one had bothered to check, thinking he was still in hiding.

"Somebody, bury this priest. Now!"

Gerard and several servants scuttled to do as he ordered, fingers pinching their noses at the stink.

By the cross! Can things get any worse? Swearing one long stream of curses before anyone else, adult or child, could make demands on him, he walked further into the great hall and yelled, "Where's the ale?"

To which his men laughed and yelled back, "Welcome home!"

Then he slipped on something squishy in the rushes and almost fell on his arse.

At which his men once again laughed and yelled, "Welcome home!"

Someone was going to get a piece . . . of her mind . . .
The first thing Breanne noticed on entering Larkspur's great hall at noon of the following day, after a long, surreptitious nighttime ride through the hills and dales of Northumbria, was the smell. The second was the number of children running about like wild animals. The third was the large number of half-eaten apples lying on the trestle tables, which should have been dismantled after the last meal. The fourth was the lack of activity by those adults who were about, some of whom appeared to be sleeping off the alehead. At the very least, there should be servants about, working.

Although they had arrived more than an hour ago, it had taken some convincing on their part to get the sentries to allow them entry. A guardsman, who had gone to get permission from the master, came back red faced, saying he could not find him.

How odd!
The sentries kept glancing at Rashid and the two Norse soldiers who accompanied Breanne and her sisters, but finally gave in after a quelling lecture by Tyra on military protocol and family hospitality. The brothers Ivan and Ivar, who comprised their two-man guard, were now in the stables taking care of the seven horses they had ridden here, being hovered over by twice that many Larkspur soldiers who were still unsure of their intentions.

"These rushes must not have been changed in a year," Breanne commented, waving a hand in front of her nose.

"Four months," the steward, Gerard, corrected her. "The master has been gone almost a year."

"But he is here now?"

Gerard nodded hesitantly. "He arrived yester-morn. Does he expect you?"

She felt her face flush.

"Not exactly, but I am certain he will welcome us," Tyra interrupted, standing to her full height, towering over the little man. "After all, he is my cousin."

That was a bit of a stretch of the truth, since Tyra's husband, Adam the Healer, had been adopted by Selik, who had been a distant cousin of Caedmon. But Breanne was not about to correct her sister in front of the steward, who kept gaping at their garments . . . and appeared to be checking out their breasts. For riding purposes, she and Tyra both wore wool tunics, held in at the waist by gold-linked belts, over slim *braies*, and boots cross-gartered up to the knees. Fur-lined shoulder mantles with gem-encrusted gold brooches completed their attire.

Vana was running a fingertip over a greasy trestle table that also had no doubt been without a scrubbing in a good while. She was sniffing at the ill odors. "Why are no servants cleaning up this filth?"

"They will not listen to me. The master has been gone too long, and they question my authority."

"We will see about that," Vana said, tiptoeing carefully through the rushes as she headed toward a slovenly maid with bosoms the size of cow udders, sitting on a hirdsman's lap. If there was anything Vana liked it was cleaning. This hall alone should occupy her for a sennight, which could be a good thing, considering all that must be on her mind.

The maid yelped when Vana grabbed her by the ear and began chastising her. "Where are the other servants? Gather them all here. They will not be given another bite of food or sip of ale if they drag their heels. Now go!"

Gerard was gaping at Vana, but then he smiled. "Thank God!"

"We have been traveling through the night," Ingrith said. "When will the noon meal be served?"

A blush once more bloomed on Gerard's face. "Cook has quit. We have been grabbing whatever is about, which is not much. I cannot recall the last time there was bread."

Ingrith, who loved to cook, tsk-tsked and made her way, carefully, toward the scullery, which was separated from the keep itself by a long covered corridor, a necessity when fire was always a concern. Soon, her shouted reprimands could be heard by one and all. Apparently, the kitchen was as untidy as the rest of the keep.

"What is she doing?" Gerard asked Breanne.

"Putting your kitchen in order. There will be a meal tonight, that I guarantee."

Gerard once again smiled and repeated, "Thank God!"

"I am going out to rescue Rashid and the men," Tyra said, then turned to Drifa, who had remained quiet behind them. "Come with me and unload those cuttings you brought with you. Did you see the condition of the garden?"

Drifa brightened and followed after Tyra.

Left alone with the steward, Breanne started to speak, but a little boy was tugging at the hem of her robe. The child with unruly, wheat-colored hair could not be much more than one year old. He wore tiny leather half boots and a drooping linen swaddling wrap. That was all. Lifting the boy up into her arms, away from her body, she asked, "And who are you, sweetling?"

"That be Piers. He does not talk yet," Gerard informed her.

She nuzzled him closer, but just his neck. Her heart nigh broke when she saw children who were so neglected. "Whom do all these children belong to, and why are they being permitted to run wild?" A half dozen or more youthlings of various ages were playing tag around the great hall.

"They belong to the master."

"The master?"

"M'lord. Caedmon."

"All of them?"

"Most of them."

"Sweet Frigg!"

"Caedmon is a good man. He takes care of his children."

"Not very well, by appearances. Where is he, by the by?"

A blond-haired god of a man emerged from one of the sleeping closets, closely followed by another buxom maid, this one much younger and fairly clean, though her bosoms were fair escaping the low neckline of her homespun *gunna*. The same had been true of the dairymaid outside. *Do all the women in this keep have big bosoms?* The man was shirtless, wearing only braies, which hung low on his hips. He smiled at her and said, "Greetings, m'lady. Geoffrey Fitzwilliam, chief hirdsman, at your service. And this is Emma."

"I am Breanne, daughter of King Thorvald of Stoneheim," she said, trying to ignore his half-clad body.

The rogue was well aware of her discomfort.

She handed the child to the maid and ordered, "Give this child a bath, and put some proper garments on him."

The woman looked as if she had been told to stand on her head in a snowstorm. "Make haste now, Emma, and I want to see the boy when you are done." The woman walked away with the now squalling child. Only then did she turn to the comely man . . .

Geoffrey, he had called himself. "Where is your master?"

"My master? Oh, you mean Caedmon?"

She folded her arms over her chest and glared at the grinning man.

Geoffrey motioned with his head toward a stairway, which presumably led to upper chambers.

Understanding dawned on her of a sudden. "He is still abed?"

"He is."

"'Tis noon!"

"He must be tired."

"I'll give him tired," Breanne muttered. "What kind of man breeds children like rabbits, then ignores them and his keep? This place is a pigpen. Nay, that is incorrect. Pigs would not live in this cesspit."

Gerard groaned and Geoffrey's eyes twinkled with merriment. Then Geoffrey called out to a black-haired giant of a man who was approaching. His hair matched a neatly trimmed mustache and beard. He would have been godly handsome, too, if not for a livid scar that ran from his forehead to his chin, causing his upper lip to be slightly raised on one side. This one was at least fully dressed, in belted tunic and braies. "Wulf, come see who has come to visit. A Norse princess."

"Actually, there are five Norse princesses," Gerard corrected him. "The others are outside. Along with a wise man from the eastern lands. Leastways he is spitting out wise sayings. And two Norse soldiers the size of warhorses."

"That is even more interesting," Geoffrey proclaimed. To Wulf, he continued, "This particular princess . . ." he motioned with his head toward her, his eyes dancing with mischief, ". . . is looking for our *master*."

They were speaking to her back by now, as she continued on her way to the stairs, trying her best to ignore them. That was impolite, she knew, but she suspected they were making mock of her princess status.

"Uh, mayhap I should go announce you first," Gerard offered.

"I will bloody well announce myself."

Laughter followed in her wake, and she thought she heard someone say, "This ought to be good."

CHAPTER FOUR

Beware of women with barbed tongues . . .
Caedmon was splatted out on his stomach,
half-awake, knowing he must rise soon. This was
a new day and a new start for getting his estate
and his family back in order.

In his head he made a list.

First, gather the entire household and
establish some authority. Someone had
been lax in assigning duties and making
sure they were completed. The overworked
Gerard, no doubt. And the absent Alys.

Second, take stock of the larder. Huntsmen
would go out for fresh meat, fishermen for
fish, and he would send someone to Jarrow
to purchases spices and various other
foodstuffs.

Third, designate Geoff and Wulf to work
with the housecarls on fighting skills and
rotating guard schedules.

Fourth, replenish the supply of weaponry.

Fifth, persuade the cook to return. The roast
boar yestereve had been tough as leather,

made palatable only by the tubfuls of feast
ale and strong mead they had consumed.

Sixth, the children . . . ah, what to do about
the children? One of the cotters' wives . . .
or John the Bowman's widow . . . could
supervise their care, and a monk from
the minster in Jorvik might be induced to
come and tutor them, although his history
with Father Luke did not bode well for his
chances.

The door to his bedchamber swung open, interrupting his mental planning. The headboard of
his bed was against the same wall as the door, so
he merely turned his head to the left and squinted
one eye open.

A red-haired woman—dressed in men's attire
. . . highborn men's attire, at that—stood glaring
at him, hands on hips. She was tall for a woman,
and thin as a lance. As for breasts, if she had any,
they must be as flat as rounds of manchet bread.
"Master Caedmon, I presume?"

"Well, I do not know about the 'Master' part.
What manner dress is that? Are you man or
woman?" He smiled, trying for levity.

She did not return the smile.

No sense of humor.

"You are surely the most loathsome lout I have
e'er encountered."

Whaaaat? He had not been expecting an attack.
In fact, he needed a moment for his sleep-hazed
brain to take in this apparition before him.

"Your keep is filthy, pigs broke through the sty

fence and are all over the bailey, I saw dozens of mice scampering in your great hall, thatch needs replacing on the cotters' huts, you beget children like an acorn tree gone wild, your staff take their ease like high nobility, there are several blubbering servants arguing over who will bury the priest who is laid out in your chapel, and you . . . you slothful sluggard, you lie abed, sleeping off a *drukkin* night, no doubt."

Whoa! One thing was for certain. This would not be yet another woman trying to crawl into his bed furs. "Stop shrieking. You will make my ears bleed." Caedmon rolled over on his side, tugging the bed linen up to cover his lower half, then sat up.

"Bestir thyself!"

"Nay!"

"Have you no shame?"

"Not much."

"Are you lackbrained?"

"No more than you for barging into my bedchamber."

"Even if you have no coin, there is no excuse for the neglect."

"Not even the fact that I have been gone nine long months in service to a king undeserving of service?"

"Where is the lady of this estate?"

'Tis just like a woman to think a woman is the answer to everything! "There is no lady."

"Hmpfh! Why am I not surprised?"

Now he was getting annoyed. "Sarcasm ill suits you, m'lady. Have you ne'er been told that?"

"The blade goes both ways, knave."

His eyes went wide at her foolhardy insults. "Who in bloody hell are you?"

"Breanne of Stoneheim."

"Is that supposed to mean something to me?"

"She's a princess," someone called out from the corridor. He saw now that a crowd of people were standing just outside the open doorway, being entertained by this shrew's railing at him. Geoff and Wulf were in the forefront, of course, laughing their arses off.

"Well, Princess Breanne, what do you in my home and my bedchamber?"

She had the grace to blush. "My sisters and I came here, on our way . . . as a stopping-off place . . . for a . . . uh, visit . . . on our journey. Your castellan offered us hospitality."

He could tell by the deepening red on her cheeks that she was either lying or stretching the truth.

"Sisters?"

"She has four sisters," Geoff offered. "All princesses."

Five princesses? Here? Oh, Lord!

"And they are accompanied by two scowling Vikings who are about this tall," Wulf added, holding a hand high above his head. And Wulf was a big man by any standard.

"They were only scowling because your archers aimed their bows at them," the lady declared, doing her own good job of scowling.

" 'Tis a comfort, your explanation is. I feel so much better."

Caedmon could practically hear the grinding of her small, white teeth.

"And there is a wise man from the eastern lands who has opinions on every bloody thing in the world, most of it involving camels." As usual, Geoff was enjoying himself at his expense.

"Why me? I mean, why stop here at Larkspur?" he asked the bothersome woman. "Surely there are better places."

"My sister Tyra is your cousin."

He frowned. "I have no cousin named Tyra." Leastways, he did not think he did, but then he was still wooly witted from sleep.

"Her husband, Adam of Hawkshire, is your cousin by marriage . . . um, slightly removed," the flame-haired witch explained.

He knew Adam, or rather he had heard of him. A famed healer. But their connection by blood was far removed.

"Did you know there is a child still in nappies walking about nigh naked? He could be trampled by dogs the size of small ponies roaming about indoors."

"Have a caution, wench. You have already passed the bounds of good sense. Any more, and you may taste the flavor of *my* wrath."

She started to respond, then stopped herself.

"I told Emma to take care of Piers," Caedmon said.

"Would that be the same Emma who spent the night spreading her thighs for the blond god?"

"She is referring to me," Geoff preened. "The blond god."

"And, by the by, why do all the females in this keep appear to have big bosoms?"

"Huh?"

Geoff and Wulf were laughing so hard they were bent over at their waists, holding their sides. When he was able to speak, Geoff said, " 'Twould seem that Gerard has a preference for big breasts when choosing maids for inside work." He gave particular emphasis to "inside work."

"Gerard? Bloody hell! He is old enough to . . . never mind."

"Not yet in his dotage, if he can still appreciate a buxom bosom," Wulf observed.

Breanne waved a hand airily. "You are not to worry. My sisters and I will set your keep aright whilst we are here."

Alarm rippled through Caedmon's body. "How long do you intend to stay?" he asked bluntly.

Another blush. "I am not certain. But you are not to worry."

"I was not reassured the first time you said that."

"You will hardly notice we are here."

"I doubt that heartily."

She went stiff as a pike, apparently not liking it when the sarcasm came from his direction, but she pressed her lips together. Very nice lips, he noticed, if he were attracted to tall, skinny, red-haired women with barbed tongues, which he was not. At least she was making an effort to be polite now.

Something very strange was going on, but he had more urgent matters to take care of. He'd drunk a tun of ale yestereve and now he needed to piss. Badly.

"Go down to the great hall and wait for me. We will discuss this later."

The shrew lifted her chin defiantly and said, "I am not leaving until you get your lazy self out of bed. If no one else cares about those children . . ." On and on she blathered in her shrill voice.

Really, this woman's tongue flaps like a loose shingle. I could rebuke her in a way she would not soon forget. Hell, I could kick her cheeky arse out the door, if I choose. But, wait. I know another way. "You say me nay? Be careful, you may find I am more than you wagered for."

"Do you threaten me, troll?"

"So be it," he said, tossing the sheet aside and standing. *How do you like that trollsome part?*

Immediately her eyes fixed on a part of his naked body, which was displaying a powerful morning thickening, standing out like a flagpole. "You, you, you . . ." she sputtered, but could not seem to raise her eyes, which he noticed, irrelevantly, were a beautiful shade of green, like summer grass on the moors.

"Do not be offended, m'lady." He pointed at his nether part. "*This* is not for you. Your virtue is not forfeit . . . from this quarter. 'Tis just that I must needs visit the garderobe."

"What an insufferable, crude, arrogant, loathsome lout!" she exclaimed as she sailed through the doorway, where the crowd had magically parted like the Red Sea of Biblical lore.

"Damn, but it is good to be home, is it not, Caedmon?" Geoff inquired sweetly, then ducked just in time to miss the pillow he sent his way.

A short time later, Caedmon realized he had one more thing to add to his list of things to do today: Get rid of princesses.

He dangled some precious jewels before her . . .

Breanne had seen naked men before. Of course she had. But there was a big difference here. Very big!

Being the daughter of a Viking king in a stronghold of two hundred randy warriors meant there had been occasions when she and her sisters had gotten a quick, unintentional view of men's "assets." Well, mayhap intentional betimes, when they had been younger and more halfbrained curious. Coming from the bathhouse. Tupping a maid in a dark corridor. As they dressed in battle gear.

None of those happenstances had prepared her for the sight of Caedmon in all his naked glory. Blessed Odin, the man was . . . endowed. All over. And arrogant as they came. Even worse, he had made mock of her by deliberately exposing his manpart to her.

"What is it about lackwit men that they think we women yearn to see their dangly bits?" she complained to Vana once she entered the great hall where her sister already had men raking the filthy rushes and women scrubbing down the trestle tables, all of them muttering under their breaths.

"What now?" Vana asked. "Did you get permission from the Larkspur lord for us to stay?"

Breanne cringed with guilt that once again she

had allowed her temper to rule her good sense. Seeing the bruises still evident on Vana's eye and neck, her first priority should have been gaining an invitation for an extended visit. "Uh, I ne'er got a chance."

Vana put her free hand on her hip, the other arm still in a sling.

"Sweet Valkyries, Vana! He was naked."

Vana just arched her eyebrows.

"I saw his phallus."

"Was it big?"

Breanne laughed. Oh, how good it was to see Vana regaining her sense of humor! "Yea, it was big. If women had such ridiculous dangly parts, they would do their best to hide them, not wave them hither and yon."

"He waved his dangly part at you?"

"Well, it was dangly, and it moved."

"Beware, m'lady," Rashid spoke up from his seat on a nearby bench where he was showing some of the children a magic trick involving walnut shells and a piece of silver. "Lust rides a fast camel."

"I thought that was death."

"Lust and death both. Allah be praised!"

"Believe me, the man had no lustsome inclinations toward me."

"Do not fool yourself, m'lady. Lust wears a mask that beguiles the best of maidens."

"I have no idea what you mean half the time, Rashid. But know this, I am not going to be beguiled by any man, let alone the lout from lustsome hell."

"The maids tell me that Caedmon is a good

man and a fair master," Vana said to her in gentle criticism.

"Would that be the maids with the big bosoms . . . or the maids with the big bosoms?"

Rashid laughed. "You know what they say about big-breasted women?"

"If it has anything to do with camels, I do not want to know," Breanne snapped.

Rashid shrugged as if he had won some argument.

Amused by their exchange, Vana grinned, then winced as the scab on her bottom lip cracked open again. If Vana's earl husband was not already dead, Breanne would have killed him with her own hands, she swore she would.

'Twas odd, the life paths the Norns of Fate ordained. From a young age, Vana had been betrothed to Rafn, the leader of their father's troops. They had loved each other dearly and planned to wed after his return from a battle campaign in the Franklands. Alas, Rafn had never returned, and in her grief, Vana had succumbed to the overtures of the then charming earl of Havenshire. Big mistake!

"What can I do to help?" Breanne asked her sister.

"Ingrith and I can handle things inside, but mayhap you could do something about the chickens and pigs running loose outside. Drifa is having a hard time getting them out of the gardens. I even had to shoo several mean roosters out of the downstairs solar."

Breanne nodded.

"The wise ones say: The enemy of my enemy is my friend. What you need to do, Breanne," Rashid advised, "is make friends with Lord Larkspur, so that those out to avenge Lord Havenshire's death will have Sir Caedmon's shield to contend with."

Breanne groaned. "Why not ask me to harness the moon?"

"The whisper of a pretty girl can be louder than the roar of a lion."

If she heard no more Arab proverbs for the rest of her life, it would be too soon for Breanne.

Keeping a keep clean . . .

Caedmon had returned from the bathhouse a short time ago and donned the first clean garments he had worn in what seemed like a year. For a certainty, he had dumped the smelly, beyond-redemption tunic and braies into the cesspit. Despite his aching alehead, he was standing in front of a brass mirror in his bedchamber, removing two sennights of bristles from his face.

Ever since he had fostered a winter and two summers in the filthy keep of a Welsh warlord and experienced the hoards of lice that burrowed into the hairs on every part of a man's body, even the nostrils, Caedmon preferred to be clean shaven. For that matter, he liked being clean all over as well, unlike many of his Saxon counterparts, and for that reason had put in the bathhouse on first arriving at Larkspur ten years past. His first wife, Elizabeth, had been grateful. His second wife, Agnes, not so grateful, somehow equating cleanliness with lustsomeness. Agnes hadn't met a passion she didn't loathe. That had included him.

He had come back from service to his king one time . . . a different king from Edgar . . . to find all the Larkspur beds infested with fleas. Agnes's remedy had been to toss white sheets over the mattresses and when they were covered with black dots, shake the sheets outside. Hah! His remedy had been to burn all the mattresses, to her disgust. Aside from hating him, lust, and baths, Agnes had also hated waste. She would have preferred fleas.

In the two days since his return to Larkspur, Caedmon had done little other than drink and sleep. Now he was ready to put his home back in shape, a daunting job but one he was looking forward to. At least there were no infestations of fleas.

Who knew when the king would call on him again, and he would have to respond or lose his holdings, which he held precariously? At this stage, he was not powerful enough to offend his liege. Of course, a man could escape service by paying scutage, but not him since he had no extra funds, due to his neglect of Larkspur caused by the same king. A circle of futility he hoped to escape by a long run of work-filled residence. Larkspur would prosper, he was determined.

He had raised the sharp blade to his soap-lathered face, when a pounding noise caused him to jerk and cut his chin.

Bang, bang, bang!

Cursing, he dabbed at the blood and resumed shaving.

Bang, bang, bang!

Another cut.

Stomping over to one of the arrow-slit windows, he tried to see down into the lower bailey, but the now continual pounding was out of his range of vision.

Bang, bang, bang, bang, bang . . . !

He quickly finished shaving and was out of his bedchamber and down the stairs within a minute, barely registering the activity in his great hall. But then he stopped, turned around, and dropped his jaw in disbelief.

A woman in a blue gown and long, open-sided white apron in the Viking style and an incongrous Saxon wimple and head rail was supervising a massive cleaning of his great hall. Servants he did not even recognize . . . and, yea, he noticed a number of the female ones were buxom . . . were busier than he had ever seen in the past. All due to orders being pelted out by the lady.

One of the princesses?

"Who are you?" he inquired bluntly.

"Vana . . . Vana Elsadottir. Daughter of King Thorvald of Stoneheim. Widow of Oswald, the earl of Havenshire." Her blue eyes dropped down to the region of his manpart, then rose quickly. With a smile twitching at her lips, she said, "I presume you are Lord of Larkspur."

Why would she ask that after looking at my crotch? Ah, the red-haired tongue flapper must have been here

afore me. "Yea, I am Larkspur, but I am not a lord,"
he said with more rudeness than warranted. "Did
you say 'widow'? I had not heard of Lord Havenshire's death."

"I meant that he disappeared, though his death
is almost a certainty by now," she mumbled, ducking her head. Then, raising her head as if with resolve, she added, "By your leave, m'lord . . . I mean,
Sir Caedmon, my sisters and I seek welcome here
for a short time," Vana said hopefully.

Of a sudden, he took note of her right eye,
framed by dark and yellowing bruises. Her
cracked lip. One arm in a sling. And the way her
free hand kept going to her ribs. That must be the
reason for the wimple, to hide finger marks on her
neck . . . or worse.

"Who beat you?" he demanded to know.

Her face bloomed with color. "I fell off a horse."
And I am a eunuch.

Without turning to face him, a man in Arab
garb surrounded by children made a snorting
sound.

"Pfff!" He snorted as well. "And I have a Scots
castle I can sell you!"

"Really?"

"Nay! Not really." He exhaled with disgust. *Oh,
Lord, spare me from lackwitted women.* "It was a jest."

"Oh." Her voice trilled into a ludicrous attempt
at laughter.

His eyes crossed with frustration at one more
boulder being placed in the path of his life. A
boulder with breasts.

The Arab was standing now. Tall, dark-skinned,

wearing a long robe with hooded cowl as Caedmon had seen in the Eastern deserts.

"And who might you be?"

"I am Ibn Rashid al Mustafa, your humble servant."

There was not a single thing humble about this man.

"You may call me Rashid. I am assistant to Adam the Healer, a far-famed physician."

"Hmmm. We could use a healer here at Larkspur."

"A thousand pardons, m'lord, but I am here only as a companion to my master's wife, Princess Tyra. I leave when she leaves."

Soon, I hope. "As you wish."

Turning his attention back to the beehive of activity in his great hall, he saw Gerard rushing up to him. "Gerard! What in bloody hell is going on?"

"Master, the wench . . . I mean, the princess Vana . . . is supervising the cleaning of the hall. New rushes, scrubbing the tables . . ."

"Did I order that to be done?" Mayhap he had been further into the alehead than he had realized.

"Nay, but it needed doing," the impudent lady interjected.

"I have been remiss," Gerard said, ducking his head with embarrassment.

He patted the old man on the shoulder. "You have done your best in trying times." *And, after all, you have given me a castle filled with big-breasted women.*

"One thing, though, m'lord."

"Please, Gerard, stop calling me 'Lord.' "

"Please, Master . . ."

He groaned. "You have known me since I was in swaddling clothes. Just call me Caedmon."

Gerard inhaled with exasperation. "The lady has ordered all dogs out of the hall."

"You have?" He turned to the woman.

"They are a peril to people's health."

"Dogs are unhealthy?" *Methinks women are the unhealthy ones . . . unhealthy to a man's well-being.*

"Well, not dogs as such. Dogs in an eating place. The dog products, I mean."

"She means shit and piss and fleas and such," Gerard explained.

"Christ's cross! I know what she means."

"And drool," she added, as if one more dog sin mattered.

"The men will not be pleased," Gerard pointed out. "They like to toss bones and rotted meat to the rushes."

"My point precisely. Rotten rushes." She preened as if she had won some important argument.

"Should I countermand her orders?" Gerard asked.

"I am standing right here. You do not have to speak over me," the lady said.

Caedmon was about to say something rude, when he sniffed the air. There was the most delicious odor.

Without asking, Lady Havenshire told him, "My sister Ingrith has taken over . . . I mean, she is helping to straighten out your kitchen. That is bread you smell baking."

He was fairly certain that his eyes had crossed again at the words "taken over." But, at the same time, his traitorous stomach growled with hunger.

"Princess Ingrith is making quail in dill-cream sauce for dinner," Gerard further informed him, indignant. "Such fancy fare for fighting men! But she would not heed my warning."

"Ingrith tends to be a bit domineering," Lady Havenshire conceded, even as she turned and ordered a maid—a maid with big bosoms fair pouring out of her ill-fitting gown—to work faster, with a sarcastic observation, "We are raking hay here, not growing it." For such a small woman, she had a booming voice that nigh made his brain explode inside his head, which was surely twice its normal size.

Just then a bare-arsed boy toddled up to him and grabbed at his knees, staring up at him with huge brown eyes. 'Twas one-year-old Piers, who was at least clean today, his hair definitely a pale blond. In truth, the mite looked more like Geoff than him. He lifted the little one up into his arms and chucked him under the chin, which caused the child to giggle and say, "Fafa."

"I think he means 'Father.'" Lady Havenshire smiled wistfully at the child.

He scowled at her. "Where is this child's nursemaid?" he yelled at the top of his lungs, causing Lady Havenshire to jump, Gerard to flinch, and the child to whimper.

A big-chested girl, no more than sixteen, came hurrying from the kitchen area. "Sorry, master, but the boy got away from me."

"Who are you?"

"Mary. Me mother is the dairymaid."

"Edgiva?"

She nodded and reached out for the child. "Come, Piers. You need a nappy and a warm gown."

"He could have fallen into one of the hearth fires," Lady Havenshire remarked, the criticism levied more at him than the child's minder.

Piers chose that moment to prove that he was all boy by aiming his little pizzle at Caedmon's chest, soaking his clean tunic. Then he flashed him a toothless grin.

Shaking his head, Caedmon handed over the child, then headed for the double doors leading out to the bailey and the still continuous pounding.

Bam, bam, bam!

"Can my life get any worse than this?" he muttered.

Turns out it could.

There was a young man . . . nay, a woman in men's braies and tunic . . . bending over between her bouts of pounding to present her nicely rounded backside to his laughing men, who stood about like idiots. She was mending a fence around the pigsty.

The pigs were not pleased.

Neither was he.

CHAPTER FIVE

❦

Oink, oink . . . there are pigs, and then there are PIGS! . . .

Breanne, straddling the top of the pigsty fence, paused to discuss some ideas with the Larkspur woodworker.

"Methinks that the lintels of the doorway leading to the keep, as well as the eaves of all these outbuildings, should have a particular design—even the stables, the chicken coop I am going to build next, and, yea, the pigsty. Mayhap matching the twining larkspur carvings that abound in the great hall's wood trim."

"Huh?" Efrim said. "What be larkspur?"

Breanne smiled. "Larkspur is a flower . . . delphinium. Look out in the fields beyond the castle. They are filled with wild larkspur, no doubt the reason for this estate's name."

"You are not decorating my pigsty with flowers."

Breanne jerked and almost fell off her perch, saved only by the strong hand that grasped her upper arm, then yanked her off the fence and to

her feet. It was the loathsome lout of the big . . .
arrogance. Caedmon of Larkspur.

Efrim had the good sense to scoot away.

"Your sty fence was broken and the pigs were
running wild," she snapped, bending over to place
her mallet and a handful of nails into a wooden
work bucket. When she began to straighten, she
looked over her shoulder . . . and caught Caedmon
staring at her buttocks.

"You really are a loathsome lout."

"Thank you, m'lady." He made an exaggerated
bow from the waist.

" 'Twas not a compliment."

"Coming from the likes of you, it is."

She bared her teeth at him. "You belong on the
other side of this fence with the other pigs."

"Dost think so?"

If he were closer, she would have given him a
mighty shove to place him exactly there.

As if reading her mind, he folded his arms over
his chest and said, "If I go over that fence, so do
you."

"Loathsome lout!"

"You are repeating yourself."

"Donkey dolt!"

"Irksome shrew!"

"Troll!"

"Harpy!"

"Stinksome warthog!"

He lifted a hand high and sniffed at his armpit.
Apparently satisfied at his smell, he smiled at her.
And, oh, it was a dangerous smile. The kind that

lured women to do things they should not. "I am capable of repairing my own fence."

"Now you will not have to. Are you not the lucky one?"

He muttered something under his breath about luck and women. She suspected there were several foul words involved.

"I was just being helpful."

He arched his brows.

"I was bored."

"And you could not go sew a tapestry, or stroll through the gardens, or strum a lute?"

"Bor-ing! I but wish to be useful. What harm is there in that?" Her eyes shifted to the right. *Uh-oh!* Now, she looked everywhere except to the right.

He, of course, had to glance at that very place on the far side of the bailey, which she was avoiding. "Do my eyes play me false? Could that be a fine-garbed woman on her knees planting something up against the castle wall? A prickle bush! God's breath! Those are the bushes that snag on horses when riding through a forest."

Breanne sighed deeply. Of course, there was a woman in fine garb, the *gunna* pulled up to her knees, the hem tucked into her belt. "That is my sister Drifa. She likes growing things, especially flowers. That is a wild rosebush she is transplanting."

His eyes widened. "A noble Viking princess is crawling around my bailey, digging in dirt, planting a prickle bush?"

Nay, 'tis a dragon building a nest. Idiot! Of course it is a woman, my sister.

The woman stood and walked over to a wooden wheelbarrow. Digging a shovel into the contents, she then emptied it onto the spot she had been weeding.

"And that is . . . ?"

"Manure." *What a dolthead! Does not even recognize animal waste, even when it smells to high heaven.*

He put his face in his hands, counted to ten . . . then twenty, before inquiring in the sweetest voice he could muster. "Where did she get the manure?"

"Your cow byre." *What? You thought she was digging in your privy?*

"Of course. How foolish of me not to know that."

That goes without saying. "You have plenty."

Something seemed to occur to him then. "Is this a jest? Did Geoff or Wulf put you up to this flummery? Are they off somewhere watching us, laughing their arses off?"

"I never met your comrades afore today."

"Oh." He seemed disappointed at her answer. "What are you doing here then?"

"That was not polite."

"I ne'er claimed to be polite, nor do I aspire to such. Why are you and your sisters here?"

I wonder what he would do if I punched him on his lofty chin. "We were just passing and thought to stop and visit."

"On your way to . . . where?"

Questions, questions, questions! "Uh, I am not certain. You should ask Tyra. 'Tis some distant kin of her husband."

"As distant as my kinship?"

That chin is looking very tempting. "You are the rudest man I have ever met."

"You have not traveled much then. I can name at least three ruder men."

Do not punch him in his arrogant chin. He would probably punch me right back. She exhaled whooshily, tired of this verbal sparring. "Do you offer us hospitality, or not?"

He hesitated, then asked, "For how long?"

"One day, or two, or so." *Or fifty.*

"The 'or so' is what bothers me."

The man was too astute by half. "All we ask is a few days of your hospitality and protection."

He straightened abruptly. "Protection . . . that is the first I have heard of protection. What do you need protection from?"

I best keep my mouth shut or I will trap myself with ill-chosen words. She waved a hand airily. "This and that."

He narrowed his eyes at her, beautiful blue eyes framed by sinfully thick lashes. "By the by, your sister mentioned being the *widow* of the earl of Havenshire. When did that villainous poor-excuse-for-a-man expire?"

Breanne could feel heat coloring her face. "Recently. He *disappeared* recently. And, yea, he was a villain."

"How did he die . . . assuming he is dead? Lord Havenshire was not that old, as I recall."

"Well, no one really knows." *Except us.* "He went out one night to visit his mistress and never came back." *How easy a liar I have become.* "But his horse did. Return, that is." *Brutus is out in your stable right now. Go check.* "Road rogues no doubt murdered him for his purse." *Whew! Lying is hard work.*

"They found no body?"

She shook her head. *I need to get away from here and his too-perceptive questions.*

"Where is the earl?" he demanded abruptly.

She jumped. "No need to yell. I already told you, he is dead."

"Mayhap he is still alive."

"Mayhap. Nay, he is more likely dead." *As a fence post.*

Just then, Ivan and Ivar, their guardsmen, stepped out of the stable, came over, and stood, legs braced, on either side of her. While she was thankful for this means of changing the subject, she could tell that Caedmon was not happy with their presence. "Go away. Shoo!" she said in a whisper.

But the thick-headed fools did not budge.

"'Tis one thing to ask for hospitality. 'Tis quite another to bring armed men into my keep." Caedmon threw the words at her like stones, and his one hand went to the hilt of his short sword.

Her guardsmen did likewise.

She motioned for the guards to halt their aggression, then told Caedmon, "They are harmless." *Unless provoked. Then, you should see how good they are at lopping off heads. Eeew!*

He gave them a thorough scrutiny. "Hah! Harmless as starving bears."

Or head-loppers.

Ivan, the guard closest to her, growled, not unlike a . . . well, bear. Ivar bared his teeth, not unlike a bear, as well.

"I meant that they intend you no harm." Turning, she scowled at her guards. "Ivan, Ivar, go. I am safe. You must needs help Tyra prepare to leave for home."

After they departed, reluctantly, Caedmon asked, "Dare I ask, who is Tyra?"

"My sister . . . your kinswoman by marriage."

"Ah, wife of my close kinsman, Adam the Healer."

"Your sarcasm is not pleasing, m'lord."

"And I do yearn to please you. I am not a m'lord."

"M'troll, then?"

He grinned. "And where is this Tyra going?"

"Home. To her husband at Hawkshire."

She could tell that he wanted to ask why they did not go with her. So, she quickly attempted to get his mind on other things. "You are bleeding," she observed.

"Huh?"

"Your face."

"Ah." He put a hand to his chin, then looked at the dab of crimson on his fingertips. "I cut myself shaving."

"Three times?"

"'Tis fortunate I am that it was not more. Every time you began that incessant pounding my hand wavered."

"Oh, so it is my fault you are so clumsy? Not your ale excesses?" She reached into a side placket of her braies and pulled out a linen cloth. She was tall for a woman, but he was taller; so, she had to go on tiptoes to reach his face, which she began to minister to.

He inhaled sharply.

"What? Did I hurt you?" *I should be so lucky!*

"Nay. 'Tis your scent."

She tilted her head to the side in question and just scarcely refrained from lifting her arm to sniff, as he had.

"You smell like flowers."

She nodded. "My sister Drifa's rose-petal soap. Would you like some?" *I could stick some down your slimy throat.*

"So I can smell like a rose?" He smiled. "That would go over well when I ride to battle. I can overcome my enemies with rose fragrance."

Grrrrrr. She smiled back through gritted teeth, despite her best intentions to keep the rogue in his place. "By the number of children inside, most of whom claim to be yours, I would say that a fair share of women, who would enjoy rose soap, reside here."

"Or women who pass by."

"Or pass by," she agreed, knowing full well that he hoped she and her sisters would soon "pass by."

One bit of blood had already dried. So, she wet the edge of her cloth with three quick darts of her tongue.

"By the rood!" he muttered.

She glanced up to see what he was muttering about.

His gaze was riveted on her mouth.

She licked her lips, assuming she must have something on them. Mayhap wood chips.

"Jesus, Mary, and Joseph!"

"What?"

"Your mouth is . . . amazing."

At first she did not understand.

And then she did.

Oh, my! Oh! My! She should have been outraged at his suggestive words. Instead, her heart began to race, and she felt her nipples harden and ache in the most annoying, wonderful way. She could swear there was a dampness pooling betwixt her legs. She tingled, all over, but especially in some forbidden places. Was this lust?

Just barely, she restrained herself from leaping on him, with her legs wrapped around his middle, the way she had seen Tyra do with Adam one time. How he would laugh at that!

But he was not laughing now. In fact, she sensed he was in the throes of his own attraction to her, and it was just as unwelcome.

"Do you blush, Breanne? By thunder, you do!" He seemed inordinately pleased by that discovery.

"'Tis just the sun."

His gaze dropped to her chest, where her breasts were heaving in and out. When had she gone so breathless? And why? Even worse, at some point she must have leaned forward, still on tiptoe, and was almost breast to chest. How mortifying! As if she would want to touch him. She quickly dropped flat on her feet.

With a shake of his head, as if to clear it, he stepped back to put distance betwixt them.

And then he smirked.

The self-sure lout!

"Two days. Two days I give you and your princess brood. Then you are gone."

She stuck out her tongue at his back as he began to stomp away, something she had not done since she was a girling.

He turned at the last moment, as if to add something else, another odious order, no doubt. His eyes widened with surprise at having caught her mid-tongue thrust. Then he chortled, "Have a caution, wench, you may find that tongue somewhere not to your liking, but definitely to mine. On the other hand, you would like it, too, methinks." He winked. He dared to wink at her.

Which caused her to tingle some more.

Therefore, she got immense pleasure when he stepped into a pile of putrid pig waste she had raked for Drifa's gardening, thus proving what she had said all along about the need for a pigsty fence. She thought about yelling, "I told you so," but decided to save that for another day. There would be many opportunities that would warrant such words around such a lackbrain.

She could not wait.

As for the two-day limit of their stay, all she could say was, "Hah!"

A woo-ing they did go, a woo-ing they did go, heigh-ho the . . .

A widow hunt.

There was no other word for the insane journey Caedmon found himself on a short time later.

He, Geoff, and Wulf were riding for Heatherby, the estate now owned by Sybil Blakeley, Lady Moreton, recent widow of Edward Blakeley, earl of Moreton. Heatherby just happened to adjoin Larkspur on the southwest, a mere one-hour ride on a good horse. Whilst Larkspur encompassed six hundred hectares of land, Heatherby was half that size. Whilst Larkspur had many fertile hides of yet-to-be-tilled land, Heatherby had a waterway leading to a seaport, albeit at some considerable distance.

Soon after he had talked with the Norse witch—and almost disgraced himself like an untried boyling by being aroused by her kissome lips—a traveling tinker arrived. Ezekial had informed them that the Earl of Moreton had passed away four days ago of a sudden heart seizure. His much younger wife, Sybil, was in deep mourning.

Caedmon wanted to make sure no other land-hungry knight nabbed her afore he had a chance to get his teeth in, so to speak. Or better yet, Geoff or Wulf's teeth, which were far more suitable. Once Edgar, like all grab-land kings, got wind of this rich land in the hands of an "unprotected" woman, he would be sure to send her a noble bridegroom, which meant some weakling under the royal thumb.

He had no wish to wed again. In fact, he loathed the idea. But he would do most anything to protect what he already had. And a foe ruling Heatherby threatened any surrounding estates.

He had been only half-attending and realized that Wulf was addressing him. "I am suspicious of your royal visitors."

"The princesses?" he asked.

Wulf nodded. "Them, the Arab who claims to be a healer but has the body of a warrior, and the two Norse bears."

"I agree," Caedmon said. "I should have kicked them out on their pretty arses the moment they crossed the moat."

"The guardsmen have pretty arses?" Geoff inquired with mock surprise.

"You know exactly who I mean."

"I understand your dilemma," Wulf said. "Hard to refuse hospitality to five women in need, especially the one who has clearly been beaten."

" 'Tis exactly what I thought. I saw finger marks on her neck." This from Geoff.

"She was married to the earl of Havenshire. You know what an evil brute he was." Caedmon drew his bottom lip in, thoughtfully. "Now he is dead . . . or missing."

"A coincidence?" Geoff asked.

He shrugged.

"Watch your back, my friend," Wulf added.

He nodded. "For now, I have more important issues to address. Like Heatherby. And the thieves who are stealing cattle from the nothern pasture. We will stop by there afore returning to Larkspur. Once we see what the situation is with the good widow."

"You should have worn your black wool surcoat with the red samite lining," Geoff told Wulf.

"Huh? Oh, nay! Do not even think it! I am just along for the ride," Wulf protested.

"Why? You are perfect for Sybil."

"I am no more perfect than you are, Geoff. Or you, Caedmon."

"It would solve your problem," Caedmon pointed out.

"How? By switching one shackle for another? If I wanted a bride, I would go home and yield to my father's wishes." Wulf was the second son of a powerful Wessex nobleman who had betrothed Wulf from birth to a Welsh princess, Gwyneth, who wanted naught to do with him. Not that he wanted her, either. None of them had ever seen Gwyneth, but considering the size of her impressive dowry, and his less-than-spectacular birthright, his maternal grandmother's pitifully small estate in Norsemandy, they figured she must be horse faced and as round as a barrel.

"Well, we agreed afore leaving Larkspur that one of us would make a bid for the lady's hand, after a period of subtle but not-too-long courtship," Caedmon reminded them.

"Subtle?" Geoff snorted.

"He means that you should not stick your tongue down Sybil's throat on first meeting," Wulf elaborated.

"Even if she wants me to?"

"How would you know?"

"Women have signals."

Caedmon speared Wulf and Geoff both with a rebuking scowl. "I meant that we come to express our sympathies. That is all at this point."

"Oh, please! We must needs do more than that," Geoff opined. "Once the king gets wind of this windfall, he will have one of his lackeys here posthaste. Or he will come himself to get a taste. Remember what he did with Ordulf's wife."

"Well, I ne'er agreed to offer *my* hand. I am going back," Wulf declared.

"You are such a lackbrain, Wulf. Do not get your beard in a blaze. Caedmon and I will do all the wooing," Geoff said. "We will see who comes out the winner."

Caedmon sighed. Somehow, it did not seem like winning to him. More like a bid for torture.

For some odd reason, an image flashed in his head of a red-haired woman with lips he was determined to taste, afore sending her on her merry way. In fact, he could swear his lips tingled in anticipation. And a certain other body part tingled, too.

Meanwhile, Geoff and Wulf blathered on about different ways to woo a woman, some so crude they could never be mentioned in mixed company. He was heartsick at the prospect of chaining himself once again in wedlock, while they seemed to look forward to this visit. Time enough to think of Sybil or Heatherby when they got there.

"Dost think the king will call us to arms again this year?" he inquired, as a means of changing the subject.

The idiots ignored him and continued their debate, now over whether pinching a woman's buttocks was unsubtle or not. And how they should be cautious around Sybil not to even mention the word *buttock*.

"We should resume training on a daily schedule so our men do not soften," Caedmon interrupted.

Still, they ignored him. Now discussing why highborn women took so long to peak during bed-sport and whether Sybil fell into that category and how Geoff once fell asleep in the midst of tupping a countess who took too long to reach her peak.

"Did a woman ever cause your cock to tingle? Just by looking at you?"

Two heads turned slowly to stare at him.

Now he had their attention!

CHAPTER SIX

⊗

And then the other shoe dropped . . .

Breanne was huddled with her sisters in the Larkspur courtyard the next morning discussing Tyra's imminent departure for her home. Hawkshire was in the southern portion of Northumbria, closer to the market town of Jorvik.

"I still think I should stay with you," Tyra insisted. She was dressed today for travel, but also for protection against brigands—who abounded here in the northern wilds, not to mention Archbishop Dunstan's men, who might already be searching for Oswald.

Once a warrior who led their father's troops, Tyra wore a soldier's short-sleeved leather tunic over slim braies covering her exceedingly long legs, but there the military similarity ended. Yea, her forearms and thighs were roped with muscle from her warrior training, but etched silver armlets, a gold-buckled belt, and a sable-lined cloak denoted her rank as a Norse princess warrior.

Although wife to Adam of Hawkshire and mother to a precious daughter, Tyra would never forget her role in life. Every person, man or woman, had gods-given skills, and Tyra's were those of a fighter.

" 'Tis best you go home to create an atmosphere of normalcy," Breanne advised. "Besides, I know you miss your husband and daughter sorely."

"I do," Tyra admitted, "but we have always stuck together in time of trouble."

"You can help us best by going home and having Adam contact his uncle Eirik at Ravenshire. Eirik will know how to help us get back to Stoneheim. Once back in the Norselands, we will be safe."

"Even if only Vana goes back at first, I will feel better." Ingrith swiped at the tears welling in her eyes.

"The rest of us can claim ignorance," Drifa said.

"I agree. Getting Vana back under Father's shield is our top priority." *Easier said than done.* Breanne bit her thumbnail nervously.

"Will you all come back to visit at Hawkshire once Vana is on her way home?" Tyra asked.

"I do not know, Tyra. Mayhap some time in the future," Drifa said. "All this excitement . . . well, a peaceful stay at home might be best. Leastways over the winter."

"Pray gods that we be home for winter," Vana interjected in a small voice.

They all linked hands, forming a circle, and entreated the Norse gods and the Christian One-God to grant their wishes.

Ivan and Ivar led the saddled horses out of the stable, and the sisters hugged once again, tears rimming all their eyes. They had been through so much of late, especially Vana, who was slowly healing from her battering, though she would wear the scars inside forever, Breanne suspected.

But enough was enough. Best that Vana, the two guards, and Rashid were on their way. Soon the Larkspur lout, and his loutish cohorts, would be home from their ludicrous bout of widow courting. There were no secrets in a keep this size. It was best the sister ranks were reduced before he ordered them to depart as a whole, as he had already done.

Just then, Rashid rushed out of the keep. "The lung fever is spreading amongst the children. I must stay."

Breanne's heart raced. "How bad is it?"

"A kitchen maid caught the fever and passed it on to two of the children. They must be isolated before others succumb, as well. The little ones are most susceptible."

"Piers? The baby?" Breanne clutched her hands to her chest with worry.

"May Allah weep, he is the worst."

Rashid was a skilled healer, having worked under Adam's tutelage for years. There could be no better medical provider in time of illness. Already, he was telling one of the housecarls and Drifa which herbs they would need and where to gather them.

Thus it was that a short time later, Tyra and the two guards had left for Hawkshire while Rashid and the four sisters were left to deal with yet another dire circumstance. The first had been a life blow, this a life threat.

Could it be that this was why they had been
sent to Larkspur, of all the places in Britain they
could have gone into hiding? Perchance the celestial beings, whether Odin or God, had destined
them to choose this remote estate because they
were going to be needed.

Breanne laughed as she entered the keep
behind Rashid and her sisters. What would Caedmon think of her being his destiny?

Where's the Pony Express when you need it? . . .

By afternoon of the next day, Breanne knew
she had to do something about the still-missing
Caedmon and his comrade friends. Three of the
children, two of the sentries, one housemaid,
and a stable boy were very ill and might not re-
cover.

The widow of Heatherby must be resisting
their wooing efforts, if they had to stay an extra
day. Smart woman. Or mayhap she was enjoying
their favors too much.

Taking a candle into the small, dark room
under the staircase where Caedmon kept his
castle records, she searched for parchment and
encaustum. There were several used pieces of
vellum on which a strong male hand had written
various tallies regarding livestock and household provender. She turned one of them over,
then dipped her pen into the treacly liquid. How
should she address her missive? Dear Loathsome
Lout. Dear Rude Oaf. She opted for graciousness
and wrote:

Greetings M'lord Caedmon:

My regrets on interrupting your most important courting. Alas, you are needed at Larkspur.

Return at once. You may resume your wooing at a later date.

> Sincerely,
> Breanne Fionadottir

It was only after sending one of the grumbling guards with the missive that she realized that she had not told him why he was needed. Well, he would find out soon enough.

His first reaction would no doubt be, "Why is she still there?"

When clueless men go a-courting . . .

Caedmon held the letter in his hands, and still, after five readings, could not believe the nerve of the Viking wench.

How dare she order him to do anything!

How dare she mock his efforts at courting! And there was no question in his mind that she was getting joy out of his predicament.

How dare she still be at Larkspur when he had ordered her to leave!

Geoff grabbed the missive out of his hands. After reading it, he passed it to Wulf. The two of them just smirked at him.

"Are you sure that you must leave today?" Lady Moreton asked, coming up to them as they stood at the entrance to the Heatherby great hall. "You have been so helpful."

It was true. They had aided her in establishing authority with the restless knights who were unsure of what to do now that their leader was gone. They had also straightened out some misunderstanding with her castellan over the disposition of livestock that had been intended for market.

As she spoke, Sybil's eyes kept going to Geoff, which was a relief to Caedmon. "I wish you joy of her," he whispered, to which Geoff just rolled his eyes.

Having a friend at Heatherby was almost as good . . . in fact, better . . . than being here himself. Although he had to admit that Sybil was an attractive package. Young . . . no more than twenty-four . . . she had been married to the much older earl by her impoverished family in need of the significant bride price. In fact, this had been her second marriage and widowhood to an older man. Not an unusual happenstance. And she was comely, with raven-black hair and gray eyes. Her front teeth were a mite crooked, giving her a lisp, and her hips were a bit wide, but those were mere trifles in the scheme of things. He and Wulf had teased Geoff about the beautiful children they would have, whereas Geoff had teased them back about all the fun he would have in the making.

Caedmon knew what it was like to be a landless knight, and he was happy for his friend if he was able to succeed with Sybil. They had been right in coming so soon. Already three other men had come sniffing after her, and more would arrive in the days ahead. Geoff surely had an advantage, being young and handsome.

"I must needs return to Larkspur. Some emergency has arisen," he told her.

"Mayhap Geoff could stay behind," she suggested, batting her long eyelashes. "Just for an extra day or two."

The three of them could scarce keep from whooping their joy.

"Are you sure you could spare me?" Geoff inquired of Caedmon, playing the innocent.

"Well, it will be difficult." He tapped his closed lips with a forefinger.

Geoff kicked him in the shin when Sybil's attention was diverted elsewhere.

"Ow!"

Sybil glanced up at him in question.

"A kink in my knee," he explained.

"Would you be able to stay?" Sybil did her eyelash batting at Geoff again, as if he needed any convincing. The two of them . . . Geoff and Sybil . . . made a great pair in the mock innocence arena.

Caedmon wagered she would be in Geoff's bed furs by nightfall.

"The housecarls have not exercised since afore Edward's death, and reivers have been stealing cattle right and left, as they have at Larkspur in your absence."

A tricky business it would be if Geoff managed to wed the lady afore the king was able to put his finger in the marriage pot, although Edgar was more like to stick his whole damn hand in, and his cock as well. Hopefully, Geoff could wed and bed her quickly, then afterward approach the

king about the earlship, or at least the land rights.
Edgar was not going to be pleased.

Thus, it was that only he and Wulf returned to
Larkspur two days and more since they had left.
He had planned to patrol the north boundary of
his lands for clues to the reivers, but decided that
it was more important he return home.

"What do you suppose has happened that
would prompt the princess's letter?"

"She must miss me," Caedmon said. And for
some odd reason, he liked that idea. *Idiot! She
would as soon kick me as kiss me.*

Wulf arched his thick black eyebrows at him.

"I am still going to send her and her sisters
on their merry way. But first I am going to make
her pay for her brassy letter." *Kicks and kisses . . .
hmmmm, that gives me an idea.*

"I would like to see that."

"Really, I have only so much time to get so many
things done at Larkspur afore Edgar goes on the
rampage again, and I have no need of distractions.
If Geoff gains Heatherby, he and I will be able to
resist together with two important holdings com-
bined, small as they are, but that is just a delaying
tactic."

"In the meantime . . . ?"

"Among other things, I want to find those
Welshmen who served with us in the Franklands
a few years past."

"The three brothers?"

"Yea. Madoc, Merrick, and Morgan. Sons of
some Welsh border king, or so they claimed.
I swear, at least three of the bratlings running

about Larkspur belong to them. Mayhap they are acquainted with your betrothed."

Wulf snorted his opinion, as if all Welshmen were related or knew each other. "We will ne'er know since I have no intention of meeting the wench."

"Methinks you doth protest too much betimes, Wulf. Why not go and meet her? She may be a great beauty, for all you know."

"It matters not to me."

Wulf's father, and not the woman in question, prompted Wulf's stubbornness, though what he had done to cause such a rift Wulf would never disclose.

"Stay and help me then. You are always welcome. But you must know that the roof leaks. The shire taxes are due, and I would not be surprised to see the reeve show up soon with his hand out. I have already been asked to oversee the next shire court, and God knows I am the least qualified to levy punishment for bad deeds. The cotters want seed for the fall plantings. And I am lustsome as a goat, not having had a woman in nigh on three months."

"Caedmon, your life is a bloody mess."

He could not argue with that.

Steam heat and then some . . .

Breanne was in the downstairs solar, which had been converted to a hospitium of sorts for the five adults and four children who lay wheezing in the warm steam.

At Rashid's direction, hot rocks were constantly

being dropped into buckets of water to create the
steam, which would clear the lung passages. That
heat, along with the warmth from the hearth fire,
made the small chamber unbearably hot.

Although most Saxon estates, and Norse as
well, had central hearths in their great halls with
smoke holes in the ceiling, few had actual fireplaces with chimneys. Larkspur, a hodgepodge of
building styles, had adopted the Frankish style of
heating and cooking. Not only were there three
central hearths in the great hall, there were also
two huge fireplaces at either end, an enormous
one in the kitchen for cooking, and smaller ones
in some of the bedchambers for heat. It was a style
that Breanne, with her building talents, liked very
much. If nothing else, it reduced the amount of
interior smoke.

Rashid had long since removed his Arab attire,
wearing only an ankle-length linen under-tunic
with the sleeves rolled up as he ministered to those
ailing with herbal potions and cool, wet cloths.
Putting aside modesty, Breanne wore a thin white
summer *gunna*, which clung to her body in the
humidity. But she could not be concerned by that
as she held the whimpering Piers.

The first day . . . *Was that yesterday or the day
before? I am losing track. . . .* they had lost one el-
derly goatherdsman. After that all the fevers had
risen, then gradually lowered until today, when
the wheezing was no longer a death rattle. Piers
was the one they had worried about most, being
so young.

"Rest, little one," she crooned, rocking his little

body in her arms, "soon you will be running about like a puppy again. Shhh. Do not cry. Shhh."

He had fallen into a restless sleep. When she was placing him in his pallet on the floor, she felt a draft of air. Caedmon stood in the open doorway. The look of utter shock on his face as he took in the scene was soon replaced by one of thunderous rage.

Then his gaze hit on her. He jabbed a finger in her direction. "You! Come with me! Now!"

She would have liked to refuse the brutish order but did not want to disturb the others.

Grabbing her by the upper arm, he nigh dragged her down the passage and into a small guest bedchamber. When he released his hand, she staggered with weariness and with the effect of the cool air after all that heat. With a groan, she dropped down to sit on the edge of the bedstead.

"What is going on here?"

She told him what had happened and the status of the sickness at this point.

He nodded. "Why did you not contact me immediately?"

We were too busy saving lives. "I did not want to interrupt your wooing."

A foul word was hurled at her.

She shrugged. "We did not know at first how bad it was. Rashid is a more than competent healer. We thought he could handle it. And he did."

"That was not a decision for you to make."

"I did . . . rather, *we* did what we thought was best at the time." *Ungrateful wretch!*

"The little mite . . . Piers . . ." he seemed to choke up, then cleared his throat ". . . How is he?"

Well, mayhap not such a wretch, if he cares about the boy. "Close to death he was at one point, I believe, but he is getting better. They are all getting better. Except for the goatherder Ufric."

Now would be the time for him to thank her. But did he do that? Nay! Instead, he studied her and said, "You look like bloody hell."

She put a hand to her head where her hair was damp and sticky. Her face was no doubt dirty. And she probably smelled. "You would, too, if you had been sitting in a steam bubble for two days. Besides, dost think I care if you find my appearance repulsive?"

"Did I say that?" A smile twitched at his lips. "Truth to tell, I find your appearance . . . delectable. Even resembling a drowned rat, you make me tingle."

What did he mean by tingling? She was the one who tingled when he was about. But then she glanced down and saw that her *gunna* was almost transparent with wetness. Her breasts and nipples were visible, as well as her nether hair.

She tried to cover herself but had not the strength. Instead, she started to laugh because, damn the man, she was tingling in those forbidden places he perused so arrogantly. But her laughter soon turned to tears of utter exhaustion.

Quickly, he walked over and picked her up in his arms.

"What?" she squawked. "Put me down."

"I am taking you to the bathhouse. And then to a bed with clean linens for a long rest."

"I must help Rashid."

"I will help Rashid. You have done enough."

"You?" she asked, skeptical.

"Dost think I am incompetent?"

Yea. "Nay. I just cannot see you wiping a sweaty brow, or cleaning a dirty bottom."

A smile turned his enticing lips upward, and, amazingly, considering her sorry state, she felt a decided tingle in her tummy. Hunger, no doubt.

While her mind had been wandering, Caedmon had still been talking. She caught the tail end. "That is the best thing about being the leader, I can delegate. Methinks Wulf would make a good bottom wiper."

So, the lout had a sense of humor. *So what?* she tried to tell herself. But then, against all good sense, she nuzzled up against his neck, inhaling his salty manscent, which was not unpleasant, mixed as it was with that of fresh air, leather, and horse. As hot as she had been in the steam heat, she was hotter now, but it was a different kind of heat, a heat generated by this man and this man only. Sex heat. "Just so it is not your bed where you deposit me," she murmured.

He murmured something back that sounded like, "We shall see."

"I am sorry to be such a bother."

He laughed. "M'lady, you have been a bother from the moment you first arrived."

"I made a wager with my sisters that the first

thing out of your mouth on your return would be a demand to know why I am still here."

"I am saving that for later."

"Did you win the fair maiden?"

"Nay. She preferred Geoff."

I doubt that.

"Wulf and I were not even in competition with the blond god present."

Will he ever let me forget that I referred to his friend in that way? "Are you very unhappy about losing the fair maiden?"

"Not at all. And Sybil is far from a maiden. She is closer to your age."

"In other words, long in the tooth?"

"Precisely."

She slapped him weakly on the chest for his teasing. "To my eyes, you are far more attractive than Geoff." *Oooh, did I say that out loud?*

He chuckled and squeezed her closer in his arms.

"One can take only so much of a blond god afore one's stomach starts to roil. They love themselves too much." *Mayhap I am getting the lung fever, too, if my tongue cannot control itself. Be still, tongue. Be still.*

"Black-haired gods are so much better."

"Yea, they are." *Tongue, you must needs stop. Oh, gods! I am talking to my tongue.*

"You are going to hate yourself on the morrow for these revelations."

"No doubt. I could give you lessons in wooing so you might better compete in future." *I surrender, tongue. Do your worst.*

"What makes you think I am interested in wooing anyone?"

"Pfff! All men are interested in wooing, as long as it gains them what they want."

"Bedsport?"

"I was thinking more along the lines of marriage."

"Methinks you think too much, wench."

And talk too much.

And then he kissed her lips ever so gently, causing her to nigh swoon, even more than she already had. The man was beguiling her, pure and simple.

Once she was rested, she was going to berate him for taking such liberty, but for now she was enjoying the tingling too much.

CHAPTER SEVEN

※

Can't we all just be friends? . . .

C For about the tenth time that day, Caedmon crept into his bedchamber at the far end of the upper corridor to check on the sleeping princess from hell. Not only was she still sleeping, for six straight uninterrupted hours, but soft snores emanated from her open mouth.

'Twas a sign of his crumbling control that he found her snores charming. Not that he would tell anyone that, least of all this feminine plague on his life.

Rashid had insisted on a hearth fire so Breanne would not get a chill. As a result, the room was hot, and she was covered with only a thin linen sheet. There was no longer any question of her having caught the lung fever, she was just exhausted, according to the healer, who also promised the six remaining patients in his care would be on their feet, good as ever, within days.

With absolutely no hesitation, he lifted the sheet to stare at her nude body. She was slim but well proportioned, with small but firm breasts crowned with raspberry-tinted areolas and nipples which were turgid even when at rest. The same red hair that covered her head comprised a curly thatch over her mons. Her arms and thighs were well defined with muscle due to the ridiculously hard labor she insisted on engaging in. Her over-generous mouth was too large for her face to be beautiful, but instead, to his mind, it gave her the sensual aura of a temptress.

Pathetic sod that he was, he smiled, knowing how much she would hate that image. Was he reverting to a boyling that he got his pleasures in such small-minded ways?

Nay, there was naught boyish about him at the moment. He would have to be a monk not to be aroused by her body, and he had ne'er leaned toward priestly abstinence. He adjusted his breeches to accommodate his thickening.

Caedmon had a problem, and not just the lust rising in him like summer sap, thick and warm. The problem was that this woman and her sisters, not to mention the talented healer, were doing too much good at Larkspur, and he feared his men and his people would expect that same standard when they departed, which they would soon.

He was closing the door softly when he noticed Lady Havenshire walking toward him.

"Are you going to the great hall for dinner?" he asked.

She nodded.

He held out his arm for her.

She flinched.

What? Did she think he was going to hit her? *Ah!*, he thought, recalling the bruises about her face and neck which were almost gone now, though her arm was still in a sling. That is precisely what she had imagined.

Before he had a chance to ask about that, she spoke. "M'lord Caedmon, I must thank you for letting us stay here under your protection."

"Protection?" *That word again!*

Her pretty face, framed by almost white Norse hair in one long braid down her back, heated with color. Vana the White, she was appropriately called in her land. "Did I say protection? I meant hospitality."

He narrowed his eyes at her.

"We will only stay until word comes from my brother-by-marriage Adam of Hawkshire or his kinsman Lord Eirik of Ravenshire. They will be arranging my safe passage back to my father's home in the Norselands."

Safe passage? Now there was another odd choice of word. "Why did you not go to Eoforwic in the first place?"

"Eoforwic? Oh. We Norse refer to it as Jorvik."

"Ships leave from the market town's port almost daily." *And Larkspur is way off course on the route from Havenshire to Eoforwic.*

Her blush deepened from pink to deep rose. "Ah . . . uh . . . there were matters to be resolved first."

Caedmon had a bad feeling about these "matters." A very bad feeling. "I have not yet offered my sympathies on the death of your husband . . . or disappearance."

She nodded her acceptance of his sympathy.

Not surprisingly, considering Oswald's character, she did not appear to be in the throes of grief.

"I assume those are the matters to be resolved ... matters related to your husband."

Her throat worked with visible gulps of distress. "We did think to stay at the monastery at Lindisfarne, despite the ill feelings there toward anyone of Norse background."

Years ago, the first Viking assaults on Britain took place at Lindisfarne, also known as Holy Island. Norsemen considered church goods ... gold chalices, bejeweled scepters, silver crosses ... to be well-deserved plunder when taken from greedy clerics.

"But Rashid angered the monk healers when he tossed out a large pottery jar of leeches. Rashid and Adam do not believe in bloodletting."

Caedmon had to smile, picturing the pompous monks being chastised by what they would consider a heathen healer and pagan princesses. But then he noted the continuing distress on her pretty face as she worried her bottom lip, staring up at him with fear.

He put a hand on her arm, ignoring her discomfort at his touch. "Is there aught I can do to help?"

"Nay! Just let us stay until help ... I mean ..."

He waved a hand dismissively. "You are welcome." *For a time. A short time.* Most of all, he could not kick them out on their lovely arses without warning, since Breanne and Rashid had cared for Piers and the others inflicted with lung fever. He owed them.

"I promise that my sisters and I will do all we can to reciprocate your kindness."

Oh, please, do not. Enough is enough. "M'lady, look about you," he said as they entered the great hall. "My keep . . . every space in it . . . is cleaner than it has ever been, thanks to your efforts." New rushes mixed with juniper tops crackled under foot and emitted sweet odors. Laundry was being done daily so that there were always fresh garments and bed linens. He would not be surprised to find one of the princesses hanging from the rafters dusting cobwebs from the high beams. To his consternation, even the swords and shields in his weapons room had been polished to a high sheen.

" 'Tis the least I could do."

I shudder to think what the best might be. He led her up to the high table and seated her next to Drifa, her half-Arab, half-Norse sister of the petite body and slanted eyes. She was the one obsessed with gardening.

Nodding to Drifa, he remarked with dry humor, "I noticed that you swept the dirt in the courtyard today and planted more rosebushes." *And disrupted my men in their military exercises every time you bent over.* Not only had she planted more bushes, but she had erected little knee-high spiked-twig fences around them to prevent the dogs from lifting their legs there.

Like her sister, she blushed prettily and announced, "The kitchen herb garden is flourishing once again," as if she were handing him a pot of gold. While he was appreciative, he would have preferred the pot of gold.

"Next I am thinking of a grape arbor."

Help me, God! He made his way to the center of the table and plopped down next to Wulf, who was staring fixedly at the food lined up before him.

"Now what?" Caedmon inquired.

"Look at this. Even King Edgar does not have such fine fare when holding a grand feast."

He surveyed the table and sighed. Thanks to Ingrith, yet another of the princesses, his kitchen was, indeed, now producing mouth-watering dishes fit for a . . . king. Usually, the regular evening meal included bread, water or ale, a *companaticum* or whatever happened to be in the broth simmering in the huge kitchen cauldron, and, if they were lucky, meat, fish, or whatever was available in season. Instead, he saw slabs and joints of mutton and venison, vinegar-brined sea trout, pigeon in lemon wine sauce, lentils with scraps of lamb, baked lamprey sprinkled with dill, mashed turnip, and a *sallat* of beets, shredded cabbage, nuts, and apples in a mustard-looking aspic.

"What is that?" he said, dipping his spoon into one wooden platter, then licking his lips at the delicious taste.

"Do you know nothing, Caedmon? 'Tis *blankmangere*. Chicken in cumin cream."

"Where would I have ever learned that?" he asked indignantly. "How did you know?"

"I asked Ingrith."

He smacked him on the arm, then remarked, "Ingrith?"

"Yea. Ingrith and I have something in common."

"What, pray tell?"

"Skin." He laughed.

"You can make mock of me, and all this," he said, waving a hand to indicate his great hall with all its cleanliness and fine food, "but it all poses a problem for me, which is no laughing matter."

"What?"

"Some of the higher-born men in my ranks are thinking about inviting their wives for extended visits."

"That could only be good for Larkspur."

"You would think so. Men longing for home do not make the best soldiers. But that presumes that conditions would stay the same here at Larkspur, and that presumes that the princesses will stay, which is not going to happen."

Digging into a melt-in-your-mouth apple tart covered with sweet cream, Caedmon closed his eyes to relish the flavors.

"There is an even worse problem," he said then. "What if word gets out that I set a finer table than the royal house of Edgar the Greedy?"

"He will be here faster than a dog on a bone. But think, Caedmon, what will he do when he sees four beautiful princesses here?"

"Bloody hell!"

"Edgar the Depraved will take them to bed, sure as sin. All of them. Mayhap even all of them together. Willing or not."

They both observed a moment of silence, taking in that mind-picture.

"If Edgar had no qualms about raping a nun

and keeping her captive, princesses would pose no obstacle," he concluded. "We have to get them out of here."

"We?"

"We."

"When?"

"On the morrow."

"I cannot wait to see this. Wake me if I over-sleep."

"By your leave, m'lords, I could not help but overhear," Rashid injected from Caedmon's other side. Caedmon had forgotten he was there. "Remember, after the game, the king and the pawn both go in the same box."

"Thank you for that wisdom," he said politely to Rashid, then turned to Wulf, mouthing silently, "What does that mean?"

Wulf shrugged, then smirked at him.

"What?"

"Nothing."

"'Tis not nothing. What amuses you so?"

"You."

"The princesses will need more than one day to depart," Rashid interjected again.

"Why?" he and Wulf both asked at the same time.

Bypassing their question, Rashid went on, "May Allah weep, but the princesses are in need of a friend. After all, the enemy of my enemy is my friend."

"Huh?" he and Wulf asked together, again. Like minds and all that. Or like lackwits, more like.

Caedmon frowned, trying to figure out what the Arab was implying. "Are you saying that the princesses and I have an enemy in common?"

"As you say." Rashid stood, seemed to touch his forehead, nose, mouth, and chest in one quick motion, then bowed from the waist at both of them, before walking away.

He and Wulf looked at each other, then both gasped.

"Edgar," Wulf guessed.

"Bloody hell!" Caedmon exclaimed, pounding his empty cup of ale on the table. "Bloody, bloody hell!"

And then the you-know-what hit the medieval fan . . .

Breanne awakened slowly in a dark room, except for the light from a single candle on a nearby low table and the embers glowing in the fireplace hearth.

She should feel guilty, having slept all afternoon and into the evening, but she felt wonderful. As she sat up, raising her arms high to stretch, the thin sheet covering her fell, revealing her nakedness.

Her nudity was of no concern. Most folks slept that way, except in the harsh winter cold. But how she got to be unclothed was a puzzle. Last she recalled was the loathsome lout picking her up from Pier's bedside and carrying her here. *Is it possible—*

Just then, the door flew open and said loathsome lout stood there, legs braced in a defiant stance, fury dancing in his hard blue eyes.

"Eeeeek!" she yelped, pulling the cloth up to her shoulders. "Get out of my bedchamber."

" 'Tis my bedchamber."

She glanced around. "Oh. Then, get out of your bedchamber whilst I put on some clothing."

He folded his arms across his chest and leaned back against the door frame. "I think not."

"Well, I am not getting out of this bed until you do."

"Mayhap I will join you."

"You would not dare."

"I would dare much in my present mood."

"What has your bowels in a knot this time?"

"Do not push me, wench. I am beyond angry."

"Why?"

"Get your arse out of that bed. I want you and the rest of your princess brood out of my keep and on your way."

"Brood?"

"Brood, horde, troop, herd, flock, passel of trouble, whatever you want to call yourselves, it matters not to me. Just begone."

"That is not nice."

"I am not trying to be nice."

"Are you not even a little bit grateful that we nursed your children and servants back to health?"

"I am very grateful. That is why I will provide six men to guard your way to wherever you want to go."

She narrowed her eyes at him. "Something has happened."

"You could say that."

"What?"

"I know your bloody secret."

Her heart skipped a beat, then began racing. "You do? Who told you?"

He shrugged.

Well, he was bound to find out sooner or later if they remained here. "You could at least offer sympathy for our plight."

"I could also turn you over my knee and paddle your arse."

"You are such a coarse creature."

He just stared at her, waiting. And waiting. And waiting.

"We did not mean to kill him."

"What?" Caedmon's eyes nigh bulged with horror, and his jaw worked, unable to speak, at first.

Oooh, this was not good.

He sank down into a chair and stared at her as if she had sprouted horns. "You killed the king?"

"Do not be silly. Of course not."

His shoulders sagged with relief. But then, his still angry gaze stabbed her. "Who *did* you kill?"

"You rat! You told me that you already knew."

"I knew that you had done something to annoy the king. How was I to guess your secret was murder?"

"Well, that is not exactly true."

"Why is that not exactly true?" he asked wearily, pinching the bridge of his nose.

How to make our dilemma more palatable? Hmmm. I hate pleading our cause to this lout. "The king might not know . . . yet. Perchance, if the gods shine favor on us, he will ne'er know."

"Firstly, who is 'us'?"

"Me and my sisters."

"What is it that you and your sisters have done?"

She mumbled her answer.

"What did you say?"

"I said we killed the earl of Havenshire," she nigh yelled.

He put his face in his hands and appeared to be counting under his breath. When he raised his head, he demanded, "Tell me everything."

Must I? "I would feel better if I were clothed first."

"I would feel better if you had never come here."

Me, too. She glared at him, then told him the entire story. By the time she was done, he appeared stunned.

It *was* a stunning story, she had to admit. "Someday you will tell this story to your grandchildren, and you will probably laugh about it."

"I sincerely doubt that." He stared at her, then shook his head with disbelief. "You put a Saxon nobleman at the bottom of a privy?" Then, "How did you fit him through the hole?"

Men! They homed in on the most irrelevant details. "It was a new garderobe, just being built."

Caedmon smiled, then went serious. "This is the worst thing that could have happened."

Dost think so, lackbrain? "I know!"

"I was not referring to you. My hold on Larkspur is tenuous at best. Edgar could take it away on a whim. My hiding the killers of one of his noblemen would constitute more than a whim."

"I did not think of that."

"I daresay you did not think at all."

I wonder what would happen if I dumped a pitcher of water over his fool head. Oh, I forgot. I would have to get out of bed first. "There is no need for sarcasm."

"M'lady, you have no idea—"

A knock interrupted what further vitriol he was about to hurl at her.

Wulf stuck his head in the doorway. "I was sent up by the three princesses. They are worried about what you are doing to their sister."

"As well they should be."

Wulf glanced her way and grinned his greeting, amused at her state of undress, no doubt. Then he arched his brows at Caedmon.

"'Twould seem that the lovely princesses are actually cold-blooded murderesses."

"Oh, please, Caedmon. I cannot wait for your explanation."

"He exaggerates," she said. *Though not by much, unfortunately.*

"Hardly," Caedmon disagreed. Turning to his friend, he said dryly, "The five princesses killed Lord Oswald and buried him in a privy."

"How did they get him through the hole?"

"Men!" Breanne rolled her eyes. "We chopped him up into little pieces. How do you think?"

"Well, Oswald always was a piece of shit," Wulf quipped, then immediately added, "Excuse my language, m'lady."

"'Tis no more than we have all said of him at one time or another, with gentler language."

Wulf was silent for a moment, then burst out laughing. "Really, Caedmon, being around you is such fun."

CHAPTER EIGHT

❧

It was raining ... babies ...

Caedmon, Wulf, and eight of his hirdsmen were riding to the far northern section of his property to investigate the further theft of cattle and the burning of a cotter's hut, leaving one man badly maimed. It did not help his foul mood that driving rain put a chill in their bones and made visibility nigh nonexistent.

His booting the arses of four princesses out of Larkspur would have to wait until his return. He could scarce wait.

It still amazed him, not only that they had the nerve to kill a man, abusive as he had been, but the lackwit women had the nerve to hide out at his estate, subjecting him to the same royal scrutiny they would no doubt get. That he could not tolerate.

And he was not going to be softened by tears, either, which was what he had faced before leaving this morning. Except for the red-haired witch. Instead of tears, she had nigh spat at him, especially when he had remarked that she had a most interesting freckle on her left buttock. Not that he had seen her buttocks, lying on her back as she had been. But the remark let her know in no uncertain terms that he had seen her nude body.

She was probably checking her backside with a brass mirror at this very moment. Oh, to be a fly on her wall!

Angry as she had been, it had not stopped her from suggesting that she ride along with him and rebuild the cotter's hut. She was no doubt still sputtering over his coarse response.

He did allow Rashid to accompany them, though, and was glad of his offer. The healer would minister to the injured man. Still, if Caedmon heard one more dumb proverb, he might very well throttle the man, despite his healing talents. And camels! The Arab was obsessed with camels. "If a camel gets his nose in your tent, the body is sure to follow." Or, "The elephant's track treads out the camel's." It mattered not that Caedmon had no clue what he meant.

Wulf just laughed. At everything. Especially him.

But then Rashid chastised Wulf on his behalf. "One camel should not make jest of another camel's hump."

To which Wulf had commented that the only hump he had was betwixt his legs.

To which Rashid had tossed out a comment about camel humps and sex that pushed the bounds of even Caedmon's sensibilities.

Caedmon was drowning in a half-brained world, and he did not just mean rain.

But the sun finally managed to peek out from

behind the clouds as they arrived at the half dozen wattle-and-daub cotters' huts with thatch roofs set out in the open in this remote region, along with the one that had been burned down. The men and women here tended the fields of oat and barley and cared for the fifty or so cattle that ranged free. It should not be a dangerous job. No one cared about the loss of an animal or two. In fact, it was expected of the Scots reivers; they even robbed each other. But now they had gone too far, with the fire, assuming it was the selfsame villains.

While Rashid worked efficiently on the injured man, taking ointments and strips of clean cloth from his leather saddlebag, he and Wulf talked to the men. They could figure no reason for the destructive act, though the shifty eyes of one of his cotters made him think there was more to this than mere deviltry. After he had dispatched Wulf and three of the men to examine the site where the cattle had been last seen, Caedmon was about to go check on the healer's progress when a youthling—no more than twelve winters, he would guess—signaled with a jerk of his head that he wished to speak with him in private.

"I know how ta trace the animals. Well, one of 'em," the boy said, right off.

"And you are . . . ?"

"Edric. Me father is Aldhelm."

Caedmon nodded.

"One of yer cattle was a special beastie ta me. Raised 'im from a calf. Bertie, I called 'im. He has an all-white face, and a shaved patch on his left haunch where me grandsire stitched 'im up after he was gored by a spiky tree limb."

"If you came with us, could you identify the animal?"

"Fer certain, I could."

Within an hour, they were riding for the Scottish border. Himself, Wulf, Edric, and four of his soldiers. Two hirdsmen had been left behind with Rashid for protection.

"Something more needs to be done here," Wulf remarked.

"True. Either I build a palisaded village of sorts, manned by a small hird of soldiers, or I pull the cotters and cattle closer to the castle keep."

"Yours is not a large estate. Methinks you need all the grazing land you can manage for cattle and sheep, and ploughlands for more grains," Wulf mused. "Do you have enough men?"

"I must needs have enough. As you say, every bit of land should be used. If I value my holding, I must protect it."

It was nightfall before they entered Scottish lands. A fire was built and cloaks laid about for men to recline, but there would be little sleep tonight in this land, which was not quite enemy, but definitely not friendly.

As he folded his arms beneath his nape and closed his eyes, the oddest image kept plaguing him. A red-haired witch with creamy skin and a sharp tongue, leaning over him, teasing, taunting. Why he should think of her was beyond him. Little more than a nuisance, she was. Once she was gone, all would be well again.

The next morning they came upon a small holding where there were several thatch-roofed, conical huts. Fences enclosed horses and livestock.

Edric drew Caedmon's attention to a particular
cow.

He nodded.

A dozen armed men with wild hair of various
shades of red and wearing furs and leather breeches
approached them on foot, from several directions.
One of them—bigger than the rest—had gray hairs
mixed with red and numerous scars covering his
bull-like body; he broke apart from his comrades
or kinsmen and stepped toward Caedmon.

This was odd, that they were not attacking. Although heavily armed, they seemed to have something to say first.

Caedmon dismounted and handed his reins to
Wulf. He and his men also had weapons at the
ready.

Stepping forth, he said, "I am Caedmon of
Larkspur. Those are my cattle over there, and you
have burned one of my cotter's huts, injuring one
man badly."

"That we did," the man answered with maddening arrogance. "I be Malcolm, laird of the Mac-
Larins."

"Why?"

"Because one of your cotters planted his seed in
one of our lasses' bellies."

Caedmon glanced toward a hut where a young
girl with a big belly stood apart from all the others.
Her eyes and nose were red from crying. "Against
her will?" he inquired.

The old man shrugged, which probably meant she had spread her thighs of her own choice.

Caedmon glanced toward Edric. "Do you know who is responsible?"

The boy's unwhiskered face flushed, and he ducked his head.

"Well?" he demanded.

"Uhtred. Me brother."

"Is he married?"

"Nay, but he has departed for parts unknown. He and me father had a . . . disagr . . . disagr . . . a fight."

Caedmon turned back to the Scotsman. "Can we sit down somewhere and talk?"

Reluctantly, Malcolm bid him welcome . . . well, not quite welcome, but at least entry into his humble home.

Hours later—after imbibing vast quantities of that potent amber brew the Scots referred to as *uisge-beatha*, or water of life, but would surely be the death of him—Caedmon and his small troop were on their way back to Larkspur, his stolen cattle left behind, and no guarantee that there would not be more missing in the future. Reiving was the way of the Scotsmen.

Traveling with them was the young woman with yet another babe to be added to his Larkspur brood. Her father had said that no man in their clan would have Maire now. The babe's future was uncertain, at best, unless the wayward Uhtred returned to his responsibilities. Why he should care, with all his other problems, was beyond him. Even in the Saxon lands, the nobility

got rid of unwanted children, most often by sending them to a convent or monastery if they had
wealth enough, or by abandoning them to woods
or cliffs to die.

Rashid offered this thought: "Sunshine all the
time makes a desert."

To which he had suggested, sweetly, that Rashid
store his advice where the sun never shone.

Wulf was calling him every kind of a fool.

He felt like a fool.

But what could he do?

A woman will do what a woman's gotta do . . .

Caedmon, Wulf, Rashid, and the small troop of
soldiers had been gone for two days. They would
not be aware . . . *thank you, gods!* . . . that Ivan and
Ivar had returned with a message from Tyra . . .
an ominous message.

Breanne was on her way to the kitchen now for
a meeting with her sisters to tell them about Tyra's
missive and to plan their strategy, in light of the
news. Breanne had never thought she would be so
anxious to go home to the Norselands.

Despite their extended trip, Breanne was not
worried about the well-being of Larkspur's master
or his minions. They were well-trained fighting
men, able to defend themselves. Even Rashid.

But she *was* worried about the fate of herself
and her sisters, knowing that Caedmon was anxious to be rid of them. Which was impossible in
light of . . . well, she would think about that after
gaining her sisters' counsel.

In truth, after chasing after Caedmon's many

children all morning, she wished she had been able to escape with Tyra. Even living under her father's constraining roof held more appeal than this wild household.

Three of the children appeared to be legitimate, including the especially needsome nine-year-old Beth, whose mother had died when she was only a few months old; Beth desperately wanted a mother and had decided that one of the four of them would do, it mattered not which. In fact, she had taken to braiding her hair and wearing an open-sided ankle length apron in the Viking style. She was above stairs now, "supervising" the housemaids in putting clean linens on the beds. It was pitiful how hard the girling tried to please.

Then there were the rascally six-year-old twins, Alfred and Aidan, who thought their goal in life was to pester and taunt every living child and animal within their range. At the moment, they were having quiet time at two different sides of the chapel for tying apples onto the dogs' tails, then releasing them into the pasture, where the horses could chase them for the tasty treats.

Breanne felt especially sorry for twelve-year-old Hugh, Caedmon's oldest child, who had been sent home in disgrace from his foster family in Mercia. Whilst performing the lowliest chores about Larkspur as punishment, he had confided in Breanne about the perverted proclivities of one of the soldiers he had fostered under. He was too ashamed to tell his father about the man's intentions, but Breanne would. You could be sure of

that. If anyone should be ashamed, it was Caedmon for not trusting his son enough to have good
judgment.

Eight-year-old Mina was another of Caedmon's
illegitimate children. The tiny, fragile-boned
beauty had black-hair and dark cat eyes. Her
mother, an Arab *houri*, had not wanted this ill-
conceived child.

Her favorite was one-year-old Piers, the tow-
headed boyling who had recovered very well
from his bout with lung fever. She did not even
mind that he followed her around like a shadow.
Some said that he was not of Caedmon's blood,
but who could say for sure?

Mina passed Breanne in the great hall. She was
holding Piers' little hand in her little hand, teaching him to walk.

Breanne smiled at them both. "My sister is making honey fig custards for tonight's dinner."

They smiled back at her, though Piers would
have no clue what she had said. In fact, he said,
"Mama," which was alarming. These children
were all so bereft of love and discipline.

Just before she entered the corridor leading to
the kitchen, she stopped to watch five-year-old
Angus, whose bouts of temper matched his fiery
hair. She would wager the boy had Scots blood
in his veins. Not a bit of Caedmon could be seen
in his features. At the moment, Angus was scrubbing egg yolks and whites off the castle walls after
tossing them at one of his brothers for teasing him
about his freckles, of which he had many. No one
was sure who had done the taunting, everyone

except Angus having magically disappeared from the scene.

"How are you doing, Angus?" she asked. "Do you need fresh water?"

He said something so foul to her that she jerked backward.

The only thing that stopped her from smacking the wretch on his little bottom was the tear tracks on his face and the realization that he probably thought she had been making mock of him.

In a far corner, she saw Oslac, Kendrick, and Joanna with their heads together, looking Angus's way repeatedly. She veered off her path to the kitchen and went up to the three seven-year-olds, all born on almost the same day. Although Caedmon had accepted them as his own, word about Larkspur was that they looked just like three Welsh brothers who had been visiting at one time, nine months afore the births. These three were a gang unto themselves. Always engaged in mischief. Always sticking together.

Well, not for long.

"I know what you have done, and I am not amused."

"Whaaat?" they said as one.

"You are all to go over and help scrub the wall. And not one word will you say to Angus, lest it be an apology. He did not tell on you, by the by."

Grumbling, they went off to do her bidding. She stayed, tapping her foot impatiently, as she watched them closely. She was not fool enough to imagine they would stay once she had left the hall.

When the wall was clean enough, she ordered

them to empty the bucket and rinse the dirty cloths in the stream outside the keep walls.

Walking into the kitchen, she saw a scene of serenity that could be taking place in their own Stoneheim kitchen, as well as here in a Saxon fortress. Drifa was tying together the stems of various flowers, which she would dry and later make into scented sachet pillows. Vana was polishing silver goblets and platters. Ingrith and two kitchen maids—with big breasts, of course—were arranging dozens of honeycombs that they had gathered that morning from conical hives located beyond the castle gardens.

The entire keep, even the outdoors, smelled of her sweet concoctions. Flies would be arriving from far and wide, drawn by the odor.

Amicia, the Larkspur cook, worked amiably beside Ingrith. Apparently, she had walked off sennights ago, aggrieved over the chaotic household and its numerous children always underfoot. She was back now that the sisters had established order.

Some of the whole honeycombs had been placed in a pottery jug with a tight cork stopper. But most were to be drained of their honey and the combs made into candles. Ingrith vowed that one day she would try to make the far-famed time-keeping candles that Adam's aunt, Eadyth of Ravenshire, had perfected. They had been invented by King Alfred.

Caedmon might not be too happy when he found out that no mead would be made from this batch of honey. Plenty would come from the second and third harvests.

Ingrith handed Breanne a fire-heated knife and indicated that she should cut off the end caps and let the honey drain through a coarse-meshed cloth hung over a kettle. Once these combs were drained, Breanne handed them to one of the maids who mashed them to a pulp in a huge bowl. Then, once again, Breanne put the combs into a straining cloth over yet another kettle. This second strain of honey would be of a poorer quality, but still good for cooking and such. The end caps and mashed combs would be thoroughly rinsed and put aside for autumn candle making. Even that rinse water was put to good use.

All this was a ritual Breanne and her sisters were accustomed to, a joint effort required in any large keep if they wanted a sweetener for their meals or fine beeswax candles for light. Ingrith was an expert in this, as in all kitchen matters.

When Amicia and the maids left the kitchen for a few moments, going out to the well to get more buckets of water, Breanne quickly pulled Tyra's parchment message from her apron flap. "Ivan and Ivar just returned from Hawkshire with a missive from Tyra."

Her sisters stilled and turned, giving her full attention. The look of fright on Vana's face was pitiful. She squeezed Vana's hand and read:

My sisters:

We arrived safely. Adam is off to Ravenshire to enlist aid of his uncle, Lord Eirik, a member of the king's Witan. Search parties are out looking, not just for the

*earl of Havenshire, but for Vana, as well. Adam fielded
their questions well, but they may return.*

*Dunstan is on a rampage. For all our sakes, stay
where you are until safe passage is arranged for home.*

*Godspeed and love,
Tyra*

"We must stay here, then," Ingrith said.

"But how can we? Lord Caedmon insists we
must leave," Breanne pointed out.

"Mayhap, with the six guardsmen he promised,
we could make it to Father's ship at Jorvik," Vana
offered hopefully.

"Or to Ravenshire. Surely Lord Eirik is powerful enough to withstand even Archbishop Dunstan's threats." This from Drifa.

"The problem is getting from here to there," Breanne said. "It is a considerable distance, fraught
with peril."

"Well, the answer is clear," Ingrith said, wiping
her hands on a clean cloth and sitting down at the
table with them. "We must convince Lord Caedmon that he should allow us to stay."

"How would we do that?" Breanne asked.

"A plan," Ingrith said. "What we need is a plan.
Recall the plan we came up with for Tyra that one
time?"

"That was a plan for Tyra to seduce Adam,"
Breanne said indignantly. "Surely you are not suggesting that one of us should seduce this lout."

Ingrith shrugged.

"I think it is a good idea." Drifa was licking the honey off her fingers as she spoke.

"Oh, really? And who would be the one of us doing the seducing?" Breanne was not amused.

Everyone stared at her.

"Nay. Oh, nay, nay, nay! I would not know how, even if I were so inclined, and I am definitely disinclined."

"We could pick straws," Vana offered. "Nay, I should do it. After all, 'tis my fault we are in this mess."

The idea that Vana would be willing to place herself in any man's close proximity so soon after her despised husband's vile conduct tugged at Breanne's heart. How could she in good conscience allow Vana to make that sacrifice?

"Oh, bloody hell! I will do it."

"Breanne! You should not curse," Drifa chastised her.

"Cursing is allowed when there is good cause," Breanne contended.

"According to whom?" Ingrith wanted to know.

"According to me. Oh, I cannot believe I am going to do this. The oaf will laugh at me, I know he will. With my womanly skills, I am incapable of enticing a goat, let alone a man."

"I could not help but overhear," Amicia said, coming back into the kitchen. "I kin give ya advice on lurin' a man ta yer bed furs, sure as Satan made sin."

Breanne and her sisters stared at Amicia, jaws agape. The cook had thirty years under her belt, and it was a wide, wide belt. Whereas most women's gowns could be cut from seven ells of cloth, Amicia's would surely require ten. She was as tall as a man—even taller than Breanne—her hefty shoulders and muscled upper arms a good framework for massive breasts jutting out in a way that caused men's eyes to bulge. And strong! Breanne had seen her wield a cleaver over a skinned red deer with the efficiency of a warrior. Her brown hair was a nest of uncombed tresses. And her front teeth protruded out over her lower lip, not unlike a horse.

A giggling Piers toddled in then with Mina in hot pursuit. He crawled up onto her lap before Mina could catch him. Breanne was wearing a tunic and braies today, figuring she might get some work done in the lout's absence.

"I tried to keep him in the hall," Mina told her, tears rimming her eyes. Really, since when did an eight-year-old girl have child-care duties? Where was Mary? Oh, she recalled now. Mary had gone out to help her mother with the milking.

Breanne handed each of them a hunk of honeycomb to suck on. Piers would no doubt get it all over her tunic. Oh, well. The tunic was old and designed for rough work. Mina scurried off, figuring she had a reprieve now that Piers was in Breanne's care.

"You were saying?" She looked to Amicia.

Amicia was helping Ingrith clean up. She even handed Breanne a wet cloth to wipe the face and hands of Piers, whose eyelids were drooping as he rested his cheek again her breast. "I heard ye

say somethin' about seducin' a man." She flashed
a lusty, knowing wink at all of them. "I know ev-
erythin' there is about that, believe you me."

What?

Amicia certainly had their attention . . . all of
them, including the two maids of uncertain age,
who looked as if they might know a thing or
two themselves. And not because they were big-
bosomed like almost all the females at Larkspur.

"I do not intend to, uh, fornicate with him. Just
get his, um, interest for a while so my sisters and
I can stay for a few sennights." Breanne felt her
face flame as she mentally chastised herself for
her stumbling words.

Amicia nodded. "The best way is ta be naked in
front of 'im. That is all it takes fer the sap ta rise in
most men. All that skin is like one of those afro-
daisy-yaks they sell in the Eastern lands."

Breanne stared at her in horror. "I will not stand
nude in front of that man." She shivered with distaste. Besides, she suspected he had viewed all she
had to offer already and had not been tempted to
jump on her with unbridled enthusiasm. She recalled his snide remark about a freckle on her buttock. Which was not there, as far as she could tell
from her view over the shoulder into a brass mirror.
She would have asked one of her sisters to check,
but then she would have had to explain why.

Amicia shrugged. "Well, the next best thing is
a goodly set of bosoms." She gave Breanne's small
ones a look of disdain. "You could try a bit of pad-
ding up there. Mayhap two molded aspics, which
would give 'em a bit of jiggle. Or if you push them

together and upwards with bindings, they might appear bigger."

Jiggle? What next?

"You are not wasting perfectly good aspics for such a dunderhead purpose," Ingrith asserted, hands on hips.

Thank you, Ingrith.

"Suddenly appearing with big breasts would make him suspicious," Vana said.

Thank you, Vana!

"Besides, big nipples are just as tempting, I understand. And Breanne has big nipples." This from Drifa, the traitor.

She glared at Drifa, who grinned back at her.

"And you have a large mouth. Men melt over women with biggish lips," Amicia told her.

"Why, for Frigg's sake?"

Almost immediately Breanne wished she hadn't asked, because Amicia told her, in explicit detail.

"I think I am going to lose the contents of my stomach," Breanne declared.

The other women at the table were dumbstruck. "Surely women do not do that willingly."

"Well, they do when it is a man they love and want to please," Vana, obviously not one of the dumbstruck, told her, not even blushing. "Like Rafn."

I do not believe I am hearing this. Well, she should not be so surprised. Long before the hated Earl Oswald, Vana and Rafn had been in love, but she had been so young. Apparently not so young for some things!

Amicia slid down onto the bench across from

Breanne. "Listen, I am going to tell you ladies somethin' few ladies know. There is one sure thing that drives men wild."

Oh, my gods and goddesses! Do I want to drive Caedmon wild?

"A woman's pleasure in the bedplay," she said with a sharp nod of her head, as if she had just imparted some great wisdom.

"Huh?" Breanne spoke for all of them.

"When a woman gains pleasure in the bedding, 'tis a man's greatest pleasure. And when he knows that she enjoys his touch . . . when she will allow him to do any wicked thing he wants . . . when she initiates certain practices . . . well, that woman can get anything from a man. Jewels, marriage, or . . . several sennights of extended hospitality."

Amicia was obviously more aware of their dilemma than they had realized.

Although Breanne was a virgin, she was not unaware that some women enjoyed sex. With the right man. Like Tyra with Adam. Like Vana with Rafn.

She wanted to ask what practices Amicia alluded to, but could not find the words without appearing ignorant.

Not so their outspoken Ingrith. "What practices?"

And Drifa. "What things might a man want to do, other than the usual?"

"Wicked things?" one of the maids inquired with decided interest, then giggled.

Another of the maids asked, "Does a woman have ta be made a certain way ta enjoy all that gruntin' an' pokin'?"

A thought came to Breanne of a sudden. "Does the master lie with all of you here at Larkspur?"

Amicia shook her head. "Nay. None that I know of. Methinks he has a mistress in Higby, or he did at one time. A widow, who is barren. The master has no wish for more bairns about the place."

"A little late for that!" Breanne snapped.

"All these children came from somewhere," Drifa added.

"Kin ya believe what the men did with apples when they came back from the wars with the master last sennight?" one of the maids said, an impish grin on her face.

"Dumb as dung some men are," Amicia proclaimed, then proceeded to tell a most outlandish tale about apples and female nether parts and preventing conception.

Breanne was shocked.

"I do not understand." Ingrith frowned with concentration. "How did they get those apple halves out afterward? What if they got stuck?"

"Oh, 'twas easy," one of the maids said. "A piece of yarn was threaded through the apple and hung outside the body."

"Like a tail?" Vana was clearly horrified, then amused.

They all burst out laughing at the image of all those apples . . . and tails.

"Actually," Drifa said, "in the Eastern lands the harem women . . . those who do not want to ruin their figures . . . have a method." She went on to speak of certain matters Breanne had never heard voiced aloud.

"Where did you hear such nonsense?" Ingrith wanted to know.

"From Rashid."

"Rashid told me as well," Vana admitted. "That is why I did not get pregnant with Oswald. I could not bear the thought of his child growing in me."

Well! Breanne thought. Just, *Well!*

"Mayhap you could get us some of those powders," Amicia said.

"I will ask Rashid," Drifa promised. "If there are such plants here, we could grow them in the kitchen garden. Make our own powders."

"Women would come from far and wide to purchase such wares," Amicia said.

"Why not just set up a stall in Jorvik's trading center?" Breanne suggested.

"Yea, that is a good idea," Drifa said with excitement, having missed her sarcasm.

Breanne covered her eyes with one hand and groaned. She was certainly not going to gain the favor of Caedmon by setting up a baby-stopping operation in his keep. *Why do things always get out of control with my sisters?* "Be careful. Men do not like women tampering with their virility."

" 'Tis not their virility that would be hindered, but a woman's fertility," Ingrith pointed out.

"Men would not see it that way. Leastways, some men measure their manhood by the number of whelps they can produce." Breanne had to snip this half-brained talk in the bud.

"Not all men. The master is not like that," Amicia contended. At the look of skepticism on Breanne's face, she went on, "I know it looks that

way with all the children about, but they are not
all his. And he is a good man to care for them."

"A lot of the children *are* his," Breanne argued.

Amicia shrugged. "He is four and thirty. And a
man. What would you expect?"

Mary came in then and carefully took the sleeping Piers from her. "I will put him in his cot," she
whispered.

"Back to the serious business at hand. Breanne's seduction of Caedmon. Dost have any
other advice?" Ingrith asked Amicia.

"I think I have had enough advice for one day."
Breanne started to rise. "Methinks 'tis time I fixed
that leak in the roof. The puddles are getting
larger and larger."

"Ah, well, I kin tell ya 'bout the candles later,
and how they can be used fer teachin' ya 'bout
lovemakin'."

Breanne plopped back down again with a long
sigh of surrender.

"I used ta work in a convent," Amicia began
with a sly grin. "We had a sayin' there. Lights out
at ten. Candles out at eleven."

Thus Breanne learned more about candles than
she ever wanted to know.

CHAPTER NINE

⟡

The highs and lows of love . . .
   Caedmon was in a foul mood.
   The trip back from the borderlands should have taken less than a day, even with the stop for Rashid and a check on the injured man. To no one's surprise, the father of the Scottish lass's bairn-to-be was nowhere to be found. Which meant that Maire traveled back to Larkspur with them. At a slooooow pace. They must have stopped two dozen times for her to relieve her bladder.
   "I wish I had never brought her with us," he muttered more than once.
   Rashid told him, "Wishing does not make a poor man rich."
   I am going to kill the man, or cut off his always-blathering tongue.
   As they crossed the moat to the lower bailey of his keep, Caedmon's temper calmed a bit. Peace seemed to have settled over the place, and he could not dispute that it was tidier than it had been on his first arrival home. And, yea, the rosebushes added a nice touch.
   Once their horses made their slow plodding

way up the incline to the upper bailey, the smell of honey permeated the air.

Wulf sniffed the air and smiled. "Three guesses who is stirring the honey pot."

"Ingrith does have a way with honey," Rashid agreed. "No doubt you will have a goodly supply of honey and candle wax from this harvest."

"And mead, I hope." This from Wulf.

Well, Caedmon could not argue with that, and, really, he was grateful, but not grateful enough to allow the murderesses to stay here. And he had to thank the stars that Rashid had refrained from one of his irksome proverbs this time.

"Uh-oh!" Wulf said.

"What?" he asked, then lifted his head to gaze where Wulf was staring. And smiling.

Bam, bam, bam!

The red-haired princess witch of the north was up at the top of Larkspur's roof, pounding at one of the slates. Thank God it was not a high-pitched roof.

Bam, bam, bam!

"Ah, Breanne is fixing your leaky roof," Rashid told him, as if he had not come to that conclusion himself, as if he could not repair his own roof.

Bam, bam, bam!

"By the cross! I swear, this time I am going to paddle her arse 'til it is black and blue."

"Oh, good! Can I watch?" Wulf asked.

Bam, bam, bam!

Maire was moaning in that way which he had come to recognize meant that she had to piss again. He ignored her. Instead, Caedmon alighted from his horse in one fluid move and stomped

over to the ladder. Within minutes he was atop
the roof as well.

Bam, bam, bam!

"You lackwitted, stubborn, outlandish excuse
for a woman!" he snarled as he made his way,
then balanced himself on the slanted roof.

She jerked backward, having been unaware of
his approach from her back, with all her pounding. With a rough snarl, she turned, slipped, and
teetered forward, hitting him in the chest.

Which caused him to totter against her, forcing
her backward. He grasped her about the waist.

For several scary moments, they swayed, forward, backward, forward again. Then they both
hit the roof at the same time. Hammers and nails
slipped downward. They did, too, for a moment
before they caught on a metal snow guard.

He lay still atop her. They appeared to be secure,
but still he waited. Finally, he lifted his head to
look down at her. Her green eyes were wide open
with shock.

"Are you all right?"

She blinked several times, then tried to push
him off. "You big oaf. You almost killed us both."

"Be still. We might die yet."

She stopped moving.

And in that moment, they both realized that
he had somehow landed betwixt her widespread
thighs, and his favorite body part was planted
smack dab up against his favorite woman's part.
And it was growing.

"Oh, good Lord!" she muttered. "Can you not
control yourself?"

"Apparently not," he replied, bracing himself with hands planted on each side of her head, "especially when you insist on squirming about."

Being stubborn, she just had to squirm against him even more.

"Oh, God!" he said on a husky moan. He felt faint-headed and excruciatingly aroused, tingling in some interesting body parts. "I need to kiss you," he said, staring down at her tempting, too-generous lips.

"Do not dare," she replied, even as she ran the tip of her tongue over said lips.

She probably moistened her lips in nervousness.

He preferred to take it as a clear invitation.

He took his time settling his lips over hers, just so. They fitted perfectly. Relishing the tactile sensation of skin on skin, nerve endings on nerve endings, he pressed, moving his mouth from side to side until her lips clung to his. Drawing back, he murmured, "You taste like honey," licked her lips, and added, "Sweet."

"You are still a loathsome lout," she said, even as she raised her head slightly to meet his next kiss.

This time he was not so gentle. "Open for me."

She refused, muttering, "Mrfpghh."

So, he nipped her bottom lip, causing her to gasp, which allowed his tongue to slide inside her honey-sweet mouth.

He could tell she was shocked. It was probably the first time any man had tongue-kissed her. If that was so, it was definitely the first time a man had lain atop her with his cock nestled in her crotch.

But then, praise God and all the saints, she relaxed and opened for him even more. Better yet, her arms went up about his shoulders and tugged him closer.

He smiled against her mouth, but did not raise his lips. Thus, a smile-kiss, he thought with a smile.

Now, not only was he kissing her voraciously, but she was responding. Sucking at his tongue when he thrust inside, moving her hips from side to side as if to create a friction in her female parts. In fact, when he put a hand to her sticky breast, she did not resist, or slap him as would be her wont in any other situation.

He used his wet tongue to stab at her ear, then blow dry, over and over. "Your breast is sticky," he told her, which was a marvel that he could notice such an irrelevant thing when her nipple was budding against his palm.

"Your son," she said, and licked his ear, then nipped at the lobe.

He felt the lick and nip all the way to his fingertips, toes, and rock-hard staff, all of which were tingling. "What?" he gasped out.

"Your son Piers got my tunic sticky with honey," she explained.

"He is not my son," he answered with lust-sodden irrelevance. "Not really."

"Well, he is adorable nonetheless, whoever his father is."

"Mayhap I am his father after all."

She took him by the ears and lifted his head. Smiling through kiss-swollen, slick lips, she said, "What are you doing to me?"

"Kissing you?"

"More than that!" she huffed. "I am tingling all over."

"Breanne, Breanne, Breanne. You should not be telling me that."

"Why not?"

"I will use it against you."

She gave him a saucy grin. "You cannot use me unless I allow you to."

"Oh, you naive wench! There are ways, believe you me."

He kissed her again, voraciously. He could not seem to get enough of her lush mouth. And her body. Cupping her buttocks, he raised her up so she was forced to brace her feet on the slate roof and bend her knees.

She began to moan.

Or mayhap it was him.

Through a haze of mind-melting arousal, he heard a discordant voice. "KAAAD-mon! KAAAD-mon!"

Raising his head, disoriented, he tried to clear his fuzzy brain.

"Someone is calling you," she told him, her voice sounding sex-husky.

"'Tis Wulf," he said when he recognized that the loud voice came from below.

He could see her slumberous facial expression change as she slowly realized where they were and what they had been doing. Soon, her cheeks and neck were a deep rose color.

"Get off of me, you big lout."

He rolled over to his side, being careful to keep his balance. He did not even try to hide his enthusiastic erection.

Which she noticed, then quickly glanced away.

"You touched my breast," she accused him with outrage.

"Oh, was that what it was? I thought it was a roof slate."

She growled. She honest-to-God growled. "I cannot believe you seduced me on top of a roof."

"Hey, you were the one who seduced me. If Wulf had not called for me, I would have been swiving you from one end of this roof to the other, and you would have been loving it."

"Modesty becomes you, braggart." She rose carefully to her feet and made her way slowly toward the ladder. Glancing down, she gasped, then looked back at him with ill-concealed disgust. "Another baby! There is a woman down there about to pop out another of your whelps, you randy goat."

He smiled, figuring he could set her straight on that matter later. For now, he was enjoying the sight of her bending over in those tight breeches . . . and wondering how soon he could get into those breeches.

But then, reality hit him like a hammer to the head, as he recalled the promise he had made himself on the long journey back to Larkspur.

The princesses would be gone by nightfall.

* * *

She was going to be nice, dammit! . . .

Breanne had never been so embarrassed in her entire life. As she climbed down the ladder, it seemed as if everyone in the world was standing below, staring at her bottom in the tight braies, including the loathsome lout who had gone before her, after kissing her senseless.

What was I thinking?

I was not thinking!

"What are you all gaping at?" she snarled. "Have you ne'er seen a woman in braies afore?"

" 'Tis not that, m'lady," Caedmon said, taking her by the waist and lifting her down the last few steps. " 'Tis a barefooted woman in braies standing atop a roof that has them stunned."

She slapped his hands away now that her feet were on the ground. "My feet are shoeless because I have learned from experience that I get better purchase with my bare feet."

"Do this a lot, do you?"

"Stop smirking, you dolt."

"That is not a smirk. 'Tis a smile."

"Well, do not smile then."

Ingrith sidled up to her and whispered in her ear, "Breanne! You are supposed to be seducing the man, not antagonizing him."

She turned to look at Caedmon. "Does he look antagonized?"

"Well, nay, now that you mention it, he looks—"

"Hail, all! Did you miss me?" Geoff, the blond god, rode up then on a black stallion fit for a king.

"Nice piece of horseflesh," Wulf remarked.

"A bride gift."

Caedmon and Wulf both grinned at their friend.

"Are you already wed, then?" Caedmon asked.

Geoff shook his head. "A sennight from now. You are all invited." He looked from Caedmon to her, then back to Caedmon, and arched a brow. "Is it possible you are to be wed again, Caedmon?"

"Huh?" Caedmon said. "What would give you that barmy idea?"

"Weeeellll," Geoff drawled, his golden brown eyes dancing mischievously, "as I rode in, from a distance I could swear I saw two people atop the roof swiv—"

"That will be enough, Geoff," Caedmon interrupted.

Breanne's face heated even more, realizing there had been a witness to her insanity.

"My apologies, m'lady. Uh, didst know that your lips look . . . ripe?"

"Ripe?" she asked on a groan. When she put her fingertips to her mouth, she realized that her lips were puffy, and no doubt abraded with color.

"Yours look ripe, too, Caedmon. Not to fear. No doubt you have both been eating berries."

A quick glance at Caedmon showed her that his lips were in the same condition as hers. Instead of groaning with dismay, he winked at her.

The man dared to wink at her.

Geoff's face turned serious of a sudden. "Did I mention that Sybil has invited Archbishop Dunstan to officiate at our wedding since he is expected in the vicinity? She sent the invitation afore I realized what she was about."

Breanne's sisters exchanged looks of horror.

Caedmon appeared equally horrified.

She wondered how soon he would be packing their bags and shooing them off to parts unknown. Belatedly, she recalled that she was supposed to be seducing Caedmon into an extension of their visit.

Releasing a long exhale, she drew her shoulders back with determination and turned to the loathsome lout. "Wouldst care to meet with me after dinner this evening?"

"Why?" the loathsome lout asked.

She fisted her hands behind her back to keep from punching him. "I would like to talk to you in private."

"Why?" he repeated.

Biting her bottom lip and counting to ten, she glanced up to the roof, then back at him. In as sultry voice as she could muster, she said, "Unfinished business."

Then she spun on her heels and rushed back to the keep, not wanting to see if he was laughing.

He was not.

"C'mere, baby," sayeth the cat to the mouse, "wanna see my cheese? . . ."

"What is this cat-and-mouse game you are playing?" Geoff asked him that evening.

Ah, that is an appropriate name for this insanity. "I do not know what you mean," Caedmon replied and continued to eat from a shank of wild boar that was covered with the most delicious sauce.

"They have been doing it all day long," Wulf spoke across him to Geoff.

"Who?" *As if I do not know!* Caedmon licked his fingers and frowned. "What is this unusual flavor?"

" 'Tis garlic and onion mixed with black pepper and a dash of wine," Geoff told him.

"You and Breanne," Wulf said.

"Wine? They are using my wine for cooking?" *One more grievance to lay at their door.*

"Tell us," Geoff insisted.

"Tell you what?"

"What is your game plan?" Geoff elaborated.

"Are you demented? I have no game plan. Why do you not go off again to woo your betrothed and leave me alone? I have enough problems without your bedevilment."

"I have done enough wooing."

"There is no such thing as too much wooing."

"I beg to differ. Any more and her expectations will be set too high."

"Well said, Geoff," Wulf said, again speaking across him. "Do as you intend to go on. Excessive wooing will wear your cock to a nub in the end."

Geoff and Wulf grinned at each other as if they had made some grand jest.

Idiots!

Then they both turned to him.

Knowing they would not cease their questions until he revealed all, Caedmon leaned back in his chair. "Which cat and which mouse?"

"You know very well which," Geoff said, slapping him on the shoulder. "You and the red-haired thorn-in-your-arse have been changing roles all day. First, you were the cat chasing her about so you could send her and her sisters on their merry way, but she evaded your chase. A milkmaid told Gerard, who told me, that she was hiding . . . I mean, working in the stable, repairing a stall door or some such. Then, when it was too late to leave this day, she was after you, attempting a meeting, and you hid from her."

"I ne'er hid from anyone." *Avoided, but not hid.*

Wulf raised his eyebrows. "Oh? There was some urgent reason why you needed to inventory the storerooms?"

"Someone needed to do it afore our supplies are depleted." *And that is the truth.*

"I saw her under the table in the steward's room at one point," Wulf remarked. He, too, was enjoying the wild boar, taking two more slices off the shank.

"She was in my steward's room?"

"Yea. On the floor. Said she was searching for a lost quill."

"That is naught," Geoff told Wulf. "I found Caedmon in the bathing house, having his toenails clipped. In the middle of the day, for saints' sake!"

"Must be he has some need for clean toes." Wulf stroked his mustache thoughtfully. "I wonder . . . oh, please tell me that it is a new perversion you are contemplating?"

"Or mayhap it has something to do with unfinished rooftop business." Geoff winked at him.

The only activity I am planning of that nature will

be a solitary endeavor. Unfortunately. "Enough! Both of you, desist!" Caedmon said, laughing.

Just then, he felt a hand clamp on his shoulder. With humor still twitching at his lips, he turned.

Oh, no!

It was the mouse.

Or is she the cat?

I wonder if her tongue is abrasive when she licks.

Does she purr?

Does she scratch when in the throes of . . .

Nay, nay, nay! I am not thinking THAT.

He stood, as did Wulf and Geoff.

"M'lord. I wish to speak with you."

Stick out your tongue, sweetling. I just want to check . . . God's breath! I am losing my mind! "Uh, mayhap later."

"Now!" she demanded, and shoved Wulf aside with her hip, sliding into his chair.

Caedmon arched his brows at her action, which had Wulf smirking as he displaced Henry from his position in front of the next chair. Truth to tell, Caedmon had to admire the lady's persistence, even if it was at his expense.

"Have a caution, Breanne," Rashid spoke up. "Spurs that are too sharp make even the mule rear."

"Shut your teeth, Rashid," she said.

"Is he referring to me as a mule?" Caedmon asked.

"Jackass would be more appropriate, I would think," Breanne said sweetly.

"Wouldst care for some boar?" he inquired just as sweetly, picking up the whole, half-eaten shank and plopping it on a wooden trencher between the two of them. Some of the juice splashed up onto her gown. "How clumsy of me!" He dipped a linen square into a cup of water and began to dab at her bodice. Immediately, he felt her nipple bud under his whisking fingers, and his fingers started to tingle with heat.

She slapped his hand away. "You oaf! I mean, that is not necessary, m'lord. It happens to all of us betimes."

And betimes it happens deliberately. "Getting aroused?"

"Oh, you are insufferable! Spilling something, that is what I meant. Blessed Freyja! How can you make the most innocent remark sexual?"

With ease.

"Mayhap because he always has sex on his mind." Geoff leaned forward to speak across him to her.

'Tis true.

Geoff continued, "My friend is very virile . . ."

Oh, good God!

". . . in case you had not noticed all the bratlings that abound here."

How can you miss them?

She glared at Geoff as if he were something objectionable beneath her shoes. Apparently being the blond god did not give him license to be a clod.

Caedmon glared, too, though he knew it would not stop Geoff when he was on a teasing tear.

"Where is your bride-to-be?" Breanne asked Geoff.

"Busy fluffing up the marriage bed."

Good retort!

She bristled. "Does she know what she is getting herself into?"

"Oh, yea, she does, but 'tis more like what she wants *me* to get into. A tight squeeze, if you get my meaning, but, not to fear, she is well-satisfied with what I got into."

"Coarse lout!" she muttered. Then turning back to Caedmon, she smiled.

A smile from the witch? I do not think so. "Why are you smiling?"

"Can a lady not smile if she wants?"

I smell the devious turns of a vixen's mind. "Do I have boar meat betwixt my teeth?"

"Nay! Stop picking your teeth. I was just smiling because . . . because I just want to talk with you. Pleasant talk."

Talk, talk, talk. She is ever chirping about talk. "You are never pleasant to me. Must be you are up to something. What?" *Look how she is gritting her teeth to stifle her temper. How odd!* "Did you go up on the roof again?"

"Of course not."

There is no "of course not" with you, m'lady. "Did you rethatch the entire village betwixt building me a new chicken coop? Or did you just make me a dozen benches in your spare time?"

"Do you enjoy making mock of me?"

Tremendously. "You wound me with your accusations."

"You make it very difficult to carry on a pleasant conversation."

Jabber, jabber, jabber. "Let us put aside all this flummery. What do you want from me?"

"A few weeks' respite."

Respite? That is a new word for being a bloody nuisance. "Explain yourself."

"My sisters and I need . . . I mean, want . . . to stay here a bit longer."

"Nay."

"Can we talk about it?"

"Nay."

She picked up the table knife and examined it closely, then glanced up through half-lidded eyes at him.

"Are you thinking about putting that through my heart?"

"Do you have a heart? I am weapon-skillful, you know."

He laughed.

"I could spear you through your laughing mouth."

"If you want a quick death, best you aim for the fat line. That is the section betwixt neck and crotch."

"Who says I want a quick death for you?"

Her sister Vana rushed up. "Breanne! You are supposed to be nice to him, not kill him."

Huh?

Another sister, Drifa, was shaking her head at Breanne as if she were a lost cause.

Ingrith, who had just come from the kitchen, assessed the situation from across the hall, then came running up. She, too, chastised Breanne. "That is not what you are supposed to do."

Huh?

Amicia, his cook, whispered something in Breanne's ear that sounded like, "Do not slice the lout, seduce him."

Seduce? Seduce whom?

Breanne's shoulders slumped. Then she straightened and turned, fluttering her eyelashes at him. "Wouldst care to walk in the garden with me?"

Oh, nay! She could not mean to seduce me. Never in a million years! Although . . . "What garden?"

"The rose garden."

"I have a rose garden?"

"Forget the bloody garden."

Progress! I got the wench to swear.

"Dost want to walk or not?" As if an idea had come to her belatedly, she fluttered her eyelashes at him.

With any other woman, he would think she was flirting. With Breanne, he had to assume she had soot in her eyes.

"We will walk," he said, standing suddenly and holding his arm out for her. He was intrigued to know what she was up to.

She stood and ignored his arm, swanning ahead of him to the end of the dais and across the great hall. He had to admit that she did have a nice bottom, which swayed from side to side. Just then, he glanced back and saw Geoff and Wulf watching him watch her backside. They grinned and gave him salutes of encouragement.

He caught up with her halfway and grabbed her hand, twining her fingers with his. She tugged, but he would not release her.

He led her then, not outside to any garden, but instead up to the wall walk on the ramparts, which were pleasant this time of night.

"Before we go any farther, there is something I must tell you," Breanne said.

"Oh, God! Not another secret." *If she killed another person, I swear I will kill her.*

"Not exactly a secret. Not my secret, anyhow. 'Tis about your son Hugh."

He stopped in his tracks, displeasure heating his blood. "You have no right to interfere with my family."

"I must speak up since he will not tell you himself. You are punishing him unjustly."

"The boy ran away from his fostering."

"Do you know why?"

Woman, you overstep yourself. "Of course I do. Earl Graystone told me that he could not accept discipline."

"Pfff! One of Earl Graystone's hersirs was trying to abuse your son."

Shock swiftly turned his displeasure to white-hot anger, mostly at the wench who dared to suggest such. "Mayhap he put a switch to his arse when he turned laggard in his duties."

"Oh, Caedmon! Do I have to speak explicitly? 'Twas not a switch the hersir wanted to put to Hugh's arse."

It took a long moment for her suggestion to sink in. *Nay! Nay, nay, nay! It cannot be so!* "Are you saying that some man tried to sodomize my son?"

She ducked her head with embarrassment at

his blunt words, but then she raised her chin with defiance. "Yea."

"Did he succeed?" His shoulders slumped.

"Nay, Hugh ran away first."

Thank you, God! "Why would Hugh not come to me?"

"He was ashamed. And I suspect you started yelling afore he could begin to explain."

"I will set things aright," he said. Then, grudgingly, he added, "I appreciate your telling me."

She nodded acceptance of his apology.

He resumed walking then, taking her with him.

"I like to come up each evening, just before dusk," he said, leaning on the ledge. He still held her hand in his, which he could tell rankled her, but was all the more reason not to let her go. His mind still dwelled on the horrific news she had laid on him.

"It is pretty, especially with all that larkspur."

"Pretty is fine," he said, "but it is land itself which is important to me." *For me, and for my children. For Hugh.*

She tilted her head at him.

"I was landless, like Geoff and Wulf, with no prospects, being a third son, but then my Uncle Richard died ten years ago and bequeathed Larkspur to me. An unexpected gift."

"But one you cherish."

"Yea, I do. You have to be homeless to appreciate what having a home means."

"Homeless? Really?"

He smiled at her and squeezed her hand. "Not really homeless, but I moved about from place to

place, wherever my military skills were needed."
*And my son Hugh, little bigger than Piers at the time,
still with his reluctant, negligent mother, a chambermaid in my father's home, who put the babe in peril
more than once. What a fool I was! A careless fool.*

"And that is why you went a-wooing this past
sennight . . . to gain more lands. Why then did
you bow out to Geoff?"

" 'Tis enough that I have a comrade-in-arms in
place at an adjoining property. And Geoff needed
a home."

"You are a good friend."

"A compliment? Forsooth! I must mark this
date in stone."

It was she who squeezed his hand then as she
leaned slightly against him. She probably did not
realize that her body pressed against his side, from
upper arms to thighs. The faint rose scent wafted
up to him from her hair. He had never been over-
fond of red-haired women, but hers was amazing,
taking on different lights through the day, from
darkish blonde to deep crimson. Tonight, in the
dimming light, even in its long single braid, it was
more like burnished silk. Forgetting himself, he
reached out a hand to touch it, but caught himself
just in time.

"And that is why you and your sisters must
leave on the morrow."

She stiffened and put a small distance between,
as much as she could with her hand still restrained.
"What has one to do with the other?"

"Everything. I walk a tight line betwixt ownership of Larkspur and duty to my king. Edgar's

court is like a vipers' pit, awash with greedy land-hungry men. If I offend my king, he could take my lands away."

"Surely the law would not allow that."

He shrugged. "The Witan would make the final decision, but many of the noble members are the king's puppets."

"Chances are he would never find out, either that Lord Havenshire was killed, or that we are responsible."

"Suspicion is enough. Mayhap if you had all stayed at Havenshire to answer questions—"

"Nay. 'Twas impossible. Other than our two Norse guardsmen, we had no one to support us there. My father and my family-by-marriage have friends in high places, but until they were at our backs, the best plan was to leave."

"No one accused you?"

"Nay, but everyone knew how Oswald was treating his wife. It was a natural conclusion that she would have just cause to get rid of him. Women have been executed for less."

He nodded. "Guilt by accusation."

"All we are asking is that you let us stay a few sennights more until . . ." She let her words trail off.

He narrowed his eyes at her. "I noticed that your two Viking bears are back. Ah! You have had word, have you not? And it is not good."

Even though the light was fading, he could see her blush.

"The truth, wench," he demanded.

"I hate it when you call me wench."

"I know," he said. "Enough evasion!"

She made a clucking sound of disgust. "Ivan and Ivar brought a missive from my sister Tyra."

He released her hand. "Give it to me."

Reaching into a side flap on her gown, she took out a piece of crackling parchment, which she unfolded. "Can you read?"

Saying a foul word under his breath, he grabbed for the letter. Once he had read through quickly, he read it again more slowly.

Handing it back to her, he stared at her with consternation, fisting his hands at his sides to keep from throttling her. "When did you receive this?"

"Several days ago."

He swore again. "Search parties are out," he repeated from the letter, "not just for the earl of Havenshire, but for Vana, as well." He glared at her. "The same Vana who is residing under my roof?"

"You know it is."

Reading again from the missive, he said, "Dunstan is on a rampage." Then he tipped her chin up so she could not avoid his gaze. "You are aware that Archbishop Dunstan nigh sits on Edgar's shoulder. If he comes here, and it appears he will be coming for Geoff's wedding—"

She gasped, having been unaware of Dunstan's upcoming visit to Heatherby.

" . . . do you not think he might stop by Larkspur?"

"We could hide Vana," she suggested.

"Where? In the new pigsty with the flower carved trim?"

"Do not be snide."

"Snide? I will give you snide. How about the rest of you? Am I to hide four princesses? And if I am found out, what then?"

"Listen, we could pay you well."

"Oh, really?"

"Yea, we could. Tyra and Vana's dowries are long gone, but Ingrith, Drifa, and I still have substantive dower wealth. We could pool our coins and give them to you."

"Not that it matters, but how much?"

She quoted a figure that gave him pause, but only for a moment. "And if any of you decides to marry, what then?"

"I am sure our father will be so happy to have Vana back, he will replenish Ingrith and Drifa's dower, and as for me," she waved a hand dismissively, "I have no intention of getting wedlocked."

I should not ask. "Why?"

"Well, look at me. I am not a great beauty . . ."

Oh, I do not know. I see a certain attraction.

" . . . and, besides, I plan to open my own market stall in Jorvik."

"How will you do that if you give me all your coin?"

Red flags appeared in her cheeks. "That is a problem I will solve when the time comes."

Typical female illogic. In other words, she would give me her future. "You insult me with your offer, woman." He grabbed her by the shoulders and shook her, so outraged was he by this whole situation and by her most of all, for laying the solving in his lap. He had not realized how hard he was shaking her until he heard her teeth chattering and looking down, saw that her breasts were jiggling. *Whaaat?*

He shook her another time to double-check the jiggling business. *Definite jiggling.* "I did not realize your breasts were so big."

"They are not," she said, squirming out of his grasp and folding her arms over her chest.

"They look big to me." *Wouldst like me to check?*

"Oh, please, can we stop talking about my non-existent breasts?"

Must we? "If they are not breasts, what are they?"

"Aspics."

That is the first I have heard them called that. Despite her slapping hands, he pressed a fingertip into one of them, and, truth be told, it was the texture of aspic.

He could not help but laugh.

She glowered at him for finding humor in her . . . bosoms.

"Why would you put aspics on your chest?" *In case your lover gets sudden hunger pangs whilst in bed?*

"Please, can we drop this subject?"

When it is just getting interesting? "Not a chance!"

"Amicia said men are attracted by big jiggling breasts."

"And you wanted big jiggling breasts to attract . . . oh, good Lord! Me?"

"Well, not precisely. I mean, yea, you, but not

because . . . Oh, what is the use!" She threw her hands in the air, as if in surrender. "Seducing you is a lost cause, and one which I find extremely distasteful."

"If that was seduction, you could have fooled me. You drew a knife on me, woman. And telling a man he is 'extremely distasteful' is not an inducement to do anything."

"I did not draw a knife on you. I only contemplated knifing you."

"Oh, that makes it better, then."

His lips twitched with humor, which would probably earn him a slap if he let it show. "Why, pray tell, were you trying to seduce me, if you find me so repugnant?"

"Not repugnant. Just insufferable."

His lips twitched some more.

"You are laughing at me," she accused.

"Not at you. It is the whole situation."

Her lips twitched with humor, too. "It *is* funny . . . that I could attract such as you, let alone tempt you to our cause."

"I do not know about that."

She raised her brows at him.

"You are tempting, all right." He ran his knuckles over the smooth skin of her cheek, then rubbed a loose strand of hair between thumb and forefinger. It *was* silky.

They both stared at each for a long moment, transfixed.

Her shoulders dropped then. "Is there really nothing we can offer that would change your mind?"

"Nay." *Except . . . nay, I will not think of that.*

"I would do anything."

He should have said nay then. He should have turned and walked away. He should not be entertaining mind images of a naked red-haired witch, spread-eagled on his bed with a come-hither smile on her face. "Anything?"

"Yea. Just name it." Her face bloomed with hope.

God, stop me. Quick, afore I jump into the quicksand of lust. All you saints, can you not put a lock on my tongue afore I say something I will surely regret? Unfortunately, all the celestial beings must have been busy elsewhere. As if drawn by a compulsion beyond his control, his fingertips traced the skin of her collarbone exposed by the round neckline of her gown. *How can a collarbone be so sensual?*

She whimpered at his touch, but did not shove him away as was usually her wont.

"Ten nights," he told her, before he could bite his tongue.

"Wha-what?"

"You want protection under my shield, you forfeit your virtue. Ten nights in my bed, dusk to dawn. Simple as that. You will let me do whatever I want. You will do whatever I ask of you." He waited for her to slap his face or kick him in the shin or lambast him with ugly descriptions of his character, but that did not happen. *The quicksand is getting deeper and deeper.*

"You cannot be serious." She looked as if she might upheave the contents of her stomach.

"Serious as sin." *Oh, this is fun. She will no doubt*

attempt to push me over the wall. I'd best be ready to sidestep her assault.

"You are a wicked man."

"Yea, that is one of my better attributes." *Come, m'lady, show me what a fierce fighter you are.*

"Why?"

He shrugged. "Because I want to." *It will come now. I am ready.*

"Any acts, you say?"

Whaaat? Is she actually considering my insane proposal? I have really gone too far. Well, what the hell! "Any and all."

"Would that include . . . perversions?"

He started to laugh, then coughed when he tried to stop. "Definitely," he said. *Oh, I wish Geoff and Wulf were here to witness this. They will never believe me.*

" 'Tis a deal," she said, reaching out to shake his hand.

At first, he did not realize the implications of what she said. When he did, he stared down at her outstretched hand as if it were a snake.

But she took the initiative and grabbed his hand to shake. The grin on her face was like that of a cat who had just licked up all the cream.

Caedmon realized, too late, that he had made a big, big mistake, underestimating a Norse witchy woman. He was caught. And he was tingling, all over.

CHAPTER TEN

❧

If kisses could talk . . .

Breanne stared up at Caedmon, trying her best to hide her dismay.

She had just agreed to his vile proposal in order to save her sister, but she did not really expect that he would follow through. Chivalry would emerge the victor in the end.

"How shall we seal this bargain?" he said, smiling at her in the most wicked way before lacing his fingers with hers again.

"Wha . . . what do you mean?" *Oh, the brute is going to bleed my humiliation for every drop.*

He tugged her back into an alcove. "If we are going to be intimate, surely a kiss would not go amiss now. A pledge, so to speak."

I knew it. Well, two can play this game. "Hmmmm. I suppose one little kiss would not hurt." She tried to free her hand and found herself against the wall. He released her hand, but his body was aligning itself with hers in a way-too-familiar manner.

"There is no such thing as a little kiss amongst lovers."

Lovers? Me? Us? "Get it over with then." She

closed her eyes and prepared for the distasteful exercise.

She heard him chuckle, but he did nothing.

With her eyes still scrunched tight, she asked, "What are you waiting for?"

"Open your lips, Breanne."

Her eyes shot open. "What?"

"Just like that, dearling." He settled his lips over hers then, and, oh, it felt so good.

Reflexively, she curved her body into his and put her hands on his shoulders.

He moaned.

Oddly, it gave her a thrill that she could make this big man moan.

"You have the most delicious mouth, lips made for kissing," he murmured, putting a hand on her chin to hold her in place. The other arm went around her waist and yanked her closer. Her suddenly aching breasts, under the aspics, were crushed against his chest, and he had somehow managed to step between her legs and press his manpart to her female part.

She almost swooned at the intensity of tortuous pleasure.

He was tongue-kissing her now, and she opened wider, wanting more of the delicious friction. Tentatively, she put the tip of her tongue in his mouth and was rewarded with another moan of pleasure.

They were both panting for breath when he leaned back to look at her. "Why is your bodice all wet?"

At first she could not speak, so aroused was

she. Finally, she managed to tell him, "You must
have squished me. My aspics are melting."

His dark eyes went incredulous. Then he burst
out laughing, hugging her to him before bracing
his arms over her on either side of her head. Her
mouth seemed to fascinate him, especially when
he traced the slickness left from their kiss with a
forefinger. Holding her gaze, he put the moist fingertip to his mouth and sucked.

She felt a reciprocal spasm low in her belly.

"Ah, Breanne," he said, forehead to forehead,
"we are going to be so good together."

That was what she was afraid of. Suddenly, she
realized that there was a strong possibility he had
been serious, that this was no game he was playing to embarrass her. Ten nights with a knight!

To her mortification, she realized that she could
not wait.

Wake-up calls can be brutal . . .

Caedmon was awakened at first light by his
children, all ten of them.

Through sleep-bleary eyes, he watched as Piers
sat his little rump down on his lower belly and
began to bounce, not the best thing to do to a man
first thing in the morning. He took him by the
waist and moved him higher up on his body.

Beth had climbed up on the bed to snuggle at
his one side, and Mina on the other. The twins,
Alfred and Aidan, along with Angus, his usual
glower in place, stood at the foot of the bedstead,
just staring at him. Oslac, Kendrick, and Joanna,
the three Welsh bratlings, were standing in the

corner in front of Hugh, who had a hand on two of their shoulders. It appeared as if he had dragged them here against their wills.

"What is amiss?" Caedmon said, trying to ignore Piers, who was doing a job on his belly, calling out, "Ha-see, ha-see!" over and over. Caedmon assumed he meant *horsey*. And he was drooling on his chest. A new tooth coming in, he supposed.

"Yer holdin' the shire court here next month," Kendrick pointed out. "We would like ta hold a family court first."

"Whaaat? I have ne'er heard of such. Why?"

"We want a mother," shy Mina said, immediately hiding her face in his side after her outburst.

Beth raised her head to look down on him. "Whilst the princesses are here, we have seen what we are missing."

"Oh? What might that be?"

"The food tastes better," Alfred pointed out.

"An' my head lice is gone," Aidan added.

"I like the roses," Joanna said, then snarled when Oslac and Kendrick elbowed her from either side. Hugh put a quick stop to that by smacking the two boys aside their heads.

"Lady Breanne helped me fight some bullies," Angus surprised him by saying even as he glared at the three Welshies.

"Mayhap ye would be happier if ye had a woman," Alfred suggested.

"I am happy enough."

"A man needs a bedmate," Aidan said. "Geoff tol' me so."

"Geoff talks too much."

"Can I be a princess when I grow up?" Mina asked.

"Only if you marry a prince."

Mina started to cry.

Beth blinked at him through tear-filled eyes. What? Did she want to be a princess, too? "Aunt Alys wants ye to wed again, Father."

"That is so she can flit off and ignore her responsibilities." Really, this was a ludicrous situation. "And you, Hugh, what do you think?"

Hugh's pale face turned paler, with rosy patches on his cheeks. Hugh did not like to call attention to himself, this son of his. "I like the Lady Breanne," he said, as if that had been the question.

"Well, I am not in the market for a wife, and neither are the princesses wanting to wed." Leastways, he did not think so.

All of their little shoulders drooped.

"Why is there a tent behind Piers's bottom?" Joanna inquired, cocking her head to the side to see better.

Everyone else, except for Piers, also looked to the section of sheet over his manpart. *Oh, my God!* He immediately raised his knees to hide his "tent."

"Do you know nothing, Joanna?" Oslac commented. "We men have morning thickenings to deal with."

We men? *Help!* Oslac was only seven years old.

"It means he has to piss," explained Kendrick, who was also only seven years old.

Coughing to clear his throat and change the

subject, he said, "I promise things will be better here at Larkspur in the future."

They did not look convinced, but there were no more arguments.

"Now, off you all go. Ask Amicia to give you some bread and honey. Except for you, Hugh. You stay."

The look of sheer horror on Hugh's face gave Caedmon pause. A son should not be fearful of his father. Respectful, of course, but not afraid.

Sitting up and swinging his legs over the side, he motioned for Hugh to sit beside him.

"Starting this morning, you will be squire to Wulf. You will do battle exercises with the men, under his mentoring. Go to the weapons room and Henry will allot you a sword, shield and other battle gear."

Tears welled in Hugh's eyes, which he quickly blinked away.

"Why?"

He shrugged. "Because it is time for you to learn a man's work. Someday you will be the master of Larkspur. It is past time you began training for such."

"Me? But I am a bastard."

Caedmon cringed at the word. "It matters not. You are the oldest. One more thing, Hugh," he said, putting a hand on Hugh's shoulder. "I would have the name of the man who tried to abuse you."

Hugh tried to rise and leave, but Caedmon held his hand firm.

"She should not have told you."

"Yea, she should have. More important, you should have told me yourself."

"You would not have listened."

"Not at first, mayhap," he conceded, "but I will be more open in the future. And know this, you did naught to be ashamed of. Men who prey on young boys are vultures who must be put down."

Hugh started for the door, a huge smile on his face, no doubt contemplating his shiny new sword. He turned at the last minute. "Are you certain you would not like to take Lady Breanne to wed?"

"Absolutely certain."

But there are other places I would like to take her. Like my bed.

From then on, Caedmon worked like a madman, catching up on all the work at Larkspur. Mayhap he was energized by his continual efforts *not* to think about Breanne and their "deal."

Or more likely he was energized by thoughts of what delights might be in store for him if he went ahead with the "deal."

First off, Caedmon met with his steward. Whilst the two of them ate hunks of manchet bread with more of the leftover boar, still delicious even with its congealed sauce, he asked Gerard for a listing of all things that needed to be done about the keep, inside and out. "In order of necessity," he added.

"The princesses have done my work for me in getting the inside in order, I must admit," said Gerard. "More linens and blankets are always needed, but once the sheep are sheared and our weavers and seamstresses set to work, they can be replenished. Huntsmen and fishermen will go out throughout the summer, to put food on the table, but also to salt and set aside for winter."

"Larkspur is self-sustaining then?"

"As long as there is no famine or drought. Even so, as you know, there are still provisions that we must get from the nearby market towns. Along with certain spices."

"Mayhap not so much since Drifa has the herb garden flourishing again."

"Possibly. But what happens when she is gone? This keep needs a woman in charge of women's duties."

"Why can men not maintain herb gardens?"

"Find me one."

"Make a list for me of everything you need. And of course I will need to know what we bring to market. Please God, let there be some income."

Gerard smiled. "We have about three dozen hogs, two sows and two dozen piglets in the new pigpen. Then there are roughly three dozen pigs pottaging loose in the woods, getting fat on acorns and such."

"How many of those are needed for fall butchering here, and how many can be sent to market? Same is true of sheep. And beef cattle. I am thinking of sending forth Wulf on an errand. He could lead a troop of men with some of these animals now."

Gerard nodded and said he would have the tally ready for him by later that day. "Methinks we should keep the sheep until autumn this year. We need all the fleece we can get for weaving. Next year mayhap we can spare some for trade."

Next up for meeting with Caedmon was Henry, his castellan. Henry was in charge of all things military. Weaponry and daily exercising of the fighting men in warcraft. Wulf would soon be taking over most of those duties.

"We have two hundred fighting men here at Larkspur, including those who came back with you," Henry told him. "I have divided them into archers, swordsmen, and those proficient with lance, mace, and battle-axe. Not that they do not all practice in all those skills."

"Let us start thrice daily exercises with the third being man-to-man combat practice." He also told Henry of his plans to establish a small fortress at the northern end of his estates to ward off the reivers. If there was protection, he was sure he could lure more of his cotters to move to those outer reaches to farm and care for cattle, especially if he offered the incentive of a share of the crops.

He talked to Amicia about the larder and what provisions they needed to supplement Larkspur's bounty. Amicia kept giving him sly looks.

"What?" he asked finally. "Have I grown a horn atop my head?"

She laughed. "Ye have already sported horns with all your deviltry. Nay, I am just trying to picture why the lass is so determined to keep you at bay."

He was not about to ask which lass, but his silence did not deter the intrusive cook.

"Do not pretend disinterest in the lady. I can see beyond yer pose."

"I am not posing."

"And do not be deterred by her lack of a bosom."

Caedmon choked on the piece of oak cake he was nibbling and had to take a long draw of ale to clear his throat. "Are you referring to the aspic bosom, or the nonexistent bosom?"

"Tsk-tsk!" she said at his pathetic attempt at humor. "Big bosoms are not everything, you know."

Oh, God! I am being given sex advice by my cook, a woman the size of a warhorse with the hint of a mustache. "When did I ever say big bosoms were the be-all and end-all?"

Amicia waved a hand dismissively. "There is not a man or boyling alive who does not lust after big breasts. Look at Gerard if you do not believe me. But I have it on good authority that the lady has big nipples. Methinks that may be some compensation."

Caedmon's jaw dropped at his cook's blunt words. *Big nipples. Now that the image is planted in my brain, I will be able to think of naught else in her presence.*

"Big-nippled women have no control over their passions," continued Amicia.

Is that true? Surely I would have heard of that before. "Where did you ever hear such a thing? Nay, do not tell me."

"I knew a man who knew a woman who ran a brothel. She said the big-nippled women were extra sensitive there." She patted her own breasts as if he would not have known where nipples are located. "One flick, and the trollops would be oozing woman dew."

Good Lord! Best I cut this conversation short afore she starts on other parts of Breanne's anatomy. "Uh . . . Lady Breanne would not like your discussing her female bits." Of course, now the only thing he could think about, with vivid mind pictures, was Breanne with big nipples.

As he walked away, quickly, he remarked to himself, *And Gerard thinks I need more women about. I think not!*

After inspecting the castle, inside and out, he thought about big nipples. Going over the ramparts and palisade for defects that needed work, he thought about big nipples. Then, working with the men in swordplay, he thought about big nipples. When he invited Geoff and Wulf to come share a cup of ale with him in the great hall, he admonished himself not to mention . . . those things he was not thinking about.

"Geoff, would you be willing to take the princesses Ingrith and Drifa to Heatherby? If asked, you could say they are needed to help plan the wedding. Cooking and decorations."

"I suppose so," Geoff said, studying him for elaboration on his request.

"And you, Wulf, would you be willing to take the princess Vana, in disguise, with you on a trip to market? You can do my trading for me, perhaps posing as my agent and his lady wife, but afterward I would like you to disappear with the lady for several sennights until we see how the wind blows with Edgar and Dunstan."

Wulf, also, agreed hesitantly. "Wouldst want me to take her to Ravenshire, or for that matter, to her father in the Norselands?"

He shook his head. "'Tis too dangerous right now. Havenshire's friends will have guards posted near both places."

"Mayhap you could take her to Wales," Geoff suggested. "You could kill two birds with one stone. Protect Lady Havenshire and meet your betrothed."

"Mayhap you could stick your wagging tongue up your arse," Wulf suggested sweetly.

Geoff just grinned.

"I know it is asking a lot of you, Wulf, to take Havenshire's widow under your wing. You could be accused of being accomplice to the murder, or at least of hiding a murderess. Same with you, Geoff, I am asking you to share a danger that is not yours."

Both men waved aside his concerns.

"Oh, and one of you should take Rashid with you."

"You anticipate trouble?" Geoff asked.

Caedmon nodded. "My bones tell me to be on the alert. This is a situation ripe for trouble."

"Why not just send the princesses on their way, as you had planned?" Wulf asked.

"Chivalry?"

Geoff snorted, and Wulf gave his opinion in one coarse word.

"I must needs scatter the prey. If they are all

here in one place, it will be easier for Edgar to pounce."

An idea seemed to come to Geoff of a sudden. His face lit up as he asked, "And what of Lady Breanne?"

"She stays here."

Two sets of eyebrows rose before they all burst out laughing.

A deal's a deal . . .

Breanne was livid by the time she located the lout outside at the exercise field.

At first, she was jarred by the sight of him, bare chested, glistening with sweat, as he finished up the day's sword play. Ne'er had Breanne been inflamed at the sight of a man's chest afore, but she was now.

"You!" she exclaimed, storming up to him, shoving him in the chest.

Caedmon finished giving directions to the two men he had been speaking to, then took her by the upper arm, nigh dragging her off to the side. "Dost want everyone to hear your latest tirade?"

"I do not . . . tirade."

"You could have fooled me."

"Stop looking at my breasts."

He grinned.

"What do you mean by sending my sisters away, without discussing it with me first?"

"You asked for my protection. I am giving it."

"By shrugging them off on others."

He explained his plan, grudgingly, "By spreading you princesses about to defray the suspicion of Edgar's hounds which will soon be sniffing about."

"That is all well and good, but you should have gotten my consent first."

"I do not need your consent." Before she knew what he was about, he ran the backs of his fingers over both of her breasts.

"You beast! Why did you do that?"

"Just checking something Amicia said."

"Oh, nay, please do not tell me that she spoke of the female sucking business."

Caedmon's jaw dropped for a moment, and he appeared to have gone speechless. "Nay, she did not mention female sucking. But you can tell me yourself. Later. When my reaction will not be so noticeable to one and all."

She considered asking what reaction he referred to, but by the continuing grin on his face, she reconsidered. "All right, mayhap it is best that my sisters scatter. Where will you send me?"

"Ah, that is the best part, m'lady. You will stay here. With me."

If her face had not been flushed with embarrassment before, it would be now. "You do not mean . . ."

He nodded.

"I thought you were teasing."

He shook his head.

Before she could say any more, he leaned down, brushed his lips quickly over hers, and whispered. "Tomorrow. Night one. I cannot wait."

And Breanne, chagrined as she was, tingled.

CHAPTER ELEVEN

❧

Partings are such sweet sorrow . . .

Caedmon stood out in the bailey, giving last-minute instructions to Wulf and Geoff.

Breanne and her sisters were in a huddle, weeping and hugging as if the world were coming to an end. Vana was unrecognizable, dressed as a boyling, with her white blonde hair plaited up under a cap. Her role would be as pig herder for some of the hogs being led to market, a role that Vana found amusing but elicited scathing commentary from Breanne. The other two sisters were actually looking forward to their trip to Heatherby. Ingrith could not wait to plan a wedding feast, and Drifa was hoping to find fresh flowers to decorate the bridal head wreath, as well as all the tables. Geoff was having great fun over the prospect of riding up to Heatherby with two beautiful women and seeing his betrothed's reaction.

Rashid was going to Heatherby, as well, it being thought he would draw too much attention to Vana if he accompanied her and Wulf. The two Viking bears, Ivan and Ivar, would accompany Wulf and Vana, against Wulf's wishes (he would have preferred a smaller party to avoid detection), insisting that they had been sent by King Thorvald to protect the sisters, and since Vana was the one in trouble, would be remiss in their duties if they stayed behind. The two Vikings were pretending to be slaves that Wulf was taking to auction.

As the ladies started to mount, Rashid came up to Caedmon and said, "So, you have developed an affection for one of the princesses."

"I have no idea what you mean," he lied.

"Are you saying that any water in a desert will do? That any woman would suffice in the bed furs, princess or not?"

"Personally I have never taken an ugly woman to bed," Geoff interjected.

"But you have awakened next to a few," Wulf countered with a laugh.

Idiots, both of them!

"Do not missay me, Rashid," Caedmon asserted. "You go too far betimes."

The Arab shrugged and said, "On occasion, God sends almonds to those with no teeth."

"What does that mean?"

"Good things sometimes go to the undeserving."

"Breanne is a good thing?"

"A very good thing." Rashid patted Caedmon on the shoulder and mounted his horse.

Breanne was bawling like a banshee as her sisters left. When she caught Caedmon watching her, however, she straightened and raised her chin high. The glower she cast his way said, unfairly, that it was his fault she was so miserable.

Ah, well, in for a saint as well as a sinner.

"Tonight, m'lady. I will be waiting."

You could say it was their first dinner date . . .

Caedmon had gone about his regular business throughout the day, but always at the back of his mind was this thought: *Tonight!* And: *Big nipples.*

He had bathed and shaved before coming to dinner, and he noticed that Breanne, at his side, must have bathed, too. Her hair, even though plaited into one long braid, was lustrous and redolent of roses from her sister's soap. Her face was shiny from being well scrubbed.

Before they left, Wulf and Geoff had handed him gifts. Since they were not wont to exchange presents, he had to assume there was some jest involved. There was.

Wulf's "gift" had been a sack of small apples.

On the other hand, Geoff's "gift" might have been given with humor, but Caedmon would damn sure make use of it. It was a small vial of clove-scented body oil from the Eastern lands, the kind harem *houris* were proficient in using on their *sheikr* masters.

Breanne sat next to him, bundled head to ankle in some Viking attire that involved a long-sleeved *gunna* overlaid with a full-length open-sided apron. If she thought that would deter him, she was sadly mistaken.

Pushing food about her trencher with a spoon, she had such a woeful face that he would have pitied her if he had not been convinced it was a ruse.

"You have no appetite, m'lady?"

She raised her eyes to look at him.

"I know the food is not as fine as that prepared by your sister, but it is better than usual fare here, believe you me." He lifted a piece of honey-oat cake in his fingers and put it to her mouth.

She glared at him, but had no choice but to open, and then lick the honey residue off her lips.

He felt each lick in his hardening staff. His loins were already tense and preparing for the feast to come.

"The food is fine," she said.

"You are peckish, then?" *Or just getting aroused, as I am? Hah! I should be so lucky!*

"Would it make any difference?"

"Not a bit." *Actually, there was that unfortunate time a wench deep in the ale-joy hurled the contents of her stomach onto my raging erection. Yecch!*

"You really are going through with this?"

He straightened. "Are you about to renege . . . already?"

"Nay, but I thought you would say it was all a jest."

"You thought I would be chivalrous?" *Not a chance, m'lady.*

"Yea."

"Nay. Until I sent your sisters away, you thought I would not take you to my bed whilst they were about. Am I right?" *The twists and whorls of a devious woman's mind are not all that hard to figure out.*

She shrugged. In other words, that is exactly what she had hoped.

"If it is your virginity that bothers you, have no

fear. I will be gentle." *Not that I have had all that many virgins.* "But do not think to make me feel guilty over taking your maidenhood."

She waved a hand dismissively. "That matters not to me."

This woman is at cross-wills to me at every turn. No matter what I say, she argues the opposite. "It would to your husband."

"Since I do not plan to wed, 'tis a moot point. Although I would care if you got me with child."

"That will not happen. I promise." *Believe you me, the last thing I want is another whelp shadowing me.*

He could tell she wanted to ask how, but dared not. Even in such a brazen lass as her, modesty still reigned. "I do not like that I have no choice, that I am being forced to do this."

"Oh, nay! Do not dare to claim such. You had a choice, all right. To make a bargain, or not. To leave with your sisters, or not."

"Do you think they will be safe?"

"For now, yea, but it will be a tightrope we walk once the king's men arrive."

"Your hold on Larkspur truly is in peril by aiding us?"

"That it is."

"Then, I owe you," she said, standing, and holding her hand out to him.

Caedmon stood, as well. It bothered him that a woman was coming to his bed out of obligation. But not enough to call it off.

One side of his brain said, *Release her from the bargain.*

The other side said, *Why should I?*

The good side said, *Mayhap if I let her go, she will come to me willingly.*

The baser side said, *Ha, ha, ha, ha!*

Wet and wild, medieval style . . .

Breanne had thought she had a fairly good idea what happened during the sex act. Holy Thor, how had she been so misguided?

Once she walked into Caedmon's bedchamber and saw the dozen candles blazing, the cozy fire in the small hearth, and clean linens on the bedstead, she knew this would not be a quick, emotionless swiving. The lout had plans, and they did not call for her lying as stiff as a board, letting him do what he will.

"What is all this?" she snapped.

The door shut behind him, followed by the ominous click of the lock. "A setting."

"For what?" She hated that her voice came out as a squeak.

He smiled. "Love play."

She hated when he smiled. "Play? What kind of rutting involves play?"

"The best kind," he said, chucking her under the chin as he walked past her and over to a large armed chair by the hearth. He toed off both boots, then sat back, legs extended casually.

"I was hoping we could get this over with quickly so I could go back to my bedchamber and get some sleep. I have been up since dawn preparing for my sisters' departure. And, by the by, when exactly is . . ." Her words trailed off as she realized she was rambling, and he was just grinning at her obvious nervousness.

"Getting this over with is far removed from what I plan. I doubt either of us will sleep this night, but if you please me, I give you permission to sleep in the morn."

"Permission? You lout! I do not need your permission to do anything."

He shrugged and wagged his fingertips, beckoning her to come closer.

She balked.

"You come here, or I come there, and since you are closer to the bed—"

She moved to stand before him so fast that the fire flickered from the wind she created.

"Take off your clothes, Breanne. Slowly."

She gasped. *No preamble. No darkened room. No romantic words.* "Dost mean to humiliate me?"

He shook his head. "I mean to make love to you, and that starts with you and I being naked. There is naught humiliating in two people enjoying each other's bodies."

Refusing would be futile. She had agreed to this bargain, and her word was bond. But, oh, she wished she could just fly away.

Despite her heated face, she removed her apron and *gunna*, standing before him in naught but her woolen hose.

"Beautiful," he said in a sex-husky voice. "You are very beautiful, Breanne."

She did not think so. "'Tis lust speaking."

"Mayhap a little. Nay, I thought the same when I saw you naked afore."

Oh, that was loathsome of him to remind her of that. She raised her chin haughtily, not about to beg him for mercy.

"Unbraid your hair and finger comb it out."

Cheeks burning, she felt a strange vulnerability raising her arms and thus her breasts for his perusal. Once the braid was undone, she shook her hair off her face.

The stunned expression on his face was priceless. You would have thought she had handed him his heart's desire.

"Turn around now, sweetling. I would see all sides of you."

Sweetling? Hah! There is naught sweet about what he would do with me.

"Remove your hose."

She was about to sit on the opposite chair to do so, but he quickly added, "Bend to take them off."

This was truly the most embarrassing thing she had ever done. When she was done, she looked up, only to be surprised that he had already removed his tunic and short hose and sat wearing naught but low-riding braises. His chest hair was dark and curly leading down to a narrow waist and then his navel. His bare feet were long and high arched and oddly attractive. Her eyes shot up to see him gazing at her hotly.

"Come here, Breanne." He spread his legs for her to stand between them.

She dragged her feet, curling her toes to fight the irksome tingles. But then she stood before him, so close she felt his body heat and more.

He performed an excruciatingly detailed examination of her body, his calloused fingertips tracing the outsides of her arms down to her wrists, her collarbones, her sides from armpits to waist, hips to thighs. When his knuckles grazed lightly over her nether hair, she jumped.

"Easy, easy," he said, as if he was gentling a horse.

Which was what she felt like, an animal being inspected for market. But she could not think on that, as his wicked fingers had moved to her breasts. He lifted them from underneath, massaged them in wide circles of his palms, then strummed the nipples with his thumbs.

She groaned, so intense was the pleasure. "This is torture," she whispered.

"Good torture, I hope. You *do* have big nipples," he added enigmatically.

Immediately she put her hands over her breasts to hide them. Did he have to call attention to her deficiencies?

"Nay, do not cover such sweet assets," he said.

"Do not attempt to sway me with false praise. I am perfectly aware that my breasts are too small, and the nipples too big."

"Bre-anne!" he chided her. "Do you not see how much your breasts please me? All of you, in truth."

As he moved her hands back to her side, she looked at his face. His blue eyes seemed lit by a sensuous flame, the long, sweeping lashes at half-mast. His nostrils flared, and his mouth parted, as if he was breathless.

Before she had a chance to anticipate his next

move, he lifted her about the waist and set her
on his lap, astraddle, her rump on his thighs, her
female parts exposed to his scrutiny. She had to
grasp his shoulders to keep from falling backward as he spread his thighs wider.

"Oh, this is so crude," she complained, trying
to escape.

He held her tight. "Love play *is* crude. And the
best love play is hot and wet and loud and, yea,
crude."

She had no idea what he meant.

"Tell me true, Breanne, how do you feel?" His
palms were stroking her thighs, from knee to
groin, lightly, over and over.

"I tingle," she confessed.

"Where?"

"My breasts and . . . and below."

He nodded as if she had given the correct
answer. "I tingle, too."

"You do?"

"I do."

"Where?"

He took her hand and placed it over his manpart, which was hard and thick. When she jerked
her hand back, she noticed that he had momentarily closed his eyes and was shuddering, as if
in pain.

"Do you tingle with all women?"

He laughed. "I ne'er have before."

She slanted him a skeptical look.

" 'Tis true."

"Would I tingle with any man?" She already
knew the answer to that because she never had

before, even when she had been kissed a time or two.

"I hope not," he said.

Why would he care? I would not care if he kissed other women. Would I? "What are we going to do now?"

"Everything."

He cupped her buttocks and tugged her closer so that her bottom now rode the hard ridge of his erection, and her breasts nestled in his chest hairs. Breanne felt light-headed and tense, waiting for . . . something.

"What do you want, Breanne?" He was kissing her ear. Nay, he was licking the whorls of her ear, stabbing the inner channel with his tongue, then blowing the wetness dry, just as he had done on the roof.

It was a revelation to Breanne that there seemed to be a direct connection between her ear channel and her female channel, which not only tingled now, but throbbed, as well. "I do not know," she answered. "Everything?"

He put a hand to her nape and drew her mouth down for a kiss, openmouthed and devouring. Without thinking, her lips became pliant and clung to his as if for sustenance. Even as he kissed her mindless, his hands were playing with her breasts. At one point, he stopped kissing her and put his mouth to her breasts. Licking. Fluttering his tongue against the nipples, then sucking deeply.

Instinctively, Breanne was undulating her hips against the hard rod beneath his braies.

"Slow down, sweetling. Slow down."

How? she wondered. *My body seems to have a mind of its own.*

He resumed kissing her then, but his lewd fingers had moved downward to her private parts, touching her with an intimacy she had never engaged in, not even imagined. She tried to back off, but he held her tight with the other hand at her back.

"You are wet for me," he announced as if it was some great triumph for him and not an embarrassment to her.

Did I piss myself? "Oh, good heavens! I am sorry," she murmured, mortified. "I am leaking."

He chuckled. "Do not be sorry. 'Tis your woman dew. Your body is readying itself for me."

Oh. But then she could think no more as his fingers explored her swollen nether lips and a raised bud of intense sensation she had not realized was there. He even put a long finger inside her.

The throbbing was tortuous now with her hips jerking spasmodically. It felt as if dozens of butterflies with cobweb-thin wings were fluttering deep in her belly. She would die if something did not happen soon.

"Look at me, Breanne. Nay, do not look away. I want to see your eyes when you peak."

"Peek at what?"

He laughed. "Your peaking. Your summit of pleasure. Now look at me and do as I say. That is it, tip backwards a bit, and hold onto my thighs. Do not let go."

He stuck his middle finger inside her grasping inner sheath, and used the middle finger of the other hand to vibrate back and forth across the distended nub.

Immediately the tension rose high and higher and higher still. Her lower body lost all control as she rode his finger. And then . . . and then it was as if she had reached the peak and fell over, shattering into a million fluttering spasms.

Her forehead was resting on his shoulder when she regained her senses. Slowly she felt him remove the finger and caress her back, spreading her wetness. So aroused was she still that she could not even care about that ignominy.

And he . . . the rogue . . . was whispering wicked things in her ear. Praise for all she had done so far. Promises of lewd things he intended to do to her yet.

What was it Rashid was wont to say: When a rogue kisses you, count your teeth.

Hah! With this rogue, she should count her teeth, her fingers, her toes, everything she had . . . and most of all, her too-vulnerable heart.

You want to put that WHERE? . . .

Caedmon lifted the bedazed woman off his lap and tossed her onto the bed, immediately crawling over her. He was a lost man. Lost, lost, lost!

She blinked, then stared up at him through eyes like shards of green glass. Apparently, she was as flummoxed as he by what had just happened. By the rood! Her receptiveness to his touch both excited him and made him wary. He could easily be smitten by this tempting witch if he was not careful.

He had gone too far.

She had gone too far.

In truth, Caedmon had intended to make bold with her, mayhap avail himself of some of her charms, just give her a lesson she would not soon forget in trying his temper. She needed bending to a man's will . . . his will. But his brutish urges had taken over once she removed her garments, and now he must needs slake his lust.   •

"Dost want me to continue, Breanne?" he asked in a raw voice as he kneeled betwixt her widespread legs and unlaced his braies, shrugging them off his painfully hard cock.

Her eyes went wide and her gaze was riveted on his erection, which of course took that as a cue to thicken even more. His enthusiasm for the bedsport was approaching embarrassment. If he was not careful, he would spill his seed like an untried boyling.

"Continue what?" she asked.

He forgot the question, for a moment, as he noticed the moisture glistening on her red fleece. "With our love play," he rasped out.

She glanced once again to his raging cock. "Dost plan to put *that* inside me?"

He laughed, painfully. "Yea, I do."

"Are you not embarrassed by *it*?"

He frowned. "Why should I be?"

"I cannot imagine the discomfort of walking around with your dangly part leading the way."

"Breanne! I do not walk around like this." *Leastways, not all the time . . . though, a great deal since you arrived, witch.*

"Can I touch it?" she asked as she half-sat up.

Good Lord! She will be the death of me yet. But what a sweet way to die! "If you must." He guided her hand down to enfold him.

But contrary as usual, she unfolded her hand, and instead ran her fingertips along the length, causing his blood to thicken and his heart to race. Every nerve in his oversensitized body was dancing, especially between his legs.

"It feels like marble, smooth and oddly hard. Why is it red on the end? Why are those veins sticking out? Does it hurt?"

Too many questions for him to answer without babbling. The feel of her fingertips wrapping about him nigh unmanned him, but then she squeezed, too hard, and he began to lose control. Prying her fingers off, he showed her how to pleasure him, and she did, intrigued by his reaction. Because her hands were rough from all her woodworking, it created the most incredible friction, like nothing he had experienced before.

"Too much too soon," he told her.

Did that stop the wench?

Nay.

She lifted his cock and stared at his ballocks, as if she had just unearthed some secret. "Eeew, it is hairy. Like peach fuzz."

Would you like a taste? Oh, that was crude, even for me. I will scare her off afore we begin. He held back a laugh, then took her hands in his, raising them above her head with her reclining again. "Now is the time to say yea or nay, sweetling. Beyond this point, I will not . . . *cannot* . . . stop."

"Was I wanton when I . . . you know? Would I be wanton if I continued?"

Definitely. "Does it matter?"

"Not much."

He had to grin at that. *God love a wanton woman!* "Actually, Breanne, there is naught that a man, even a husband, cherishes more than a good woman who can be bad in bed."

"You jest."

He shook his head. "I do not. If you must know, Breanne, I want you to be uninhibited with me."

"I would not know how."

"I will teach you." *Said the spider to the ant.* "So, yea or nay?"

"You would let me renege on our bargain? You would be satisfied without actual fornication?"

"I would not be satisfied, but . . ." He shrugged. *Do not overplay the meekness game, Caedmon.*

"Would you take back protection of my sisters?"

Probably not. "Probably."

She seemed to consider his words. She was no doubt trying to figure a diplomatic way of saying she did not want him, but then she surprised him, good and well. "That thing that happened to me afore . . . the peaking . . . will it happen again?"

"I guarantee it will." *Well, practically guarantee.* "Hopefully, more than once."

"Go ahead, then. Do it."

Was there e'er a more romantic prelude to lovemaking? As if I care! I am about to have my wicked way with the wicked witch of the north.

CHAPTER TWELVE

It was a hairy situation . . .

Breanne's entire body was humming. Truly, it was amazing, as if every portion of her skin, all the nooks and crannies, was being alerted to something stupendous about to happen.

Caedmon lowered himself to lie atop her.

Oh. My. Gods! She gasped at the feel of his chest hairs against her breasts.

He raised himself slightly, and, as if he could read her mind, moved his chest from side to side so the coarse hairs could abrade her already erect nipples. She closed her eyes and saw bright lights behind the lids, so intense was the pleasure. *Do it again. Do it again. Do it again.*

"Do you like that, dearling?" he whispered. When she did not . . . could not . . . answer, he urged, "Open your eyes, Breanne, and tell me."

I like it overmuch. "I suppose it is all right." *Do it again.*

He nipped her chin with his teeth, not convinced, but lout that he was, he stopped the chest caresses. Instead, he began to kiss her again, another form of sweet torment.

Unlike the earlier hungry kisses, these were gentle and slow and slumberous, as if he had all the time in the world. Taking him by the ears, she lifted his head. "Not like that." *Do the other thing with your chest hairs.*

A laugh rumbled up from deep in his throat. "Now you are an expert on kissing?"

"I know what I like." *Chest hairs.*

"You do not like soft, coaxing kisses?"

"Bloody hell, man! I am already coaxed. Move on to something more . . . more . . ."

"Vigorous?"

Exactly. "If you insist."

He was smiling down at her, and, oh, the lout had a smile that would tempt a saint. "Like this?" He traced the outline of her lips with his tongue and murmured, "Didst know you have a siren mouth?"

"I beg your pardon!" She was trying her best to be a compliant sex partner, and he insulted her!

"That was a compliment. I meant that your mouth is lush and so kissome, it draws a man, like a siren. It gives men ideas."

"Seems to me you have ideas enough," she huffed out. *If you do not give me a chest-hair caress again, and soon, I am going to wallop you over your fool head.*

He rubbed the wetness on her bottom lip with the pad of his thumb. She tried to nip at it, but he pulled away just in time, his eyes crinkling with humor. When their mouths melded now, he pushed his tongue into her mouth, slowly, buried deep, then slid back out. In. Then out. In. Then out. Breanne was not too clear on the details of swiving, but she was fairly certain this rhythm matched what he would be doing to her below. *All right, then. Mayhap I could give up the chest-hair caressing for tongue caressing.*

Next time he thrust into her mouth, she sucked on his tongue, causing his body to jerk. But then she felt him smile against her mouth; so, she assumed she had done the right thing. Thus encouraged, she sucked some more, then tentatively tried dipping her tongue into his mouth.

He groaned.

Breanne was mentally congratulating herself as she came to understand that groans were good in bedplay. She vowed then to make the knave do a lot of groaning before the night was over.

Now, while his kiss turned lustsome, his hands were busy on other parts of her body. Her aching breasts, her buttocks, the backs of her knees. *By the gods! Who knew the backs of my knees could be so sensitive to touch?* Suddenly, he raised his head and said, with chagrin, "Breanne! Your eyes are open. Why?"

She liked the way his lips were a bit puffy from her kisses and his breathing was ragged. 'Twas a heady feeling, knowing she could do this to him. "I am trying to concentrate."

"On what, pray tell?"

"Everything. You are doing so many things at once. Can you not finish one task at a time?"

"Task?" The grinning lackwit was having great fun at her expense.

"Besides, how will I know what you are doing if I cannot see?"

"Just close your eyes, sweetling, and I will tell you when there is something good to see."

She succumbed to the forceful domination of his kisses then and only closed her eyes when he moved down her body and began to suckle at her breasts. Turns out that big breasts were not a necessity for lovemaking. Turns out big nipples were good for something.

Ribbons of heat unfurled in her as he brought her to another of those peaking things, just by fondling her breasts and dipping his talented fingers into her woman folds. She had scarce caught her breath when he whispered, "Now you can look."

With arms levered on either side of her head, he was positioned betwixt her thighs, his phallus at her woman's portal. "Are you ready?"

"How would I know?" she snapped.

Slowly he pushed himself inside her, only a little, then pulled out. Then, in a little more, then out again.

"You are so tight," he grunted out. "So wonderfully tight."

She could tell when he hit her maidenhead, but it only pinched a bit, and the pain was soon gone, replaced by the most amazing fullness. Sweat beading his forehead, he rocked in and out of her until finally he was buried to the hilt. He rested then, forehead to forehead, and asked, "Have I hurt you?"

"Just a little. Do not stop."

He grinned. "Not a chance."

While he rested inside her, her inner muscles stretched and shifted to accommodate his size.

"You feel like a hot velvet sheath," he whispered. "Oh. My. God! Keep welcoming me like that."

She had no idea she had been doing any welcoming. "It feels as if my womanparts are weeping around your hardness."

"Your woman dew," he explained. "Like warm honey, it is."

"Are we done fornicating?" *If so, I liked the chesthair caresses better.*

He laughed heartily, and she felt the ripples of his humor inside, along her inner . . . *yea, I notice now* . . . clasping folds.

He began to move then, long tortuous strokes, so slow she wanted to hit him, so delicious she wanted to bite his shoulder to hold back a scream of ecstacy. When he alternated with hard, shorter pummels, he actually lifted her body, so strong were the thrusts. By now she was mindless and writhing in tortuous pleasure.

And then he stopped.

He bloody hell stopped.

It took her a moment to see through the haze of arousal. He was clearly as aroused as she was, if not more, but he was fighting it.

"What?" she whimpered. *If this is all, I am going to be very, very disappointed.*

With a grim smile, he rolled over, his manpart still inside her, taking her with him. Now she lay atop him. Gently, he took her by the shoulders, pressing until she sat up, astride him.

For a second, he closed his eyes and hissed through gritted teeth. She had that effect on him, she realized with glee, and swung her hips from side to side to test her powers.

"Witch!" he said, putting his hands on her waist to hold her in place. Then he said, "Your turn."

At first, she was confused. She had no clue what to do. But then she realized what a position she was in, and she did the only thing she could.

She leaned forward and rubbed her breasts back and forth across his bristly chest hairs.

Off to the races . . .

Caedmon had always prided himself on his stamina in the bedsport, but this was ridiculous. If he did not peak soon, he was going to set some kind of record for male virility.

He had to smile at that notion.

But then he could not smile anymore.

Breanne sat atop his belly like a bloody queen. Due to the heat and their exertions, her red hair had turned curly, with wild waves framing her face and falling on her shoulders and back. Her lips were reddened and swollen more than usual. Her raspberry nipples pointed at him like fingers of accusation.

Flipping her hair back, she leaned forward and brushed her breasts over and over, side to side, over him. The nipples kept snagging in his chest hairs.

Gaaaaaaaaa!

"Does that feel as good to you as it does to me?" She slanted him a sultry look.

Gaaaaaaaaa! "You know very well it does. Every time you move, my cock smiles inside you."

"A smiling cock?" She arched her brows provocatively.

What kind of monster have I created here?

Nay, not a monster: a goddess of sex.

"Why are you grinning like the cat who swallowed all the cream?" said Caedmon.

"Because I feel like the cat who swallowed all the cream."

He cupped her small breasts from underneath and lifted them. *If I am to die from overstimulation, this will surely be the way to go.*

She looked down and inhaled sharply.

He gloried in the fact that she was so responsive. He had not expected this bounty. "Do you ride, Breanne?"

"Of course I ride." She frowned. "What an odd question to ask at a time like this."

"Not so odd." *Come closer, little ant. Lord Spider has something to show you.*

"How could you think of horses when . . . oh, my!"

He had lifted her by the hips until she almost escaped his impalement, then down. Up. Down. Her jaw was gaping open with wonder.

Making women gape in bed was his second-best talent. Next to . . . "Not horses, dearling. Men. This man, in particular. Dost think you could ride me?"

She still knelt astride him, unmoving once again, her rump raised slightly. He put one hand to the back of her waist, and used the other hand

to strum the pearl of her arousal, which he could
see peeking through her nether hair. Like a pink
jewel amongst red fleece.

She gaped some more before bursting forth
with laughter. A joyous tingling sound.

Then she challenged him.

"Canter or gallop, m'lord?"

Lout sex, oh, yeah! . . .

Breanne was stunned.

Well, that was an understatement. But, really,
she was going to have words with Tyra next time
she saw her. How could her sister have kept this
information from her? Why had she never mentioned that sex could be so . . . so exciting? Aside
from the bone-melting excitement, it had been satisfying physically, and it had been fun.

If sex with a lout could be so amazing, she could
only imagine what it would be like with a man
she loved. Truly, Breanne's perceptions of men
and women, marriage, and relationships were un-
dergoing a change. She would need to rethink all
her old ideas.

Glancing to her side where the lout was asleep,
splayed out on his back, she had to smile that she
had depleted him so.

From his finely sculpted face, over broad shoulders and wide chest, narrow waist and hips, muscular thighs and calves, and, yea, the now limp
manpart, she had to admit he was an attractive
man. And what he had been able to do with that
body was commendable.

Now, however, she was not sure what women

did in situations such as this. Was she supposed to just lie here until he awakened and had need of her again? Hah! Not bloody likely.

Easing her hair out from under one of his arms, she slid across the mattress, when a hand shot out and grabbed her by the wrist. "Where do you think you are going?"

She half turned from where she sat at the side of the bed. He was gazing at her sleepily, an insufferable smile of triumph lifting the edges of his lips. "Back to my bedchamber."

"Why?"

"To sleep?"

He shook his head. "You sleep here, with me, for the next nine and a half nights." He put particular emphasis on the half night part, to remind her, she supposed, that she had not yet fulfilled her bargain.

As if to emphasize that fact, he yanked on her arm, pulling her back and over him. On the way, her hip met the wet spot where he had released his seed, to prevent a pregnancy. When she tried to roll off, he secured her with arms like manacles about her waist.

He stared up at her for a long time, saying nothing.

"What?" she finally asked, uncomfortable with his scrutiny.

His head lifted so he could brush his lips against hers, ever so gently. "Thank you."

"For what?"

"The most satisfying bedplay I have ever engaged in."

She cast him a skeptical glance.

"You were wonderful, dearling. A great surprise."

"Didst think I would be like a broom in bed?"

"Something like that." He chuckled. "Did you enjoy it?"

She thought about lying, but it was no use. She had behaved like a strumpet. "Yea, I did. And you were a surprise, too."

"How so?"

"I will not tell you. Your ego is too large as it is."

"There are other parts of me that are large, too." He waggled his eyebrows at her.

He did not need to tell her that. She felt it growing against her hip.

"There are so many things I want to do with you," he said, his voice husky in a masculine way.

"What sort of things?" she asked before she could bite her tongue.

"Ah, sweetling, I thought you would never ask." He proceeded to tell her, in detail.

"You jest," she said at one point.

Which prompted him to elaborate on even more wicked, incredible activities.

"It would take a month, in fact, many months to do all that."

"And we have only nine and a half nights. Guess we need to get to work quick then. What would you like to do first?"

"I would like you to bathe me," she said, surprising even herself.

"And will you bathe me in return?"

She tapped her lips as if pondering. "Would there be massaging oil involved?"

"For a certainty."

"Well, then, lout, it is a deal."

He was always on her mind . . . and other places . . .

Four days later, after having sex in more ways and in more places than she would have ever imagined possible, Breanne's lips and nipples were raw from Caedmon's constant attentions. Raw in a nice way. Even air felt like a lover's caress, so that when he wasn't around, she was still reminded of him.

But then, Caedmon had told her just this morn that his manpart was raw, quickly adding, "Not that I am complaining."

Thus, she was in her bedchamber, with the upper part of her *gunna* hanging down to her hips, applying some ointment to her breasts when Amicia came in, without knocking. "Oh, sorry ta disturb ye, but I need some help down in the kitchen with . . . oh, blessed Mary!" The cook burst out laughing, so hard that she was soon bent over at the waist, and tears welled in her eyes.

"What is so funny?" Breanne asked, tugging her dress back up and lacing it at the neck.

"You? You have succumbed to the master's seduction. I tol' ya he was a devil with the wimmen. They cannot resist his charms."

If only Amicia knew! It hadn't taken much charming to get her in his bed.

"What is the problem in the kitchen?"

"I forget the directions fer the eel brine that yer sister makes."

She walked alongside the cook down to the kitchen.

Before they got there, Amicia put a halting hand on her arm. "Methinks ya could use some of the powders Rashid gave ta me."

"I have no head megrims." *Just another kind of ache.*

"Not that kind of powder. These are the kind that prevent the babes from comin'. Remember, Lady Havenshire told us of them some days ago."

Hmmmm! "Do they work?"

Amicia shrugged. "Be damned if I know, but he says they be used by them harem harlots. Love slaves." Motioning for Breanne to stay there, Amicia rushed off, then came back with a small palm-sized sack lined with parchment. Inside was the powder.

Well, if it was good enough for harem harlots, she supposed it would be good enough for her. In truth, that was what she was, in some ways. Caedmon's love slave.

She could not wait to tell him.

No doubt he would have some ideas related to harems. She had a few ideas herself.

Whaaat?

What is happening to me?

Was I always wicked beneath the surface? Or is it only this man who turns me wanton?

Aaarrgh!

With those horrific ideas riddling her brain, Breanne decided to go build a bench . . . or a cow byre . . . or just pull her hair out, one strand at a time.

On the way, she was stalled in the great hall, where Caedmon was holding shire court. While he was hearing the complaint of a man who said his neighbor had stolen a cow, Caedmon glanced up and saw her. She could not break the eye contact for a long moment while they both thought of all that had gone on between them, and what was yet to come. That was what went through her frazzled mind. The air fair sizzled. Then he smiled, and Breanne's bones almost melted. Truly, that was the unacceptable effect the lout was having on her.

Despite the small amount of sleep she had been getting, she seemed to be bright-eyed and energetic during the daytime as she attempted to take over the duties that Vana and Ingrith had organized so well. As for the outside and Drifa's flowers and herbs, they would have to live or die without her help. She had no talent with growing things. But, no matter what she was doing, Caedmon appeared to be always on her mind.

With an exhale of disgust, she sank down to a bench at the back of the hall, and watched and listened as Caedmon wielded his own brand of justice. And she was impressed. He listened carefully, he weighed all sides, he displayed a rare sense of humor, and was firm when he finally made a decision. And the cases ran the gamut from petty theft to murder to failure to pay taxes.

As she sat, all his children, one by one—except for Hugh, who sat at Caedmon's right—plopped down beside and across from her. They were like burrs in the wind, and she the shaggy sheep in their path. They followed her everywhere, except to Caedmon's bedchamber, and then only because he locked them out.

She wasn't surprised by Piers coming to her with outstretched hands, climbing up onto her lap, but she was surprised by Angus sitting on the bench next to her, up close. The surly little boy, who looked so different from the rest, was the butt of numerous pranks, many of them just harmless youthling teases, but he did not see them that way. And, rather than break out in tears, he stiffened his little back and hurled insults back at them.

Right off, they besieged her with their complaints and entreaties.

"Kendrick pinched my arse."

"I did not! I was flicking off some pig snot."

"Can I ride a horse? If Beth can have a pony, why do I get naught?"

"I am bigger than you, bratling. Ride a goat, if you must."

"Go bugger yerself."

"What is a bugger?"

"Why are your lips so red?"

"Father kisses her, that is why."

"Oh, you! Kisses do not make lips red."

"He looks at her like he could eat her up, like that tasty boar sauce."

"Oslac, you are daft. How could he eat her up?"

"I could tell you—"

Beth slapped a hand over Oslac's mouth. "Desist

with that kind of talk." Beth smiled slyly at Breanne then and said, "We must needs be polite to Lady Breanne if we want her to stay."

"You want me to stay? How nice! But I cannot stay indefinitely. Just until my sisters return."

Mina began to cry at that news, and Angus sniffled.

"We took a vote," Alfred said, as if that meant she had no choice.

"You are gonna be our mother," Aidan finished for his twin.

"You are better than the last trollop who shared our father's bed," Joanna remarked.

"Thank you for the compliment," Breanne said, then sighed inwardly. Even the children knew she was behind locked door with the lout every night, engaged in bedplay.

But Joanna was not done with her observations. "Phew! 'Twas a close call, that one. Lady Anise had already buried four husbands and was looking toward Larkspur for a new acquisition."

"She smelled funny," Angus said.

"Perfume," Beth replied. "She used splashes of perfume, rather than bathing."

"Well, we got rid of her, did we not? Methinks it was the frog in her washbowl," Kendrick observed, a mischievous gleam in his big brown eyes.

"Or the worms in her porridge," Joanna added, a matching gleam in her brown eyes.

"I farted every time she walked by." Oslac grinned, as if that were some great feat.

Enough was enough! Breanne was able to

escape because Hugh had just come up behind her and said, "Father wants you to come up to the dais and give him counsel on a difficult case."

"Me?"

"Yea. You may have an opinion that would help."

She glanced up, and Caedmon was indeed looking her way, and beckoning with his fingertip.

"I will take the children outdoors," Hugh offered.

When she sat down on the right of Caedmon behind the table, she told him, "I hate when you do that fingers-beckoning thing. It makes me feel like a pet dog."

"I know," he said and tugged her chair closer to his. Then, as if she had not even spoken, he whispered in her ear, "Greetings, my lady love." For everyone else's benefit, he said loudly, "Lady Breanne, we need a woman's view on this particular matter."

Since when? Suspicious of the rogue's intent, she studied the three people before them. Two women—*big-bosomed, of course*—bracketed one of Caedmon's hersirs, whose face was flushed with a combination of anger and embarrassment.

"Repeat the complaint for us, Gerard," Caedmon said.

Even as Gerard stood up to speak, Breanne was shocked to feel Caedmon's hand in her lap, though he appeared to be listening intently to Gerard. Or pretending to listen.

"Our bargain was only for nighttime," she hissed at him.

"You fell asleep on me last night afore dawn.
You owe me an hour."

"Lady Breanne . . ." Gerard was saying.

She gave the steward her attention, or as much
as she could whilst Caedmon's wicked fingers
were gathering the hem of her robe up her leg in
a leisurely exploration, causing her to lose focus
and setting her aflame.

When she glared at him, he bestowed one of his
lazy heated smiles on her, knowing full well its
effect. "Loathsome lout!" she muttered.

"Winsome wench!" he countered, staring
straight ahead with the innocence of a wolf at the
chicken-coop fence.

Gerard was still introducing the complaint.
"Thomas of Hexham has been in Lord Caedmon's service for nigh on ten years . . ." Thomas,
a bull-like soldier with a crooked nose that had
undoubtedly been broken more than once, raised
his chin high.

Breanne grabbed at Caedmon's meandering
hand, under the table, but he merely flipped it
over, his covering hers. In effect, he was moving
her own hand to raise the hem, which was now
thigh-high. To her dismay, as her blood thickened
and pulsed in her lips, her breasts, and betwixt
her legs, Breanne realized that she was becoming
enslaved by her passions, under Caedmon's tutelage. "Stop it. Stop it right now."

"What?" Gerard asked.

Not having intended to speak aloud, she waved
a hand for him to continue.

Caedmon smothered a laugh, then took a long

draw on his cup of ale, presumably to clear his throat.

"Thomas of Hexham has been wed to Maude for five years . . ."

His teary-eyed wife was more than thirty and a bit on the plump side, but comely.

Meanwhile Caedmon's hand had released hers and was now entering forbidden territory. He nigh did a victory dance when he realized she wore no undergarments, then said in an undertone, still staring ahead, "Witch! You will pay."

I am already paying, rogue.

" . . . but Eadgifu claims Thomas to be the father of her unborn bairn." Eadgifu was a big-breasted, brazen hussy that Breanne had seen about the keep, flirting with one and all, as long as they had a male part. And the lackwit men had no problem swiving a very pregnant woman.

Caedmon's fingertips brushed across her nether hair, and it took all her strength to keep from moaning and opening her legs to him. Truly, the man could make her knees sweat with a mere touch.

"Now, the question afore this court," Gerard continued, "is whether Thomas will claim this new child? And if so, will he provide for the child and its mother, and will there be a penalty for adultery?"

"I contend this is a question for the church, not a shire court," Caedmon said. Then, proving he could do more than one thing at a time, he managed to insert a foot behind her two, which were pressed close together, and yanked. In that second of surprise, her legs spread slightly, and he got a hand betwixt her legs. "Is that not so, m'lady?"

"Huh?" She had no idea what Caedmon was referring to as his fingers were already delving into her cleft.

"Should I hear this case, or pass it on to the church?"

"Begging your leave, m'lord," Eadgifu said, "I be due in a few sennights. I cannot wait fer some church ta get around ta my situation." She hefted her big stomach up for emphasis, which called attention to her big udders. In truth, the coarse woman could be the prow on a longship with all her protruding assets.

"What is it you want?" Breanne managed to ask, despite the fluttering exercise Caedmon was doing with his lewd fingertips. She blinked several times as blood drained from her head and rushed to other, more intimate parts.

"I want him ta take care of me and me babe." Eadgifu shot a smug look at Thomas and his wife.

"He has four children of his own ta care for," Maude protested. "I believe my Thomas is innocent, but if he has been strayin', I will cut off his cock and give it ta yon harlot, wrapped in a riband."

Breanne put a hand to her mouth to hide her smile. *I do like this woman.*

Thomas crossed his legs and cast his wife a sheepish glance. "I have ne'er lain with this woman," he contended.

"Liar!" Eadgifu shouted.

Breanne was fast losing control with the rogue drawing circles around her nubbin of pleasure. She must leave soon or humiliate herself by peaking in front of one and all. Raising a hand, she said in a rush, "Thomas and Maude, you are to remain silent whilst I ask Eadgifu a question."

"I do love a woman who gives orders," Caedmon remarked low enough that only she could hear.

"Shut your teeth."

"Methinks I may just swoon."

Eadgifu preened, figuring she was about to win her case.

"Eadgifu," Breanne said, "Thomas has a birthmark few people are aware of. Where is it located on his body?"

At first, Eadgifu's eyes darted right and left, trapped like a doe in a bramble bush, but then she noticed Breanne staring at Thomas's belly.

"On his gut," Eadgifu announced.

Thomas grinned and before he could be told to halt, he unlaced and dropped his braies to show a stomach devoid of any birthmark. Of course, he also showed them a manpart, as well.

"Oh, good Lord!" Breanne put her hands to her eyes until he raised his braies back up.

Maude began to weep with relief and told her husband, "I believed ya the whole time, dearling."

Thomas was not convinced. "I am aggrieved, wife. Ye must prove ta me how sorry ye are."

Breanne could pretty well guess what that involved.

"Thomas, you have proven your case, with Lady Breanne's help," Caedmon ruled, then gave Breanne a winning smile. "Go in peace, Thomas. And, you, Eadgifu, do not let me see you in this court again. If you know not who the father is, have the good sense to pick a man you have actually tupped with."

"I thought I had," Eadgifu shot back. "But then all men are the same in the dark, are they not?"

A lot of sniggering and hoots of laughter rippled through those gathered in the hall as an audience. But Breanne would not have known that. She was too busy peaking all over Caedmon's busy fingers.

She arched her neck and closed her eyes to prevent herself from shouting out her bliss. When she opened her eyes, the lout was watching her. "You look flushed, m'lady," he said. "Wouldst care for a cool drink?" He removed his wandering hand and reached for a cup of ale.

"Nay, I do not want a drink. You think you are so clever. Well, how do you like this?" It was her hand now in his lap, embracing his already hard phallus. She began to rub up and down.

Caedmon made a gurgling sound, deep in his throat, and shuddered.

"You look flushed, m'lord," she said coyly. "Mayhap you need a cup of ale . . ." In a whisper, she added, "poured over a certain body part."

With a laugh, she released him, stood, and began to walk away, figuring she had had the last word.

But behind her, she heard Caedmon tell those

left in the great hall, including those in line to be heard. "Let us break for an hour or so. I have an important matter to settle elsewhere."

Glancing back over her shoulder, Breanne saw Caedmon coming after her, and she knew, without a doubt, the way he wanted to settle said matter. She ran till she reached the small-accounts room and attempted to slam the door, but his booted foot was already inside.

"Well, well, well," Caedmon said, leaning back against the closed door. "What shall we do now?"

CHAPTER THIRTEEN

A *wall banger, for sure . . .*
    How could he have been so blind?

Breanne . . . the princess, the witch, the wench, the lady, the for God's sake carpenter, or whatever she chose to be at any given time . . . was every man's dream of a bedmate. When he first met her, he had thought she was naught more than a shrewish, irksome, plain woman of no particular attraction. She was just the opposite. Oh, she was still irksome and shrewish on occasion, but her attributes were beyond beautiful. To him, if no one else.

Leaning back against the closed door, he stared at her as she fidgeted behind a table in the center. Then she began to arrange in neat piles a Far East abacus, several sheets of vellum, an ink pot, a thick candle, wax, and a seal. There were also beaded sticks of different colors, which he used to keep a tally on the number of sheep, cattle, hogs, goats, and other animals in his possession.

"I could help you with your accounts."

"Gerard does that for me."

"Pfff! Look at this mess."

He shrugged. "And when would you have time for this? Before or after you build me a new keep, take care of the household and kitchens, arrange the butchering, and what else? Oh, I know . . . share my bed."

"Well, I am thinking about teaching the children their numbers and letters until a new Godman comes for your chapel and tutoring, or until I leave here, whichever comes first."

He stiffened. "You overstep your bounds. I did not ask you to do all these things."

"They needed doing. I am only trying to help."

"And yet you fail to complete the one duty I ask of you."

"What would that be?"

He waved a hand toward his crotch. "You cannot tease a man to enthusiasm, then leave him hard and wanting."

Her laughter was a big mistake.

He moved toward the table.

She moved to the other side.

He moved again, and took the ink pot off the table, setting it on a shelf. That is all he would need, to return to the shire court covered in ink.

She feinted right, then left.

Hah! He was an expert swordsman. He could parry any move she made. But then he tired of the game and lunged over the table, taking her with him, up against the wall.

"Ooomph! You big oaf! You knocked the wind out of me."

"I intend to knock more than wind out of you afore I am done." While she had been talking, he was busy unlacing the neckline of her gown. He shrugged the gown and its sleeveless surcoat off her shoulders and down to her elbows, thus confining her arms at her side.

"You brute! 'Tis daylight and there are folks about, waiting for your return."

He was nibbling a line along her jaw, from ear to chin, and up the other side. "They can wait. As for daylight, take another hour off the tail end of our bargain."

"An hour!" she squealed, whether at the amount of time, or the fact he was rubbing his rock-hard cock against her cleft. If not for her gown and his breeches, he would be swiving her by now. But then he noticed her breasts. "Breanne! What is this grease?"

A blush started on her face and moved downward over her neck and chest and, yea, said breasts. "'Tis an ointment for soothing raw skin."

"I hurt you?" He used his fingertips to rub the ointment into the skin, everywhere except the rosy nipples.

She moaned.

"That hurts, too?"

"It hurts good."

He smiled. "I know what you mean. I hurt good, too, but my hurt is down lower." He tugged her sleeves down and off so that her arms were free. Then, taking her hand, he encouraged her to explore his "hurt." When she obliged, using the movement he had taught her, he closed his eyes, lest she see that they were crossed. He closed his mouth as well, lest he yell out his pleasure.

Even though she had been a virgin just days ago, she was a bold and brazen lover. A prize any man would cherish. Not that he cherished her, precisely. Nay, but he did appreciate her.

"This is impossible, you know."

His eyes shot open. "Why?"

"There is no bed, and it is daylight, and—"

He laughed. Bold and brazen, she may be, but she was still innocent in so many ways. "Lift your gown up to your waist."

"Wha—"

He was already doing it for her. When she was bare to the waist, and he had unlaced and dropped his breeches, he instructed, "Put your arms around my shoulders." Then he lifted her by the buttocks and showed her how to lock her legs behind his waist.

"Oh." That was all she said, but it was enough.

In one fell swoop, without foresport or even a kiss, he entered her. And she was ready for him, thank the saints!

"Gaaaaaaaaa!" Breanne looked stunned, even as her inner muscles gave him welcome with throbbing, repetitive clasps. "What you do to me, knave!"

"You do not like it?"

She slapped him playfully on the chest. "You know I do." Then she leaned her face down toward him and licked a line around the edges of his lips.

"Witch!" he choked out. "You ensorcell me, I swear you do."

Her first peaking was about to hit, as evidenced

by her eyes glazing over. She made little panting sounds of escalating passion.

"I never knew. I. Never. Knew."

Hey, I have done this about a thousand times, and I never knew, either.

He turned them so that her back was against the wall. Glancing downward, he saw her short curls intermixed with his, like black and red fleece, spun together. Cradling her face in trembling hands, he whispered against her open mouth, "You make me breathless with need."

"Any ready female would do, I warrant."

I wish that were so. "Nay. Just you. This is naught like anything I have ever experienced afore. Believe that, if naught else."

"What does it mean?" she asked.

It means I am sinking fast in quicksand . . . and loving it. He could not answer because his lower body had taken over. Long, slow thrusts that quickly became short and hard, pummeling her against the door.

"Oh. Oh. Oh. Oh . . ." she keened with each stroke.

Passion licked through his body. His senses reeled. He was consumed with his want of her.

She was equally abandoned. He could see by her eyes, which were large and liquid, by her wails of pleasure, and by the way she arched her hips forward against his belly, then matched his rhythm, undulation for undulation.

'Twas a wonder that he was able to pull out at the last moment before spilling his seed inside her womb. It was a wonder, as well, that he really,

really wanted to stay, to throw caution to the wind, to be fulfilled totally as men were meant to be.

He helped her to stand on wobbly legs, then leaned down to kiss her lightly on the lips. Next he pulled up and laced his breeches. She still stared at him, stunned. He loved that he could stun her. Adjusting her gown, he kept kissing her, unable to stop. Finally, when he was about to drop the hem of her *gunna* back down, he heard a crackling sound.

"What is that?"

"Hmmmm?" she said dreamily.

He chuckled. "Breanne! You must get control of yourself afore you go back into the hall. In truth, I heard one of the children knocking on the door, looking for you." *More like all the children, but she does not need to know that.*

"Oh, my gods! What must everyone think?"

That I have been swiving you silly? "No one will have noticed your absence, except mayhap one of the children, and they are too young to know what we were about." *Hah! My children were born knowing all the things they should not.*

She pulled a small cloth sack out of a side placket in her gown, squeezing it to indicate that this was the source of the crackling noise. "Amicia gave it to me. Rashid gave it to her."

"And?"

"It prevents conception."

"What? Oh, this is too much, even for you. Dost mean it kills the babe in the womb? Toss it away."

"Nay. Mixed in hot water with a dollop of honey to mask its taste, it *prevents* a man's seed from fertilizing a woman's egg, or so Rashid told Amicia."

Caedmon smiled.

"'Tis no laughing matter." She moved to the other side of the small room, trying her best to smooth her gown and finger comb her hair.

"I agree, but 'tis a joyous matter if the powder works. Just think, I could engage in sex the way God intended." *And no more babies, thank you, God!*

"I do not think God intended people to prevent birthing babies."

How like a woman! Give a man a gift, then take it back. "Why would God have invented such herbs if not to be used?"

"You have a point, I suppose. And, leastways, it is not some lackwit idea about apples."

God's toenails! She knows about THAT? "Hey, 'twas not my idea, and I ne'er tried it, either. Geoff told the men of that practice. In any case, I must needs get back to the shire court afore they bring me up for neglect of duty," he told her. Opening the door, he let her go through first, then smacked her on her bottom.

"What was that for?"

"Just to remind you. Drink a cup of that brew this afternoon. In fact, drink five cups. One for each time I will be—"

"Impossible man!" She laughed. Then she was the one to smack his rump.

He liked it.

Lick that, bozo! . . .

Breanne was trying her bloody damn best not

to fall in love with the loathsome lout. She feared it was a losing battle.

As she lay on his bed, waiting for him like a sheep with no mind of its own, Breanne had much to consider. It was day five of their bargain. At the end of the next five days, what would their relationship be? Would he release her, or expect her to continue as his mistress? Would she want to? Or would he offer more?

Everything was turned upside down in her life, starting with the murder, the escape and hiding out, the departure of her sisters, and now her lewd activities with the loathsome lout.

And he *was* a loathsome lout. That had not changed. With ease, she could tick off the list of his faults on her fingers.

He ruled his keep, especially his children, with a lax hand. Thus the mess they had encountered on first arriving here.

He made jest of her constantly. What was wrong with a woman having talents outside the bedchamber or sewing solar? And carpentry was a time-honored skill, good enough even for God's son. Not that she was comparing herself to Jesus.

He begat babies like a randy rabbit. Ten at last count.

He was lustsome all the time, ready to engage in sex at a moment's notice, in the most outrageous ways and places. She had drawn the line at his taking her in a wheelbarrow position, her being the wheelbarrow.

He left Larkspur sparsely armed on too many
   occasions when he went off to fight in the
   king's army.

On the other hand, she had to admit that:

He had taken a passel of children under his
   wing, many of whom were not of his blood.
Even as he teased her, he had a great capacity
   for laughing at his own foibles, as well.
He was a great lover, always ready to try
   something new. And, to her dismay, she was
   enjoying that virility very much.
Much as he loathed King Edgar, he served
   him well in order to preserve his heritage.
He offered protection for her and her sisters,
   albeit at a price, but a price she was finding
   increasingly easy to pay.

But wait. Here he was now.

Without knocking, Caedmon walked into his
bedchamber and locked the door behind him. He
had forgotten to engage the lock yesterday and
therefore given the twins Alfred and Aidan more
than an eyeful when they barged in just after dawn.
Fortunately, they were both too young to understand what it meant when a naked woman knelt
on all fours on the bed with a naked man taking
her from behind. They had accepted Caedmon's
explanation that they were playing "horsey." And,
nay, they were not permitted to join in the game.

"You are smiling," Caedmon said.

I am happy to see you. Oh, nay! I cannot say that.

'Tis too soon. He will use it against me. "I am counting the days till my punishment ends."

A flash of hurt in his eyes was quickly masked
over. "Punishment? You consider our bedplay
punishment?"

Of the most painfully delicious kind. "What would
you call it?"

"Pleasure."

"That, too," she conceded.

And just like that the vulnerability turned into
arrogance. "Ah, well, then, I am about to punish
you with so much pleasure you will beg me never
to stop."

Please do. "You are little inclined toward meekness, m'lord."

He was already shucking off his braies and
tunic, his blue eyes glinting with approval as he
noticed her enjoying his unclothing. "Did you
drink any of the powders today?"

"I did."

"How much?"

"So much I had to go to the privy five times to
relieve my bladder."

"Good." He leaped onto the bed, causing the
ropes to creak.

"You will land us on the floor, fool." She
laughed.

He pinched her bottom.

"Ouch! What was that for?"

"For telling me that our lovemaking is punishment."

"Well, it is."

"Liar!" He rolled over on his back, folded his

hands behind his neck, and grinned over at her, not at all embarrassed by his nudity or his rising enthusiasm. "Take off your clothes for me, dearling."

She was wearing only a thin bed rail, but she balked nonetheless. It was part of the game they played behind doors.

"What will you give me if I do?"

He glanced downward.

"That goes without saying."

"I do have another gift for you, but you must be naked for me to give it to you."

"I cannot imagine—"

"No guessing. Just do it."

She slid off the bed and prepared to do so. Even though she wore only the one garment, she took a long time removing it. First, baring one shoulder, then the other. Holding the loose garment to her breasts, she turned and flashed him a saucy smile over her shoulder. Then she let loose the fabric and wriggled it down to her ankles, giving him a tempting view of her swaying bottom on the way down.

"Come here, witch." He held his arms out to her.

She meant to jump on top of him on the bed, but he caught her about the waist and turned her over on her back. "Do not move." Slipping off the bed, he went over to a table near the door where he had placed a small pottery jar.

"What is that?" she asked suspiciously.

"Something to heal your abraded breasts and to soothe my hunger."

"Huh?" She leaned forward and sniffed. "Honey?"

He nodded, then ran a thin stream over her lips. "Have you ever had a honey kiss?"

"You know I have not. Have you?"

He shook his head. "A first for me, too. In truth, you bring the creativity out in me."

She did not believe that for one moment, but she liked hearing it. And she liked even more his honey kisses, which he bestowed with expertise, bending over the bed, his one hand braced over her, the other on the pulsing hollow at the base of her throat.

"You want me," he declared, with satisfaction.

"You want me," she declared right back, equally satisfied.

They smiled at each other.

"For a woman with such a sour tongue, you do taste sweet." To prove his point, he lapped at her honeyed lips. Then he kissed the honey and nipped it with his teeth. He laved her lips and the surrounding skin.

The need to touch him was overpowering. She ran her hands over his back, delighting in every knob of his spine, every supple, bunching muscle in his shoulders and upper arms, even the strong tendons in his straining neck. When his tongue pressed into her mouth, she drew on him and would not let go.

"Bre-anne! You will be the death of me." He ground the words out between his teeth.

And myself, as well. "A good death, or a bad death?"

"A very good death, as you well know. Now, behave." He ran the pad of his thumb over her still slick bottom lip, then kissed it off. It was not a neat kiss. How could it be, with both of them so sticky?

A sennight ago, Breanne never would have imagined all the different kinds of kisses there were, or how a mere kiss could turn her weak and wanting. "I can taste the honey on you," she remarked when he came up for air. "And your lust."

"Honey lust? I like it."

"I never knew the mating could be so fun," she told him. "I thought it was a serious, sometimes distasteful business."

"It is for some women, and, nay, before you get the wrong idea, enjoying sex does not make you a harlot. In truth, a woman who enjoys bedplay is man's greatest gift."

The things this man does say! He wields charm like an erotic sword. "You are just saying that so I will not feel guilty."

"Do you feel guilty?"

She shook her head. "Not now, but I probably will later."

"Do not," he urged. "We are hurting no one by being together."

That was debatable because she sensed sure as sin that she was going to be hurt in the end.

When he stood once again, moving away from her, she sighed her disappointment.

"Miss me already, do you?" he asked.

Nothing escapes this man, I swear. "Lout!"

"But a loveable lout, am I not?"

She got no chance to answer because he was using a wooden spoon to put a dollop of honey

on each nipple. They both watched as the honey
spread in all directions till the areolas were covered. "Beautiful!" he murmured. "Absolutely
beautiful! Do you have any idea what you do to
me, Breanne?"

She surveyed his body. He was aroused. She
could tell by his erection, of course, but also by
the murkiness of his blue eyes and by his short-
ness of breath.

"We do it to each other." How could she say
otherwise, when her nipples stood up like little
flags announcing her excitement?

Laying himself down on his side, propped on
an elbow, he traced the honey with a forefinger,
making increasingly smaller circles, starting with
the edge of her areola and moving closer and
closer to the taut nipple. Giving the other breast
the same attention, he then began to retrace his
steps, but now with the tip of his tongue.

"Please," she whimpered.

"What?"

"You know."

"You are sore. I do not want to hurt you."

"If you do not suckle me soon, I am going to
hurt *you*."

He laughed, then moved to kneel between her
legs. With one arm under her back, he arched her
up off the mattress so she was at his mercy, with
no choice but to hold onto him or fall. Leaning
forward, he took one breast into his open mouth,
almost all of it, but then she was not that big. With
his phallus hitting her belly, he began to suck
tightly, pulling upward, stretching the breast with

him. By the time his hard sucking reached her nipple, she was shuddering with her first peaking, scarce realizing that he had moved to the other breast. And then he hooked his arms under her knees, which he raised up to his shoulders.

"Aaarrgh!" She clutched at the bed linens and tried to move, but she was at his mercy in this ignoble position. "Release me, knave."

"Why?"

Oh, good gods! What is he doing now? Honey . . . he is pouring honey THERE. "Because I feel like a fool hanging from you like this. Eeeeek! What are you doing?"

"Bringing the feast table closer." He began to lap up the honey.

And she began to tingle, all over, but especially where he was "feasting." She closed her eyes, which were no doubt rolling back in their sockets. She made huffing sounds to keep from peaking again. She stiffened her body to resist all the sensations battering her body like pellets of warm rain.

"Relax," he said, playing with her breasts while his tongue was busy torturing her below.

"You jest. I could no more relax than . . . oh! Ooooooh!"

"Didst like that, sweetling?" he asked after licking his way up one side and down the other of her female folds, then sticking his tongue inside her.

"I will be pissing honey water for a fortnight," she chuffed out.

He chuckled, and she felt his breath over her sensitized mons. "You do have a way with bluntness, m'lady."

She told him what he could do with his bluntness, and he chuckled some more. Best she keep
her coarse words to herself, because they only
gave him fodder for humor.

"Surely this is a perversion," she observed on a
moan of rising passion.

"Of the best kind," he agreed.

"I do not want to peak again like this. I want
you inside me."

"I thought you would never ask, sweetling."
He lowered her legs back to the bed, kneed her
thighs farther apart, and levered himself over her.
"Ready?"

"Are you serious? I am overready."

"Good," he said, then mounted her with a
mighty thrust into her female channel, which
caused her traitorous inner muscles to milk him
in welcome. In truth, her body had a choke hold
on him that would not let go.

"Oh. My. God!" he gritted out. "You are killing
me."

"Good," she was the one to say now, but she
was soon at a loss for words as he stretched her
as never before with a penetration so deep she
feared he would break something inside her. Nay,
that was not so, she realized, as her body melted
around his hot staff, easing his way.

"You feel . . ." he gasped, "like heaven."

"And you, as well." She kissed his neck.

"I cannot wait. I cannot." In the throes of his
escalating passion, which ignited hers, as well, he
locked fingers with hers.

She was almost frightened by the intensity of

his feverish arousal, except that his guttural endearments and the tremors rippling over his body were a reflection of her own excitement. They fed off each other.

When his thrusts became short and rough, when he reared his neck back, and let loose with an exultant shout of triumph, she realized that he was still inside her, and his hot seed was hitting the wall of her womb. With a loud roaring in her ears, desire and love . . . yea, love, damn his eyes . . . filled her to overflowing, and she cried out her peaking.

For a long time afterward, she lay in his arms, enveloped by a dreamy afterglow of satisfaction. Neither of them was capable of speech in the wake of what had been more than an act of sex. Much more. She was shocked by the depth of her feelings for this man and knew she had to keep her emotions to herself, lest she scare him off for the short time they had left together.

"You are amazing," he said finally. "*We* were amazing." His hands were caressing her back, brushing wisps of hair off her face, giving her feathery kisses on her chin and shoulders.

"You make me feel beautiful and prized." She took his hand and kissed the palm.

"You *are* beautiful, and any man would prize you."

She could argue with that, based on her past experience, but she wanted to maintain the harmony that enveloped them at the moment. She cleared her throat. "I want to say something."

"Uh-oh. Sounds serious."

"It is. To me. I just want you to know that when

this . . . this . . ." she waved a hand to indicate the two of them in bed ". . . is over, I will be thankful."

He cocked his head to the side. "Why?"

"Because you have shown me that lovemaking, or bedplay, or whatever you call it, can be a wondrous thing. This has to be the way that God . . . or the gods . . . intended it to be."

"There are priests who would disagree with that sentiment."

"They are biased, then. What I am trying to say, and obviously failing, is that I no longer hate you for forcing me into this bargain."

"Uh-huh," he said hesitantly. "Listen, Breanne, do not make more of this than it is."

"Oh?" The hairs on the back of her neck stood up.

" 'Tis lust and naught else. I would not want you to fancy it up."

"Fancy it up?" *You lout! You foolish, foolish lout! You are going to ruin it all.*

"You know, love and all that other nonsense. Lust is all it is. Wonderful lust and bedplay, for a certainty, but that is all. Some women start dreaming of softer emotions, but you are more sensible than that. Do you understand what I mean?"

Clear as ice. Breanne's heart felt as if it were cracking. "I am beginning to understand."

"Whew! 'Tis a relief. I was afeared you were thinking of extending our . . . our relationship into something more, like marriage." The lout shivered with distaste.

I shiver, too, fool, but for a different reason. Before he had come into the bedchamber tonight, she had been musing over the possibility that she was falling in love with the scoundrel, and hoping he was feeling the same. But not because she expected a marriage proposal. Still, she was insulted that he would equate all they had just shared to mere lust, no more significant than scratching an itch.

Sliding off the bed, she stared down at him for a moment.

"Breanne?" At last he was beginning to wonder whether he had misspoken. "Are you all right?"

"I am just fine," she said, reaching for the honey pot. With the wooden spoon, she poured a huge dollop along the length of his already reburgeoning phallus. Then another. And another.

He smiled, figuring she was amenable to his insulting words.

"And what are you going to do about all this honey?" he asked, beckoning her closer.

I thought you would never ask. "'Tis not what I am going to do about it, but you are." She was already drawing her sleep rail over her head.

"Huh?"

"Lick it off yourself, dolthead. Lust is all you want from me? Fine. But, wonder of wonders, I am all out of lust." *How I wish that were true!*

She had already unlocked the door and was halfway out before he got her message. He jumped off the bed, honey dripping down to the floor. "What about our bargain?"

She looked at him as if he were a halfwit. He was. "I am done with you and your bloody bargain."

"Like hell you are!"

But she was already gone.

CHAPTER FOURTEEN

❧

Hide-and-go-seek, medieval style . . .
Women! Who could figure them out? Their
minds were like mazes designed to confuse the
average man.

It was after midnight. Where could she have
disappeared to? And why, for God's sake? All he
had done was spell out exactly what they both
knew already.

After she had slammed the bedchamber door
on him, he had pulled on a pair of breeches and
rushed after her. But she had not gone to her bedchamber. Nor to the kitchens or even out on the
ramparts. Well, he was done chasing her. When
she had settled down and become biddable, he
would talk some sense into her.

For now, he had to do something about all
that honey still covering his cock and seeping through the wool of his breeches. He was
standing in front of the washstand, using a cloth
dipped in the cold water from the pitcher and
bowl. And wasn't that a shock to his overheated
enthusiasm?

There was a soft knock on the door.

"Come in," he said, relieved that she had come back, despite his rancor over her behavior.

But it was not Breanne. It was Geoff.

"What are you doing here?"

"Greetings to you, too, Caedmon."

"What are you doing here this time of night? What has happened?"

"We just got word at Heatherby that Dunstan and his entourage are overnighting at St. George's monastery and will arrive in the morn."

"Arrive where? Heatherby? Or Larkspur? *Bloody damn hell! What next?*

Geoff shrugged. "Methinks he will visit both Larkspur *and* Heatherby, but I am not sure which will come first."

"How many in his company?"

"Two dozen, more or less."

"That is all I need." He was scrubbing at his genitals with vigor.

"What in the name of St. Cuthbert are you doing?"

"Washing the honey off my cock." He winced at the coldness of the water.

"Dare I ask why you have honey on your cock?"

"You may ask, but I will not answer."

"If you are able to lick your own cock, I am going to be very upset."

"Why?"

"Because I always wanted to do that."

Caedmon laughed, despite the seriousness of the impending situation.

Geoff sat down on the edge of the bed, then

immediately shot back up. Wiping a hand across his arse, he said, "There is honey on your bed linens."

As if he did not already know that!

"I saw Lady Breanne on my way up here."

I hope you tripped her. "Oh? What is she doing up at this time of night? Building a new Roman wall?"

"Going to the bathing house. Come to think on it, she smelled like honey, too." Geoff glanced from Caedmon's honey-coated cock to the bed, then back to Caedmon's heated face. "Please tell me you have not been swiving a princess."

Only about twenty times. "And if I was?"

"That, my friend, is a sure path to matrimony."

"Not with us. We have an agreement." *Or we HAD an agreement.*

Geoff arched his brows.

He declined to answer. Finally clean, he tossed the rag in the bowl of dirty water and pulled up his breeches. "Let us go find some ale."

Geoff nodded. "Ale would be welcome, but I must needs return tonight. I just wanted you to have fair warning. Be prepared."

Once they were seated at the back of his great hall, where most everyone was asleep on benches and in bed closets, he turned to his friend, "How are the two princesses doing?"

Geoff rolled his eyes. "They have become great friends with Sybil, and the three of them are turning the estate upside down in plans for the marriage ceremony and feast."

"I have not heard from Wulf. Have you?"

Geoff shook his head. "But then, I did not expect to. You know how Wulf is when on a mission."

"I can only assume that no news is good news. Are you not fearful that Dunstan may put a stop to your wedding?"

"We held a handfast ritual as a safeguard, and, of course, consummated the union." He grinned at him to show it had been a satisfying consummation. "But just in case, I should be there when they arrive."

The first thing Caedmon did after seeing Geoff off, promising he would come for his wedding, was to wake Henry. "Take fifty of the hirdsmen and patrol the northern borders. In fact, erect some temporary quarters for them there. And do not return until you have word from me that it is safe."

Henry did not need to be told that Dunstan would take one look at the hundred and twenty-five and more soldiers residing here and force a goodly number of them to return with him to Winchester to join the royal troops.

"I will be out shortly to see them off."

Henry scurried off. He might be old, but he knew what to do in an emergency, without any fuss and bother.

Gerard must have been alerted by the sudden activity and was pulling up his breeches as Caedmon approached. "What is amiss, m'lord?"

Caedmon explained briefly and said, "We will need to make provision for sleeping quarters for the archbishop and of any nobility traveling with them, in the event they stay overnight, God forbid! Henry will take care of the guardsmen who accompany him. Make sure there are clean bed linens. *Including mine.*

"Also, check to see what shape the chapel is in. I will send out huntsmen for more game, and fishermen for fresh fish."

"What about the children?"

Caedmon pondered the problem of ten children, mostly illegitimate, running about under the priest's judgmental nose. "Lady Breanne will take care of them."

Gerard raised his bushy eyebrows.

"I will leave it to you to make that chore known to her. Mayhap you could teach her that whistling trick."

After that, Caedmon went searching for Amicia. Finally, he found her in one of the bed closets with Dafydd, the Welsh stable hand. It was a sight he would not want to see ever again. Amicia was as tall as he was, and some might say just as muscular. Dafydd came about chest high on both of them and gave proof that the size of the boot had naught to do with the size of the cock, by huffing and puffing like a stallion as he plowed a squealing Amicia good and well.

Caedmon turned his back until they were done. Then he told Amicia, "Come. You have much work to do. Archbishop Dunstan and his group are on their way."

With no embarrassment at all, Amicia stood and adjusted her gown. Dafydd was splatted out on his back, already half asleep.

Caedmon nudged him with his boot.

"Wh-what?" Dafydd sat up.

"Two dozen of the king's men, including Archbishop Dunstan, will be here on the morrow. Make sure there is enough feed in the stables and that the stalls are mucked out."

Grumbling something about bothersome holy men, Dafydd rose and tugged up his breeches, which had been bunched at his ankles. Before he stomped off, he gave Amicia a lustsome wink.

Now that she had tasted Dafydd's "charms," Amicia seemed to be uninterested in the stable hand, and so she ignored his wink. "Dunstan? Fer goodness sake! I need to go find a few of the kitchen maids so we kin get started on the bread making. The monks and their minions are allus picky about their bread bein' fresh."

Caedmon nodded, and while they walked side by side, he told her that fish and game would be forthcoming, hopefully by noon.

And not to worry about making the meals fancy, as Ingrith had been teaching her. "We do not want them to get too comfortable here with fine fare and soft beds."

"So I should put out some of that maggoty venison that has been in the scullery since God was a child."

And end up in a pillory. "I would not go that far." She grinned at him.

"I mean it, Amicia. Toss out the bad meat."

"No one ever lets me have fun."

"Seems to me you were having plenty of fun a short time ago."

She smirked. "Yea, I was. Everyone knows that Dafydd has a manroot the size of a cucumber."

Everyone except me! He choked as air went down the wrong throat passage. Way too much detail!

By the time he had everything set in motion that he could in preparation for Dunstan's visit, Caedmon decided he would try to get some sleep, even if it was only a few hours until dawn.

But then he remembered some unfinished business. Red-haired witchy business.

First he checked his bedchamber. Empty, as he had expected. Then hers. Also empty. But wait, a pillow and some bed linens were missing. He stood in the corridor, tapping his thinned lips thoughtfully. Where would she go to sleep where she thought he would never find her?

"Aha!"

A short time later, opening the chapel door quietly, he saw her lying on a bench, the linen cloth wrapped around her like a shroud, her hands folded together under her cheek, as if in prayer. He was going to give her plenty cause to pray.

Without warning, he went up to her, lifted her high, then tossed her over his shoulder. With her squawking like a chicken facing the cook's axe, he walked through the hall and up the stairs to his bedchamber. Tossing her on the bed, which still had honey on it—on the side where she would be sleeping, not he—Caedmon walked over to the door and locked it, pocketing the key.

She had a full-blown screaming tantrum while he removed his garments, and she tried to escape her shroud. The more she squirmed, the more she tangled the sheet.

"This is not funny." She glared at him.

"I beg to differ."

"And put some clothes on. You are not sticking that thing in me again."

He glanced downward and saw that he was, in fact, aroused. Nothing new in that. He was always at the ready around her.

"I will stick this *thing* in you again, if I want to, but methinks I will wait until you beg me this time."

"When pigs dance!"

"I went to a fair one time where they had a dancing pig."

She had managed to get out of the linen and was adjusting her bed rail, which was by now half off one shoulder.

He walked over, grabbed the neckline and yanked until it was torn right down the middle.

She gasped. "Why did you do that?"

"Because you annoy me." *And, truth to tell, all your blathering is annoying me, too.*

He crawled up onto his side of the bed, facing away from her, and pulled a linen sheet up over his body to the waist. There was no fire, but it was not overly cold tonight.

"This side of the bed is sticky," she observed.

"I know." *If she keeps on talking, I am going to stick a wad of linen in her mouth . . . or something else. Hmmm.*

"Change sides with me."

Are you barmy? "Nay!"

"Well, if you think I am going to beg, you are more demented than usual." He heard rustling noises and assumed she was laying her bed linen

over the top of the damp spots. She cursed once,
then twice.

What now? "A problem?" he inquired without
turning over to see for himself.

" 'Tis too wet. And sticky." Without glancing her
way, he could tell that she was now standing. "It
seeps through everything." When he said nothing
more, she finally asked, "Where shall I sleep?"

With a long sigh of exasperation, he turned over
and lifted the sheet next to him.

Muttering her disgust, she started to climb up.

"Take off that bed rail afore you strangle yourself."

"If I do, you are not to touch me."

He rolled his eyes. *Right now, the only touching
that appeals is you, naked, over my knees, arse pointed
northward, being paddled with my palm.* Much as that
image appealed, he decided to save it for another
day. "Breanne, Archbishop Dunstan and his cohorts are on their way here. Geoff came to give me
the news. I have spent the last three hours making
arrangements. I need sleep now."

"You lout! Why did you not tell me that to begin
with?"

*Mayhap I was too blistering angry with you. Mayhap
I had more important things on my mind. Mayhap
your wagging tongue put me off.* He shrugged and
bided his time while she worked her way around
the honey spots and under the linen.

He gave her only a second to relax and let her
defenses down. Then he rolled over on top of her.

"You promised not to touch me."

"I did not."

"Well, do not."

He was already working her hair out of its damp braid and adjusting his body so that his cock was right where he wanted it to be. It felt as if there was moisture where his staff was resting, but just to make sure, he tested her female channel with a finger. "You are wet for me," he hooted out with a joyous laugh, holding said finger up for her to see.

"Nay, I am not. 'Tis just dampness from my bath."

"You took your bath hours ago."

"How do you know that?"

"My spies told me." He put his finger into his mouth to taste, then declared, with deliberate irksome glee, "Woman dew. Wet for me."

"That is the most disgusting thing I have ever seen."

"Really? When I think of disgusting, I think of . . ." He told her about a form of bedplay that was, in fact, more disgusting.

She clicked her jaw shut when she realized she was gaping. "You said you needed to sleep."

"I do, and the best way to insure a good sleep is to tup first." Before she had a chance to protest, he lifted her hips and plunged inside.

He had not intended to do that. Really, he had not. He was just going to tease her. *So, now what do I do?* "Shall I stop?" *Oh, please, say nay. Be amenable for once.* He rubbed his chest hairs across her nipples. Just once.

"Do not dare."

He smiled, but then he recalled something.

With a grunt for his self-inflicted pain, he withdrew from her.

"What are you doing?" She tried to pull him back by tugging on his buttocks, but he remained rigid outside her body.

"I recalled that I told you just moments ago that I would not swive you again until you begged. Are you ready to beg?"

"Hah!"

Betimes drawing a battle line was not a good decision. He was having second thoughts, but his pride would not allow him to give in. Putting his back to her, he said, "Sleep well, m'lady witch."

"You cannot fool me," she said, smacking him on the back. "You will not be able to rest, now that you are aroused, until you are sated."

"I can always pleasure myself . . . unless you are ready to beg."

"Not a chance!" Then, "How dost one pleasure oneself?"

He began to laugh and could not stop, even when she battered his shoulders with her small fists.

"If you will not tell me, I will ask Amicia."

"Good. Perchance you will then give me a demonstration later."

"How would I . . . I mean . . . never mind."

Amazingly, he did fall asleep, only to awaken near dawn with a sleeping princess snuggled up against his back . . . her knees behind his knees, her mons behind his buttocks, her breasts against his back. She would hate herself for crossing the line.

If he were chivalrous, he would slip out of bed and let her sleep, unaware of how, even in sleep, she sought his body. That is what he should do, but, never having been chivalrous to any great extent, he instead put a hand over her hand which was cradling his ballocks and spoke over his shoulder.

"Ooooooh, Bre-aaaaanne!"

He was not entirely loathsome . . .

Breanne was impressed.

Just as she had come to the conclusion that Caedmon was a stubborn, lackwitted, lazy, loathsome troll of a man, albeit an accomplished lover, she got to see him in a new light. From the instant he had embarrassed her in bed by proving that she had been the one who could not keep her hands off of him, he had changed before her eyes. He was now an efficient, in-control, no-nonsense master of Larkspur, a warrior at heart.

He had Hugh at his side everywhere he went, whilst Breanne took charge of the other children, gladly, especially since there was an air of fear about the place. Archbishop Dunstan was a powerful man, some said even more influential than the king. If he was not pleased, Larkspur could suffer. And Breanne could not help but feel she and her sisters were responsible for this dire situation.

She had the children looking clean and well groomed after a battle at the bathing house early this morn. The three terrors . . . Kendrick, Oslac, and Joanna . . . were particularly difficult. You would think she had asked them to peel off a layer of skin, when all she had insisted on was a good scrubbing.

Putting two fingers in her mouth, she let loose with a most unfeminine whistle, and, amazingly, the children all lined up in order of height. It was a trick Gerard had taught her. Unfortunately, she had not yet mastered the trick of keeping them in place, and they soon began to scatter.

"Wait!" she shouted.

In an attempt to evade Dunstan's scrutiny, she was about to lead them all on an "adventure" outside the castle grounds, down by the river. But first she stopped in the kitchen to put bread, cheese, oat cakes, and apples in a leather bag. Amicia and her helpers were all in a tizzy, dressing the deer one of the hunters had brought in, along with two ducks and a brace of rabbits. Another man handed the cook a string of fish.

"I could use yer sister now," Amicia remarked to Breanne.

"I would offer to help, but Caedmon asked me to take care of the children. Make them presentable. Keep them out of the way."

Amicia nodded. "Wish we could all go hide fer a sennight or so. I hear the God-man hates wimmen."

On that happy note, Breanne went through the open corridor to the great hall, where her group awaited her. Her heart swelled seeing how nice they looked with their grubby faces washed and their hair slicked down. Every one of them, except Piers, was scowling with discomfort at the new garments they had been forced to wear.

"No grumpiness today," she said cheerily. "We are going to have a good time."

Kendrick said something that sounded like "Bugger good times."

"I wanna go swimming," Joanna demanded. "And catch some frogs and roast the legs. Yum!"

Yecch!

"Las' time, ye made the fire too big, and Gerard whopped yer bottom," Angus said gleefully. "Ye could not sit down fer a whole day."

Joanna stuck her tongue out at Angus.

Piers was hunkered down on his little haunches watching a spider. She took his hand quickly before he decided to put the creature in his mouth.

Oslac broke wind apurpose, just to show her who was really in charge.

Beth and Mina blushed with mortification. If they could disown their brothers, they surely would.

Alfred and Aidan were making buzzing noises. Apparently rumors were rife this morn about honey and swiving, as evidenced by sticky bed linens. Not that the twins knew what swiving was, but they clearly understood it was a forbidden subject, and therefore of interest.

With a whooshy exhale of disgust, she led the little varmints out to the upper bailey, not unlike a goose with its goslings, then stopped dead in her tracks. It was too late. Archbishop Dunstan and his entourage had already arrived. With the outer door shut behind them, she pressed up against the castle wall with the children and, using hand signals, tried to sidle away. Unfortunately, one of

Dunstan's soldiers was eyeing them suspiciously. As if a woman and nine children could do them harm!

Caedmon, Henry, and some of the higher-ranking hirdsmen were bowing from the waist at Archbishop Dunstan as he dismounted. The horses were being led off to the stables. She had to admit, Caedmon looked godly handsome in a blue tunic with a gold link belt over black breeches tucked into knee-high polished boots. His dark hair had been trimmed and combed off his face.

"Welcome to Larkspur, Your Grace," Caedmon said, leaning forward to kiss the priest's ring.

I am not noticing the pull of fabric over his firm buttocks. Really. I am surely not that wanton. Well, mayhap a wee bit wanton. Aaarrgh!

The archbishop made the sign of the cross with two raised fingers over Caedmon. "May the Lord bless and keep you."

Bless all of us, Lord. We are in deep trouble here.

The white-haired and white-bearded Dunstan had to be in his fifties. He was dressed in a simple cowled robe, but the fabric was of softest wool with an under-robe, or vestment, of finest Irish lace, peeking out at the wrists and neck and ankles, and the rope belt was threaded with strands of silver. A large gold crucifix hung from a heavy chain around his neck, and on his fingers were several rings.

A monk in tonsured haircut and coarser robe carried the elaborate, pointed headdress known as a mitre, which would be worn during official duties. Yet another priest placed a jewel-encrusted

crosier in the archbishop's right hand, the crooked
shepherd-like staff being a symbol of his office.

The stern-faced archbishop's eyes darted here
and there, taking everything in. No doubt he
would be able to report back to the king the exact
condition of the keep right down to the number of
soldiers and sheep for shearing. She could swear
his rheumy eyes went wide on noticing the twining larkspur carvings she had made in the eaves
of the pigsty. He probably thought they were some
pagan symbols.

"Wouldst like to break your fast, Your Eminence?" Caedmon inquired. "I have set my cook
to prepare a meal for you."

Dunstan shook his head. "First we will say Mass
in thanksgiving for our safe journey through this
primitive land."

Breanne could only be thankful that Caedmon
had the foresight to set the housemaids to cleaning the small chapel this morn.

"The bathhouse is ready, if need be, and a private bedchamber for you," Caedmon added.

Once again, Dunstan shook his head. "Mass
first."

No thanks for Caedmon's thoughtfulness, just
a judgmental haughtiness, as if any consideration
was his due.

They were all walking up the step to the double
doors leading into the great hall when the archbishop noticed her and the children, still propping up the wall. The children had the good sense
not to misbehave, for once. "*Who* are they?" he demanded of Caedmon.

Caedmon did not even look her way. The grimness of his expression was telling to Breanne. He knew he was walking a fine line here. One misstep and he could lose all. "Those are my children," he said, "along with Hugh here, my oldest." He put a hand on Hugh's shoulder.

"And the woman?" It was clear as a bell the disdain Dunstan held for women. His eagle eyes took her measure from head to toe. "Those fine garments are not of a housemaid."

"This is Breanne of Stoneheim, daughter of King Thorvald."

She bowed to the archbishop but, not sure of the protocol, did not dare try to kiss his ring.

"Stoneheim?"

"In the Norselands," Caedmon elaborated, with obvious reluctance.

"A heathen Viking!" Dunstan's nostrils flared with outrage. If she were closer, he might have tried to smite her with his staff.

"I believe she has been baptized," Caedmon said before she could speak up and probably say something objectionable. He frowned at her in warning not to disagree with what he had said. What he did not know was that her father and all her sisters practiced both the Norse and Christian religions.

Something seemed to occur to Dunstan then. "Are you sister to Lady Havenshire?"

Oh, gods! Here it comes! "Yea, I am."

"Is she here?" His eagle eyes scanned the surroundings.

Breanne shook her head.

"Where is she?"

She shrugged. "Back in the Norselands, I believe."

Dunstan pointed a bony finger at her and said, "I will speak to you after Mass, and you will tell me the truth, or suffer the consequences. Do you understand me, wench?"

How could she not understand him? He was practically spitting his displeasure.

Caedmon hung back as the group went inside toward the chapel, which could be entered both from the inside of the keep, or through an exterior door. "You did well," he told her in an undertone.

"You jest. I did terribly. My voice shook, and my eyes probably belied my lack of honesty."

"I will make sure to be with you any time you speak with the archbishop," he promised. "Do not fear. This will soon be over, and we can resume our bargain."

"Whaaat?" she screeched. "How can you think of that at a time like this?"

"Breanne, Breanne, Breanne! I think of *that* all the time."

To emphasize his words, the rogue cupped her buttock and squeezed before anyone could notice.

Except for his children, who began to make bzzzzing noises.

CHAPTER FIFTEEN

✥

When dumb men hear dum-dum-dee-dum . . .

It was late afternoon and the archbishop could be put off no longer. He wanted to speak with Breanne. Now!

Caedmon had to give Breanne credit. She had managed to make herself and the children nigh invisible. It could have been disastrous if he had had to cope with the antics of the bratlings along with the verbal traps set by Dunstan.

And there were traps aplenty, he had soon learned, when Dunstan revealed the primary reason for his visit. Despite his being joined at the hip with King Edgar and way too involved for a priest in the cesspit of royal politics, the archbishop was in the midst of a monastic revival in Britain, building churches, abbeys, and monasteries hither and yon. Probably trying to earn points with God toward sainthood when he died. In fact, he wanted to build a bloody damn monastery on Larkspur lands, as if Caedmon had land to spare. And even if he were willing to part with his Odal rights to a portion of Larkspur, that would not be the end of it. Next, workers would be required to

help build the monastery. Then cattle and sheep
for subsistence. Guardsmen to protect the clergy
from raiders. Then the monks would be baptizing
every living body in sight and demanding dona-
tions in God's name. Worst of all, having Dunstan
or his minions so close would mean that Caedmon would have the church and King Edgar's
spies constantly looking over his shoulder.

He took Hugh with him in his search for Breanne. They finally found her down by the river,
sitting on a blanket where food had been spread
out. Piers was asleep beside her, his little buttocks
up in her air, one of his thumbs in his mouth.
Joanna and Kendrick were in the water, swimming, whilst all the others were playing some
kind of run-and-hide game. Mina was the first to
see him, and she made a running leap. He caught
her up in his arms and kissed the top of her head
where the hair was still damp, no doubt from her
swimming, too. Beth was next. She wrapped her
arms around his waist and rested her face against
his abdomen. Aidan and Alfred had death holds
on his thigh, on the other side.

Breanne looked up, then looked again. She
appeared amazed at the affection his children
showed toward him, or was it perchance his own
affection toward them that caused her astonishment? The expression on her face soon turned to
wariness, but was probably because of the way
he had embarrassed her in bed this morn. *By the
saints! Was it only this morn that she shared my bed?
It feels like a lifetime ago.*

"You are summoned," he said, disengaging

himself from his children's clutches. Holding out a hand, he pulled her to her feet.

"Archbishop Dunstan?"

"One and the same. He wants to talk with you. Immediately."

She shivered, but then straightened herself as if gathering courage. "So be it."

"I will stay with you, regardless of what he says."

"What he says?" she repeated.

"He will no doubt try to question you separately from anyone else, in order to trick you."

She moaned.

"Hugh, you will stay with the children. When it is time to return to the castle, go through the scullery. Whatever you do"—he was speaking to all the children now—"you are to stay out of sight and do not speak, other than answering yea or nay. Do you understand? This is important."

One by one, they all nodded.

Walking back across the grassy field studded with fragrant larkspur, he put a hand to her waist, tugging her to his side. It was a sign of her nervousness that she did not swat him away. In fact, she looped her arm around his waist, as well.

Trying to distract her, he remarked, "Didst know that when you touch me, I tingle?" *And grow hard as a pike.*

Instead of laughing, she said, "Me, too."

"Huh?"

"I may not like you much, but there is no denying your sizzling charms."

"Sizzling charms? I like that."

She did swat him then on the chest with her free hand. "How are things going with Dunstan?"

"Precarious?"

She tilted her head to look up at him. "How so?"

"He wants a portion of Larkspur land to build a monastery."

"Uh-oh!"

"You got that right. Mine is not a big estate, and the last thing I need is a horde of monks nearby, watching my every move."

"Will he take the land, regardless of your wishes?"

"Probably not. I am trying to convince him that the southern border of Larkspur, which is mostly moors, is not conducive to farming or raising cattle or grape growing for wine, which are the usual sources of income for the churchmen. Besides, I warned them of Scottish reivers who covet aught of Saxon ownership and of Vikings who consider the golden chalices and silver plate of the clergy fair game."

"I am scared."

"For whom? Me or yourself?"

"Both."

He squeezed her closer. "Naught will happen to you whilst under my shield. That I promise."

"And yourself?"

"I have been playing these cat-and-mouse games with King Edgar and his cohorts for years, and King Edwy afore him. I will not let them take what is mine."

They were back at the keep now, and he had

managed to distract her with their conversation, but he could feel the tremors of fear in her brave body.

"How do I look?" she asked.

She had plaited her hair, then formed the braids into an intricate coronet atop her head, no doubt to soften the wildness of her red hair. The pale skin of her face was rather golden today from the sun, which caused a few more freckles to emerge. Instead of the Saxon attire she usually wore— *and thank God she was not wearing breeches*—she had donned a belted Viking undergown of pure white linen, covered by an open-sided green calf-length apron, embroidered on the edges and held together at both shoulders with brooches of gold in the pattern of writhing dragons.

"You look just fine. Wonderful."

Breanne knew that she should not let his compliments go to her head, but pitiful as she was, she did just that. "You do not need to go that far, scoundrel." She flashed him a shaky smile, then squirmed out of his embrace and walked ahead of him to the open door of the solar, which was empty, except for Archbishop Dunstan and Father Edward, who would be staying at Larkspur as chaplain and tutor for the children.

Dunstan was sitting in an armed chair, his head bowed as if in prayer. Father Edward was doing likewise, telling his beads with a soft murmur from his seat on a bench near the window.

"Your Grace?" Caedmon said.

The archbishop's head shot up, his eyes alert. He put up a halting hand when they started to enter the room. Staring at Breanne, he asked, "Are you in the midst of your monthly courses?"

She gasped. It was the last thing she had expected from him. From any man, actually. "Wh-what?"

"You heard me. I will not be in the same room with a woman having the bloody flux. 'Tis unclean. A mark of Eve's sin on all women."

Flustered by the outrageousness of Dunstan's observation, Breanne replied, "I am not unclean." Her hands fisted as she was scarce able to restrain her temper.

"Sit then." Dunstan motioned to the two other chairs in the room. "You do not need to stay, Caedmon."

Oh, nay! I cannot handle the archbishop alone.

"I stay," Caedmon insisted.

Thank you, gods. She shot Caedmon a glance of thanks, but he ignored her.

It was clear that the archbishop did not like Caedmon's tone, but he finally agreed with a nod of his head.

One hurdle handled.

"You are daughter to King Thorvald of Stoneheim. A princess."

She hesitated, then said, "I am, but I do not use the title."

"You and your sisters, including Lady Vana, were at Havenshire when the earl went missing."

So, he knows more than we expected. "We were."

"Dost know where the earl is?"

Under a pile of . . . nay, I cannot even think of that. "I do not."

"Did you kill him? You or your sisters?"

Bloody hell! I must needs tell one lie after another, and I am no expert at lying. "What? You wound with me your words, Your Grace. You have no reason to say that to me."

"The man has disappeared off the face of the earth. What else can I think?"

Who asked you to think? "Mayhap he is with his mistress."

"He is not."

He does not seem at all perturbed that Oswald had a mistress. How typical of a man! And a priest, at that!

"She believes your sister is responsible for his disappearance."

"She would, would she not? To divert attention from herself." *By thunder, how much longer will the questioning go on? He is sure to catch me in my web of lies if I am not careful.* She could not help herself then. "You do know that Oswald was a vicious, cruel man who beat my sister?"

Dunstan waved a hand dismissively. "She no doubt deserved disciplining."

Breanne was about to launch herself at the misogynistic, poor excuse for a priest, but Caedmon put a hand on her forearm and spoke first. "You have to know, Your Grace, that Lady Havenshire is a small woman in stature and strength. How would she have been able to kill and then hide such a big man as Oswald . . . if he is in fact dead?"

"With help," Dunstan replied, staring at Breanne accusingly, as if his stare would cause her to reveal all.

I have been stared down by better than you, priest. My father, for example, has guilt staring down to an art. "If you are accusing me and my sisters of some conspiracy to kill the earl of Havenshire, you are wrong."

"Why did you leave?" The archbishop's questions pelted her like little stones.

"My sister . . . Vana . . . was in such distress, grieving over the loss of her husband, that we felt she needed a change of scenery."

Dunstan arched an eyebrow. "A husband whom you claim abused her?"

Breanne shrugged. "Some women love men who are not good for them." *Where did that load of nonsense come from?*

"Why Larkspur? Why not some place closer?" Dunstan narrowed his eyes at her.

He is suspicious. "Caedmon is kin to my sister Tyra's husband. We decided to visit."

"You came all the way from Havenshire to Larkspur . . . *for a visit*?"

"Yea, we did. And Caedmon has been generous in offering us hospitality." *Believe that and I have a fjord I can sell you in Trondheim.*

"Where are your sisters now? Where is Lady Havenshire?"

"Two of my sisters have gone to nearby Heatherby to help prepare a wedding. And Vana has returned to Stoneheim."

"What wedding?" Dunstan's stiffened posture in the chair bespoke the fury to come.

"My friend Geoffrey Fitzwilliam is to marry Lady Sybil of Heatherby, Lord Moreton's widow,"

Caedmon interjected. "I was under the impression you had come this far north to officiate."

"Never! I was told that Lady Moreton would marry the king's choice in due time after her period of mourning. This is a disgrace. Her husband is scarce cold in the ground."

"Well, I am sure you will be able to settle the matter once you go there." Caedmon paused. "When might that be?"

"Not until I settle matters here first," he said icily. "Back to you, m'lady. What are you doing here alone in a keep full of men?"

"Uh . . ."

"She has a chaperon," Caedmon inserted quickly.

I do?

"And who might that be?"

Caedmon's face turned red. She could tell he was stumped for what to say. But never did she expect him to say what he did. "Lady Amicia."

Breanne barely stifled a snort of disbelief.

"Why have I not seen her?"

"A megrim," Breanne told him. *Good Lord! We are telling one lie after another here. To a holy priest, at that.* "Her head was aching; so I told her to lie down and rest."

"You will present her at dinner this evening."

By the stars, how will we ever manage that?

"Of course," Caedmon agreed.

"And, by the by, Caedmon, you will seat no women above the salt whilst I am here. Too many men are lax in putting their women above themselves."

"That is what I always say, Your Grace. Keep women in their place."

She was going to throttle Caedmon when they left this room.

"Now, m'lady, I will have the truth from you. Why are you here at Larkspur? And no more lies."

There was a long pause before Caedmon raised a hand for permission to speak for her.

"The princess Breanne is too shy to disclose the real reason why she is here." He cast her a false smile of besottedness, before telling the archbishop, "We are betrothed."

Breanne blinked several times and clicked her gaping jaw shut. *Whaaaaat?*

"Do you not think it would have been wiser to get the king's permission first?"

"We are in love," Caedmon said, batting his eyelashes at her like a cow-eyed youthling.

"Pfff!" was the archbishop's opinion of love. He turned to Breanne then. "Do you have a dowry?"

She nodded hesitantly.

"How much?"

She really resented this invasion of her privacy, but felt compelled to answer, naming the generous sum her father had settled on each of his daughters.

Caedmon turned slowly to look at her in astonishment, while Dunstan was practically wringing his hands with anticipation at the cut he and the king might gain as their portion. She had told Caedmon before; he must have forgotten.

After that, things went downhill faster than a

snowball in a Norse avalanche, ending with the archbishop saying, "I will bless your betrothal this evening, my children."

With this ring, I thee tup . . .

"Have you lost your bloody mind?" Breanne hissed at him as soon as they left the solar.

"Shhhh!" he said and put a fingertip to her mouth to indicate silence until they put distance betwixt themselves and Dunstan.

She attempted to bite his finger.

He was almost certain it was not a love bite.

"Have a caution, wench. I am in no mood for your antics today."

"*My* antics?"

He nigh dragged her along with him through the keep and up the stairs to his bedchamber, where they would not be overheard. Along the way, he nodded to various housecarls of his and members of the archbishop's retinue, as if his yanking on a reluctant woman was usual fare at Larkspur. They probably thought he was going to beat her. Shoving her inside his room, he closed and locked the door.

Dazed, she glanced around. "Why did you bring me here? Oh, you randy goat! If you think I am going to—"

"Hush, Breanne! I brought you here for privacy, and naught else." *Although now you mention it, mayhap there would be time for a bit of bedplay.*

"Lady Amicia? A betrothal? How could you, Caedmon?"

"I had to think quick, and that was the best I

could come up with. Dost think I have any desire to be married again? I would sooner cut off a limb."

"Dumb, dumb, dumb."

"At least I tried. What did you offer, except a bit of stuttering?"

"I do not stutter."

"Stutter, stutter, stutter."

"How immature of you!"

"Listen, we are accomplishing naught with this bickering. We need to decide what to do next."

She inhaled and exhaled several times, then sat on the edge of the bed.

He sank down into a chair, close by.

"I will do my best to make Amicia into a lady," she said.

He had to grin. He just had to.

"'Tis not funny."

"I beg to differ. You must needs find a gown long enough to fit her and with wide enough shoulders, but beyond that, who will shave her mustache?"

"Tsk-tsk!" she clucked, trying to hide the smile that was tugging at her lips. "Amicia has a slight fuzz above her lip, but not enough to be called a mustache."

That was debatable. "We cannot let her speak. If Dunstan insults her the way he does all women, Amicia is likely to tell him to go bugger himself."

"I will tell her to pretend that she is folk-shy."

They both rolled their eyes at that.

"Why in the name of all the gods did you tell him we were betrothed?"

"Hah! You could show a little appreciation. Dunstan's questions were leading in a direction that could very well have ended with you being dragged naked behind a cart with your head shaved. The mark of an adulterous woman."

"How about an adulterous man?"

"No such thing."

Her face went deathly white. "He would not."

Caedmon shrugged. "I have seen worse done by God-men in the name of the church. And Dunstan is a power unto himself."

"Besides, neither of us is married. So adultery does not come into the picture."

He waved a hand dismissively. "You are naive if you think that matters." He went on to tell her stories of things he had witnessed done by churchmen, including the skin of a man tacked to a church door, not to mention all the depravities the king himself had performed.

"I had no idea." Her shoulders drooped.

"You are not to worry, Breanne." He got up and went to sit beside her on the bed. Putting an arm over her shoulder, he tucked her into his side and kissed the top of her head. "I will protect you."

She sniffled, then straightened. "If we work together, mayhap we can survive this mire of quicksand."

He smiled. "That is the spirit. Now, first off, I think you should wear my ring." He tugged the signet ring off his middle finger and pushed it onto her right hand. "Nay, do not protest. 'Tis the first of my *arrha* gifts for you. If we were really getting married, you would move the ring to your left hand during the ceremony, signifying that you will be obedient to your new husband."

"Never!"

"I am just saying." He smirked at her.

The lout! She adjusted it on her finger, then made a fist to ensure it did not fall off. "I like it," she said, staring up at him through lashes that sparkled with tears, like burnished copper.

His heart swelled for some odd reason. "It is too big," he said gruffly.

"I will fix it with yarn."

"Once Dunstan leaves, we can dissolve the betrothal," he pointed out. "So do not worry in that regard."

"Seems to me that we are spinning so many lies we are bound to be caught."

"Too bad Rashid is not here. He would no doubt have a wisdom parable to suit."

She laughed and swiped at her damp eyes. "Definitely, and it would involve camels."

"Dost think we should seal our betrothal?" he asked then.

"With a kiss?"

"Nay. I was thinking more in the line of a swiving." *Or two.*

"That is all I would need . . . to be discovered by the archbishop in the midst of fornication. Not that I am interested."

"Your nose twitches when you tell a lie."

"It does not." She put a hand over her nose to make sure.

"I could make you be interested."

"I doubt that. I have built up a resistance to your tempting charms."

I have tempting charms? I had no idea. "Did I ever tell you about the time I spent in the Arab lands?"

"You pop from one subject to another like fleas on a white dog."

" 'Tis the same subject. Whilst there, in Baghdad, I learned the most amazing things about sex."

She examined her fingernails, pretending disinterest. But she was interested, all right. Bloody hell, *he* was interested, too, because he sure as spit did not know what he was going to say next. But then, an idea came to him, unbidden. *Ask me, little mouse. This cat sitting next to you is in the mood for a juicy mouse stew.*

"What amazing things?"

Meow! "There is one particular position, a favorite of mine, truth to tell, where the female ends up peaking over and over and over. So well-pleasured is she that her bones nigh melt."

"What position? Seems to me we have tried them all."

"Oh, nay, how can you say that? There are dozens and dozens, mayhap hundreds of positions to try yet."

"I do not believe you."

"You wound me." He pretended great affront. "Name one."

"How about the 'Butterfly,' or 'Row the Boat.' "

Her eyes widened and her cheeks flushed. "Do

you stay up all night dreaming these outrageous tales?"

"You may laugh, but did you know there is a famous book written a thousand years ago that explains many, many ways to make love, illustrated with drawings. 'Tis called the *Kamasutram*."

"You surely jest."

He shook his head. "Well, the only way to prove it is to demonstrate." He batted his eyelashes at her.

She stared at him for a long moment, clearly tempted. Then she stood and shook her head, laughing. "You are incredible."

"Thank you."

" 'Twas not a compliment."

CHAPTER SIXTEEN

❦

I can do WHAT with a candle? . . .

"Does my rump look too big?"

Breanne rolled her eyes at Amicia's question. *Like the back end of a cow.* "It looks just fine. Stop worrying."

It had taken several hours and ten ells of fabric to turn Amicia into anything remotely resembling a noble lady. In truth, she looked like a big blue tent.

"I was noted fer my rump at one time."

Too much information! Breanne started to laugh, then choked on air going down the wrong way. Amicia clapped her on the back so hard she launched into a new round of choking. When her breathing returned to normal, she said, "Nay, I did not know that."

"That was afore it dropped and spread."

Sweet Valkyries!

"A sad thing, really, 'cause men do like buttocks what are high and curved jist right. I usta be able ta twitch me nether cheeks, one at a time. My man at the time loved it."

I cannot believe I am having a conversation about women's back ends.

"How is yers?"

I thought my sisters were blunt, but this conversation passes all bounds of woman talk. "Since I have no way of seeing back there, it would be impossible for me to have an opinion."

"Hah! If ya have a good arse, yer man will tell ya so, believe you me. Arses are right up there with jiggly bosoms when it comes ta men and their appetites."

"Since I have no man, it is a moot question." *Now, please, can we end this kind of talk?*

"If ye say so. What you two been doin' up there in the master's bedchamber with the door locked? Dancin'?"

Breanne's face heated. "Just because I might have been a little bit intimate with your master, does not mean he is my man."

"Who ya tryin' ta convince? Me or yerself?"

Changing the subject, Breanne asked, "Have you ever heard of the 'Butterfly' or 'Row the Boat?'" Then immediately regretted her question.

"Huh?"

"They are supposedly sexual positions."

"Oh, that! I prob'ly did, but gave it no name. I will tell ya one trick, though. One that drives a man wild in bed."

Do I want a wild man in bed? Breanne waited for Amicia to continue, but she did not. "Tell me," she finally demanded.

With a conspiratorial grin, Amicia told her how to use her inner female muscles—*Who knew I had inner female muscles?*—to clutch and unclutch a

man's member. " 'Tis jist like what ya do when ya
need ta piss but need ta hold it in. Practice and
ya will soon see what I mean. Actually, I heard
that in some of them Eastern harems, the *houris*
. . . thass what they call the whores . . . practice
with little marble wands inside them the size of a
man's middle finger. A candle works jist as well."

*And you would know that about candles . . . how?
Nay, I cannot ask her that because she would probably
tell me, in detail.* "That is the most outrageous tale
I have e'er heard."

"I allus wanted ta be a lady. Mayhap I will be
able ta latch onto some handsome knight and we
will go off and live in his castle."

Oh, my gods! "Uh, I am fairly certain that Lord
Caedmon will be wanting you to return to your
cooking duties once the archbishop is gone."

"Should I curtsy when I meet the old buzzard?"
Amicia proceeded to do the most demented bending of one knee down almost to the floor, which
resulted in her head rail falling off and her almost
toppling over, saved only by Breanne's hold on
her arm.

"Nay, a curtsy will not be necessary," she said,
"and do not refer to him as a buzzard, please."

"Some monks are sodomites, ya know. That
means they likes ta bugger men, not women."

*She bounces from one idea to another like water in
hot grease.* "I doubt there are any more sodomites
in the priesthood than in regular society."

"I rather like that young priest what will be
stayin' here at Larkspur."

"Amicia! You are not to seduce a priest."

Fortunately, or not so fortunately, Caedmon arrived then. To say he was startled by Amicia's appearance would be a vast understatement. To give him credit, he managed to immediately mask his feelings of shock, followed by humor. Instead, he said, "How nice you look, Lady Amicia."

Amicia beamed.

"I will escort you both to dinner. I must warn you, Archbishop Dunstan is not very fond of females."

"See, I told ya. Sodomites," Amicia said to Breanne.

"Whaaaat?" Caedmon looked as if he had swallowed his tongue.

"Nay, nay, nay! Archbishop Dunstan is not a sodomite, Amicia. And you must never repeat that again." *Lest we all end up in a dungeon somewhere . . . or skinned.*

"What I started to say, *Lady* Amicia . . . and, Breanne, you must remember to refer to her in that way . . . is that Archbishop Dunstan has a warped view of religion in which women are to blame for just about everything wrong in the world. As a result, neither of you will be sitting at the high table."

Which is just as well if he is going to insult us, Breanne thought. "As I told you before, Amicia . . . I mean, Lady Amicia . . . you and I should not speak at all, unless a direct question is asked of us."

"Even then, do not volunteer any information," Caedmon cautioned. "Try to appear meek, Amicia."

Breanne snorted at that prospect.

Amicia moved ahead of them then, gleefully enjoying her stroll through the great hall, hips swinging from side to side, as Caedmon's men dropped their jaws, then made lewd remarks.

"Bloody damn hell! I told them that she is to be Lady Amicia tonight and that they were not to pay any particular notice of her when she comes in."

"Hard not to notice the transformation," Breanne replied.

Caedmon nodded, bent his neck to the left, then to the right. "I do not think I have ever seen a female rump that size afore."

Liar, liar, your braies are on fire . . .

Caedmon seated Breanne and Amicia at the trestle table closest to the dais, just below the salt. Instead of being insulted, Breanne looked scared to death, and Amicia was having the time of her life.

He did not know if Dunstan would be offended by having the two women within view of his seat at the high table, but at this point, he just did not care. He was done groveling to satisfy every little whim of the cleric, like his bed remade with special scratchy linens he carried everywhere with him as a sort of self-flagellation, or incense burned in the chapel to purify it from Father Luke's death, or a lamb to be slaughtered and cooked for him, specially, instead of the usual fare. He had even ordered one of Caedmon's irate servants to launder and iron all his garments, including some finely laced vestments, and have them done within three hours.

"Do not be afeared," he told Breanne, placing a comforting hand on her shoulder. *I am afeared enough for both of us.* "Dunstan will leave tomorrow for Heatherby." *Even if I have to push him out the door.*

"I have a bad feeling."

You have no idea. "Do not be looking for trouble. A good soldier knows to take one battle at a time to win a war."

"That sounds like something Rashid would say," she replied with a laugh.

Yea, that is me. A wisdom skald. More like a lackwit skald. He shrugged. "You look pretty tonight."

She cast him a skeptical glance. For some reason, she had ne'er been confident about her beauty. And she *was* beautiful.

Her hair was loose with a fillet of braided gold holding it in place, across her forehead and scalp. The red strands sparkled from the light of the wall torches. She wore a crimson gown with Norse embroidery along the wrists and along the edges of the sleeveless surcoat of the same color that covered her almost to her ankles. The gold brooch that held a short shoulder mantle, the gold-linked belt that tucked her kirtle to her waist, and the gold stars that dangled on thin chains from ear ornaments bespoke the wealth she had hinted at earlier in the day, when Dunstan had asked about her dowry. A well-dowered bride she would be for some man. Too bad he was not in the market for a bride.

Just then, he noticed something glittering on her hand. It was his signet ring.

His eyes shot up to meet her gaze, and held.

"How do you do that?" she husked out.

He tilted his head in question.

"Make me tingle."

He smiled. He could not help himself. "Where?"

"Where what?"

He squeezed her shoulder where his one hand still rested. "You know very well. Where do you tingle?"

"As if I am going to answer that, rogue!"

"If it is any comfort to you, you make me tingle, too."

They were spared any further discussion on the matter by the arrival of Archbishop Dunstan, who was followed by his retinue of sycophants and clergy. Most of them took seats on this lower level, but the three priests were obviously going to the dais.

Dunstan stopped when he saw them.

"Lady Breanne," he said with a nod. "And this, I assume, is Lady Amicia. You were derelict in your duty today, m'lady. I hope it will not happen again."

Amicia looked puzzled. "Dairy Lick?" Then outraged. "Is he sayin' I lick cows?"

God's breath! Would everything be ruined by a mere choice of language?

"She had a fierce megrim," Caedmon said quickly, "no doubt due to the chastity belt that was put on her by her father long ago." He rolled his eyes meaningfully at the archbishop.

The archbishop's face flushed red. "I did not think they did that anymore."

" 'Twas a long time ago," Amicia chimed in.

Thank God that Amicia got in the spirit of things. Now she was caught in the lies, like him and Breanne.

"Well, bless you, my child, for your chastity." He made the sign of the cross in the air over her.

Some of his housecarls snickered at Amicia being described as chaste, and he flashed them glowers of warning.

"So, Caedmon, when would you like to hold the betrothal ceremony?" the archbishop asked then.

How could I have forgotten that? " 'Tis really unnecessary, Your Grace. We will wed soon enough."

"And I would much prefer to have my father present," Breanne interjected.

"Females are to be seen and not heard," Dunstan said, scowling at Breanne, before adding, "Is King Thorvald on his way?"

"Uh, yea, he is, but I am not sure when he will arrive." Breanne's eyes caught his, pleading for help.

"We sent a missive to Breanne's father sennights ago," Caedmon lied, realizing too late that he was digging them deeper into the hole of deceit, "but you know how long the voyages to the Norselands are, to and fro. Dependent on the wind, storms, and God himself." Caedmon patted himself on the back for adding that last bit about God. Surely, the archbishop would be impressed.

"I go to Heatherby from here. If King Thorvald has not arrived by the time I depart for Glastonbury, we will hold the betrothal ceremony forthwith. Provided that this meets with King Edgar's approval, of course. He will already be angry over Lady Moreton's marriage; he had plans for her."

He left then to go to his seat, his two sheeplike priests following after him, heads bowed, arms crossed with hands inside the opposite sleeves.

Whilst Amicia was busy gawking all around from her novel position near the high table, Caedmon sank down to the bench next to Breanne, just for a second. He had to nudge her with his hip to get her to move over. "It appears that you and I are going to have to get betrothed."

"One lie leads to another and another and another. Where will it end?"

He had an idea, a horrific idea, but if she did not suspect, he was not going to be the one to tell her.

"Exactly what happens in a betrothal ceremony?" she asked.

"I have ne'er had one afore, but it seems to me that it is just two people pledging to get married within a year."

"A year? Phew! A year will give us plenty of time to unbetroth ourselves."

"I have missed you, Breanne. Have you missed me?"

"How could I miss you? You are always there."

"Not always."

She studied him for a moment. "You mean, in bed."

Definitely. "That, too."

"I slept with you last night."

"That is the problem. You slept." He let the fingers of one hand walk up her arm, from wrist to shoulder. He could almost imagine the goosebumps rising on her skin. Bloody hell, he had goosebumps, too.

She lifted his errant hand and placed it on the table. "Bedplay! Is that all you can think of?"

"It is when I am around you."

"I do not like being a lady," Amicia interrupted their flirtsome game.

He and Breanne both said, "Why?"

" 'Tis boring. If I were sitting at the other end of the hall, some lusty man would have his hand up me robe, or I would be tickling his manpart under the table."

Caedmon burst out laughing, then looked at Breanne.

"Do not dare!"

"Oh, well, I kin always practice me exercises 'til this bloody dinner is over."

"Do not ask," Breanne said.

At the same time he did just that. "What exercise would that be?"

Ignoring his question, Amicia addressed Breanne, "Yer face looks red. Are ya practicin' yer exercises, too?"

"You both look like your bowels are blocked," Caedmon grumbled, irritated at being ignored.

But then Amicia, to Breanne's dismay, told him in graphic detail exactly what exercise she referred to. His jaw dropped lower with each word.

Breanne buried her face in her hands.

An idea came unbidden to him. Caedmon knew

what his second bridal gift to Breanne would be.
A candle.

His fruit was yummy . . .

There was good news, and there was bad news
the next day.

Good news: The archbishop was leaving Larkspur.

Bad news: She and Caedmon were going with
him to Heatherby.

Good news: Lady Amicia was staying home.

Bad news: A betrothal ceremony would be
held within a few days if Breanne's father did not
arrive, which he would not, since he had never
been summoned to begin with.

Breanne drew her horse up beside Caedmon's
as they rode out of Larkspur, twenty guardsmen
accompanying them. Northumbria was still a
wild, ungoverned land where villains and reivers
abounded. Thieves had no qualms over killing
a person for a few pieces of gold, no matter that
they be high church officials.

Caedmon was a handsome man, no doubt
about it. Looking out one of the arrow slit windows this morn, she had seen him practicing
swordplay with his men on the exercise fields. He
must have bathed afterward before dressing in a
tunic of finest dark blue wool, held in at the waist
with a wide leather belt, over black, brushed-hide
braies. He was clean shaven and his still-wet hair
had been trimmed yet again.

Noticing her scrutiny, he asked, "Is something
amiss?"

She could not tell him that he made her tingle just looking at him. "What a mess you got us in now!" she hissed. Even though the archbishop and his retinue rode in the forefront, she would not want anyone to overhear.

"Me? I am not the one who said we could not be formally betrothed until your father arrived."

"Perchance you could pretend to get some deadly illness."

"Why do I have to be the one to get sick? Besides, knowing Dunstan, he would perform a deathbed marriage, followed by Extreme Unction, just so he and the king could get a portion of your dowry."

"Even if we were getting married, I would not be willing to give any of my dowry to them."

"You would have no choice."

"Methinks Britain is not a hospitable land for women."

"'Tis no worse here than any other country, and in truth, I am not given a choice in all things, either."

"What do you mean?"

"Until my uncle died and deeded me Larkspur I was a landless knight with no prospects. You cannot know what it is like to finally have a home when you had none."

"And now I have jeopardized that for you."

He shrugged. "I had a choice, as did you when you agreed to our bargain. But a man like me, with no powerful political connections, is always at risk with greedy kings . . . and influential churchmen."

"How horrible!"

" 'Tis the way of the world. But do not think I am sitting here waiting for doom and gloom to fall on my head. Little by little I am building up my troop of housecarls and hirdsmen. Eventually, I would like to add more rooms onto the keep, and build a village beyond the castle grounds, to attract men with families."

All that building made Breanne nigh salivate. "What is stopping you?"

"Money, mostly. But more than that, when the king calls me into service, as he did for the past nine months, I am unable to work my land. And the scutage is too high. This is a small estate, compared to others, and in a remote, undesirable location, so close to the borders, but even so, I have to be careful not to gain attention."

"If it is all about money . . . or at least partly . . . why not wed again to some wealthy heiress?"

He grinned. "Like you?"

"Nay! Of course not. I have no interest in marriage."

"Nor have I."

"You are not even tempted?"

"Oh, I am tempted, m'lady, but not by your coins." He waggled his eyebrows at her. "By the by, I would imagine that horseback riding is a good time for doing your exercises."

"You will ne'er let me hear the end of that, will you?"

"M'lady, that mind picture of you with a candle will be in my head forever."

And mine, as well. "Why do you resist marriage so much?"

"I have traveled that path twice, and both were agonizing. I will not willingly undertake that torture again, not for any amount of wealth."

"Geoff is doing so, for land, is he not?"

"Yea, but Geoff has ne'er been wed afore. He will learn."

"You have a jaded view of marriage. Were you never in love?"

He snorted.

"Could be that your marriages were unhappy because you did not love your wives. Nay, before you scoff, know this: There are men and women who fall in love and wed because they cannot live without that other person."

"You know such as those?" He was clearly unconvinced.

She nodded. "I do. My sister Tyra and her husband, Adam. Lord Eirik of Ravenshire and his wife, Eadyth. Eirik's brother Tykir and his wife, Alinor. Just to name a few."

He shrugged. "If you say so. Still, 'tis not for me."

"Nor me."

"Why? A woman's place is in the marriage bed, big with child, keeping her husband's household."

"Is that so, lunkhead?"

He grinned, and she knew he was teasing her.

"Why have I ne'er wed? I will tell you why. I am not beautiful, like my sisters, and—"

"I think you are beautiful."

She waved a hand dismissively. "'Tis true I have a sizeable dowry, but the men who have come

courting with that in mind have not gained favor
with me. In truth, I would rather not marry, and
instead use my dowry to open a woodworker's
trading stall in Coppergate, have my own home,
be dependent on no one, especially not a husband.
I make special hand-carved chairs that would do
well for a start. And I could make matching tables
and benches."

He put up his hands, as if in surrender. "I did
not mean to give offense."

"Yea, you did. You enjoy pricking me to ill
temper."

"May I say one last thing on the subject without
you flaying me with your tongue?"

"Why stop now?" *Is that what I have become? Am
I now a shrew?*

"You are a passionate woman. Do not try to
deny it. I have seen and felt the evidence of that
passion. How will you do without?"

I do not yearn for sex play. I yearn for you, fool.
"What makes you think that I will deprive myself
now that I have tasted of this forbidden fruit?"

"Am I your forbidden fruit?"

*Hah! If we were in that Christian Garden of Eden,
you would be the apple AND the snake.* "You are at
the moment, but I am sure there will be other fruit
in my future."

She could tell he did not like her answer, for he
heeled his horse into a gallop and rode off.

CHAPTER SEVENTEEN

⊕

Some knots are harder to unravel than others . . .

S   There was so much hugging and weeping between Breanne and her sisters that you would have thought they had been separated for years, not days.

Caedmon had never yearned for a close family, not having experienced it himself, growing up the third son of a third son of a hardened man always struggling for daily bread. It was through his mother's side of the family that noble blood flowed through his body, and then just a trickle. 'Twas only mischance that his maternal uncle had no heirs, thus granting him Larkspur. Mayhap that was why he was so quick to welcome all those children into his "family," because in truth that was the only family he would ever have. Mayhap that was why Larkspur was so important to him, small as it was by other standards.

The archbishop and his group had already dismounted and gone inside with Geoff, who had rolled his eyes at him when Dunstan was not looking. The women had not yet reunited, and Lady Moreton had been delayed by some last-minute clothing disaster . . . soot on a white apron, or some such thing.

Dunstan had seen Rashid, though, and made a remark about heathen Arabs. Rashid just pretended to speak no English.

Rashid walked up to Caedmon now, and they both stared at the women.

"What is it about women and tears?" Caedmon mused, not really expecting an answer.

However, Rashid never was one to be without an opinion. " 'Tis not just women. Men cry on occasion, too, even if they keep the tears inside."

Caedmon raised his eyes skeptically. He could not recall the last time he had succumbed to leaking eyes. Mayhap when he was nine and his mother had died.

"If there were no tears, our ribs would burn," Rashid pontificated.

What a load of rubbish! "Tears are a sign of weakness."

"A thousand pardons, but I notice how your gaze keeps going to Lady Breanne," Rashid observed. "And one of your men mentioned something about a betrothal ceremony. Is there a need for such?"

"Huh?" *Does he mean pregnancy?* "Oh, good Lord, nay. 'Tis just a ruse we have concocted to account for the princess's having been at my castle without a chaperon." At Rashid's disapproving expression, he added, "No offense to the princess or her family, but I have no intention of marrying ever again. Twice was enough, thank you very much."

"He who is bitten by a snake is ofttimes scared of any rope on the ground."

By the time Caedmon figured out what he meant, the Arab was off on another subject, "Have you heard from Lady Havenshire?"

He shook his head. "Do not fret, though. She is in good hands with Wulf."

"And with her two Norse guards," Rashid added.

"That, too. 'Tis my hope that she is on a long-ship back to her father in the Norselands. Edgar and Dunstan would have no way of reaching her there."

Rashid frowned. "But then it will appear as if she is guilty. Never will she get a fair hearing to prove that she had just cause."

"If there is such a thing as a fair hearing for a woman killing a nobleman! Nay, I think 'tis best to go on as they started. If there is no body, there can be no proof of murder."

"From what I have been told of Oswald's cruelties, he is in the proper resting place. Allah be praised!"

"Leave it to a woman to think of putting a piece of shit under a pile of shit."

They grinned at each other.

Caedmon sighed. "I cannot imagine where this will all end."

"Every knot has some way to undo it, my friend."

Caedmon looked up then and saw that Breanne was staring at him. As their gazes held for a long moment, his heart swelled, and yea, he began to tingle in all his extremities, one in particular.

He realized in that moment that the biggest knot in his life was standing before him, with wisps of red hair blowing in the breeze and green eyes liquid with some emotion he could not name. It was a knot he feared would never unravel.

A short time later, Geoff came up to him with two cups of mead. The idiot was wearing a gold-embroidered green samite surcoat over a black tunic and braies with a gold-linked belt. Dumb as a goose! Did he not realize that fine apparel would make Dunstan greedy?

They sat down on a low bench in the bailey, which was bracketed on either side by wild rose-bushes. Drifa's handiwork, he supposed, wondering how soon Breanne would be itching to build something. If so, it had better be something religious, like a life-size crucifix.

"You are smiling, Caedmon."

Caedmon smiled wider. "I was just noticing all of the princess Drifa's live decorations. For your wedding?"

Geoff nodded. "Inside, as well. Flowers everywhere, even in the garderobe. And the food! We will all grow fat as lazy summer bears. But Sybil is pleased, and that is what matters."

Caedmon arched his brows. "No second thoughts?"

"None. I did not realize how much I yearned for land of my own, but beyond that, Sybil and I are well suited." Geoff's cheeks flushed of a sudden. "The ceremony takes place day after tomorrow. Will you stand with me?"

"Of course." He studied the still-blooming color

on Geoff's face. "You are smitten. God's bones, you are!"

"Not smitten, precisely, but I must needs thank you for stepping back and allowing me this opportunity." He squeezed Caedmon's forearm.

"You are wrong, my friend. Sybil had eyes only for you from the beginning."

"Speaking of which, I notice that you and Lady Breanne cannot keep your eyes off each other. Mayhap 'smitten' is in the eye of the beholder."

Caedmon felt his face heat, too. "The woman is driving me barmy." Instead of mentioning the one, most important, way in which Breanne was making him crazy, he told Geoff about the whole scenario with "Lady Amicia," even the clenching woman-muscle business.

Geoff was howling with laughter by the time they noticed a lone rider on a fast horse approaching Heatherby. The man was an advance guard, carrying the Golden Dragon flag of the House of Wessex. Turns out the folks at Heatherby were to be given a great—some might say dubious— honor. King Edgar, two thanes, an ealdorman, and a troop of four dozen hirdsmen would be arriving for the wedding.

"That wily slyboots! It appears Dunstan has his own hidden agenda," Geoff observed.

"You have no idea!" Caedmon proceeded to tell him of the archbishop's request for land to build a monastery. "I daresay he knew all along that the king was on his way, to reinforce his grab-land appetite."

"They bode ill for Heatherby *and* Larkspur."

"For a certainty!"

"And for us," Breanne said, coming up to them. "I suspect the disappearance of the earl of Havenshire is in this mix, as well. Now that we are forewarned, however, we can concoct our own plans to deflect their questions."

Plans? She and her lackwit sisters are going to make plans? Caedmon turned to Geoff. "Shoot me with an arrow through the heart and put me out of my misery right now."

"Oh, nay, you do not escape so easily!" Breanne put her hands to hips and glared down at him. "If we are going to suffer, you are going to suffer with us."

So, Caedmon said, "What the bloody hell!" and, with Geoff's hoots of encouraging laughter, he did what he had been wanting to do all day. He pulled Breanne forward so suddenly that she fell against him with a squeal, a sure sign that she wanted him, in his opinion. Leastways, that is what he told himself. Then he bent her back over one arm and kissed her.

And kissed her.

And kissed her, openmouthed, with teeth, and tongue, and hard-pressed lips, until both of them stood on wobbly legs staring at each other, dazed. Only then did they realize that they had an audience, with one important member.

Archbishop Dunstan had come back outside.

He was not pleased.

Warts and hunchbacks and big butts, oh, my! . . .

Several hours later, Caedmon was entering the

Heatherby great hall with Geoff at his side. What they saw nigh caused them both to fall over with shock.

"Oh, good Lord!" they said as one.

Other than Breanne, Archbishop Dunstan had not yet met any of the women, including Lady Moreton. All of them were evading the priest. No surprise there! Everyone within a sulong of Heatherby would like to go into hiding for the next sennight or so, Caedmon included.

Especially in light of what Geoff and Caedmon now beheld.

First there was Breanne, with red spots covering her face and neck and an ugly wart on the tip of her nose that resembled green snot. *How can she be beautiful to me, even with a wart? My brain must be melting.* Ingrith had doubled her weight and now had a back end that rivaled Amicia's. *I wonder if she can get through the scullery door.* Drifa had done something to blacken all of her front teeth, and she was cackling. *That is all we need ... a slant-eyed crone with leaky black teeth.* And Sybil had a hunchback. *I wonder if she knows her pillow back is slipping?*

Rashid, passing by with a stack of firewood in hand, was not surprised. He remarked blithely, "The heart of woman is given to folly."

He and Geoff stared at the women, slack-jawed, for a long moment before Geoff said, "By thunder, Caedmon, I forgot how much fun it is to be around you."

"I had naught to do with this." Turning to the four women, he asked, "What in bloody hell is going on?"

"You told us to beware of King Edgar when he comes," Breanne defended herself to Caedmon.

Sybil addressed Geoff in her faint lisp, "You said Edgar would tup a goat if it could stand on two legs and have breasts." On her tongue, breasts sounded like "blests."

"I am not so sure that a hunchback would deter our king," Geoff remarked.

"Mayhap I could put some malodorous substance on my *gunna*," Sybil offered. "Like manure."

"That would do it," Geoff replied.

"Nice freckles!" Caedmon said to Breanne.

"These are not freckles, you lackwit!" she replied indignantly. "They are spots."

"Oh?"

"Caused by the red pilfin bush I touched when we stopped to water the horses today. Very contagious."

Caedmon turned to Drifa, the plant expert. "Red pilfin?"

Drifa cackled and winked at him. Not an attractive sight.

"I take it there is no such thing."

"No matter!" Breanne interjected. "As long as Dunstan and the king believe there is, they will not want to get close enough to check."

"I will be in the kitchen helping cook with the wedding feast preparations," Ingrith said. "Methinks lutefisk and a heap of gammelost would be enough to turn the archbishop and the king off my food." At his frown of puzzlement, she explained, "Gammelost is a cheese so stinksome that legend says some warrior kings fed it to their men afore battle to turn them berserk."

"That is all we need . . . a berserk archbishop."

With a mischievous grin, Ingrith waddled away. They all stared at her huge bottom, transfixed.

"I need to gather flowers for the bridal head wreath." Drifa made for the outer door.

"Will you help me fix my hump?" Sybil asked Geoff.

"You want me to hump you?" he inquired with mock innocence.

"Have you ever made love with a hunchback afore?" Sybil glanced up at Geoff as he wrapped an arm over her hump.

"Not lately."

They were both laughing as they walked off.

" 'Twould seem that Geoff and Sybil are a good match," Breanne remarked.

He shrugged. "Both of my wives were biddable afore the weddings, too. You cannot trust women that way. They change afore a man's very eyes. From angel to devil's spawn in a heartbeat."

"That is the kind of drivel Archbishop Dunstan would spout." She smacked him on the arm. "You do not believe that. Besides, since when is a biddable woman an asset to be desired?"

"Oh, I do not know about that. I am thinking of something right now where I would bid and you would agree."

"Can you think of naught else but bedplay?"

"Nothing so enjoyable." He winked at her. "What is that thing on your nose?"

"Porridge and peas, smashed together."

"It is sliding off."

"Not to worry. I have spares."

He leaned in closer, sniffing. "And that fruity scent?"

"Raspberries. I used the juice to make my spots."

"I love raspberries." He licked a line from chin to ear. "Yum!"

She sighed, swaying on that line betwixt stubborn and biddable.

I am so good! Really, I amaze myself betimes.

"Stop it! I will have to repaint myself now." Her words were strong, but her voice was weak.

One more push and she will sway right over that line. "Let me lick you all over, and I will help you respot yourself. In fact, there are several special places I am inclined to paint on you. Using a feather." *How do I come up with this stuff? Must be one of Geoff's talents wearing off on me.*

Her tongue darted out and flicked across her suddenly dry lips. He had caught her interest. Even so, she resisted. "After the blistering lecture Archbishop Dunstan gave us over the kiss out in the bailey, I have decided to be good."

Oh, please, do not! "There is no fun in that."

"There is no fun in being labeled a strumpet, either."

The cleric had warned them of temptation, fornication, impure thoughts and deeds. And laid most of the blame at her door.

"He ne'er used the word *strumpet*."

"He implied it. And did you notice his mention of Eve's wicked ways, but no mention of Adam's wicked ways?"

"He did mention women being Satan's whips." Caedmon chuckled.

" 'Tis not funny. You would have thought I was a harlot, all because of a mere kiss."

"It did not feel 'mere' to me, sweetling." *In fact, hot and wild would be a better description.*

"To me, neither," she conceded.

"Will you come to me tonight?" He ran a hand along her arm, from shoulder to wrist, caressingly.

She shook her head, even as she nigh purred at his touch. "I am sharing a bedchamber with my sisters and Sybil. I cannot imagine you having your own room with all the guests here or about to arrive."

"You are correct. Geoff, Rashid, and I have reserved one horse stall in the stables for ourselves."

"A step down in the world for you."

"Not so much. The straw is clean, and believe you me I have made my bed in worse places, especially when off to war."

"Everything is happening too fast."

He nodded. "Will you be returning to Larkspur with me once the wedding is over?" He had no idea where that question had come from, but suddenly the answer was very important to him.

"I do not know. It depends on whether Dunstan and the king are satisfied with our explanations for Oswald's disappearance. The safest

route would be for me and my sisters to return to
Stoneheim, except for Tyra, of course, who lives
at Hawkshire with her husband. Are you worried
that I have not fulfilled our bargain?"

"Yea, you do owe me four more nights. Or is it
five?" He grinned at her, then twined the fingers
of one of her hands with his and raised the fist to
his mouth where he kissed the knuckles.

She just stared up at him, aroused already, he
could tell.

"Come, let us walk outside. Soon, the king will
arrive, and there will be no opportunity," he said.

"'Tis a good thing you did not bring the children. With all the tension here, the least bit of mis-
conduct might set off a disaster."

"For a certainty. And they will be safe under
Hugh's guidance, along with Amicia and Mary."

"I will miss them when I depart Northumbria.
They are fine children, Caedmon, even if they are
not all yours."

"You will miss the children? What about me?
Will you miss me, wench?"

She laughed and swung their linked hands between them. "Fishing for compliments, are you?"

"You do not give them readily . . . not to me,
leastways."

"Yea, I will miss you."

He gazed at her for a long moment. "Would you
stay if I asked?" *Damn, damn, damn, I must be daft to
mention such a possibility.*

"As what? Nay, do not answer. No matter how
I might feel, my father would consider it a grave
insult if you wanted me only for a mistress. Wait

. . . do not get your bowels in an uproar. I am not asking for matrimony from you. That was understood from the beginning. So, long way of getting to my answer. Nay, I would not stay if you asked."

A reprieve for my hasty tongue, he thought, *but why does it feel like a stab to the heart?* He remained silent as they walked across the angled bridge that led from the upper motte to the bailey below and then through the drawbridge outside the keep toward an orchard of cherry and apple and pear trees, still in blossom.

"I would say one more thing, Caedmon. I am appreciative of the protection you offered me and my sisters, and if, by some mischance you lose Larkspur as a result, I am certain that my father would offer you an estate in the Norselands to reestablish yourself."

He grinned at that. "You would make me into a Viking?"

"There are worse things."

"Would you buy me a longship? Would I be able to rape and pillage?"

"No Norsemen I know rape and pillage. Plunder is a different matter. Some folks deserve to be plundered. You have been listening to too many biased priest historians." Offended at his teasing, she tried to pull away from him, but he held on tight.

"Now who is getting their bowels in an uproar?" Backing her up against a tree, he dropped her hand, but imprisoned her with elbows braced on either side of her head. He watched with fascination as a shower of white flower petals dusted her head and his.

She turned her face away from him, but he just used that opportunity to lick the red spots on that side. When she pivoted to chastise him, he kissed her. "Raspberry kisses," he said against her open mouth. "Have you e'er been tupped against a tree?"

"You know I have not." Try as she might, a smile twitched at her plump lips.

In between kisses, he was ruching up the hem of her *gunna*, bit by bit, until she was bare from the waist down. "There are so many ways I want to make love with you. So many things to do that I have not yet had a chance. How can you think of leaving afore then?"

She was busy, too. Bemused, he had not realized that she had already unlaced his breeches and had them shoved down to his knees.

"Mayhap I will have to find another man to show me those things," she offered.

"Nay!" he exclaimed, surprised himself by the vehemence of his response. He lifted her by the buttocks and arranged her legs around his hips. With one mighty thrust, he was inside her tight sheath. "You are mine! Dost hear me?"

"They heard you all the way to Larkspur."

He tried to laugh, but it came out as a gurgle. So overaroused was he that he could not move for fear of peaking, way too early.

"Help me," he said against her ear.

She cupped his face in her palms. "How?"

"Touch," he grunted out, taking one of her

hands to touch that place where they were joined. Guiding one of her fingers, he showed her how to strum that nubbin of woman-pleasure.

Almost immediately, she began to whimper and her inner muscles spasmed around him. Only then did he began his strokes, in and out, only a few times afore he came to a blinding peak within her still convulsing insides.

With his forehead pressed against her forehead, he panted, fighting for breath. "Sorry," he finally said.

"For what?"

"Being too quick."

"I was ready, Caedmon."

He drew back a bit and smiled. "Yea, you were."

She smiled back at him, reaching up to brush a strand of hair off his face.

His heart turned over, he swore it did.

"I cannot bear to think of you doing this with another woman," she confessed.

"I think I would kill the man who takes you to bed," he confessed, as well.

" 'Twould seem we have a problem."

He turned and sank down to the ground with his back to the tree. She landed on her knees astride him, sitting on her haunches, with his limp member still inside her.

"Does this count as one of my remaining nights with you?" she teased.

"Hah! I figure one night accounts for at least six bouts of lovemaking. So, what we just did merits, oh, let us say, a sixth of a night." *Never did I realize that my talent for numbers would come in so handy.*

She laughed. "You are an optimist."

"Four times then, and a quarter of a night."

"I cannot believe I am bargaining like this for my virtue."

"You lost your virtue to me more than five nights ago, sweetling." He shook his head at the ridiculous position he was in . . . making love out in the open with his breeches about his ankles and her gown hiked up to her waist. " 'Tis insanity, the risks I take to be with you." *And well worth the risk!*

"*Your* risks? All my plans for my own woodworking business teeter on the edge. I will tell you what is insanity. It is me spreading my thighs for any man, let alone you."

"What is wrong with me?"

"You have ten children. You want no more. You have been twice wed, unsuccessfully, according to your own accounts. Any woman holding out for marriage will be sore disappointed. You hold on to your lands by a thread, at the whim of a greedy overlord."

'Tis true. 'Tis all true. He tilted his head to the side. "So, what is wrong with me?" he repeated, disregarding what she had just said as unimportant.

She shook her head at his hopelessness.

I am. Hopeless, that is. "Rashid says that we cast lustsome glances at each other all the time, that anyone with even a speck of a brain could guess what we have been doing."

"Just so Dunstan and the king do not suspect."

"Will someone tell your father of our doings

when you go home?" *That is all I need . . . an angry father with a sword at my throat.*

"Nay, but Rashid might tell Adam, my brother-by-marriage."

That could be just as bad. He started to say something, then stopped. His nostrils flared, and his heart skipped a beat, then began to race. He looked downward, where they were still joined, then back to her face. "By the saints! *What* are you doing?"

"Practicing my exercises."

His thankful, growing cock, if it could talk, would be saying about now, "Insanity be damned!"

CHAPTER EIGHTEEN

*H*elp came from the lone stranger . . .
Caedmon and Geoff had been sitting before
a reduced version of the Witan, "holding court" at
a long table in the solar for more than two hours
and no end in sight. You would have thought they
were being tried for some high crime.

When Archbishop Dunstan announced the
meeting several hours after the king's arrival,
he said there were three things on the agenda.
Geoff's wedding to Lady Moreton. Caedmon's betrothal to Lady Breanne. The disappearance and
possible murder of Lord Oswald, earl of Havenshire. Why the king's council would need to be involved in those first two was beyond Caedmon's
understanding, and he had told the members so,
to no avail. Ealdorman Orm of Donchester, the
royal magistrate, had informed him in no uncertain terms, "Lands held by the nobility in Britain
may be gained by Odal rights, but they are still
under the king's sufferance."

"I take exception! Geoff and I have both served
you well, Your Grace," Caedmon told the king,
who was leaning back in his chair, indolently ex-

amining his fingernails. "You have no cause to think we have acted in any way contrary to your wishes, had we known of them."

King Edgar was very short—coming barely to Caedmon's shoulder—towheaded, and pudgy, but he considered himself a prize to females, none of whom dared to disagree. Of late, he had been encouraging the title "Edgar the Peaceable," because he had managed to avoid any new wars, no matter that he paid Viking brigands to stay away.

And he had been giving Dunstan free reign to build one monastery after another, reinstating the Benedictine rule of poverty, chastity, and obedience, none of which applied to himself, of course, whose style of living was anything but religious. Secular clergy were being ejected without warning, and to date he had built twenty-five new monasteries and repaired that many existing ones.

An odd dichotomy, really. A king with a legendary sexual appetite aligned with a priest who hated women.

"We do not question your loyalty, Caedmon. Nor yours, Geoffrey," the king said, although his tone said otherwise. "But we do question your timing. Why the haste?"

"I fell in love on first sight," Geoff said with a perfectly serious expression on his face.

"With a hunchback?" the king scoffed.

"Who lisps," Lord Orm added, also with skepticism.

"Sybil is beautiful on the inside," Geoff claimed with a long sigh.

Caedmon almost bit his tongue. Geoff was the

most superficial man when it came to appearances, his own and his women.

"Well said, Geoffrey. A good sentiment," Archbishop Dunstan said, impressed with Geoff's piety.

What an idiot!

"Truth to tell, Geoffrey, I came here this morn, expecting to dissolve your presumptuous handfast marriage. There are others of more merit who could benefit from the Heatherby estates." The king glanced pointedly at the two thanes, sons of his cousins, who sat on either side of him, sulking. "However, after some consideration, methinks that the marriage should go forward on the morrow." Under his breath, he muttered to the two thanes, "And I wish him joy of her."

In other words, the two thanes did not want the lands enough to bed a hunchback. Caedmon had no idea what would happen in future times if Geoff and a beautified Sybil ran into any of them. He supposed they could say that a holy relic rubbed over the hump had caused it to disappear. Bloody hell!

"That is not to say there will be no penalty," Dunstan was quick to add. "Let us say, twenty mancuses of gold."

Geoff was about to protest, but Caedmon squeezed his forearm in warning. Now was not the time to argue.

"Now, 'tis your turn, Lord Caedmon," Dunstan said.

"You may leave us, Geoffrey," Dunstan added.

"Oh, I do not mind staying," Geoff started to say, looking to Caedmon for guidance.

" 'Tis not necessary," he whispered to his friend. "Make sure the women are ready." Breanne and her two sisters were presumably sitting outside this room all this time, waiting for their own interrogation.

Once Geoff left, Edgar sat up straighter. Caedmon was fairly certain he had a cushion under his arse to give him height. "Last time I heard, and 'twas only a few months ago, you were adamant about not remarrying. Tell us of your relationship with the Viking princess? What made you change your mind?"

The two thanes bracketing Edgar sat up straighter, too. It became apparent to Caedmon that while Heatherby was no longer of interest to them because the hunchbacked Sybil went with the package, Larkspur was not so encumbered. They wanted his land.

Caedmon warned himself to tread carefully. "That is how I felt at the time, but then I met Lady Breanne."

"Is she the one with red spots?" Edgar asked Dunstan.

The archbishop nodded.

"How long will she have them?" Edgar wanted to know.

Why in bloody hell does he care? If he thinks to force her to his bed, he will have to plow through me first! "I have no idea. Is there a reason why you ask?" Caedmon's voice was icy with affront. No one in the room could doubt that he was giving the king a silent warning.

Edgar tented his short fingers in front of his

face, staring at him with barely concealed hostility. "Why should we give our permission for this betrothal?"

Caedmon would have liked to ask since when was a royal approval needed for anything involving this remote, small estate?

Just then, the door swung open and in strode a man clearly of noble stature. He was tall, his black hair sprinkled with gray, wearing a fine wool cloak over soft leather breeches and tunic. Gold shone from his shoulder brooch and belt. It was Eirik, earl of Ravenshire, kin-by-marriage to Breanne's sister Tyra. Caedmon did not know him personally, but he had seen him at a distance in the past at royal events.

Geoff followed Eirik in and sat down beside Caedmon, whispering, "The women are primed for battle."

"Please tell me that you jest."

Eirik made a short bow from the waist at the "royal" table and said, "Greetings, Your Eminence. Greetings, Your Highness. I came as soon as I heard a meeting of the Witan was being called. I must have missed my invitation." Without being asked, Eirik pulled a chair up to the table where the others sat. He turned then and winked at Caedmon, so quickly no one else saw it.

"This is not a formal meeting of the Witan," King Edgar said in his usual whiny voice.

Caedmon had mixed feelings about Lord Ravenshire's arrival. On the one hand, he resented the implication that he could not handle his own affairs. On the other hand, a good soldier never looked a gift horse in the mouth. Or, as Rashid would say, "Never look a gift camel in the mouth." It was a sign of his melting brain that he was making up camel proverbs in his head.

"Continue as you were." Eirik motioned toward them with a wave of his hand. "Do not let my presence inhibit you." The latter was ludicrous, considering how uncomfortable he was making the other Witan members.

"King Edgar asked why he should give permission for my betrothal to Lady Breanne," Caedmon explained to Eirik, whose eyes widened just the tiniest bit at the news of a betrothal. "I was about to say that I married twice to satisfy the crown's wishes, and I vowed that I would ne'er wed again, but that was afore I met my lady love, a gentle, sweet lass. She is everything a man could want in a wife." He was sure that Geoff and Wulf would laugh their arses off one day in recounting his description of his fierce Viking lass. Breanne would, too, for that matter.

"But she is a heathen Viking," Dunstan protested.

"I told you afore that her family has been baptized."

"Do not think that I am unaware of the Norsemen's practice of being baptized as a convenience to travel in our lands." Dunstan sneered. "They are no more Christians than camels."

Good thing Rashid was not here. He would not like the maligning of camels.

"Have a caution whom you speak ill of, Your Eminence," Eirik warned. "I am half Viking."

Dunstan made a harrumphing sound.

"I understand the wench has a sizeable dowry," Edgar said. "How much and how is it to be allocated?"

What he really meant was, how much would he get if he allowed the marriage? A marriage that would never be happening. What a mess!

"I have not even talked with her father yet. Until that happens, I cannot say."

"What is this really about?" Eirik wanted to know. "The king, two thanes, an archbishop, and an ealdorman do not travel to the far reaches of the kingdom to discuss a betrothal that represents a pittance compared to the rest of the realm."

Dunstan tapped his fingertips on the tabletop. "The murder of the earl of Havenshire . . . that is what this is about, and we have reason to believe his widow is the culprit."

Eirik turned to Caedmon with mock dismay on his face. "Is this true?"

Caedmon shrugged. "I did not know they found a body."

Dunstan's face flushed with chagrin. "We do not need a body to know there has been foul play."

"Are you saying that this whole flummery is being played over a murder that might not have taken place?" Eirik's face was livid with outrage.

"Call in the women. Let us get to the bottom of this vile situation." Edgar was probably bored by now. "Know this, Caedmon, any persons who helped Lady Havenshire escape are considered accomplices and will be judged and punished accordingly, and that includes you and the sisters."

"Escape? How can someone escape when they have never been charged?" Eirik glowered at the other Witan members. "This is an exercise in stupidity, if you ask me."

Caedmon stood and snarled at the king. "Accomplice? The injustice of your insult cuts deep. Do not threaten me, Your Highness, when I have done naught but give you good service over the years."

Now it was Edgar's turn to flush with embarrassment. Backtracking, he said, "My apologies, Caedmon. I do value your service. Understand our dilemma, though. A valued nobleman and close friend is missing, and the only clues to his whereabouts lie with the women under your protection."

"Get the women, and let us be done with it," Dunstan ordered.

And then the terrible trouble just got more terrible . . .

The longer they waited, the more nervous they got.

Breanne and her sisters had been sitting at the far end of the great hall, closest to the solar, for more than two hours, waiting their turn. The only thing that gave them hope was the arrival of Lord Ravenshire and his wife.

Lady Ravenshire, who asked to be called Eadyth, was a fascinating woman, and beautiful. Even though she must have been close to fifty, her naturally silvered hair and clear skin belied her years. In fact, she had once been known as the Silver Jewel of Northumbria because of her beauty. Right now, she was in deep conversation with Drifa and Ingrith about her beekeeping operation. She had already promised Breanne help in setting up her woodworking stall in Jorvik when she was ready.

Rashid sat with them, but he had been advised to remain quiet or stay as far away as possible from Dunstan, who hated Arabs almost as much as he hated women. Never mind that Rashid was a far-famed healer and comrade of some well-placed men. "Even the camel knows not to stand in a place of danger and trust in miracles."

"What does that mean?" Breanne asked on a deep sigh.

"It means that Allah helps those who help themselves. You and your sisters have done well." Rashid patted her hand. "Making yourselves scarce and unattractive. Huddling behind the shield of strong men. Speaking up when all else fails. You are fighters, all of you, and that is good in the eyes of Allah."

"There is fighting, and then there is fighting. King Edgar does not play by the rules. He is a vile man," Breanne answered.

Rashid shrugged. "An ass is an ass even if laden with gold."

Hearing Rashid's words of wisdom, Eadyth smiled, then took note of Breanne's nervousness as her fingers kept going to her wart to make sure it was still in place. The kind lady said, "Do not fret over your disguises. Did I tell you how I fooled Lord Ravenshire into believing I was an old crone when we were first married? For months and months, by ashing my face, cackling, and using the transparent beekeeping net material, my husband never suspected. 'Tis my belief that men see what they anticipate seeing, not the real thing."

"In other words, men are clueless?" Breanne said.

"Definitely," Eadyth replied.

"I heard that," Eirik said, coming up to them. He leaned down and kissed his wife on the cheek before telling them, "Time for you to go in."

They all stood and Eirik turned away from his wife. "Oh, my God!" he said, taking one look, then almost jumping back in shock. It was the first he had seen them since his arrival when he had gone directly to the solar. Now, eyes wide with amazement, he burst out in laughter.

Breanne's hair was braided and arranged on top of her head to expose more skin covered with the "contagious" spots. Caedmon had helped her apply her wart earlier in the kitchen, an exercise that involved lots of touching, very little of it near her nose.

Ingrith was in her fat costume and had even put wads of fleece inside her mouth to give herself puffy cheeks, which meant that she slurred when she talked, as if she was *drukkin*. Vana was all croned up with blackened teeth, bent posture, and a cane. And, of course, Sybil had her hunchback.

They all hurried toward the solar and what they hoped would not be their doom. Caedmon and Geoff stood outside in the hall, ready to escort them inside. The serious expressions on their faces would be enough to scare them witless, if they were not already at that point.

The women, along with Caedmon and Geoffrey, sat on benches facing the long table where Eirik had rejoined the other Witan members.

King Edgar's beady eyes examined the women before he curled his upper lip with distaste. "Let us get on with it. I am hungry."

Every person in the room knew what his appetite was for, even Dunstan, who whispered some admonishment in his ear. King Edgar just shrugged. He would do as he willed, then go build a church or two in penance.

Lord Orm, the magistrate, started the inquiry. "Where is Lady Havenshire?"

At first, no one spoke, but then Breanne realized her sisters were looking to her to be spokesman. "I do not know."

"When did you see her last?"

Breanne glanced at her two sisters, each of whom shrugged.

"A sennight or two ago."

She could tell that Lord Orm was getting impatient with her terse answers. Caedmon had advised her to volunteer nothing.

Dunstan slammed a hand on the table. "Where did you see her last? Why did she leave? Who traveled with her? Where was she going?"

She raised her chin bravely, trying her best not to be intimidated, but her voice came out wobbly when she started to speak, helped only when Caedmon surreptitiously squeezed her thigh.

"Vana was grieving for her husband, who had disappeared, but she was being questioned in a threatening manner . . . as you are questioning us now."

Every member of the Witan glared at her audacity, except Lord Ravenshire, who favored her with a wink and a small smile of encouragement.

"With no one to protect Vana, except for our two Norse guards, my sisters and I convinced Vana to come north with us to visit my betrothed's estate." She flashed Caedmon a simpering smile, and he reciprocated by lacing the fingers of one hand with hers. "After we were here a few days, Vana yearned to return to Stoneheim and my father's care. Our Norse guards, Ivan and Ivar, accompanied her. Once her husband returns home to Havenshire, she will, of course, return."

"Why did you and your sisters not go with her?"

"Because I wanted to spend some time with my betrothed, and my sisters agreed to stay until the wedding . . . or at least until the formal betrothal ceremony." Breanne gulped over the lump in her dry throat. Lying drained a person, she found.

And King Edgar was still suspicious.

Breanne was repulsed by the Saxon king's shifty eyes and loose lips, which bespoke a lecherous disposition. He was renowned for surveying every room he encountered for his next prey, sexual or otherwise. He was scare older than twenty-one, but his dissipated face made him look a decade older. Sybil had told them this morning of some of the punishments Edgar had levied in the past, sometimes on a whim: slitting the nose, cutting off hands or feet, plucking out eyes, leaving a body out in the elements exposed to the pecking of vultures. Thank Odin that she and her sisters and Sybil had had the foresight to make themselves unattractive. Now, if only they could convince him they were not guilty of murder.

"As for you, Caedmon, you have been a good soldier for me," King Edgar was continuing, "but I am convinced that your princess knows more than she is telling. Which therefore follows that you know, too."

Caedmon jumped to his feet and yelled, "You have no right to dishonor me."

The king jumped to his feet, yelling back, "I have every right." Pointing to two of his soldiers propped against a far wall. "Restrain him in the dungeon."

Breanne stood, too, at Caedmon's side. "If you put him in a dungeon, you will have to imprison me, too."

"Shhh. Sit down, Breanne," Caedmon told her, trying to shove her back down to the bench by pressing on her shoulder, to no avail. Then he hissed at her, "Your wart has fallen off."

Turning her face away from the Witan, she reached into a placket of her gown, then attached another wart. "How do I look?"

"Ridiculous. Sit down."

"If Breanne is going to the dungeon, then I am, too," slurred Ingrith, who stood with difficulty, considering her bulk, and folded her arms over her hugely padded chest.

"Me, too," said Drifa, with a cackle, exposing her blackened teeth.

"We have no dungeons at Heatherby," Geoff said, standing at Caedmon's other side. "Do we?" he asked Sybil.

"Nay. Just a cold-storage room that we use for the occasional villain."

"That will do," Edgar said.

"Enough!" Eirik said, stomping over to hover above King Edgar's much smaller frame. "You cannot imprison your subjects for an imaginary murder just because you suspect they know something."

"I can do whate'er I want," the king said petulantly.

Everyone started yelling and talking at once, including Dunstan, who was trying to calm down the king.

Thus it was, in the midst of all the chaos, that at first no one heard the guardsmen at the door announce new arrivals in great numbers on the horizon, coming to Heatherby. Mayhap as many as a hundred heavily armed horsemen.

"Who is it?" the king demanded to know. "Friend or foe?"

The guardsman said, "They are too far away yet. But they do carry a black flag with what looks like blood dripping from a stone."

"Uh-oh!" three Viking princesses said as one.

As everyone rushed to get out of the door and up to the ramparts, Caedmon turned slowly to look at her. He lifted one eyebrow in question. "What now?"

"Vikings."

"Vikings?"

"Stoneheim Vikings. And if they carry the banner, my father is with them."

"Is that good news or bad news?"

"Well, let me just say, my father has seen more than fifty winters, and he has not left the Norselands in twenty years."

It was Caedmon then who said, "Uh-oh!"

CHAPTER NINETEEN

❧

Daddy knows best . . .
  Caedmon walked up behind Breanne as she stood at the ramparts and kissed the back of her neck.

He sniffed deeply and said, "You smell of raspberries and roses.

At first, she leaned back into him and allowed him to wrap his arms around her waist, but then she shrugged him off. "Behave, lest someone see us."

He glanced around. Most everyone was at the other end of the ramparts, or down in the bailey preparing for the "visitors."

Dunstan and the king had not been happy to learn that a "horde" of Norsemen were on their way, even when assured by Caedmon, Geoff, Eirik, and the princesses that they probably came in peace.

"Why are you so distressed?" he asked Breanne. "You should be happy that your father comes to your rescue." Assuming that was why he was here.

"I suspect that my father is beyond furious and will ride in with sword and battle-axe raised."

He had been thinking that all would be well now that her father and his hirdsmen had come to escort the princesses home. "You do not mean that he would kill Edgar and Dunstan."

She shrugged. "There is no telling what an angry Viking will do. He has been known to lop off a head and then sit down to eat."

My head is beginning to ache.

"I should forewarn you . . ."

Bloody hell! I do not like that look on her face.

" . . . if my father hears of our bargain, or even the false betrothal, he might be a tiny bit upset."

Forget head lopping. Perchance my brain might just explode inside by head.

"Oh, look, there is Tyra. In full battle gear." At first she giggled, then went more serious when she realized the significance of that apparel. "That is Adam and their little boy Edward riding farther back."

Caedmon had never seen a woman in armor, weighed down with sword and axe, although Saxons grew up on tales of the warrior queen Boadicea, who had fought bravely against the Romans.

Just then, Breanne went stiff and gasped.

"What?"

"Oh my gods and goddesses! 'Tis Rafn." She pointed to a Viking warrior who rode at the head of the hird, beside the king.

"Who the hell is Rafn?" he asked but Breanne was already running away.

He followed her across the ramparts, down the stairs, through the great hall, across the upper, then the lower bailey. Her sisters were following close behind them. The drawbridge had been lowered and on the other side of the moat the troops had come to a halt with the man Rafn dismounting.

"Rafn!" Breanne screamed and rushed into his open arms as he limped toward her. He was a tall man, even taller than Caedmon, though slim and almost gaunt. He supposed some women would find his dark good looks appealing. He did not. Breanne was laughing and kissing the Viking's neck.

With muttered imprecations, he stepped forward and yanked Breanne out of the man's arms. The warrior immediately reached for his short sword.

Caedmon did likewise.

"Caedmon! What are you doing? This is Rafn."

"And who are you to touch one of the princesses?" Rafn shouted.

Caedmon was about to say he was her betrothed, but Breanne slapped a hand over his mouth. "Caedmon is a friend and kinsman-by-marriage. He offered us protection." Then, she turned to Caedmon with a tsk-ing sound of disgust. "And this is Rafn, Vana's long-ago betrothed, who was supposed to be dead."

"Hmpfh!" He was not consoled.

"What happened?" she asked Rafn.

"I will tell you all later." He smiled at her.

Caedmon did not like other men smiling at her. Not one bit. Even a man presumably linked to her

sister. And wasn't that a fine mess of another color!
An alleged murderess and a come-from-the-dead
Viking warrior.

Meanwhile the other sisters had caught up and
were surrounding Rafn, giving him hugs and
kisses.

There was a coughing noise behind them.

He and Breanne turned to face a glowering old
man with long white hair and war braids twined
with crystals framing his leathery face. "Vikings
are meant to ride longships, not horses," he complained as two men helped him dismount. When
he stood before them, Caedmon could see that he
was a big man, and very fit for his age. Breanne
had told him that she and her sisters were all legitimate, though born of different deceased mothers.
Thorvald, apparently, had married all his women,
sometimes more than one at a time.

A teary-eyed Breanne rushed up to her father,
who opened his arms to embrace her. Patting her
on the back, he kept telling her, "Hush now. Everything will soon be aright."

Swiping at her eyes, Breanne stepped back, and
Caedmon immediately put his arms around her
shoulders. For some reason, he wanted to be the
one to reassure her.

"And who are you to be touching my daughter
so?" the aged warrior inquired.

"Sir Caedmon, this is my father, His Royal Highness the King of Stoneheim, Thorvald. Father, this
is Sir Caedmon of Larkspur. You must be kind to
him. He has protected us all these sennights when
we were alone and had nowhere else to go."

"Is that so?" He eyed Caedmon suspiciously, but only for a moment. With a gruff laugh, he grabbed Caedmon and yanked him into a hug that about broke his ribs and cut off his breathing.

"I owe you much, Saxon. Do you want gold, lands . . . or, ha, ha, ha . . . one of my daughters?"

The three princesses all groaned.

"It is a jest our father plays everywhere we go," Breanne explained. "He pretends he wants us all married off."

"I do," the king disagreed.

"He is just teasing," Breanne contended.

The king rolled his eyes at Caedmon. Just then, he seemed to really look at his daughters, and he swore a blue Viking streak. "What has happened to my beautiful daughters?"

Breanne's red spots were smudged from her father's hug, but Ingrith was still fat, and Drifa still crone-like. Breanne told him quickly that there was a reason for the disguises, which she would explain later.

The king just nodded, looking over their shoulders as Archbishop Dunstan approached, using his crozier as a walking stick. He was flanked by two of his tonsured monks. Dunstan's face was flushed from the exertion, or perchance he was angry. Probably both.

"King Thorvald!" Dunstan greeted the old man who was eyeing him warily. "I see you have arrived in time for the betrothal ceremony."

Caedmon and Breanne looked at each other . . . and grimaced.

"What betrothal ceremony?" King Thorvald demanded to know, regarding the archbishop with as much distaste as the clergyman regarded him.

Dunstan glanced at Caedman and Breanne, an evil grin tugging at his thin lips, as if he had caught them finally in his wily trap. "Caedmon and Breanne, of course."

The quicksand Caedmon had been sinking in for days just pulled him under. He could swear he heard the loud sucking noise. No way out of this mess! He was one dead Saxon duck.

The tic pulsing at the edge of King Thorvald's mustache was the only clue he gave that he was ignorant of these happenings. "My darling Breanne and her beloved Caedmon? How could I forget?"

The sly king then smiled.

Beware a Viking's wrath . . .

First things first.

Breanne, her sisters, her father, Rafn, Eirik, and Eadyth were in the solar. They drank cups of Eadyth's fine mead, which she had brought with her from Ravenshire, and nibbled at manchet bread and hunks of cheese whilst catching up on all that had happened these past few sennights.

Geoff and Sybil were making arrangements to feed and house another hundred bodies in addition to those who had come with Dunstan and King Edgar. Adam and Rashid had taken little Adela for a walk to see some newborn lambs. The archbishop and his clergy were resting or praying somewhere in the keep. The ealdorman was off drinking ale to assuage his impatience over the way the Witan hearings were going, or not going.

And Caedman, may the gods bless him, had taken the king and his cohorts out hunting with falcons. It was either that or let Edgar make merry with one or several of the Heatherby maids, willing or not. Besides that, he had been eyeing Breanne's fading spots with suspicion.

"I do not blame you, daughters, for killing Havenshire," Thorvald told them. "I only wish I had been there."

"Not nearly as much as I do." Rafn was feeling immense guilt over all that Vana had suffered, thinking him passed to the Other World. He had fallen in battle and had been presumed dead, but in fact he had been taken into slavery by a vicious outlaw band of Danes. His original wound, a deep sword cut to his thigh, had never been treated properly, and thus he limped slightly. "I but wish that Caedmon would tell me where Vana is hiding so that I can take her home with me." *And marry her* was left unspoken, but inevitable.

"He honestly does not know, Rafn," Breanne told him. " 'Twas better that none of us knew. Be assured that she is safe under the care of Wulf. And Ivan and Ivar, as well."

"We owe these people so much," Rafn told Thorvald.

"Rest assured. We will reward them for their help."

"I am not sure they will want or take a reward, Father, but this is a small estate, and they do not have the resources to feed all of you," Ingrith pointed out, her mind ever on food. "There will be enough to last through the wedding feast on the morrow, but not much else." The Norse troops were settled in tents in the fields beyond the castle, but they still needed food and drink.

"Rafn, send someone to the nearest market town for supplies."

Rafn nodded.

"We will be going back to Larkspur right after the ceremony. Caedmon advised me that would be the best place for us to wait for Vana to return. She will have heard of our presence here in Northumbria."

"I only wish it could be now. 'Tis hard to wait, doing nothing," Rafn remarked.

"Father, Larkspur is not a grand estate, either," Breanne said.

"We will worry about that when the time comes, daughter. Now, back to Oswald. Are you certain the body will not be found?"

"He is at the bottom of a privy . . . a very deep privy," she remarked dryly.

Her father and Rafn gaped at her before breaking out in grins. Then Rafn asked, "How did you get him through the hole?"

Breanne and her sisters just rolled their eyes.

"Believe me, Rafn," Tyra said, "I would have had no problem making a bonfire of him, beast that he was, but there was an easier solution." She explained how they had disposed of the body and then pretended that Oswald had ridden out of the castle.

"Oh, Rafn, you should have seen Vana. Black and blue marks on her face, finger marks on her neck, a broken arm, and . . ." Drifa's words trailed off as she saw the horror on Rafn's face. "I am so sorry. I did not mean—"

But Rafn stood abruptly, appearing as if he might hurl the contents of his stomach, and staggered out of the room.

"Nice work, Drifa," Ingrith remarked.

Drifa started to cry.

"'Tis not your fault," her father said, pulling her onto his lap. "We had to learn the details eventually. Why the disguises?"

They told him of King Edgar's reputation for sexual assaults, whether the women be lowborn or noble.

Their father bristled with indignation. "Did he touch any of you?"

"Nay, but I am not sure how long we will be able to fool him," Breanne said.

"Well, keep your distance 'til we are ready to leave. And, believe you me, when I meet with these Saxon miscreants later today, I will make it clear that no complaints will be filed against any of my daughters. If there are, they will have not just me to deal with, but many of our Viking neighbors. Eirik's brother Tykir at Dragonstead and Brandr of Bear's Lair have pledged hirds of soldiers, if need be."

"Not to mention Ravenshire men," Eirik pointed out.

"Now, tell me, daughter, why it is that you stayed back at Larkspur whilst your sisters came here? And what is this about a betrothal?"

The door was opening as her father started to speak.

Caedman entered and said, "Forget about the betrothal for now. Edgar has a dairymaid trapped in a locked milk shed, and her father is heading that way with a battle-axe."

"Let me take care of it," Rafn said, coming in behind Caedmon. "I am in the mood for killing someone."

That was all they needed.

It all comes down to money, honey . . .

The meeting of the Witan later that day was vastly different from the one held that morning.

It was difficult . . . nay, impossible . . . to ignore King Thorvald's presence. Equally difficult to ignore was King Edgar's surly disposition. He was not a happy king, having been thwarted in his swiving of the dairymaid, not that the maid was objecting, but her father was. It had taken Arch-bishop Dunstan's intervention to pry the king away and to appease the angry father with a handful of coin. No one knew where the two thanes were. They had disappeared after the Vikings' arrival, mayhap gone back to their Wessex homes.

Thorvald had taken one bite of food at an earlier meal and spat it out with contempt. Disregarding any of their arguments, he ordered Ingrith to the kitchen to prepare her usual sumptuous fare. That was where she and the other princesses were now. They would dine royally tonight.

Rather than the ealdorman magistrate, Eirik was the one to open this meeting. "We are here to discuss the disappearance of Lord Havenshire."

"More like murder," King Edgar grumbled.

"Until you find a body, there will be no talk of murder," King Thorvald asserted.

"Putting aside any accusations of murder, why do you seek Lady Havenshire?" Eirik inquired.

"She had cause to want him gone," Edgar snarled.

"Oh?" Eirik lifted one haughty eyebrow.

"Havenshire beat her regularly, no doubt because she needed it," Dunstan elaborated. "All women do at one time or another."

Rafn let out a roar of outrage, and it took both Caedmon and Geoff to hold him down in his seat. Even so, Rafn managed to yell, "You bloody bastards! Vana was a gentle woman, the least deserving of any soul I have e'er met. Personally, if he were here now, I would lop off his head. Then you would not have to search for his vile body."

"Rafn, you are not helping matters," Caedmon whispered.

With a snarl of disgust, Rafn plopped down in his seat, stone-faced with fury.

Caedmon pinched the bridge of his nose as he contemplated how this mess was going to be ironed out. "Do you have a headache?" Geoff asked him.

"Why? Is blood seeping out of my eyeballs?"

"That bad, huh? Methinks you need a bout of bedsport."

"Hah! That is not likely to happen in the near future."

"I could lend you my hunchback."

"Geoff! You are getting married on the morrow?"

"I was just teasing, lackwit."

"I wonder if Sybil would appreciate the jest."

"Do not dare tell her."

"We cannot resume our meeting until you two stop chattering," Lord Orm said.

"Back to your comment about Lady Havenshire having cause to kill her husband," Eirik said to Dunstan. "Are you aware that the earl has many enemies?"

Caedman noticed that Eirik always spoke of Oswald as if he were still alive, saying he "has" enemies, and not "had" enemies. It was a lesson he would follow.

"In fact, I have been told that Lord Havenshire has a reputation for whipping or striking anyone who displeases him . . . housecarls, maids, even his own hirdsmen," Eirik went on. "Therefore, if you want to make accusations of murder, or some other foul act against the earl, why not accuse them?"

Dunstan and Edgar were at a loss for words.

"Do not throw the arrow that can come back to you," Rashid muttered behind him.

Caedmon had no idea what that meant, but he did know that it was a good thing the king or Dunstan could not hear him.

"Here is the situation," Dunstan said. "The four princesses were at the castle the night the earl went missing. It is very suspicious that they were in the earl's bedchamber just before his demise."

"Demise?" Thorvald hollered. "There you go again, dreaming up murder when you have no proof it ever happened."

Dunstan held up a hand. "Let me finish. We are trying to piece together what happened at Havenshire from the time Lady Havenshire's sisters arrived until the earl's disappearance was noted."

Caedmon inhaled deeply. This was the do-or-die moment.

"When we arrived at Havenshire, 'twas early evening. I recall because most of the Havenshire folks were still in the great hall, eating dinner," Ingrith interjected, her speech slurry from the fleecy cheeks.

"Our sister Vana was not present, and we were not looking for Lord Havenshire; so, we do not know if he was there. We went directly upstairs," Drifa said.

Breanne picked up the lie . . . uh, story . . . from there. "Our sister was badly injured. Black eyes, neck-strangling marks, a broken arm. All our attention was focused on helping our sister. Did Lord Havenshire cross our minds? Yea, but only as we cursed the man who would do this to a woman. We assumed that he had beaten his wife, then left to visit his mistress, which I understand was his routine."

Dunstan was not happy with her story because it not only put Havenshire in a bad light but also himself, as Dunstan had claimed on more than one occasion that beating a woman was not only acceptable but a good thing. "I find your story highly implausible," Dunstan spat out, drool pooling at the edges of his mouth. "Methinks a torture test to determine your truthfulness might be in order."

There was a ludicrous method of ferreting out liars. Have them put a hand in boiling water. If the skin did not blister or peel off, they were telling the truth.

King Thorvald stood to his impressive height and pointed a long finger at the archbishop. "You will perform no torture on my daughters. You can accept what they say or not, but this farce is over."

"And how do we know that none of you is responsible?" Rafn added, looking pointedly at Dunstan and the king.

"How dare you!" Edgar jumped to his feet.

"I understand you want lands . . . Heatherby, Larkspur," Rafn blundered on. "Why not Havenshire, which is a much more prosperous estate?"

"Your question is insulting and inappropriate," Dunstan said, ice coating his words. Turning to Lord Ravenshire, he demanded, "Remove him from our presence."

Eirik made some silent signals to Caedmon and Rafn, and the Viking got up and walked out. But just before he exited, he said, "If any of you does one single thing to harm Vana, you will feed the raven so fast you will not know what hit you."

"That . . . that man threatened us. Take him into custody," Edgar shouted.

The two soldiers in the room looked from the king to Dunstan to the magistrate, Lord Orm, to Lord Ravenshire, confused about what to do. Dunstan waved a hand and said, "Let him go. For now."

"You were saying . . . ?" Lord Orm prodded Lord Ravenshire.

"I was saying that Lord Havenshire had many enemies. Seems to me that you have concentrated so much on Lady Havenshire you have failed to investigate anyone else. If naught else, you have prematurely judged this woman."

King Edgar's response was a crude Anglo-Saxon word.

Dunstan flashed him a warning glare, then surprised them all by saying, "Your words are well worth heeding, Ravenshire. On the issue of Lord Havenshire," he looked at his fellow Witan members, "I suggest we do more investigation."

Neither Orm or the king was happy with Dunstan's suggestion, but the archbishop was a powerful figure. Even the king rarely disagreed with him in public.

Dunstan addressed King Thorvald then: "Do I have your word that you will make Lady Havenshire available for further questioning if need be?"

King Thorvald hesitated, then nodded, but Caedmon knew there was no chance in hell that Vana would come back on Saxon soil once she was gone.

"The last thing we are to discuss is Caedmon's hasty betrothal to Lady Breanne," the king said.

Caedmon and Thorvald both tried to speak at the same time. Caedmon won. "There has never been a formal betrothal, just talk of one."

"By the runes! That matters not. My daughter will be betrothed only when I say so." Thorvald glanced at Caedmon. "No offense, but I know nothing of you and your affections for Breanne. You are aware she has this tiny little quirk."

Dost mean she likes to brush her naked breasts against my chest hairs. Caedmon grinned. "Dost refer to her woodworking skills?"

"For a certainty. She cannot be left alone for even one day without building something. We have more benches at Stoneheim than we have people to sit on them.".

Ravenshire cleared his throat. "Uh, could we go on here?"

"Listen," King Edgar said to King Thorvald, "you surely understand that noble marriages are arranged here for political reasons. Favors granted. Adjoining estates. Pacts with other nations. And, yea, Caedmon, your estate is small compared to some, but we believe there is merit in your remarrying some Saxon lady who brings profit or merit."

To the crown, Caedmon finished for him.

"I know what you mean," Thorvald said. "That is true in the Norselands, as well, but in my family it is different. I have promised each of my daughters that she may choose her own husband . . . a decision that has come back to bite me in the arse since only two of them have wed, and one of those badly. But that is neither here nor there. It should be noted that their dowries go to them, not their husbands, on marriage. Unless they choose to gift their husbands."

"Will you at least put off the betrothal ceremony, if there is to be one, until we can discuss a certain widow we had in mind for you?" Dunstan asked Caedmon.

"What widow?" Caedmon eyed the king and Dunstan with suspicion.

Reluctantly, Edgar told him, "Lady Helen of Lockhaven. She brings two castles, many hectares of land, and a good annual profit from her sheep."

"Whaaat? She is more than forty . . . closer to fifty." And homely as the back end of a hog. Not to mention the sheep smell that followed her everywhere.

Geoff was scarce hiding his mirth beside him, but Caedmon considered it no laughing matter.

"All the more reason for it to be a good match," Dunstan opined, "since you have said on more than one occasion that you have too many children already."

King Thorvald leaned forward on his bench to address Caedmon over the two people between them. "You do not intend to have any more children? Well, that does it then. No betrothal with my daughter. If naught else, my daughters owe me a grandson. I am sick to death of an all-female household."

For some reason, Thorvald's dismissal of him as a prospective groom cut deep. He should not have been offended, but he was.

"Have you been dallying with my daughter?" Thorvald asked of a sudden.

What exactly is dallying? Less than swiving, I would wager.

"Nay," Caedmon lied.

"Well, do not, lest you want at least five more children."

Whaaat?

Geoff chuckled and pretended to be counting on his fingers, up to fifteen, counting this current five.

"Never!" Caedmon mouthed silently to Geoff.

"Definitely," Thorvald insisted, having interpreted their silent exchange.

Everyone started talking at once.

But then Geoff stood and spoke over all the voices, " 'Tis past time we held a wedding. Mine."

Caedmon breathed a sigh of relief then as the room began to empty. It would be a short-lived relief, though, because nothing had been settled.

Fifteen children? He almost gagged.

And Lady Helen? Hah! He would sooner wed a camel.

It was appropriate then that Rashid, in passing, tossed one of his proverbs his way: "He who rides the camel should not be afraid of dogs."

"We have a similar Saxon saying, Rashid," Geoff interjected.

Caedmon could not wait to hear this one.

"He who tups the keg must take the foam with the ale."

"Well said!" Rashid congratulated Geoff.

Caedmon just put his face in his hands.

CHAPTER TWENTY

&

The path to true love is mighty rocky . . .
It was by far the most unusual wedding that had ever occurred in Northumbria, perhaps the whole world. The blond godly handsome knight and the hunchbacked lady.

Breanne and her sisters could not stop giggling, even during the overlong ceremony performed by Archbishop Dunstan. The king and his troop had left afterward, having accomplished or not having accomplished what he had wanted. Besides, they had no way of knowing there would a real feast to follow, no more of that bland fare fit for only peasants.

Because it was a wedding feast, Dunstan had been forced to allow women at the high table, but he did not like it, and made sure he was at the opposite end. Working with the Heatherby cook, Ingrith had surpassed herself with the food.

The archbishop kept criticizing Sybil for providing such a merry feast when, in fact, she should still be in mourning. But Breanne noticed that the priests ate heartily; no fasting for them.

While several young girls played lutes, the

kitchen helpers were carrying in trenchers of food. Among the meats were roast boar in Ingrith's special sauce, mutton, several pigs cooked whole in hot coals, calf brains, and the organs of all the animals. If meat was not to the feast goers' taste, there were five kinds of freshwater fishes: trout in honey cream, oat-stuffed pike, gingered carp, poached perch in mustard sauce, and pickled eels. Egg and mushroom pies, various cheeses including the Viking *skyr*, manchet bread, and honey-oat cakes accompanied various vegetable dishes, like creamed turnip, lentils with lamb, marrow-thickened cabbage, herbed beets, buttered peas. If that weren't enough, there were savory puddings and apple tarts. And of course, mead and ale, lots of it.

"I think we should leave for Larkspur this evening, whilst there is still light," Breanne's father said to her. He was seated at her right, and Caedmon on her left.

"I have already sent word ahead to prepare for you and your army," Caedmon told him. "You are welcome at Larkspur, but do not expect much."

"Caedmon! Why would you say that? Larkspur is a lovely place," said Breanne.

His face flushed. "I only meant it is not as grand as what you might be accustomed to."

"Hah!" Thorvald said. "You would be surprised at where I have put my head down on occasion." He studied Caedmon for a few moments, then added, "I like you. Too bad you will not suit for my Breanne."

"What? Father! Caedmon has not offered for

me. We merely pretended an upcoming betrothal to divert the archbishop and king's attention. So, discussion of his suitability is unseemly."

Her father and Caedmon both grinned.

"Furthermore, if I wanted to marry this loathsome lout, I would be the one to judge his suitability, which would be more than satisfactory."

"Huh?" Caedmon said.

Her father let loose with a chortle of laughter. "I merely meant that Caedmon wants no more children, whilst I yearn for a grandson."

It was Breanne's turn to blush.

The subject was changed when her father said to Caedmon, "Didst know that Adam, my son-by-marriage, drilled a hole in my head one time? Save me from death, it did."

The two of them carried on a conversation around her then, but that was just as well because she felt a vise closing over her heart at the prospect of leaving Caedmon behind when she left with her father. They would all return to Larkspur to await Vana's return, which might be only a matter of days.

And Breanne realized something horrible in that instant.

She had fallen in love with the loathsome lout.

And she was not the only one to come to that realization.

Rashid was just passing by behind her, and he leaned down to whisper in her ear, "To love and be loved is to feel the sun from both sides."

Unfortunately, this was only a one-sided love.

And Caedmon must never find out.

* * *

The only gift he wanted was . . . you know what . . .

They had been back at Larkspur for two days, and Vana had not yet returned. King Thorvald and his followers were restless. And Caedman was miserable beyond anything he had ever imagined.

The first thing Thorvald had done was order wagonloads of goods to be delivered to Larkspur. Food, spices, barrels of ale, cattle, horses, sheep, goats, even a flock of noisesome peacocks.

When Caedmon protested, the old man had pulled him into another of those rib-crushing bear hugs, and he had even kissed him on the cheek. " 'Tis the least I can do to repay you for what you have done for my daughters. You risked much, and I must needs show my gratitude."

What I have done is swive your daughter. So, please, no more gifts.

Caedmon would have argued more, but the king had chosen that moment to ask, "Is there any chance you might marry Breanne?"

Oh, good Lord. Did I say that aloud? "Huh? What? Uh, why do you ask that?"

"Your stuttering is answer enough." Thorvald had sighed with disappointment. "I see the way you two look at each other betimes when you think no one is looking. I just thought . . ."

He shrugged.

I look at her like that because I cannot not look. I am like a starving man watching a juicy boar steak float by. "Thorvald . . . I mean, Your Highness—"

The king waved that higher address aside.

" . . . I have great respect for your daughter, and if I were ever going to marry again, I would be honored to have Breanne. But you can see how things are here. Children everywhere. A man reaches a point where it is just too much."

" 'Tis a sad thing when a man disdains the gifts the gods give him. No matter what you say, children are gifts."

"I know they are, but I have too many gifts."

He had stormed away then.

But speaking, or thinking, about his children brought him to the problems they were currently causing him. Not a one would speak to him, except Piers, who could not speak anyhow. Angus, angry all the time anyway, had walked up and kicked him in the shin, hard, and without speaking just stomped away on his little legs. They wanted Breanne to stay, and they blamed him for her imminent departure. He also suspected that they felt responsible by their mere existence . . . which in some ways was true.

When had his life become so complicated?

He knew the answer to that without thinking. When the princesses had arrived at his door.

Right now he had another bone to pick with King Thorvald. He found him sitting outside in an armed chair he had ordered one of his men to bring out so he could watch the soldiers exercise, both his and the Larkspur hird.

"What is the meaning of this?" he said right off, dropping the two heavy leather bags onto the king's lap.

Thorvald jerked back with surprise. "A gift."

"What for?"

"Does there have to be a reason? We Vikings like to give gifts. Wouldst begrudge me that?"

The sly old bird! "Listen, there has to be several hundred mancuses of gold in those bags. I cannot accept it." *Even if I need it.*

"Yea, you can. Did your mother never teach you manners, how to accept a gift graciously?"

"My mother died when I was nine." *Try learning manners from a father who favored a heavy hand with his children.*

"That explains it then."

"Explains what?" *Good Lord! Shut your teeth, Caedmon!*

He just smiled at him. "Take these heavy things off my lap afore you give me a cramp. You know I will find a way to leave them behind if you do not take them openly."

Walking back to the keep, muttering curse words under his breath, he ran into Breanne, knocking her to the ground. Which was an amazing thing in itself. He had been avoiding her like a . . . well, rash. No good would be served by them being together anymore.

But wait. She had been blathering something about visitors.

"What is it?" he asked, helping her to stand.

"Four riders are approaching. I think it might be Vana."

Caedman put the bags of gold inside, then followed after her, but at a slower pace because he recognized in that moment that if Vana was here it meant they would all soon be departing, never to return.

How would he bear it?

Sometimes true love does run smooth. . .

Breanne and her sisters were waiting in the upper courtyard for Vana, their father having insisted on their staying with him.

Wulf, Ivan, and Ivar dismounted, then helped Vana off her horse. Without skipping a beat, she smiled widely and ran toward them. First into her father's big arms. Then, hugging and kissing each of them. "At last, my sweet, I can take you home," her father said, swiping at the tears in his eyes.

Holding her away from him, he examined her features. Luckily, all the bruises had faded, and she no longer had her arm in a sling. In fact, she looked better than she ever had, having gained some weight, and her skin had a healthy color.

Vana turned again to her four sisters, who enclosed her in a group hug, with more tears and hugs. What a relief that their dangerous escapade was over!

Just then, their father interrupted them. "Now, let your sister breathe. Step back. Vana, I have a surprise for you."

"Oh, please, no more surprises. My life has been too full of surprises of late. I want to go home and live a calm, uneventful existence."

"I do not think that is going to happen." Her father turned Vana by the shoulders so she could see the man approaching with a slight limp.

Vana gasped and put a hand over her mouth. Tears rolled down her cheeks. "Rafn, is it truly you? Oh, please, gods, do not let this be a dream."

"Heartling," Rafn choked out.

They ran toward each other.

In a shout of joyous triumph, he lifted her in his arms so her feet dangled off the ground and hugged her tightly. He was crying, too. "I never thought I would see you again."

"I thought you were dead."

They kissed then, long and passionate.

"You look thinner."

"You look more beautiful than ever."

More kisses and disbelieving caresses as if to prove the other was actually there.

"Will you marry me?"

"How soon? Can we do it today?"

"I blame myself for your horrible treatment at the hands of that brute."

She shook her head. " 'Twas my fault. I should have had more faith."

"I love you so much. I will never let you go again."

"All the pain . . . all the worry these past sen-nights . . . having you back makes it all worthwhile."

There wasn't a dry eye amongst them. Vana had suffered so much. She deserved this reward. Rafn, too.

"I think it is time for us to go inside and give them privacy," Breanne said.

She looked up then and saw Caedmon lean-ing against the wall of the keep, watching her.

She wanted to rush into his arms, to beg him to ask her to stay, to say that he loved her. And she wanted to say, "Look at Rafn and Vana. Deep, abiding love does exist." But his arms were folded over his chest, and his eyes were blank, without emotion.

"Thank you, Caedmon, for all you have done to bring us to this happy conclusion." *Please ask me to stay.*

He shrugged. "Your father has thanked me enough. Too much, actually."

"We will probably be leaving on the morrow," she said. *Plese ask me to stay.*

His jaw seemed to clench at her words, and if she had expected him to say something, she was sorely disappointed.

He just spun on his heels and walked away.

He does not want me to stay.

Good-byes are such sweet sorrow . . .

Caedmon was drowning in family. It was bad enough coping with his ten children, but Breanne's family and kin were overwhelming.

Even though Archbishop Dunstan had departed with his group, leaving Father Edward behind, there was still King Thorvald, the five princesses, Rashid, Ivan and Ivar, Rafn, Adam the Healer and his child, Lord and Lady Ravenshire. If they stayed much longer, he feared Eirik and Eadyth's grown children and their spouses, along with Eirik's brother Tykir and his family, would be descending on Larkspur like locusts. And they all wanted to help him. Sending unusual beehives to increase his production of honey. A new bull. Grains for planting. A better market source for his cattle. And of course the damn noisy bothersome peacocks, which were driving his cotters barmy.

In order to get rid of Dunstan, he had promised to go meet Lady Helen. A promise he had no intention of fulfilling. Breanne had overheard and looked as if he had stabbed her in the back.

He was sick of hugs, and tears, and more hugs, and good wishes, and gifts, and good wishes, and all that bloody happiness. Wulf, who was a mite folk-shy in crowds, shared his opinion and decided to go visit Geoff. Unfortunately, Caedmon could not leave his own keep. Besides, he had to be here when Breanne left, even if it was like sticking needles in his heart, a self-inflicted pain.

And his children were still not speaking to him. Not that he viewed that as any great hardship. Quiet children could be a blessing.

He just wished this ache in his chest would go away. It had been difficult avoiding Breanne these past few days, but the yearning for her remained. In some ways it was like he had a pig bladder in his chest that was being blown up, and blown up, and blown up. Eventually it was going to burst, and then where would he be? Shattered, he supposed.

"Do you love her?" Wulf had asked.

"Nay! Of course not. But I have a mighty lust for her."

Wulf had just shaken his head at Caedmon's hopelessness. "Lust for a highborn lady equals marriage, my friend."

"Not for me!"

"Why do you resist so much?"

"I want a peaceful, orderly life. No more up-heavals. I deserve as much. My children do, too. Breanne turns me upside down and inside out. Chaos reigns when she is around."

Matters had not been helped by Rashid, who told him, "Even the camel knows that love is suffering."

Thank God he would be hearing no more camel proverbs after tomorrow. Well, today, actually, since it was just past midnight.

He was lying on his bed, arms folded behind his head, staring up at the ceiling, waiting for dawn to come. There would be no sleep for him tonight as his mind swirled with what-ifs.

Just then he heard a creaking sound and the door opening slowly. He shot up into a sitting position.

It was Breanne, wearing only a bed rail and carrying a candle, which she set down on a table by the door. Her hair was unbound, with long curly strands going every which way.

"Breanne?" *Thank you, God!*

"I drank ten cups of Amicia's potion today . . . the one Rashid gave her. I figured I owe you four more nights on our bargain. Mayhap you would accept this one night as final payment."

"Breanne, your father and your family have given me so many gifts of goods and money, it would be mean-spirited of me to demand any more from you." *Bloody damn hell! Forget sacks of gold and peacocks. I want you.*

"You do not want me then?" She sighed deeply and seemed unsure what to do next.

Huh? How can you even think that? "Your father would be on me like a dog on a bone if he knew you were here. He would have me before the priest saying my wedding vows before I could say one word in my defense. Ahhhh!" he said then. "You have plotted a way to get me to marry you. Is your father in the hall waiting to pounce?" *At this point, do I care?*

Her green eyes went wide with shock.

"I have taken your maidenhead, Breanne. No way of repairing that cracked egg. For that alone, your father would kill me, or force me into matrimony. You have to know that. And yet here you are. How do you explain that?" *Stop flapping, tongue. Take what she offers. Stop thinking, Caedmon.*

"You loathsome, arrogant lout!" Tears were already leaking from her eyes, which she swiped away with the back of her hand. "What makes you think I would wed with you, even if asked? You do not want me? Fine! I would not have you on a silver platter with an apple in your lying teeth. Our bargain is over! Good night and good riddance!"

She had already opened the door and was about to leave when he jumped off the bed and lunged for her, knocking her to the floor. *Oh, nay! You cannot offer me heaven and leave me in hell.*

"Ooomph! Get off of me, you big, ignorant maggot. You are crushing me."

"Shhhh!" he said, picking her up. "Or your

father *will* be coming after me." He carried her squirming body back into the bedchamber, locking the door behind him.

Tossing her to the center of the bed, he crawled up over her. He was naked. She would soon be naked. *Is there anything more sensuous than the feel of skin on skin?*

She thrashed and tossed from side to side, trying to escape. She truly did not want to be with him now.

"Breanne . . . sweetling, I am sorry. I did not mean to hurt you."

"The only way you could hurt me would be if I cared, and I do not care a whit for you."

He used a thumb to wipe the tears from her cheek. "Never say that I do not want you. I want you too much. I hurt in here . . ." he pounded his chest for emphasis, " . . . with my yearning for you." *And that, my dearling, is more than I can admit without baring my soul.*

She stilled. "If you want me, why did you say what you did about my father?"

"Because it is true. Now, do not get your blood boiling again . . . leastways, not in temper." *They should rename me Caedmon the Tongue Flapper.* "I meant that he would have good cause for attacking me. I have taken something precious from his daughter."

"You have taken naught that I was not willing to give, but I deserve more."

He stared at her, drinking in her beauty. He wished he had Geoff's talent for charming love words, but the best he could come up with was,

"Will you stay with me tonight, Breanne? Just this night?"

"That is why I came. Not to trap you. In fact, not for you, at all. For me. To close the door on our . . . relationship, for want of a better word. But I have changed my mind."

Oh, nay, nay, nay! Think quick, you blundering fool. "I am so confused. Divided in heart and head. By responsibilities. And loyalty. Love of my land. Concern for my children. And caring for you. Yea, I do care, but it all comes at the wrong time. In truth, there probably was never a good time for our *relationship*."

"Let me up, Caedmon. This was a mistake. I realize now that I did come here expecting more from you than a tupping or two, enjoyable as they might be. I admire you, Caedmon, but you are a coward."

What? He rolled over to release her. "I would kill any man who called me that."

"Good thing I am not a man then." She stood and stared down at him, her expression sad but rigid with determination. When she got to the door and unlocked it, she said, "I will say good-bye to you tonight. Know this . . . I could have loved you, and that would have been a priceless gift, but you would have viewed it as yet another shackle, like your children. Shame on you."

With those stinging words, she was gone.

CHAPTER TWENTY-ONE

☙

$\mathcal{T}$*he army was a mite on the young side . . .*
Nine children were huddled in a long-abandoned root cellar some distance from the keep, making plans. It was well past their bedtime, but they had to act now, under cover of darkness.

Hugh looked around the small space. There were piles of blankets. Plenty of candles, including some that were already lit. Food and pottery jars of fresh water. Buckets of water, with soap and drying cloths, for bathing. Even a screen taken from one of the bedchambers with covered bowls for privy matters behind it.

"Father is going to kill us for this," Mina pointed out.

"Or mayhap he will thank us," Hugh said. "We all agreed that we want Lady Breanne for our mother."

"Yea. Think how bad things were afore she arrived," Oslac added.

"I like to sit on her lap." Six-year-old Alfred sighed.

"Me, too." This from his twin Aidan.

"She smells good." Mina sniffed the air as if

she could actually smelly Breanne's rose-scented soap.

"And father wants her, too, I am convinced of that, or I would not have been involved in this." Hugh was the oldest and most responsible. He would be the one to suffer if the plan did not work.

"I agree." Beth patted him on the arm. "Father is not so grumpy since she arrived."

"Mayhap we should have involved Rashid. He is the one who gave us the idea when he told us about all those knights of old," Joanna reminded them. "They kidnapped their brides and made them fall in love."

"Either that, or they lopped off their heads." Kendrick elbowed Joanna, who elbowed him right back.

"Behave," Hugh cautioned.

Kendrick's response was to break wind, loudly.

"Phew! You stink," Joanna said.

Kendrick pretended to fan air from his backside toward her.

"If this does not work, I am going to run away and live with the fairies," Angus said, sticking his lower lip out with belligerence.

"There is no such thing," Oslac hooted.

Angus head-butted Oslac, and the two of them wrestled about on the dirt floor.

The twins, Aidan and Arden, just watched, in between yawns. If they did not leave soon, the two would be asleep.

"Let us go now," Beth suggested. "We accomplish naught standing about here."

"Yea, we must give Father plenty of time to tup

Breanne silly so that she will want to stay with him forever." Kendrick thought he knew everything about grown-up things.

"Eeew!" Mina exclaimed. "Why would any lady want to do that?"

"What is tup?" Arden asked.

Hugh felt like pulling his own hair out, one strand at a time. In some ways, he could understand why his father abhorred having any more children. He could not stand them himself, and he was one of them.

"Listen. One more time." Hugh looked at each of them, one at a time, to get their attention, which had a tendency to wander. "Aidan and Arden will stay here to open the door for us." It was a door slanted on an incline to open upward, exposing the underground room. It could be locked from the outside. "Angus, you will keep guard outside. Joanna, you will make sure the wheelbarrow is ready near the back door of the keep and that no one sees you. The rest of you will come with me. Do we have the ropes and gags?"

They all nodded.

"To victory!" Hugh shouted with an arm raised, as he had heard some chieftains did before battle.

The rest of them just gaped at him as if he had lost his mind.

"When this is all over, I will get the last of those honey cakes from the storeroom, and we will celebrate," Hugh offered.

That did the trick, because his brothers and sisters then yelled, "To victory!"

* * *

Little soldiers are allowed to fight dirty . . .

It was the middle of the night, and Caedmon slipped on a pair of braies and naught else, going down to the hall to get a cup of ale. Mayhap that would help him fall asleep.

He was surprised to see Lord Ravenshire sitting alone before a low fire, sipping a cup of ale. After Caedmon found a pitcher and cup, he sat down next to him.

"Is something amiss?" he asked.

Eirik shook his head. "Nay. I get head megrims betimes, and a cup of my wife's mead often soothes the pain. I was just about to go back to our bed." He studied Caedmon for a moment. "How about you? Something troubling you?"

He shrugged, then admitted, "Breanne."

"And?"

Is that not enough? "I care for her." He chose his words carefully.

"Does she not return the sentiment?"

He laughed. "I think she does, but not at the moment." *More like, she would carve me into a chair if she could.*

"I see the way you look at each other when you think no one is looking."

"Everyone says that." *I must practice not looking at her so much.*

"Ask the lady to marry you." Eirik's suggestion was blunt and unexpected. "That is what this is all about, is it not?"

At first Caedmon resisted answering. It was none of Eirik's business, after all. But the man was only trying to be helpful.

"I have been wed twice afore. Disasters." *They were right when they named it wed-LOCK and referred to the BONDS of matrimony.*

"That happens betimes."

"I have ten children."

"Congratulations."

He shot Eirik a glare. "'Tis naught to be congratulated over. Besides, they are not all mine." *And someday I am going to find those three Welsh brothers. But, nay, those three whelps have been with me too long. They are more mine than theirs now.*

Eirik waited for him to say more.

"I do not want to marry again. I do not want any more children. I want a life of peace and tranquility."

"You keep saying I want, I want. This is not all about you."

He sighed. "You are right. I am being selfish."

"Life is all about balances, in my opinion. Good and bad.

"We have choices and they are not always the ones we want to make. Mayhap you need to weigh all the good things that would come from marriage to Breanne against the bad things. See what the scales show then. Compromise is not a bad word."

"That is good advice." He laughed then. "But far too late."

"'Tis ne'er too late."

"My only saving grace tonight is that Rashid is not here to give me a camel proverb."

"You think that is bad. You should meet my friend Bolthor, the world's worst skald. He would be telling sagas about all your embarrassing events to one and all. He once wrote a saga about my brother's cock."

Laughing, Caedmon stood and downed the rest of his ale in one long swallow before heading for the downstairs garderobe to relieve himself. Then he would go back to his bed and, hopefully, sleep.

He had just relaced his braies and gone out into the corridor when a small animal jumped on his back. The hands of the animal went around his neck and stuffed what seemed to be a pair of hose in his mouth. Other animals were knocking him to the floor and tying his hands behind his back and his ankles together. Turning his head to the side, he was shocked to see that the villains were his children. Hugh, Beth, Mina, Kendrick, and Oslac tried to lift him several times, but kept dropping him because of his weight and their relatively small size. *What game is this? I am going to kill the little buggers.*

After whispered consultation among the lack-wits, they began dragging him along the hall, then outside, where they lifted him into a wheelbarrow. He would have bruises all over his body. *Some small people I know are going to have bruises on their little rumps when I am done.*

By the time they arrived at the cold cellar, where little Angus was standing guard with a wooden sword in his hand, Caedmon was swearing behind his gag. *God's teeth! This is no longer funny, if it ever was.* There were going to be blistered arses aplenty in this castle come morning.

Once they got him down the steps, one rough

bump at a time, he saw Alfred and Aidan rise from where they had been nodding off.

Propping him up against the wall in a seated position on a blanket, Hugh told him, "Father, we are doing this for your own good. You will thank us on the morrow . . . or the next day."

Mayhap I should send you to a monastery, boy, to show how thankful I am. Caedmon hoped his eyes told Hugh how grateful he was going to be.

They all left then, even Alfred and Aidan. He could hear them up above, outside the door, talking with Angus.

He had no idea what this was all about until, a short time later, the door opened again, and another body was dragged down the steps. Muffled sounds of protest came from said body, which was wearing a white bed rail. They dumped the body next to him on the blanket.

Guess who? he jested with himself. He even laughed, or tried to, under his gag.

All of his children . . . well, nine of them . . . Piers presumably being too young to participate . . . stood looking down at them. Hugh, the spokesman, said, "I know this looks bad, but we are doing this for your own good."

"All ye gotta do is tup 'er 'til her eyes roll in her head and she agrees ta be yer bride," Joanna said.

I cannot believe she said that. Does she even know what tupping is?

"Joanna! You were not to tell them that," Hugh chastised her.

You can say that again!

Joanna ducked her head. "Well, 'tis true," she mumbled.

Breanne's eyes widened, then darted to the side to glare at him.

Hey, it was not my idea.

"You have plenty of food and blankets and stuff," Beth pointed to various baskets.

"We will check on you once every day to see . . . well, to see how you are progressing."

Hugh looked at his little band of lackwits and raised a hand in the air, yelling, "To victory!"

"To victory!" the rest of the scamps echoed.

Then they ran up and out the door, but Hugh ran back and said, "Oops. I forgot." He quickly loosened the ropes on Breanne's hands, enough so she would be able to undo them the rest of the way. Then he ran up and outside again. This time, the door slammed down, and he heard the lock being engaged.

A short time later, he and Breanne were both free. Well, free but captives of his own children.

"Yell for help," Breanne suggested.

"No one will hear us. We are down too low and far away from the keep. The only way shouting would help is if people come searching for us out this way."

"Did you put them up to this?"

I was hoping it was you. "Are you barmy? Why would I do that?"

"Sex."

"You are barmy. If I wanted sex, it would not be in a root cellar on the hard floor with a shrew." *Though I would not turn it away.*

"Sorry. I should not have said that. What are we going to do?"

"Hell if I know." He feasted his eyes on her, from her wild red hair to her bare toes. Then he smiled. "Wanna tup?"

Breanne surprised the spit of him by saying, "Sure. Why not?"

Caedmon was fairly certain this was a dream.

He was a hard nut to crack . . .

"I must say life is never dull around you, Caedmon."

Breanne was walking around the small underground room, which had once housed root vegetables and salted meats.

"That is what Geoff and Wulf say about me all the time, but I do not seek these kinds of things. Must be I attract them, though." He stood and shrugged out of his braies, then beckoned her with his forefinger. "Come here, Breanne."

The intent was clear in his deep blue devil eyes and in his staff, which stood at attention down below.

She could play coy and wait for persuasion, but she had lain awake after leaving Caedmon's bedchamber, berating herself for leaving. Yea, he had told her that marriage would never be in the offing, but she could have one more night of loving. More memories to store for what would surely be a lonely future.

This was her second chance.

She raised her night rail up and over her head,

dropping it to the floor. Then she walked toward him in as sultry a fashion as she could manage.

He laughed. "Temptress," he said against her ear. Then he kissed her and at the same time lifted her up off the floor and walked to the blanket, where he lay her down, himself at her side, never once breaking the kiss. "I want you. I want you more than I have ever wanted anyone or anything."

You do not know what "want" is, lackwit. I have it in much greater abundance, thank you very much. "I am here."

"Yea, you are." He smiled down at her, then surveyed her body, slowly, running a fingertip along her collarbone, down between her breasts, over her belly and navel, stopping at her nether hair. "Do you have any idea how beautiful you are?"

She would have disagreed, knowing her attributes, or lack of them, but mayhap he saw her through the daze of arousal. No matter.

His calloused hands traced the same path again, but this time he used his palms to worship the skin of her arms, inside and out, under her breasts, her belly, the backs of her knees, with throaty endearments at each place, telling what he saw and liked. Just that had her moaning her ardor as all her senses leaped to life. *He is ruining me for other men. No one else could possibly make me feel this way.*

Eyes brimming with passion, he framed her face between his trembling hands and kissed her, softly, entreatingly, like a true lover. His love.

Oh, if only that were true.

He made a rough sound when she pressed the tip of her tongue into his mouth, then proceeded with an in-and-out rhythm that matched what was to come below.

The first time she peaked was when he played with her breasts. Teasing fingers. Nipping teeth. Lapping tongue. And rough, insistent sucking.

I will never look at my breasts in the future, or touch them, without remembering this.

"Look at me," he insisted. "I want you to see how much you please me."

He moved lower then, parting her female folds, spreading the wetness there, searching and then finding a nub of such intense pleasure that she cried out.

"Did I hurt you?"

Just the opposite. She shook her head.

He knelt between her legs, then spread her thighs wider, and moved himself lower. When she realized what he was about to do, she protested. "No!" *He could not possibly be going to . . .*

"Let me."

"Oh . . . oh, I never thought. Do people do this?" *If they do not, they should. Holy Thor!*

"We do, dearling. We do." With those words, he showed her what a man could do, making love to a woman's parts. So intense was the pleasure, she could not object. And she peaked again with whimpers of cascading spasms, starting inside, then spreading out and over her entire body.

When he moved to arrange himself at her

woman's portal, she asked, "Do women do that to men, as well?"

He seemed surprised by her question at first, and then he said, "They do."

Caedmon's manpart was long and thick, poised for entry. She knew because she was raised on her elbows watching him. Glancing up, he noticed her scrutiny and smiled ... a smile that not only tugged at his lips, but danced in his eyes. Then he thrust inside her, and she had to close her eyes against all the sensations assaulting her. She melted around his stretching fullness. The fine hairs stood out all over her body. Her nipples ached.

His eyes were closed now as he seemed to be fighting for control, but she would have none of that. She reached around and cupped his buttocks, pressing for more. *Do not think you have all the control, my lord of sin.*

Opening his eyes, he laughed and began long, lazy strokes that nigh drove her into a demented state of endless moaning. It was too much, and not enough. Her hips were rocking wildly. There was a roaring in her ears. As he pounded into her, she realized that somehow her legs had locked around his hips. Straining, straining, straining toward the most incredible, shattering explosion of the senses, which left them both weak and depleted.

This is surely heaven and Valhalla all rolled into one.

As they lay side by side facing each other, his limp member still inside her, he lazily slipped his

tongue in and out of her mouth, a reminder of
what they had just done. She put her hands to his
face, holding him back a bit. "I love you," she said.
That was all. She had no idea how he would react,
but it had to be said.

He just stared at her, his fingers gently pushing
wet strands of hair off her face. "I am glad."

That was all, but it was enough . . . for now.

He did not know it yet, but she was not leaving
on the morrow. He might be a hard nut to crack,
but she was going to crack him eventually. After
all, she had nine helpers for that endeavor.

Lest he worry about her getting too serious, she
lifted one leg up over his thigh and said, "Wanna
see how good I am at my exercises?"

Turns out she was very good, if male groans
and pleas for mercy were any indication.

*The way to a man's heart is NOT through his stomach,
ladies . . .*

Caedmon stared down at a sleeping Breanne.
Finally, he had worn her out. Hah! He was the one
worn out. In the best possible way.

She had milked him with her new inner muscle
exercises until he thought he had died and gone
to Valhalla. *Thank heavens for the female body and
all its nuances.* They had tried the Butterfly position after that, the one he had mentioned to her
before. *Who knew I could do THAT?* Then she had
put her mouth to him and caused his heart to stop
before thundering into rhythm again. *Un-be-liev-
able!* She would be the death of him yet . . . a good
death, he had to admit.

What was he going to do with her?

I have a few ideas.

One thing was certain, he was not going to let her go.

He lay down then, spooning himself into her back, and pulled a blanket over the top of them. It would soon be daylight and God only knew what would happen then.

For now, he was where he wanted to be.

CHAPTER TWENTY-TWO

&

The games children . . . uh, adults play . . .

"Where is she?" King Thorvald bellowed. He was outside in the bailey, ready to mount his horse and take off for Jorvik, where he had eight longships waiting to take them back to the Norselands. All of the troops below were ready to ride. His daughters, as well. Except for Breanne.

"I have looked everywhere," Tyra said, putting a hand over her barely raised belly. She had told him earlier this morning that she was breeding another grandchild for him. She and her family would be traveling with them to Jorvik, then off to her own home at Hawkshire with her husband, Adam, Rashid, and little Adela. "Breanne is nowhere to be found."

"When did you see her last?" Rafn asked.

"She went to bed when we did," Vana told him, "but she was not there when we awakened this morn."

King Thorvald's blood went hot. "Where is Caedman?" he shouted to anyone who would answer.

"Uh, he has not been seen today, either," Gerard, the steward, answered, from a distance.

Does he think I am about to lop his head off? Nay, it is that knave Caedmon for whom I am reserving that honor.

"Mayhap Caedmon went to Heatherby to join his friend Wulf, who went there last night," Tyra offered.

"He has not left Larkspur," the stable master said from the back of the crowd that was gathering. "His horse is still in its stall, and the sentries would have noted his departure."

"Rafn, give orders for the hird to dismount," Thorvald ordered. "We will not be leaving today. Adam, can you help organize a search party?"

"Where shall we look?" Drifa wanted to know.

"Somewhere with a bed would be my guess," Thorvald said. And then he chuckled to himself. *'Twould seem that another of my daughters is going to leave the nest.* "Where is Ingrith?"

"Here I am, Father."

"Best you start arrangements for a wedding feast."

"But I want to be married at Stoneheim," Vana protested.

"'Tis not for you."

It took five hours of useless searching before someone noticed that Caedmon's children were acting strange. After another hour of intense questioning, a crowd of about twenty was heading out the back door of the keep. The children, wisely, went into deep hiding.

Thorvald had not had so much fun since Adam had drilled a hole in his head, and he had pretended to be unconscious so he could plot the marriage of one of his daughters. Suffice it to say, he was smarter than his daughters gave him credit for. Never underestimate a Viking, he always said.

Welcome to the light, son . . .

Caedmon and Breanne were eating their first meal of the day, manchet bread, hard cheese, and apples, when they heard the sound of many voices approaching.

"Uh-oh! We are about to be rescued." He smiled at Breanne and helped her to her feet.

She smiled back at him.

There was no longer an ache in his chest. Instead, he was filled with a fierce joy. He was not sure what that meant, but it had to be good.

"I will take care of this," he said, leaning down to give her a soft kiss. "Do not be afeared."

"I am not afraid. What will be will be. How do I look?" She was smoothing her wrinkled bed rail, which she had not worn until this morn.

"Like you have made love with a sinfully handsome man six times in the past twelve hours. Mayhap seven if you count . . . never mind." He reached over and ran his thumb over her lips, which were raw and swollen from his kisses. Wisps of damp hair framed her glowing face. Whisker burns marred her face and throat and chest. "How do I look?"

She gave him a saucy head-to-toe survey. He

was wearing naught but braies. There were scratch marks on his chest and back. His lips were puffy. His eyes gleamed with some secret. "Like a man who has been thoroughly satisfied numerous times by a temptress of the highest order."

The door opened, letting sunlight in.

Caedmon took her hand and led her up the steps. At first, he was blinded, but then he realized that a stunned crowd was watching them emerge. At the head was Breanne's father, King Thorvald.

Holding a hand for silence, Thorvald studied both of them thoroughly. Then he smiled and yelled over his shoulder, "Someone get the priest."

Surprisingly, Caedmon did not shudder or make protests of his innocence. This was inevitable. He knew that now. It had been ordained from the moment she entered his castle.

He noticed that Breanne remained silent, too. Had she come to the same conclusion?

With a surge of possessiveness, he put an arm around her shoulder and started to walk them back to the keep, the crowd following after them like ducklings.

"One thing," he said, stopping to shout, "where are my children?"

To the surprise of everyone, Caedmon most of all, Breanne put two fingers in her mouth and let loose a shrill whistle. Even more surprising, ten children, even little Piers, came running to stand in a line in front of him.

They were all smiling.

* * *

Here comes the (Viking) bride . . .

They were about to be married the next afternoon in the new grape arbor at Larkspur, the trellises having been built by the bride and the grapes vines planted and arranged in an arch by her sister Drifa. Succulent smells came from the kitchen, where a wedding feast was being prepared.

Breanne had not spoken to Caedmon alone since yestermorn when they were "rescued." She did not know what he had said to his children, but she had seen from a distance that he spoke to them seriously and at length. But at the end, they were all laughing, and he placed a fatherly arm over the shoulders of Hugh, who had been the instigator.

She had also seen him talking with her father over cups of ale. It had been a long conversation, but it could not have been too bad since her father had not lopped off his head or done him bodily harm.

Caedmon had not wanted to be married. He probably still did not. But she was going to marry him anyhow. She would teach him to love her over time.

Somehow, amongst her sisters, Sybil, and Lady Ravenshire, an exquisite bridal gown had been put together. One of Sybil's gowns of sky blue edged with silver embroidery. It was covered by a surcoat of sable-lined samite in a darker, slate-blue color, with embroidery in a larkspur design; someone had found it in a chest left by the former

owner of this estate. Eadyth managed to make one
of her beekeeping veils into a bridal veil hanging
from a circlet of Drifa's flowers. All this attire was
more Saxon than Norse. So she wore her hair in
one long braid, Viking style, and at her shoulder
was a brooch in a writhing, intertwined animal
design.

Her sisters looked just as lovely in their bright
gowns, Tyra's Saxon style, but the others pure
Viking. Her father would be giving her away, and
her sisters would stand as witnesses. On Caedmon's side would stand Geoff, Wulf, Hugh, and
Rashid.

"It is time," Ingrith said, sticking her head in
the door.

Breanne sighed deeply and began to walk out
with Eadyth. "Are you nervous, dearling?"

"Surprisingly, I am not."

But that was not true once she got outside in
the bright sunshine. Caedmon stood near the trel-
lis waiting for her. He looked so handsome in a
new dark blue fustian tunic over matching blue
braies. The sun reflected like stars on his silver-
hilted short sword in its side sheath and his gold-
linked belt.

He was being forced into this wedding. Despite her earlier claims not to care, to be willing to
wait for his love to come, she was having second
thoughts now. It was so unfair to this man, who
had not been treated fairly much of his life.

But then he smiled at her, and Breanne put her
hand on her father's extended arm and began to
walk toward him.

They were to be married in two ceremonies, one Christian and one Norse. Father Edward was not pleased. So he rushed through his ritual and sat down in a huff. Breanne hardly felt as if she was married. She had not even raised her veil yet. She and Caedmon exchanged looks, then shrugged.

Now it was time for the Norse wedding ritual, which would be officiated by both her father and Rafn.

A small table was brought over, under the arbor, and on it was a silver-chased goblet of wine, an ornately jeweled knife, a gold braided cord, a hammer, a polished stone, and a bowl of oat seeds. They were both jarred with surprise when her father began to chant primitive words in Norse. For the benefit of those who did not understand Norse, Rafn interpreted, "King Thorvald called out to god and man, family and friends to come witness today the marriage of Caedmon of Larkspur and Princess Breanne of Stoneheim."

"Dunstan would have a screaming fit if he were here," Caedmon whispered to her out of the side of his mouth.

"He would have barred all women from the ceremony, even the bride," she replied.

Caedmon chuckled.

"Shhh!" her father said and handed to Caedmon the goblet of wine. "Odin, we draw this nectar from your well of knowledge. May you bring this couple the wisdom to deal well with each other in this marriage journey they begin today. Especially give these two stubborn people the wisdom to know when to give up the fight."

"Hah!" Breanne said.

Caedmon just grinned. He took a sip of the wine, then turned the goblet and pressed it to her lips so she could drink from the same spot. She could swear the metal carried the warmth of his mouth.

Her father must have given Caedmon instructions ahead of time, because after she took a tiny sip of the red wine, he set the goblet down, then picked up the hammer. "Thor, god of thunder, I take in hand your mighty hammer, *Mjollnir*—well, actually, 'tis Breanne's hammer. This I pledge: I will protect you, Breanne, my wife, from all peril. I will use my fighting skills to crush your enemies. Let it be known forevermore. Your foe are now my foe. My foe are your foe. The shield of Larkspur is now *our* shield." With that, he raised the hammer and crushed the stone.

Breanne jerked back with surprise.

Then her father took over again. He picked up the bowl of seeds, taking a handful. "Frey, god of fertility and prosperity," he began.

Caedmon stiffened beside her.

Are you demented, Father? How could you bring up that most hated subject to Caedmon on this of all days?

Her father continued, "We implore not fertility or great wealth in this marriage, oh, great Frey. What we seek, instead, is that you bless them with a rich love and richer passion . . . and if a child, or five, comes along, so be it!" Before his words could sink in, he sprinkled a pinch of the seeds over her breasts, and a much larger amount over

Caedman's chest, enough that they floated down
to his crotch.

Caedmon looked horrified.

My father is a total idiot.

Her father, the total idiot, was barely stifling a
grin.

Taking her left hand and Caedmon's right, her
father tied them together loosely with a gold cord.
Then, before she realized what he was about, Rafn
took the knife, put shallow slits on each of their
wrists, then pressed the two cuts together.

*That is just wonderful. Bloodshed on top of every-
thing else!*

"As Caedman's blood melds with Breanne's, so
shall his seed," her father proclaimed.

Children again. Must you keep reminding him?

"I am doomed," Caedman whispered, but he
flashed her a wink.

Huh? What does that wink mean?

Finishing, her father said, "From this day forth,
Breanne is Caedmon's beloved, and he is hers.
With this mingling of their blood, they pledge
their troth. From the beginning of time, to the
end of time, let it be known that . . ." he nodded
to Caedman, who began to recite words that must
have been rehearsed:

"I, Caedmon, give my heart to thee, Breanne."

Then he nodded to Breanne, who repeated back
to him, "I, Breanne, give my heart to thee, Caedmon." *Oh, this is awful. I had no idea Caedmon would
be required to say all these false words. He must be furious. But, oh, they are beautiful sentiments.*

"It is done," her father said, and the crowd began to clap.

Caedmon lifted her veil and looked at her long and hard before leaning down to kiss her lips. She thought he whispered against her mouth, "My bride!"

Some time later, just before the bridal feast was to began, Caedmon realized that Breanne was missing. He found her in one of the storerooms, weeping.

His heart seized up. "Breanne! What is amiss? Please do not tell me that you are already regretting our marriage. You told me when we were in the root cellar that you loved me. I thought . . ."

She shook her head and continued to sob. He held her until the tears stopped, and he wiped her wet face with a cloth.

"Tell me," he said.

"Oh, Caedman, I feel so bad. I am not regretting the marriage. Of course I am not, but you were forced into this. I could have prevailed with my father, but I did not."

If you only knew, sweetling. He cocked his head to the side. "I was not forced."

"Of course you were. You do not love me."

"I do so." *Heart and soul.*

"What? Oh, please, do not feel the need to placate me. I will be aright in a moment. Go back to the hall, and I will join you shortly."

"Absolutely not! Where did you get the idea that I do not love you?"

"You never said so."

"I did not? Are you sure?"

She slapped him on the chest. "Of course I am sure. Do you think I would forget something so important?"

"I could swear I told you a hundred times whilst we were in captivity." *Or mayhap I was too busy enjoying your body.*

"You did not."

"Then I showed you." *Many, many times, if I do say so myself.*

She folded her arms over her chest and glared at him.

"I love you, Breanne. You are probably going to turn my home into a madhouse. You are probably never going to be biddable. You are probably going to have five daughters, just to plague me. But I love you and am proud to be your husband." *I am good. I had no idea I could be so good. Ah! Mayhap it is because the words come from my heart.*

They kissed to seal his words, and Breanne did not think she could be happier than she was this day. To think, killing an earl led to this event.

"Oh, before I forget, I have a little bridal present for you," she said. *By thunder! Do I ever!*

He unraveled the red cloth tied with a yellow riband. Inside was a candle. He held it in his hand. He frowned and examined it on top and bottom and sides. Then, he let out a hoot of laughter. "You are priceless, Breanne. But I will have to give you my bridal gift later when we are in bed."

"I think I have already seen that 'gift.'" *And very nice it is, too.*

"Not that, heartling." He pinched her bottom.

"I was talking to Rafn and he told me about this secret Viking trick."

"A bed trick? I do not like the sound of that." *Liar! It sounds intriguing, truth to tell.*

"Oh, you will like this. It is called the famous Viking S-Spot."

Breanne's eyes lit up. "Can we skip the wedding feast?"

READER LETTER

Dear Reader:

I hope you liked what I call my medieval version of the Dixie Chicks song video, "Good-bye Earl."

Tenth-century Vikings and Saxon knights are particular favorites of mine. It was such a colorful time. And, believe me, women could be treated badly, as the earl's wife was in this book. But there were also many instances of women being strong.

Most important to me as a writer of romantic fiction is the fact that humor has survived through the ages. We know from the Viking sagas that these attractive folks had an incredible ability to laugh at themselves.

Lest you think it incredible that Vikings and Saxons might mix freely, let me tell you that, throughout the ninth and tenth centuries, Vikings moved comfortably throughout Britain, sometimes as invaders, but most often as settlers. And they could understand each other; Old Norse (not to be confused with modern Norwegian) and Saxon English were similar.

Yes, the Vikings could be rapers and pillagers at times, but generally, that is a deliberate fabrication of the biased monk historians of the times. Believe me, Saxons could be just as vicious. There are historical reports of enemies being skinned alive and their skins being tacked on church doors.

Because most of the Scandinavian countries were mountainous and had little arable land to accommodate the increasing populations, Viking men continually had to seek new homes to live. And blending into these countries was aided by the fact that the Viking men were so tall and good-looking (and bathed more often than other men of that time), thus attracting women in all countries. Their sometimes frigid climate forced them to become tough and aggressive, though they had great respect for the law. The same could be said of the women.

Thus, it would not have been uncommon for a Viking woman, like Vana in this book, to be married to an English earl, or a Norse nobleman (jarl) to marry a Saxon lady. In fact, many people do not realize that Vikings once actually ruled portions of Britain, particularly Northumbria and its Norse capitol, Jorvik, modern-day York.

Some even say that the modern nursery rhyme, "London bridge is falling down . . ." was actually based on the Viking overthrow of London in 1014 by Olaf I of Norway.

I've said it before and will say it again: I have particular reason to be fascinated by the Viking culture. I can trace my paternal family tree all the way back to the tenth-century Hrolf the Ganger, first duke of Normandy (called Norsemandy at that time).

And that bit about fruit as a method of birth control . . . hey, Casanova was reputed to have a thing about lemons. When he was entertaining one of his mistresses, he would order a tray of halved lemons, which were to be inserted . . . well, you get the picture. So, I just extrapolated to apples since lemons were not available in the tenth century in Britain. A caution: Do not try it at home. I have visions of some female showing up at a hospital emergency room with an apple or lemon stuck in never-never land, telling the doctor, "But I read about it in a Sandra Hill book."

What would you like to see next? A story about one of the other Viking princesses? How about Wulf and his Welsh lady? Or Alrek the Clumsy Viking? I could return to Scotland with The Scots Viking; surely Jamie the rascal should have his own story.

The Viking orphanage in Jorvik? So many possibilities.

I love hearing from you readers. You can contact me at shill733@aol.com, or by visiting my website at www.sandrahill.net,where there are novellas, genealogy charts, book videos, and other freebies.

As always, I wish you smiles in your reading.

Sandra Hill

GLOSSARY

braies—slim pants worn by men, breeches.

brynja—a flexible chain-mail shirt.

companaticum—"That which goes with bread," which usually meant whatever was in the stockpot of thick broth always simmering in the huge kitchen cauldron. Usually with chunks of meat. Unfortunately, not cleaned out for long periods of time.

Coppergate—a busy, prosperous section of tenth-century York (known then as Jorvik or Eoforwic) where merchants and craftsmen set up their stalls for trading.

drukkin (various spellings)—drunk, in Old Norse

Ealdormen—chief magistrates, or king's deputies, in Anglo-Saxon England. Later referred to as earls. Appointed by the king; most often were noblemen.

ell—a linear measure, usually of cloth, equal to 45 inches.

encaustum—tenth-century type of ink made by crushing the galls from an oak tree (boil-like pimples on the bark), which contain an acid. Mixed with vinegar or rainwater, the substance was thickened with gum arabic. Iron salts added color to the ink.

Eoforwic—Roman (and later Saxon) name for early York.

fillet—band worn around the head.

hand—a measure equal to 4 inches.

handfast—betrothal sealed by joining hands in order to cohabitate before actual marriage.

hauberk—a long defensive shirt or coat, usually made of chain links or leather.

hectare—a unit of land measure equal to 2.471 acres.

hersir—military commander.

hide—a primitive measure of land that originally equaled the normal holding that would support a peasant and his family, roughly 120 arable acres, but could actually be as little as 40.

hird—a permanent troop that a chieftain or nobleman might have.

hirdsman—one of the hird.

housecarls—troops assigned to a king's or lord's household on a long-term, sometimes permanent basis.

Jorvik—Viking-age York, known by the Saxons as Eoforwic.

mancus—a weight of gold of about 70 grains, or equal to six shillings or thirty pennies/pence (one shilling = five pennies). A pound then and now equaled 240 pence. The Anglo-Saxon pence was made of silver and had high purchasing power. For example, thirty pence could buy an ox; four or five pence, a sheep.

Norsemandy—tenth-century name for Normandy.

Northumbria—one of the Anglo-Saxon kingdoms, bordered by the English kingdoms to the south and in the north and northwest by the Scots, Cumbrians, and Strathclyde Welsh.

Odal rights—laws of heredity.

pace—a measure equal to 2.5 feet.

scutage—a sum paid to an overlord in lieu of military service.

seneschal—an agent or steward.

sennight—one week.

skald—poet.

skyr—a Norse cheese similar to cottage cheese.

steward—a man responsible for day-to-day running of the castle or keep.

sulung—the area that could be kept under cultivation by a single plough team of eight oxen, equal to two hides.

thane—a member of the noble class below earls but above freemen. Usually a landowner.

thrall—slave.

tun—252 gallons, as of ale.

vassal—a freeman who owns land.

wattle and daub—an early method of building.

wergild—a man's worth.

Witan (or Witenagemot)—a king's advisory council, made up of nobles and ecclesiatics.

Dark and Dangerous Ways . . .

Dearest Reader,

Why is it that the unrepentant rake, brooding duke, or wicked rogue never fails to set even the most sensible hearts aflutter?

And what happens when a sensible lady plays with fire, unafraid to get burned?

This winter feel the heat with four new, delicious romances—from *New York Times* bestselling authors Elizabeth Boyle, Sandra Hill, and Kerrelyn Sparks and talented debut author Sarah MacLean—in which scandalous heroes meet their matches at last, in ladies who know that sometimes bad can be gloriously good . . .

Coming January 2010

How I Met My Countess

The first in a new series
from *New York Times* bestselling author

Elizabeth Boyle

When Lucy Ellyson, the improper daughter of an infamous spy, saves the Earl of Clifton's life, he decides to make her his countess. But then the irresistible chit vanishes and Clifton is certain he's lost her forever . . . until he discovers she's living in Mayfair, as scandalous as ever and in the sort of trouble only a hasty marriage can solve. But before Clifton can step in, secrets from the past emerge, threatening to ruin them both.

While the Earl of Clifton had been expecting a scullery maid or even a housekeeper to respond to Mr. Ellyson's shouted orders, the gel who arrived in the man's study left him taken aback.

Her glorious black hair sat piled atop her head, the pins barely holding it there, the strands shimmering with raven lights and rich, deep hues. They were the sort of strands that made one think of the most expensive courtesans, the most elegant and desirable ladies.

Yet this miss wore a plain muslin gown, over which she'd thrown an old patched green sweater. There were mitts on her hands, for the rest of the house was cold, and out from beneath the less than tidy hem of her gown, a pair of very serviceable boots stuck out.

This was all topped off with the large splotch of soot decorating her nose and chin.

She took barely a glance at Clifton or his brother before her hands fisted to her hips. "Whatever are you doing shouting like that? I'm not deaf, but I fear I will be if you insist on bellowing so."

Crossing the room, she swatted Ellyson's hand off the map he was in the process of unrolling. Plucking off her mitts and swiping her hand over her skirts—as if that would do the task and clean them—she caught up the map and reshelved it. "I doubt you need Paris as yet."

There was a presumptuous note of disdain in her voice, as if she, like Ellyson himself, had shelved their guests with the same disparagement that she had just given the errant map.

And in confirmation, when she cast a glance over her shoulder and took stock of them, it was with a gaze that was both calculating and dismissive all at once. "Why not begin with ensuring that they know how to get to the coast," she replied, no small measure of sarcasm dripping from her words.

Ellyson barked a short laugh, if one could call it a laugh. But her sharp words amused the man. "Easy girl, they've Pymm's blessing. We're to train them up."

"Harrumph," she muttered, putting one more stamp of disapproval on the notion.

Clifton straightened. It was one thing to be dismissed by a man of Ellyson's stature, but by a mere servant? Well, it wasn't to be borne. He opened his mouth to protest, but Malcolm nudged him.

Don't wade into this one, little brother, his dark eyes implored.

"I need to start with Lisbon," Ellyson said. "But demmed if I can find it."

"Here," she said, easily locating the map from the collection. "Anything else?" Her chapped hands were back

on her hips and she shot another glance over her shoulder
at Clifton, her bright green eyes revealing nothing but
dismay, especially when her gaze fell to the puddles of
water at his feet and the trail of mud from his boots.

Then she looked up at him with a gaze that said one
thing: *You'd best not expect me to clean that up.*

Clifton could only gape at her. He'd never met such a
woman.

Well, not outside of a public house.

Bossy termagant of a chit, still he couldn't stop watching
her, for there was a spark to this Lucy that dared to settle
inside his chest.

She was, with that hair and flashing eyes, a pretty sort
of thing in an odd way. But she held herself so that a man
would have to have a devilish bit of nerve to tell her so.

Then she shocked him, or at least, he thought it was the
most shocking thing he'd ever heard.

"Papa, I haven't all day and I've a roast to see to, as well
as the pudding to mix."

Papa? Clifton's mouth fell open. This bossy chit was
Ellyson's daughter?

No, in the world of the Ellysons, Clifton quickly discovered, such a notion wasn't shocking in the least.

Not when weighed against what her father said in
reply. "Yes, yes, of course. But before you see to dinner,
I have it in mind for you to become Lord Clifton's new
mistress. What say you, Goosie?" he asked his daughter as
casually as one might inquire if the pudding was going to
include extra plums. "How would you like to fall in love
with an earl?"

Lucy glanced over her shoulder and looked at the man
standing beside the door. Very quickly, she pressed her lips
together to keep from bursting out with laughter at the
sight of the complete and utter shock dressing the poor

earl's features. He had to be the earl, for the other man hadn't the look of a man possessing a title and fortune.

Oh, heavens! He thinks Papa is serious. And in a panic over how to refuse him.

Not that a very feminine part of her felt a large stab of pique.

Well, you could do worse, she'd have told him, if the other man in the room, the one by the window, the earl's brother from the looks of him, hadn't said, "Good God, Gilby! Close your mouth. You look like a mackerel."

The fellow then doubled over with laughter. " 'Sides I doubt Ellyson is serious."

Lucy didn't reply, nor did her father, but that was to be expected, for Papa was already onto the next step of his plans for the earl and his natural brother, and therefore saw no polite need to reply.

"Sir, I can hardly . . . I mean as a gentleman . . ." the earl began.

Lucy turned toward him, one brow cocked and her hands back on her hips. It was the stance she took when the butcher tried to sell her less than fresh mutton.

The butcher was a devilish cheat, so it made ruffling this gentleman's fine and honorable notions akin to child's play.

Clifton swallowed and took a step back, which brought him right up against the wall.

Literally and figuratively.

"What I mean to say is that while Miss Ellyson is . . . is . . . that is to say I am . . ." He closed his eyes and shuddered.

Actually shuddered.

Well, a lady could only take so much.

Lucy sauntered past him, flicked a piece of lint off the shoulder of his otherwise meticulous jacket, and tossed a smile up at him. "Don't worry, *Gilby*," she purred, using the familiar name his brother had called him. "You don't have to bed me." She took another long glance at him—from his dark hair, the chiseled set of his aristocratic jaw, the breadth of his shoulders, the long lines of his legs, to his perfectly polished boots—everything that was wealthy, noble, and elegant, then continued toward her father's desk, tossing one more glance over her shoulder. "For truly, you aren't my type."

Which was quite true. Well, there was no arguing that the Earl of Clifon was one of the most handsome men who'd ever walked into her father's house seeking his training to take on secretive "work" for the King, but Lucy also found his lofty stance and rigid features troubling.

He'll not do, Papa, she wanted to say. For she considered herself an excellent judge of character. And this Clifton would have to set himself down a notch or two if he was going to stay alive, at the very least, let alone complete the tasks he would be sent to do.

No, he is too utterly English. Too proud. Too . . . too . . . noble.

And Lucy knew this all too well. For she'd spent a good part of her life watching the agents come and go from her father's house. She knew them all.

And she also knew the very real truth about their situation: They may never come back. As much as she found it amusing to give this stuffy earl a bit of a tease, there was a niggle of worry that ran down her spine.

What if he doesn't come back?

Well, I don't care, she told herself, crossing the room and putting her back to the earl. She opened a drawer and handed a folder to her father, who through this exchange had been muttering over the mess of papers and correspondence atop his desk. "I think you need these," she said softly.

Her father opened it up, squinted at the pages inside, and then nodded. "Ah, yes. Good gel, Goosie." He turned back to Clifton. "Whatever has you so pale? I don't expect you to deflower the gel, just carry her love letters."

"Letters?" Clifton managed.

"Yes, letters," Lucy explained. "I write coded letters to you as if I were your mistress and you carry them to Lisbon." She strolled over, reached up, and patted his chest. "You put them right next to your heart." She paused and gazed up at him. "You have one of those, don't you?"

Coming February 2010

Viking in Love

The first in a new series
from *New York Times* bestselling author

Sandra Hill

Breanne and her sisters are more than capable of taking care of themselves—just ask the last man who crossed them. But when a hasty escape lands them in the care of a Viking warrior, the ladies know they have at last met a worthy quarry. After nine long months in the king's service, all Caedmon wanted was . . . well, certainly not five Norse princesses running his keep. And after the fiery redhead bursts into his chamber on the very first morning . . . Caedmon settles on a wicked plan far more delightful than kicking her out.

*B*eware of women with barbed tongues . . .

Caedmon was splatted out on his stomach, half-awake, knowing he must rise soon. This was a new day and a new start for getting his estate and his family back in order. In his head he made a list.

First, gather the entire household and establish some authority. Someone had been lax in assigning duties and making sure they were completed. The overworked Gerard, no doubt. And the absent Alys.

Second, take stock of the larder. Huntsmen would go out for fresh meat, fishermen for fish, and he would send someone to Jarrow to purchases spices and various other foodstuffs.

Third, designate Geoff and Wulf to work with the housecarls on fighting skills and rotating guard schedules.

Fourth, replenish the supply of weaponry.

Fifth, persuade the cook to return. The roast boar yestereve had been tough as leather, made palatable only by the tubfuls of feast ale and strong mead they had consumed.

Sixth, the children . . . ah, what to do about the children? One of the cotters' wives . . . or John the Bowman's widow . . . could supervise their care, and a monk from the minster in Jorvik might be induced to come and tutor them, although his history with Father Luke did not bode well for his chances.

The door to his bedchamber swung open, interrupting his mental planning. The headboard of his bed was against the same wall as the door, so he merely turned his head to the left and squinted one eye open.

A red-haired woman—dressed in men's attire . . . high-born men's attire, at that—stood glaring at him, hands on hips. She was tall for a woman, and thin as a lance. As for breasts, if she had any, they must be as flat as rounds of manchet bread. "Master Caedmon, I presume?"

"Well, I do not know about the 'Master' part. What manner dress is that? Are you man or woman?" He smiled, trying for levity.

She did not return the smile.

No sense of humor.

"You are surely the most loathsome lout I have e'er encountered."

Whaaaat? He had not been expecting an attack. In fact, he needed a moment for his sleep-hazed brain to take in this apparition before him.

"Your keep is filthy, pigs broke through the sty fence and are all over the bailey, I saw dozens of mice scampering in your great hall, thatch needs replacing on the cotters' huts, you beget children like an acorn tree gone wild, your staff take their ease like high nobility, there are several blubbering servants arguing over who will bury the priest who is laid out in your chapel, and you . . . you slothful sluggard, you lie abed, sleeping off a *drukkin* night, no doubt."

Whoa! One thing was for certain. This would not be yet another woman trying to crawl into his bed furs. "Stop shrieking. You will make my ears bleed." Caedmon rolled over on his side, tugging the bed linen up to cover his lower half, then sat up.

"Bestir thyself!"

"Nay!"

"Have you no shame?"

"Not much."

"Are you lackbrained?"

"No more than you for barging into my bedchamber."

"Even if you have no coin, there is no excuse for the neglect."

"Not even the fact that I have been gone nine long months in service to a king undeserving of service?"

"Where is the lady of this estate?"

'Tis just like a woman to think a woman is the answer to everything! "There is no lady."

"Hmpfh! Why am I not surprised?"

Now he was getting annoyed. "Sarcasm ill suits you, m'lady. Have you ne'er been told that?"

"The blade goes both ways, knave."

His eyes went wide at her foolhardy insults. "Who in bloody hell are you?"

"Breanne of Stoneheim."

"Is that supposed to mean something to me?"

"She's a princess," someone called out from the corridor. He saw now that a crowd of people were standing just outside the open doorway, being entertained by this shrew's railing at him. Geoff and Wulf were in the forefront, of course, laughing their arses off.

"Well, Princess Breanne, what do you in my home and my bedchamber?"

She had the grace to blush. "My sisters and I came here, on our way ... as a stopping-off place ... for a ... uh, visit ... on our journey. Your castellan offered us hospitality."

He could tell by the deepening red on her cheeks that she was either lying or stretching the truth.

"Sisters?"

"She has four sisters," Geoff offered. "All princesses."

Five princesses? Here? Oh, Lord!

"And they are accompanied by two scowling Vikings who are about this tall," Wulf added, holding a hand high above his head. And Wulf was a big man by any standard.

"They were only scowling because your archers aimed their bows at them," the lady declared, doing her own good job of scowling.

" 'Tis a comfort, your explanation is. I feel so much better."

Caedmon could practically hear the grinding of her small, white teeth.

"And there is a wise man from the eastern lands who has opinions on every bloody thing in the world, most of it involving camels." As usual, Geoff was enjoying himself at his expense.

"Why me? I mean, why stop here at Larkspur?" he asked the bothersome woman. "Surely there are better places."

"My sister Tyra is your cousin."

He frowned. "I have no cousin named Tyra." Leastways, he did not think he did, but then he was still wooly-witted from sleep.

"Her husband, Adam of Hawkshire, is your cousin by marriage . . . um, slightly removed," the flame-haired witch explained.

He knew Adam, or rather he had heard of him. A famed healer. But their connection by blood was far removed.

"Did you know there is a child still in nappies walking about nigh naked? He could be trampled by dogs the size of small ponies roaming about indoors."

"Have a caution, wench. You have already passed the bounds of good sense. Any more, and you may taste the flavor of *my* wrath."

She started to respond, then stopped herself.

"I told Emma to take care of Piers," Caedmon said.

"Would that be the same Emma who spent the night spreading her thighs for the blond god?"

"She is referring to me," Geoff preened. "The blond god."

"And, by the by, why do all the females in this keep appear to have big bosoms?"

"Huh?"

Geoff and Wulf were laughing so hard they were bent over at their waists, holding their sides. When he was able to speak, Geoff said, " 'Twould seem that Gerard has a preference for big breasts when choosing maids for inside work." He gave particular emphasis to "inside work."

"Gerard? Bloody hell! He is old enough to . . . never mind."

"Not yet in his dotage, if he can still appreciate a buxom bosom," Wulf observed.

Breanne waved a hand airily. "You are not to worry. My sisters and I will set your keep aright whilst we are here."

Alarm rippled through Caedmon's body. "How long do you intend to stay?" he asked bluntly.

Another blush. "I am not certain. But you are not to worry."

"I was not reassured the first time you said that."

"You will hardly notice we are here."

"I doubt that heartily."

She went stiff as a pike, apparently not liking it when the sarcasm came from his direction, but she pressed her lips together. Very nice lips, he noticed, if he were attracted to tall, skinny, red-haired women with barbed tongues, which he was not. At least she was making an effort to be polite now.

Something very strange was going on, but he had more urgent matters to take care of. He'd drunk a tun of ale yestereve and now he needed to piss. Badly.

"Go down to the great hall and wait for me. We will discuss this later."

The shrew lifted her chin defiantly and said, "I am not leaving until you get your lazy self out of bed. If no one else cares about those children . . ." On and on she blathered in her shrill voice.

Really, this woman's tongue flaps like a loose shingle. I could rebuke her in a way she would not soon forget. Hell, I could kick her cheeky arse out the door, if I choose. But wait. I know another way. "You say me nay? Be careful, you may find I am more than you wagered for."

"Do you threaten me, troll?"

"So be it," he said, tossing the sheet aside and standing. *How do you like that trollsome part?*

Immediately her eyes fixed on a part of his naked body, which was displaying a powerful morning thickening, standing out like a flagpole. "You, you, you . . ." she sputtered, but could not seem to raise her eyes, which he noticed, irrelevantly, were a beautiful shade of green, like summer grass on the moors.

"Do not be offended, m'lady." He pointed at his nether part. "*This* is not for you. Your virtue is not forfeit from this quarter. 'Tis just that I must needs visit the garderobe."

"What an insufferable, crude, arrogant, loathsome lout!" she exclaimed as she sailed through the doorway, where the crowd had magically parted like the Red Sea of Biblical lore.

"Damn, but it is good to be home, is it not, Caedmon?" Geoff inquired sweetly, then ducked just in time to miss the pillow he sent his way.

A short time later, Caedmon realized he had one more thing to add to his list of things to do today: Get rid of princesses.

Coming March 2010

The Vampire and the Virgin

from *New York Times* bestselling author

Kerrelyn Sparks's

Love at Stake series

After doing battle with evil vampires intent on world domination, Robby MacKay is in dire need of a vacation. And calm, cool nights on a tropical island are exactly what the doctor ordered . . . but there's nothing cool about Olivia Sotiris. Also on vacation, the very sexy, very hot psychologist can make Robby's eyebrows singe with just one look. Soon, those nights aren't calm or cool . . .

Olivia rested her elbows on the patio wall and gazed at the beach below. A breeze swept a tendril of hair across her face, and she shoved it aside. Most of her long hair was secured on the back of her head with a big claw clip, but as usual, there were always a few unruly strands that managed to escape.

She took a deep breath, savoring her solitude. There were times, like during the party that evening, when the constant bombardment of everyone's emotions became hard to bear. It would feel like she was drowning, her own emotions submerged under the flood of those around her, to the point that she feared losing herself entirely. She'd learned over the years to handle it, but still, every now and then, she had to escape the maddening crowd.

Being an empath had certainly helped her with her job. Unfortunately, her unique abilities had also caused the monster to become obsessed with her. *Don't think about him. You're safe here.*

A movement far to the left caught her eye. She focused on a grove of tamarisk trees but only saw them swaying with a breeze. Nothing strange there.

Then she saw him. A lone figure emerging from the dark shadow of the trees. He was jogging along the beach. At this time of night? He reached a clear, sandy expanse where the moon shone brightly, and Olivia forgot to breathe.

His body was beautiful and she suspected his face was, too, but it was hard to tell at this distance. Dressed in dark jogging shorts and a plain white T-shirt, he moved quickly and easily along the beach. His skin seemed pale, but that could be caused by the moonlight.

She sucked in a deep breath as he came closer. He was a big man. His T-shirt was stretched across wonderfully broad shoulders, the short sleeves tight around his biceps.

If only she could see his face better. Her gaze drifted over to the telescope. Why not? She rushed over, pointed the telescope in the man's direction, and peered through the eyepiece.

Oh, yeah, he did not disappoint. His eyes looked sharp and intelligent, pale, though she couldn't tell the color. Green, she hoped, since that was her favorite. He had a straight, strong nose, a wide mouth, and a strong jaw with a sexy hint of dark whiskers. There was a grim expression on his face, but it didn't make him unattractive. Quite the opposite. It added to his aura of masculine power.

He passed by the house, and she admired his sharp profile for a few seconds, then lowered the scope to his body. His chest expanded with each deep breath, and she found herself matching her breaths to his. Even lower, she noted his muscular thighs and calves. His white running shoes pounded on the sand, leaving a steady trail.

He continued down the beach toward the rock known as Petra, giving her a glorious view of his backside.

"Opa," she muttered as she continued to spy on him through the telescope. She'd seen plenty of fit men during her training days for the Bureau, but this guy put them to shame. While their muscles had seemed forced and clumpy, this guy looked completely natural, moving with an easy, graceful control.

She was still focused on his rump when she noticed the attached legs were no longer moving. Did he run out of steam? He hadn't seemed tired. His jogging shorts slowly turned, affording her a long look at his groin. She gulped.

She raised the scope to his chest. Oh dear. That huge expanse of chest was now facing her direction. Surely, he wasn't . . . she lifted the scope to his face and gasped.

He was looking straight at her!

She jumped back, pulling her blanket tight around her. How could he see her? The courtyard was dark and the walls reached to her waist. But then the walls were white-washed and she was cocooned in a white blanket, and the moon and stars were bright. Maybe he *could* see this far. Surely he hadn't been able to hear her? She'd barely spoken over a whisper.

He stepped toward her, gazing at her with intense eyes. Oh God, he'd caught her ogling him with a telescope! She pressed a hand against her mouth to keep from groaning out loud. Apparently, the smallest of sounds was carrying across the beach.

He took another step toward her, and the moon glinted off his hair. Red? She hadn't met any redheaded men at the party that night. Who was this man?

"Olivia," Eleni called through the open door. "Your tea is steeping."

She strode into the kitchen and waited impatiently for her mug of tea. "There's a man on the beach."

"Are you sure? It's almost two in the morning."

"Come and see. Maybe you know him." Olivia wandered back to the patio and peered over the wall.

He was gone.

"He—he was there." Olivia pointed south toward Petra. There was no sign of him anywhere.

Eleni gave her a sympathetic look. "You're exhausted and seeing shadows. Drink your tea, child, and go to bed."

"He was real," she whispered. And the most beautiful man she'd ever seen. *Dear God, please let him be real.*

Coming April 2010

Nine Rules to Break When Romancing a Rake

A delightful new romance from debut author

Sarah MacLean

Kiss someone passionately, fire a pistol, attend a duel . . .

Lady Calpurnia Hartwell has had enough. Sick and tired of following rules and never having any fun, the inveterate spinster decides it's time to throw caution to the wind . . . at least just this once. But when a little fun leads her into the arms of a devastating rake, good Lady Callie must decide if she'll retreat to the life she knows . . . or succumb to a most ruinous temptation.

W ho are you?" The Marquess of Ralston's eyes narrowed in the darkness, taking in the soft angles of Callie's face. "Wait . . ." She imagined his eyes flashing with recognition. "You're Allendale's daughter. I noticed you earlier."

She could not contain her sarcastic response. "I'm sure you did, my lord. It would be rather hard to miss me." She covered her mouth immediately, shocked that she had spoken so boldly.

He chuckled. "Yes. Well, it isn't the most flattering of gowns."

She couldn't help her own laughter from slipping out. "How very diplomatic of you, my lord. You may admit it. I look rather too much like an apricot."

This time, he laughed aloud. "An apt comparison. But

I wonder, is there ever a point where one looks *enough* like an apricot?" He indicated that she should resume her place on the bench and, after a moment's hesitation, she did so.

"Likely not." She smiled broadly, amazed that she wasn't nearly as humiliated by his agreement as she would have expected. No, indeed, she found it rather freeing. "My mother . . . she's desperate for a daughter she can dress like a fashion plate. Sadly, I shall never be such a child. How I long for my sister to come out and distract the countess from my person."

He joined her on the bench. "How old is your sister?"

"Eight," she said mournfully.

"Ah. Not ideal."

"An understatement." She looked up at the star-filled sky. "No, I shall be long on the shelf by the time she makes her debut."

"What makes you so certain you're shelf-bound?"

She cast him a sidelong glance. "While I appreciate your chivalry, my lord, your feigned ignorance insults us both." When he failed to reply, she stared down at her hands and replied, "My choices are rather limited."

"How so?"

"I seem able to have my pick of the impoverished, the aged, and the deadly dull," she said, ticking the categories off on her fingers as she spoke.

He chuckled. "I find that difficult to believe."

"Oh, it's true. I'm not the type of young lady who brings gentlemen to heel. Anyone with eyes can see that."

"I have eyes. And I see no such thing." His voice lowered, soft and rich as velvet as he reached out to stroke her cheek. Her breath caught and she wondered at the intense wave of awareness coursing through her.

She leaned into his caress, unable to resist, as he moved

his hand to grasp her chin. "What is your name?" he asked softly.

She winced, knowing what was to come. "Calpurnia." She closed her eyes again, embarrassed by the extravagant name—a name with which no one but a hopelessly romantic mother with an unhealthy obsession with Shakespeare would have considered saddling a child.

"Calpurnia." He tested the name on his tongue. "As in, Caesar's wife?"

The blush flared higher as she nodded. "The very same."

He smiled. "I must make it a point to better acquaint myself with your parents. That is a bold name, to be sure."

"It's a horrible name."

"Nonsense. Calpurnia was Empress of Rome—strong and beautiful and smarter than the men who surrounded her. She saw the future. She stood strong in the face of her husband's assassination. She is a marvelous namesake." He shook her chin firmly as he spoke. "It is a name to be lived up to. And I think you are well able to do so, if only you would attempt it."

She was speechless in the wake of his frank lecture. Before she had a chance to reply, he continued. "Now, I must take my leave. And you, Lady Calpurnia, must return to the ballroom, head held high. Do you think you can do that?" He gave her chin a final tap and stood, leaving her cold in the wake of his departure.

She stood with him and nodded, starry-eyed. "Yes, my lord."

"Good girl." He leaned closer and whispered, his breath fanning the hair at her nape and sending a thrill through her, warming her in the cool April night. "Remember, you are an empress. Behave as one and they will have no choice but to see you as such. I already do . . ." He paused, and she held her breath, waiting for his words. "Your Highness."

And with that, he was off, disappearing deeper into the maze and leaving Callie with a silly grin on her face. She did not think twice before following him, so keen she was to be near him. At that moment, she would have followed him anywhere, this prince among men who had noticed *her*, not her dowry or her horrible dress, but *her!*

If I am an empress, he is the only man worthy enough to be my emperor.

She did not have to go far to catch him. Several yards in, the maze opened on a clearing that featured a large, gleaming fountain adorned with cherubs. There, bathed in a silvery glow was her prince, all broad shoulders and long legs. Callie held her breath at the sight of him—exquisite, as though he himself had been carved from marble.

And then she noticed the woman in his arms. Her mouth opened in a silent gasp, her hand flying to her lips as her eyes widened. In all her seventeen years she'd never witnessed something so . . . wonderfully scandalous.

The moonlight cast his paramour in an ethereal glow, her blonde hair turned white, her pale gown gossamer in the darkness. Callie stepped back into the shadows, peering around the corner of the hedge, half wishing she hadn't followed, entirely unable to turn away from their embrace. My, how they kissed.

And in the deep pit of her stomach, youthful surprise was replaced with a slow burn of jealousy, for she had never in all her life wanted to be someone else so very much. For a moment, she allowed herself to imagine it was she in his arms: her long, delicate fingers threading through his dark, gleaming hair; her lithe body that his strong hands stroked and molded; her lips he nibbled; her moans coursing through the night air at his caresses.

As she watched his lips trail down the long column of the woman's throat, Callie ran her fingers down the same path on her own neck, unable to resist pretending that the feather-light touch was his. She stared as his hand stroked up his lover's smooth, contoured bodice and he grasped the edge of the delicate gown, pulling it down, baring one high, small breast to the night. His teeth flashed wickedly as he looked down at the perfect mound and spoke a single word, "Gorgeous," before lowering his lips to its dark tip, pebbled by the cool air and his warm embrace. His paramour threw her head back in ecstasy, unable to control her pleasure in his arms, and Callie could not tear her eyes from the spectacle of them, brushing her hand across her own breast, feeling its tip harden beneath the silk of her gown, imagining it was his hand, his mouth, upon her.

"Ralston . . ."

The name, carried on a feminine moan, sliced through the clearing, shaking Callie from her reverie. In shock, she dropped her hand and whirled away from the scene upon which she had intruded. She rushed through the maze, desperate for escape, and stopped once more at the marble bench where her garden excursion had begun. Breathing heavily, she collected herself, shocked by her behavior. Ladies did not eavesdrop. And they *certainly* did not fantasize in such a manner.

Besides, fantasies would do her no good.

She pushed aside a devastating pang of sorrow as the truth coursed through her. She would never have the magnificent Marquess of Ralston, nor anyone like him. She felt an acute certainty that the things he had said to her earlier were not truth, but instead the lies of an inveterate seducer, carefully chosen to appease her and send her blithely off, easing his dark tryst with his ravishing beauty. He hadn't believed a word of it.

No, she was not Calpurnia, Empress of Rome. She was plain old Callie. And she always would be.

At Avon Books, we know your passion for romance—once you finish one of our novels, you find yourself wanting more.

May we tempt you with . . .

- **Excerpts** from our upcoming releases.
- Entertaining **extras**, including authors' personal photo albums and book lists.
- Behind-the-scenes **scoop** on your favorite characters and series.
- **Sweepstakes** for the chance to win free books, romantic getaways, and other fun prizes.
- Writing **tips** from our authors and editors.
- **Blog** with our authors and find out why they love to write romance.
- **Exclusive content** that's not contained within the pages of our novels.

Join us at
www.avonbooks.com